THE DREAMTIME OF THE ARTFUL DODGER

Norman Eshley   Elizabeth Revill

Published in 2021 by
AG Books
www.agbooks.co.uk

Distributed worldwide by
Andrews UK Limited
www.andrewsuk.com

Contents

Acknowledgements

Norman and Liz would like to thank the whole team at AUK for their hard work in taking this novel through to publication; to Rachel and Andrew for their unfailing support and Otto Indiana Taylor-Rickard's artwork ideas; to Simon Golding & Simon Farquhar for their continued encouragement, to Barnaby Eaton Jones for his introduction to AUK and Francoise Pascal for her help in navigating the tricky world of publishing.

Special thanks to Jeff Jones, our diligent proofreader who edited the novel for us.

When Liz read Norman's screenplay she was incredibly excited by the project and its unique concept. Simon Golding suggested that it should be expanded and would make an excellent novel and so Liz got together with Norman to research this period in history and write the novel, an experience she thoroughly enjoyed. Perfectly in tune with the storyline, Norman allowed Liz free rein to develop new characters and subplots, which help to make it a real adventure.

We hope you will enjoy it, too, and discover what happened to Jack Dawkins, the Artful Dodger.

For Rachel, Gail, Jane and Andrew

About the Authors

Norman Eshley has been a professional actor since 1966 appearing in many notable TV series and films as well as starring in numerous commercial theatre tours. He feels truly blessed to be married to Rachel. This is his first novel.

Elizabeth Revill is a multi-optioned screenwriter, a novelist with fifteen titles and a produced playwright who began her career as a professional actress after winning the Carleton Hobbs Award from the BBC. She lives on a farm in Devon with her husband Andrew, dog Pippin and Ashton the cat.

Prologue: Fagin Meets His Maker

The morning of Fagin's hanging had dawned.

Water dripped monotonously down the rocky walls in one of Newgate's filthy, dank cells. The sound echoed hollowly in the cramped space as it bounced and splashed on the dirt floor. Moss was growing together with algae that had formed on the rough edges of the hewn stone blocks where prisoners had carved their initials and scratched lines marking the days of their incarceration. It was more akin to an underground cavern than a prison cell and the air was stale; stinking of unwashed flesh, excrement, other bodily fluids and the stench of fear.

A dark haired, scrawny youth of about twelve years crouched in the corner, away from the iron bars fettered by chains. Jack Dawkins' eyes that once lit with mischief, looked despairing and desperate. His normally cheeky, engaging smile had been replaced by a solemn look that screamed misery. The Artful Dodger, as he had been known, wondered what was in store for him.

**

Further down that same corridor Fagin had more than enough time to reflect. He sat in his rags on the damp, cold stone bench and thought of all the men he had known who had danced the jig of death on the scaffold. Some of those men, he thought, had met their demise because of him. His conscience had never worried him even when he had watched some of them die, knowing that he was responsible. He remembered their final moments, bodies twitching into a swinging stillness and the sound of the creaking rope that chafed their broken necks. He marvelled at how quickly strong vigorous men were transformed into dangling rag bags of clothes with no substance.

Footsteps echoed dully along the stone corridor leading to his cell. The jangling of the gaoler's keys grated as they clanged together and wrestled with a rusty lock that imprisoned the now gaunt and lice ridden, thief who had controlled an empire of child pickpockets and worse.

His clothes, now ragged and torn made him look more like a scarecrow than a man. He looked up wide-eyed as the gaoler stood back to allow two turnkeys to enter his cell. Fagin spat onto the earth floor and some spittle remained dangling from his wizened lips, which he wiped off on his tattered sleeve.

The turnkeys moved purposefully and pinioned Fagin's twig like arms. The disbelief and horror of what was to happen to him had finally taken hold but instead of panic an inexplicable calm seemed to fill him. The guards led him away and the door clanged shut. There was finality in the sound, Fagin thought.

They arrived at the door to the courtyard and as they crossed the threshold Fagin felt the rain on his face, dew dropping into his straggly beard and coursing a path down his dirt streaked cheeks. Fagin shuddered.

"Tis all very well for you, Fagin," remarked one of the turnkeys; "but we must walk back in this." Both turnkeys guffawed.

Fagin turned his face up to view the drab grey sky and wondered at how all colour seemed to have drained from the day. But, then the tumultuous noise appeared to wake him from his stupor. He looked ahead and saw that despite the weather a great multitude had assembled. Hanging was sport and considered fine entertainment. People had travelled for miles to watch him die.

The windows overlooking the scaffold were filled with people, smoking and playing cards to pass the time until the execution; the ribald crowd were pushing, quarrelling and joking, jostling for the best position to watch the show. Everything in the stark surroundings shouted life and animation save for one dark cluster of objects in the centre of the all black stage, the crossbeam and all the hideous apparatus of death.

It was then that full realisation took hold and Fagin stared in horror and tried to pull back from the fate that awaited but the turnkeys had too firm a grasp on him and dragged him forward. "I am but an old man... I am an old man," he muttered in thin reedy tones.

He was marched forward, propelled up the steps and pushed onto the trap. The hangman, his face grotesquely masked, slipped the noose over Fagin's head followed by a white hood. A hush fell over the crowd that had become silent in eager anticipation. They sighed, almost as one, as the hangman released the trap and Fagin dropped to what his detractors hoped would be his eternal damnation.

A cry of glee filled the air.

***

From his cell the Dodger heard the mob screaming for joy and knew that Fagin had taken the morning drop. Jack Ketch had claimed another soul. But Dodger felt nothing. He was numb to it all and closed his eyes. Memories and Fagin's words reverberated in and around his head, "We must welcome a good hanging, cause when the poor devil drops that's the best time to dip the crowd's pockets, Dodger."

The grinding sound of the key in the lock broke his thoughts. Jack opened his eyes. He looked towards the door, which scraped open, and a guard entered and sniffed. "Right! Come on, then," he ordered.

The Dodger followed him out. His shoulders were drooped and showed none of his usual bravado and confidence. The skip had gone from his step and was more of a dogged plod and his eyes were downcast as he stoically placed one foot in front of the other. It was almost as if he'd lost all hope but in the way he shook his head, as if to dislodge some irritating insect, there were remnants of Jack Dawkins' real self, even if the glimpses were fleeting.

The crowds were beginning to melt away. They were dispersing to hostelries where they could continue their enjoyment of a day out. But, before the last stragglers left, three carts were driven to the front of the forbidding prison with four soldiers in each wagon. There they waited.

A stout metal studded wooden door opened and thirty prisoners in shackles were led to the drays. They filed past Fagin's lifeless, hanging body. Jack Dawkins tried to avert his eyes but the draw was too strong and it was inevitable that his gaze fell upon his old master; he couldn't avoid it. One of Fagin's shoes had fallen off and his big toe poked through a hole in his stocking. There was no dignity in death. A wave of regret washed over him as the last person he knew as master was no more. Jack shook his head determined to perk up and be watchful. This was how he could protect himself and survive.

Amongst the motley collection of prisoners was an even smaller boy who answered to the name of Edward. He was terrified and whistled constantly to hide his nerves. The remaining spectators lingered seeing new sport was to be had. They shrieked abuse and pelted the prisoners with rotten fruit as they were loaded onto the carts, which finally rumbled out onto the road and away.

It was the last time The Dodger saw London.

1: The Dodger's Journey Begins

Young Jack was forced onto the wagon and like all the prisoners still wore old and worn manacles, leg irons and chains. They were heavy for one so short and chafed his skin, now painfully red and sore. His emaciated legs were bruised and his wrists tender with abrasions. He struggled to get into the designated cart and was propelled in by one of the prison guards, who cursed and rasped, "Get in there, you varmint. You're holding the others up. Move it or you'll feel my stick on your back."

Jack didn't need telling twice as he was squashed up against a greasy beefy man with hands the size of dinner plates. He was soon pushed tighter into the brawny man whose broken nose and scars testified that he was used to brawling. The man sniffed loudly trying to prevent the ever permanent dew drop from splashing down his mouth and chin. He lifted his arm to wipe his nose on his threadbare sleeve and the chains clanked, invading the space of his neighbour on the other side of him.

"Watch yourself!" threatened the slighter man who had a cruel twist to his lips.

"Or what?" came back the bellow. "We're in this together and need to make the best of it. We don't want no cause for them to batter us with their sticks," the hulking man said jerking his head at the soldiers. "Or worse."

Jack kept his head down and said nothing even when the next prisoner leaned hard against him almost popping him out of his place like pus from a pimple.

Conversation stopped abruptly as the captain in charge thundered his order. "Quiet! Keep your thoughts and voices to yourself."

A shrill whistling continued in the background that was penetrating Jack's head. He wanted to clamp his hands over his ears as the screeching tone was irritating him beyond belief, but of course, he couldn't move wedged as he was between two large men.

"Oi, you!" shouted a soldier indicating Edward. "Shut your rattle or we'll shut it for you. How would you like to have your lips stitched together?" That threat alone was enough to silence little Edward for a while.

"Nice tune," said the hulk. "What is it?"

His neighbour piped up, "I know it… It's on the tip of my tongue… Got it! Nah! The name escapes me. But I know, I know it. It'll annoy me now until I remember."

"Know it or not," said the soldier, threateningly. "If you speak again, I'll cut your tongue out."

The convicts in that wagon shuffled their feet nervously. There were a few coughs and splutters together with the metallic rattle of their restraints but no one spoke, at least not audibly. Soon, all three carts were loaded and the cob horses drawing them moved off from the prison gates in the direction of the docks at Woolwich.

They were a miserable sight in the drizzling grey of the solemn afternoon. The horses' convoy plodded along the cobbled streets, their hooves punching holes in the muffled silence, as the heavily clouded sky hung above them oppressively and the rain continued to fall.

***

Now, well into their journey, Jack dared to lift his eyes and scour the faces of his compatriots. They were a rough looking lot but none so scary as Bill Sikes, thought Jack. That brute always had a dangerous, unpredictable glint in his eye, as both he, Sikes' girlfriend, Nancy, and the other urchins could attest. Jack was glad Bill was dead. The man was unhinged, his violent nature well known amongst them all. Even Fagin was afraid of him. It was good he was gone and could hurt no one else again.

The cloud formation in the dreary sky began to take on more definitive shapes rather than the dull, blanket of monochrome grey. The cumulous nimbus clouds had started to roll in, threatening sharper showers and more. Jack prepared to get wet. In fact, he thought, it would be quite a relief. He wished he could move his dirt warm hands and refresh his face with the rain; not that he liked washing but the stench of those surrounding him made him more aware of the unpleasant odours a man's body could create.

People passing the wagons stared and shouted lewd comments, making menacing gestures, and mocking the prisoners. Jack cast his eyes down once more to shut out the bullying abuse that was hurled from the roadside and blinked back the hot stinging salt tears that promised to course down his cheeks. He knew he mustn't cry. It was a sign of weakness and that would never do in this company. He swallowed hard.

The clip clop of horses' hooves seemed endless and time dragged on until Jack could smell the sewage and rubbish on the Thames quayside in Woolwich where the great prison hulk, HMS Dasher was moored. It looked like a gypsy camp hung with bedding, clothes, and rotting rigging; a floating shanty town. The carts progressed to the small jetty and stopped. The accompanying captain barked an order and the former inmates of Newgate prison were forced to unload. One by one they clanked out of the wagons onto the ground and shuffled into line to wait.

One of the soldiers marched to the cannon sitting on the jetty and loaded it. On the captain's order it was fired. The resounding boom alerted those on the ship and two boats were seen to be lowered into the debris strewn, fetid water rowed by convicts with several soldiers in each watching them. They headed for the shore, each pull accompanied by a metronome count shouted out to keep the strokes in time, all oars working together.

Once moored, the captives clambered aboard. The soldiers on shore gave each boat a shove to propel them on their way and they were rowed to the great decaying prison ship.

Finally onboard the prisoners were counted and forced to strip wash using some disinfectant soap to kill the parasites that had hidden in their clothes and bodies. Each one was given fresh, clean but shabby prison garb and their old clothes were destroyed.

From there they were herded in groups to await instruction. The youngest kept together before the adults. Jack found himself next to young Edward. The whole journey had been exhausting and as they sat waiting on the wooden deck the two lads fell into a fitful sleep.

They were rudely awoken by a gruff, ruddy faced man who prodded them awake. "On your feet, both of you," he hissed at them. They awoke with a start and for a moment Jack wondered where he was, then he remembered.

Here the weather could change in an instant and the remnants of the rain laden clouds from earlier had been chased away by a southerly wind that warmed the boys' chill bones. The sun beamed down gracing the deck and prisoners with its glow as Jack and Edward stood in line waiting for their next orders.

After the brief sleep, some of Jack's cheekiness and lively personality resurfaced. He attempted to parade his clobber to his new companion, "Lovely bit of smutter I've got. Known for it, I am," he said perkily in his cockney accent.

Edward admired his own garb, "At least this fits."

Jack boasted, "I'm used to standing out from the crowd. Clothes maketh the man. That's what Fagin used to say to me."

"Who's Fagin?"

Jack paused slightly as he remembered his old life and said quietly, "No one... Not now." He changed the subject and sounded brighter, more friendly, "What do they call you?"

"Edward."

Jack thrust out his hand, as would a gentleman, "Pleased to meet you, Ted."

"No, Edward," he insisted. "It's what my mother used to call me," he said with a hint of sadness.

"Suit yourself."

"What do they call you?" asked Edward.

"Me? I'm Jack Dawkins. They call me The Artful Dodger."

Soon the gruff man's voice boomed out, "Move out, now. Down below! Watch your step." The crocodile line of convicts filed down to the prisoners' area. Jack gazed about him. It was a hell on earth; a floating dungeon with continual rattling of chains, the aura of departed souls, the smell of dirt and fear, and the noise of vermin, oaths and execrations.

Rats emboldened by living cheek to jowl with convicts ran freely below deck, scratching, nipping, gnawing and attacking the soft flesh of men. Their sharp clawed feet quick enough to evade a swiping hand, their pointed teeth tearing at cloth to reach human tissue and their appetites for blood growing with each new batch of arrivals.

Guards clamped young Jack into irons. He almost said that there was no need. He wasn't going anywhere. He was hardly a threat to anyone given his size.

Edward was next. He, too, was chained and fettered. Jack glanced at the young boy. He felt for him. He didn't know why the young lad should touch his heart, as he'd always looked out for himself, just for himself, you could only count on number one, he'd been told in the past. It was something he'd always lived by. That way, there were no expectations and no disappointments.

Behind young Jack and Edward stood a tall thin, middle-aged prisoner, Gipps. He wore a black eye patch and spoke in the heavy lilting tones of Ireland. His shoulders were slumped wearily but in spite of everything he maintained a merry twinkle in his eye.

The guard standing behind him gave him a prod with his baton, "You, move it!"

"Yes, sir." Gipps fell in behind Jack and Edward. It was his turn to be put in irons. "Oh, yer a terrible man, so you are."

"Yeah? Well, you can't be no saint else you wouldn't be here, would ya?" was the response.

Jack had fallen silent as he took in the squalid surroundings and conditions. A couple of slop buckets in the corner for urine and faeces. Tattered, mildewing patches of straw, lay in clumps, most of it wet and dirty. It was far worse than any place he had dwelt before, even the derelict, poverty stricken back to back houses in the east end of London were luxurious compared to this. The boards of the deck above made a ceiling so low that Gipps was forced to stoop.

The guard went to a hay bale stuffed in the corner that had started to moulder. He then proceeded to pull it apart and tossed it to the prisoners, "Here's your bedding. Don't get too comfortable." He grinned revealing a mouthful of crooked and broken teeth.

"Is this where we sleep?" asked Jack of no one in particular as he looked around the filthy conditions.

"Bout all you could do here," mused Gipps answering for the guard.

The guard shrugged and returned to the top deck, while Jack, Edward and Gipps struggled to make themselves comfortable.

"Down in this dungeon, there is no day and no night. It will all be one, as you will learn, my little friends; so, you will," said Gipps, who spoke with assured certainty.

***

The pleasant day had turned to coal black night, not that the prisoners were aware. It was as Gipps had said, day and night had become one. Jack had attempted to focus his eyes on the gaps in the decking where fingers of light had tried to poke through. However, it had little effect on the pitch black of that crypt of disease and death where they were housed.

A tedious routine had been established and each prisoner had been furnished with a clay bowl and enamel mug. They were ordered to take care of them. If they lost them or broke them they would starve or die of thirst. They had to protect these utensils as they would their own life, for their existence depended on it.

A thin faced young man with piercing blue eyes carried a pot of a thin soupy type substance with bits of cabbage leaves floating in it. Behind him was another elderly man who stooped from the waist clearly suffering from some spinal disorder. He carried a wooden bucket of water and a ladle.

Each prisoner was commanded to hold out their bowl and mug, to be filled.

The cramped space was now filled with convicts all secured to the rings on the floor of the deck. The crushing pressure of so many bodies pressed up against each other produced a strong, sour odour that made Jack want to gag.

Gipps, Jack and Edward sat manacled to the floor, still restrained in irons in the grim dusty dark. The lean faced man with a saturnine look rasped an order. His voice sounded as if his vocal chords had been cut and stitched together with cat gut. "Bowls up."

All along the side of the deck, prisoners in regimented fashion raised their bowls and cups as one. The guards walked along the lines and a meagre portion of broth was slopped into each one. The stooped elderly man dipped his ladle in the water and poured it into the upturned cups. From a rough cloth apron pocket, he produced some mouldy biscuits, some alive with weevils, and handed one to each captive.

Gipps studied the murky water in his mug. It had a dark cobweb like mass that had settled at the bottom and complained, "The water's damn filthy. I wouldn't drink it, Patrick."

"Jack, me name's Jack."

"Jack," said Gipps resolutely. "Okay, Patrick."

Edward peered at his biscuit and shuddered as a weevil dropped from it onto his lap. "I can't eat this."

Jack, who had known what it was to be without, tried to chivvy the young lad up, "A day or so without food and you eat anything, trust me."

As if on cue, a black ship rat scurried between their feet. Gipps eyed the creature with his one good eye and agreed, "Aye, even him."

Jack studied Gipps; "How long do they keep us here?"

"Till a ship's free to take us away I s'pose. Could be anytime. Ah well. Things'll be better when we get on the boat."

"But, what if we get ill?" asked Edward timidly.

"Reckon that'd be the least of our worries," said Gipps with a sigh and momentarily closed his good eye.

Once the round of prisoners had been fed and watered the convicts were left to try and sleep. It was almost impossible shackled as they were. Their only concession to comfort was a little bit of straw, which they could place to alleviate sore limbs and buttocks. Some men found it easier to sleep than others and those lucky ones soon fell into a roaring medley of snores.

Edward was filled with nerves and began to whistle shrilly that same tune that he had on the wagon as they had travelled. It was only then that Jack realised the irritating noise, which had so annoyed him before, had been coming from his new companion. Jack sighed in resignation and rolled over as best he could to escape the screeching in his ear.

This repetitive procedure was the same day in and day out. There was no respite, no escape and it was almost impossible to tell how long they had all been holed up in this inhuman place.

***

Three months later there was a change in the air. Footsteps resounded on the upper deck. Voices could be heard rumbling above. Gipps jerked his head aloft, "Reckon that's the sign."

"Why? What's happening?" asked Jack.

"Think we be on the move, so we are," said Gipps in his lilting tones.

"Anything to get out of here. It'll be good to feel the air on my face," murmured Edward.

A flinty-eyed soldier came down the steps to their deck. He had a handkerchief tied around his face to help prevent the putrid smell from invading his nostrils. He had with him a younger soldier whose face began to take on a greenish yellow hue as he saw the conditions and smelt the thick rancid odour. He walked along the line and his hands trembled as he fumbled with the rusty key to unlock the prisoners from the floor. The lead guard bellowed, "On your feet. All of you, now." He punctuated his order with a cough as the acrid stink hit his throat.

The prisoners rose unsteadily, the distinct lack of exercise showing, as many were weak and unsteady on their feet. Another order was roared although this time the guard's voice cracked somewhat. "Forward march."

The convicts shuffled ahead disturbing the rats who had huddled into the bodies of the captives seeking warmth and a chance to nip at their withered flesh. The men moved towards the companionway that led to the upper deck, albeit slowly. The lead guard smacked his baton in his hand and wasn't afraid to crack it on the legs of those he deemed to be too slow. Some buckled under the beating, which threatened to take down others in the line.

The boys finally reached the rickety wooden steps and Jack climbed up them quite nimbly for one so malnourished and small, eager to reach the light. Edward followed as quickly as he could, not wanting to lose the one friend he believed he had made. Gipps was close behind. Soon, they were on the top deck blinking in the bright light that made their eyes twinge.

Jack and Edward joined the line of men who were shuffling down a gangway and dropping into boats tied up alongside. Jack squinted in the sunshine and could see three horse-drawn drays waiting on the river bank together with a team of armed soldiers.

Jack, Edward and Gipps were loaded into the middle boat, where prisoners took the oars and rowed back, paddling in time to the metronome count, just as before.

Edward whispered to Jack, "Are we going to the ship?"

"Looks like it," said Jack, a hint of optimism in his voice.

"Is it a long way?" asked Edward.

Jack rolled his eyes, "How the hell should I know?"

Edward bit his lip and went quiet as they watched the carts approaching the jetty to pick them up. They could hear soldiers yelling orders as the first wagon went on its way and the second drew up. The impatient horses stamped and their nostrils steamed in the morning air. Jack looked sideways at his flaxen haired companion who seemed determined to stick close to him. His irritation with the repetitive whistling was slightly diminished and the Dodger felt somewhat sorry for the little boy. He couldn't think for the life of him what the kiddie had done to be incarcerated. He thought that at some point he would ask him; when he felt more comfortable to do that.

The boat skulled to the side of the jetty and a soldier hollered for them to prepare to land. Edward and Jack were hauled out by guards on the other side and propelled towards the waiting wagon where they were boarded in their group, Edward firmly following Jack with Gipps behind.

One sad faced man with a balding head who muttered to himself, struggled to get in the dray and suffered a beating from the guard. He was cracked on his legs, back and head and fell onto the cold, slippery stone. His head split and began to bleed profusely congealing in a pool under him. The man's eyes appeared to have rolled back in his head. The soldier dragged him out of the way as the others were loaded. Every now and again he would kick the still man, who didn't stir.

The order was given and the cart moved off on its journey. Jack stared out of the back of the wagon and watched other prisoners being loaded. The fallen convict was still on the ground and Jack supposed he must be dead and a shiver ran through him. Lastly, he gazed back at the hulking prison ship that dominated the skyline. It sat there waiting like a predatory giant insect with its rancid rigging fluttering like shredded bats' wings to lure, engulf and devour the next batch of men that would be deposited in that hell hole. With that image in his head Jack pulled his gaze away and felt sorrowful for those who would be the next inmates.

The cart plodded onwards.

***

Hours later the sun had died sinking to the horizon in a blaze of fire. The unloaded prisoners sat down by a huge fire. It cheered their spirits and some of Jack's cheekiness returned as he watched the guards tending the horses at the side of the road. One guard, a large man who walked with a swagger, strolled around them. He clearly enjoyed his position of authority.

Jack buoyed up by the warmth of the fire braved asking a question. His face broke into a lopsided grin, "When do we get our grub?"

"After the horses," came the brusque response as the guard ambled off.

Another soldier, carrying a wooden bucket containing water and a ladle, spooned some water into the cups they had been given. Another soldier carried a sack and dished out hunks of bread and a biscuit.

"At least this water's clean," said Jack in approval as he took a sip.

Edward glanced across at Gipps who appeared to be grinning inanely, "What you smiling at, sir?"

Gipps still beaming wildly, looked up at the sky and back to the others before sighing contentedly, "I'm happy, so I am."

Jack exchanged a look with Edward and rolled his eyes raising his finger to his temple in a circular motion, which made Edward grin. Jack, his curiosity piqued, turned to Gipps, "What you got to be happy about?"

"Doesn't matter."

Jack shrugged and drank some more of the water before tearing into the bread that was somewhat fresher than they were given on the hulk. He examined his biscuit and that, too, appeared more wholesome. 'Maybe that's what made Gipps happy,' thought Jack. And then mumbled, "He doesn't take much pleasing."

"What you say?" asked Edward.

"Nothin', no matter."

"Still, it's better here in the fresh air by the fire, ain't it?" said Edward.

"I suppose. We still don't know what's gonna happen. Anything could," said Jack with a flicker of worry crossing his puckish face.

***

The cargo of convicts had finally arrived in Portsmouth after two days of travelling. The tangy smell of the salt air assailed their nostrils and Jack was filled with an inexplicable feeling of hope and yet he knew that he had nothing to be hopeful about but at least the sun was smiling down on them as they gazed at a tall ship, the Aurora, which waited in the dock, ready to transport them to Australia.

The prisoners, still in their original groupings, were ordered to board and shuffled along the gangplank to the decks where they were commanded to wait. Every man stood there cowed, broken and in trepidation of what was to come. Rumours had abounded and stories had reached the criminals' ears, told by sadistic guards who enjoyed seeing the men's discomfort. The tall tales had reached unimaginable proportions and filled many with acute dread and fear. Jack was more resigned and always believed to take gossip as exaggerated chit-chat. He believed it best to reserve an opinion until he knew the truth. It was no good frightening people for entertainment. The journey to come couldn't be as bad as already experienced, he thought. He needed to think positively and look forward to the new country as an opportunity and a chance to start again. At least, that is what he hoped.

2: The Voyage to Australia into the Unknown Gets Underway

The prisoners were grouped on deck as it waited in Portsmouth dock preparing to transport them to Australia. As the crew readied themselves to depart, the men, still manacled, remained silent, their eyes fixed on Captain Dowson, a formidable looking man, with a shock of wild, white hair. He appeared to tower over them, standing, as he did, above them on the bridge deck. He clutched a heavy black leather bound Bible in one hand and surveyed those in front of him. As his eyes locked on various individuals in front of him they averted his gaze; such was the power in this man's presence.

A hush even fell over the working crew as the captain prepared to speak. His voice boomed out, "I am Captain Dowson. I am the law onboard this ship; the only higher authority is God." He held the Bible aloft emblazoned with a gold cross for all to see. His lips curved disdainfully as he dropped his arms and continued, "I have the power to flog you, box you, or hang you."

A look of puzzlement flickered across Jack's face. He whispered out of the side of his mouth to Edward, "What does he mean, box us? With his fists?"

Captain Dowson raised the Bible once more as he recited words said many times before. "For we ourselves were also foolish, but according to his mercy he saved us. You men are deserters. You have deserted God and had you been in the military and deserted, you would have been executed. In their infinite mercy God and the law have given you a second chance. There will not be a third." He turned to the guards and ordered them with a sweeping gesture, "Take them below."

Jack, Edward and Gipps were propelled forward with the others and forced to shuffle below to the prisoners' quarters where a young guard assigned them their berths, which were cages containing bunks. He pressed his baton into Gipps' back, "Right you three, in there. Move."

The ship lurched suddenly. There was a roar of men's voices shouting above the rising wind and the scream of mewling gulls, which could just be heard below deck as the increasing gusts blew through the sails and gaps in the wooden deck.

Edward looked up startled, "What's that? What's happening?"

Gipps face broke into a grin and he sighed in satisfaction, "We've set sail."

***

A few hours later, the ship was well on its way, rising and dipping in the waves and troughs of the Atlantic Ocean being blown by the strong, westerly wind. The timbers of the vessel groaned combining with the shriek of the wind as it funnelled through the gaps and cracks in the decking.

Jack, with his eyes stubbornly closed, was lying down struggling to sleep in the wild cacophony. Finally, his eyes blinked open. It was impossible to slumber. He leaned up on one elbow to hear Edward ask Gipps something that he was curious about, too.

"What did you do? To be on here?"

Gipps scratched his stubbly beard and with a hint of a sparkle in his eye smiled as he replied, "Me? Just a bit of light thieving. Gipps is a master," and he grinned even more broadly.

Jack piped up, "Oh, pockets?"

"No, vases and things."

"That's a daft thing to steal, Gipps. You get seen carting big stuff about."

"Aye, well I wanted to be seen. I was only doing it to get caught."

"You must be touched," said Jack scornfully.

"No, I just wanted to see my daughter. She's already over there, you see."

"Why's she over there?" asked Edward.

"She was transported over a year ago. She was expecting a baby but they still lagged her. I didn't have no money to get out there. So, I thought I'd get them to take me. I've conned the bastards." Gipps grinned.

"What? You did this deliberate?" said Jack incredulously.

"Yeah. But I couldn't get arrested for ages. An' I had to be careful not to do anything too malicious or I'd get the drop. Be no use to anyone then."

"We're none of us much use now. How d'you know you'll find her when you get there?" said Jack.

"Well, can't be that big a place, can it? Australia?" said Gipps with a look of hope on his face. "I'll find her."

Jack didn't look too certain and screwed his face up in an impish way. "I wonder when we'll get out from here? We've been stuck down here for nearly a week."

How do you know it's a week?" asked Edward.

"Easy. I look at the tiny bit of light that shows through the decking. When it gets dark that's one day. Then I wait for the next light to show through and so on. I make marks on the floor by my bunk. If I count them that's five. So, nearly a week. Seven days in a week ain't there?"

Gipps nodded, "Yes, me lad, there is. They'll have to let us up on deck soon, so they will."

"Why?" asked Edward.

"We need to move, get our legs working. If we don't we won't be able to walk proper. How can they get us to work when we get there, if we're too weak to move?"

"Makes sense," said Jack perkily. "Remember on that horrible hulk?"

"The prison one, Dasher or whatever it was called?"

"Yeah. Well, some of the others could hardly walk after being chained to the floor for so long."

"Yes, and they got a beating for it," remembered Edward.

"We'll be fine, all of us," reassured Gipps.

"How do you know?" asked Edward.

"I just do."

The trio fell silent and watched as the light coming through the cracks faded and they were left in the pitch black dark of night. All that could be heard were the creaking timbers and the sonorous snoring of prisoners, interspersed with whistles, snorts and grunts. Jack covered his head with his arms and struggled to sleep. But, finally, with the rocking of the boat he managed to block out all the extraneous sounds and fell asleep.

***

At first light, the rays of the sun poked through the gaps in the decking casting bar-like shadows on the sleeping forms. There was a clatter of feet as a portly guard with a red face descended the rickety wooden steps. He rattled his baton on the wooden struts of their cages. "Wakey, wakey!" he shouted in his gravelly voice.

Men were startled awake by the sound. Jack's eyes blinked open, "Think we'd be used to that by now," he whispered.

"I ain't never gonna get used to it," said Edward mournfully.

"Come on!" shouted the guard. "Rouse yourselves." He marched along the line of cages opening the doors and ordered, "Right! Up on deck all of ya!"

Jack looked around in consternation, "What's happening?"

The guard yelled back, "You're getting your exercise. Get some fresh air."

Jack and the others rose up. Jack, rubbed his eyes and stifled a yawn. "How often do we get this?"

Back came the prompt response, "Once a week."

Keen to see the sun and feel the wind on their faces they scrambled out eagerly and filed out of their cages to the ladder that led to the top deck. The guard stood at the base and watched carefully as each prisoner climbed up. He tapped a few with his stick, not to hurt them, but to urge them on. "Hurry up! Don't keep everyone waiting. Come on. Move along."

Jack and Edward climbed steadily with a hint of enthusiasm in their movements. Gipps was following close behind them. As they reached the top and clambered out onto the deck they forgot their stiff limbs and weakened muscles, and gazed in amazement at their surroundings. Everywhere they looked they saw sea. The vessel fell and rose in the troughs as gusts of wind occasionally whipped up the deep blue water.

The sky had scattered rolling heavy clouds that were being bowled along by breezes that sometimes made the boat roll. Every so often the convicts, shaky on their feet, were forced to grasp the thick chandlers' ropes that ran alongside the inner edge of the deck's rails to prevent themselves from tumbling over. The boat felt very small on the vast ocean that stretched around them in every direction with no sight of land anywhere.

Edward's mouth dropped open in awe, "Cor, where's the world gone?"

Jack rubbed his eyes again as if he couldn't believe what he was seeing and stared about him, "Dunno. It was here yesterday."

"Start moving!" roared the plump guard. "On you go, walk the deck until I tell you to stop."

The prisoners moved forward slowly in twos and threes to march around the perimeter of the deck. Jack, Edward and Gipps walked together aware that Captain Dowson was watching them all closely from the bridge.

Gipps muttered quietly, "Shame. I'd like to have seen England one last time. I got to see Ireland as we pulled away from it. Ain't never gonna see England again, now." A note of regret had entered his voice. Jack and Edward risked a look at their fellow prisoner. Jack could swear he saw the beginning of a tear in the older man's eye.

"Don't expect we'll ever get the chance either," said Edward as much to Jack as to himself.

"S'pect not," said Jack before turning to Gipps. "How long were you in England?"

"I came over in a cattle boat forty year ago. Now, I'm leaving it in much the same way."

"See, you've kept your sense of humour, Gipps."

"Aye, well you're quick with your patter, too, young Jack. You remind me of me at your age."

Jack taken aback at the words turned to Edward, "Hope I don't remind you of him when I'm his age," he said with a wink. "If I live that long."

At that moment a freak wave crashed against the hull and seawater splashed over the deck. Gipps slipped in the pooling water and fell into one of the guards who lost his own footing and tumbled over, sliding across the deck. He struck his head on the capstan. A trickle of blood ran down his face, he lifted his hand and looked in surprise at the amount of blood that transferred to his hand.

Gipps looked on in horror as Captain Dowson, with a wicked gleam in his eye, bawled out, pointing at him, "Bring me that man!" The prisoners all stopped and froze in fear. Captain Dowson bellowed again, "Keep moving." The convicts continued to walk on. All stepped very carefully and most didn't dare to look at Gipps who was being hustled to the bottom of a companionway, which Captain Dowson was descending brandishing his Bible as if it was a weapon, his face as black as Newgate Knocker. His coat tails flapped behind him like some marauding evil creature of the night. His eyes glinted with a malevolent, feral light. He spoke with obvious glee as he approached Gipps who stood trembling. "Assaulting one of my officers. How dare you?"

In panic, Gipps protested, "It was the sea. I fell. It was an accident, so it was." Gipps' face filled with alarm.

Dowson's tone was icy, "I don't tolerate excuses." There was a pause before he added with some pleasure in his voice, "Box him."

The guards hurried to drag Gipps across to part of the deck where a sunken wooden box of about nine foot square with bars on the lid was just visible. One of them opened it up. It contained, ropes, netting and other seafaring paraphernalia leaving little room inside. Dowson ordered Gipps, "Get in."

Gipps stared at the small space in horror and attempted to plead with the cold, intransigent captain, "I'm an old man, Captain."

"And yet you've still not learned to toe the line," the captain sneered.

Gipps began to jabber in protest, "Please, have mercy, sir. Please."

Strong arms lifted him off his feet and thrust him inside the box. Wild with fear, Gipps began to scream as he was crammed inside; the lid was slammed shut and locked. Dowson's mouth twisted into a cruel grin as he saw the pitiful sight of Gipps' fingers poking up through the bars as if reaching to the heavens in supplication.

Young Edward and Jack passed the torture crate and exchanged looks of horror and disbelief at what had just happened. Neither dared to speak. Behind them a gaunt prisoner stopped and stared at the spectacle with a haunted expression on his face before he was shoved in the back and forced to move on.

Dowson's words rang around the deck above the sound of the thundering waves, "You will stay in there for a few hours until you have learned to behave."

Dowson returned to his spot to watch the prisoners continue their marching exercise, but each man was filled with dread with the knowledge of what could happen to any one of them. They walked gingerly around the deck, careful not to do anything that would attract unwarranted attention. By the way they walked it was clear that most prisoners had, had their spirits crushed.

***

Later that night, the wind had all but disappeared. It was much slower going. The sea was calm almost glass-like. The clouds had been chased away to reveal a myriad of stars and the face of a leprous moon, which shone its silver ribbons of light on the water.

Jack and Edward lay on their beds in miserable silence. Gipps' bunk was empty and Jack was visibly losing some of his regained cheeky swagger. Edward had just withdrawn into himself, lost in his own thoughts. It seemed an eternity before they both fell asleep.

***

The next morning, they didn't wake to the spindly fingers of sun poking through the gaps and patterning their faces but by the gruff voice of a guard, which roused them and the others, as he ordered, "Up! Get up the lot of ya!" He rattled his baton back and forth across the bars of the cages rendering further sleep impossible.

Jack awoke rubbing his eyes in the half-light and blinked at the guard. He stretched his arms as much as he could in the confined space and stepped back to allow the guard to enter their cage and give him room to move. Edward stood up meekly and waited silently.

The other prisoners awoken by the noise all stepped out from their bunks and stood up to await their instructions. The guard that had entered Jack and Edward's berth began to strip Gipps' bunk, tossing the meagre bedding on the floor and gathering it up.

Jack watched in confusion, quietly at first until curiosity got the better of him and he dared to speak, "Why you doing that?"

"He won't be needing it again."

"Why's that?"

"He's dead," said the guard with a crooked grin. "Gone. Why? Do you want to join him?"

Jack shook his head vehemently as Edward whispered, "Dead? Gipps is dead?" and Jack moved across to him and put his arm around his shoulder. The guard snorted in derision and left as Jack and Edward swapped a look of abject despair.

After getting over the shock of losing Gipps both Jack and Edward kept to themselves, neither wishing to attract undue attention from any of the guards or the captain whose searching look terrified them. They kept their heads and their eyes down. Nothing was said officially about the big man, they didn't know how he died or what had happened to his body. In hushed whispers at night Jack supposed the gentle giant had been tossed overboard for whatever sea creatures that followed the sailing vessel to devour. "It's a bloomin' shame," muttered Jack. "Ain't never gonna see his daughter or grandkids until they die and then they might never meet."

"Is that what happens?" asked Edward.

"Dunno, really. Only what I've heard."

"Tell me."

"Some say that when you die that's it. Gone for good and nothin' else. But, I had a friend who believed that when your time come, all the folks who'd passed before you and thought a lot of you would come and get you. Take you across to the other side."

"How does that work?"

"Dunno. It's only what I heard."

"Does that mean when my time comes my mother will be there?"

"I s'pect so. Never really thought about it since it was said."

"Then, I'll believe it. It's a lovely thought. It means poor old Gipps will see his family again. He wasn't a bad man."

"No, he wasn't," murmured Jack as he settled down to sleep.

***

The days rolled on melding into each other and life on board the Aurora seemed long and hard. They were forced to listen to Captain Dowson reading religious passages from the Bible. His voice would boom out across the deck of the ship as he repeatedly read his favourite verses. One of which was The Suffering Servant from the book of Isaiah. Often he would stand on the bridge reading dire words of punishment and chastisement to accompany the lashings of the cat o'nine tails used to flog unlucky prisoners whose crimes could be no more than a careless word or not moving quickly enough for the guards when forced to exercise. Their agonised screams would mingle with the captain's monotonous recitation. This man had no mercy, no compassion and appeared to enjoy the suffering of those in his care. Jack and Edward were determined not to be singled out for anything.

In the next cage sat the gaunt prisoner with straggly grey hair that hung in greasy locks around his sallow saturnine face, whose emaciated form was covered in bruises and welts. His face had a troubled look and he would sometimes gaze blankly at

Edward and Jack, never wishing to communicate, never uttering a word, just looking at them with dead eyes, a blank stare that was devoid of any emotion.

***

One night, many weeks into their voyage, Edward began to shiver uncontrollably. He was unable to move, seeming paralysed and running a fever. He lay on his bunk sweating, his face covered with an unhealthy sheen but was too ill to care. The gaunt prisoner watched young Edward with dull glazed eyes that looked but didn't appear to see. Jack stayed at Edward's side willing him to improve. It was Jack who moistened his lips with water and helped him to drink. It was Jack who tried to cool the young lad down with rags soaked in water. It was Jack who sat with him while he shivered and helped him to eat.

The guards took no notice. No one worried about the boy or asked after him and Jack thought it best not to say anything but kept a vigil next to him. One evening Edward's food ration was placed at the side of his bunk but lay there untouched. One weasely faced convict with hooded savage eyes and a reasonably well defined body, for living in such circumstances, watched and waited for his moment to strike and steal away young Edward's helping of food but Jack was too quick; he stood his ground and prevented the man from taking it. The whole altercation was surveyed by the silent gaunt prisoner who was looking more wraith-like with each passing day.

Jack continued to help Edward to sips of water and tried to encourage him to eat something to build up his strength. He persevered to get him to take some thin broth and nibble on a hunk of bread. His persistence paid off and days later Edward began to regain his colour. His lips were no longer blue and he looked more alert, which was just as well, as the portly guard came down below and issued the order, "Everybody up and out, exercise time." He rattled his baton on the struts of the cages as the prisoners filed out ready to ascend the ladder to the deck.

Although still weak, Jack helped Edward out and up onto the deck where the order was barked at them to start moving. On the bridge the captain began his impassioned rhetoric interspersed with quotes from the Bible. The men shuffled around the rocking deck in time to the slow beat of the captain's words that punched through the sound of the crashing waves.

Edward paused momentarily in his weary weekly plod as the gaunt man stopped, his eyes still blank and staring. He gazed at Edward with a look that penetrated through to Edward's psyche. Then, without warning he clambered over the rail and threw himself into the surging ocean. The guards rushed towards the incident as Edward looked down in horror at the man's half-starved body floating in the water. The man made no attempt to swim but allowed himself to be dragged down slowly by the swirling sea. Edward was rooted to the spot his eyes fixed on the disappearing body. He suddenly came to when the guards pushed him out of the way. Jack caught Edward by the arm and propelled him forward in line with the other convicts engaged on their relentless march around the deck. He prayed that Captain Dowson hadn't noticed.

Time passed painfully slowly until they were commanded to return below. Almost gratefully Jack helped to usher Edward back down the ladder to their cage. Edward's eyes were drawn to the adjacent berth, which had housed the gaunt prisoner who had thrown himself to his death. Jack tried to cheer Edward up with some of his chirpy chatter, when a guard appeared and entered the next cage to dismantle the dead prisoner's bunk and gather up the bedding. The boys fell silent and watched.

There was a subdued hush amongst those convicts back in their places as Captain Dowson did something he never did. He came down the ladder and walked along the line of cages scrutinising each inmate. Jack and Edward kept their heads down and their eyes lowered, when suddenly a huge hullaballoo broke out further down the line. Forgetting his fear and hesitance Jack rushed up to the front of the bars and tried to crane his head through to see what the disturbance was all about. Dowson was arresting a man the others called, 'The Preacher'. The man was flanked by two guards, forced to the bottom of the ladder and made to ascend.

Dowson's voice reverberated around the lower deck. "I will not tolerate disobedience or any kind of disruption on the Aurora. Prisoners found guilty of misconduct or crimes aboard will be punished severely. Be warned, I am not afraid to pronounce the death penalty. I am the law on this ship, the authority that you will answer to. You will do well to remember that."

The silence hung heavily in the confined space. The prisoners hardly dared to breathe. Dowson's lips curved up with enjoyment at being able to wield his absolute supremacy as he strutted past the rows of cages. He coughed slightly as the acrid, sour stench of the men caught in the back of his throat. He took out a handkerchief and pressed it against his nose and mouth before following the guards and the man up the ladder.

Jack turned to Edward, "What was that all about?"

Edward shrugged, "No idea. But I wouldn't want to be him, would you?"

***

It was a day later and for once the air was still and warm. The boat pitched gently in the unusually calm sea. The sky was cloudless and a brilliant azure blue. The blazing sun burned down relentlessly on the deck of the Aurora and on the heads of the assembled prisoners that were amassed on the deck. Captain Dowson, clutching his Bible, and his officers were gathered on the aft deck.

Jack and Edward both wondered what was going on and stared about them in bewilderment. On the aft deck stood an officer with a drum, looking as if he was ready to beat out a tattoo. There were a number of other soldiers including the Marine sergeant, a tall and sturdy man with a large bushy moustache, who waited by the stepped entrance to the deck. At the end of the deck, close to the edge of the ship, dangled a noose, which caught the eyes of all the prisoners who gazed at it with trepidation.

Jack whispered to Edward fearfully, "The evergreen, the gibbet..."

Edward's mouth dropped open, "A hanging?" Jack nodded and swallowed hard.

Captain Dowson signalled to the Marine sergeant who disappeared from view.

The drummer with great ceremony struck out a sustained drum roll as the middle-aged convict known as 'The Preacher' was brought up on the deck. The man was forced to his knees and made to look up at Captain Dowson who gave the pronouncement that all could hear, "You have been found guilty of attacking another convict with a knife and have been sentenced to death. The sentence will be carried out with immediate effect... Do you have anything to say?"

The officers hauled the man to his feet who spoke in a soft educated tone, "To what end? You would not listen at my so-called trial and you will not listen now. I told you I had been attacked and had been forced to defend myself. Captain Dowson, you know that I am a man of the cloth and would not lie, yet you seem determined to get rid of me. So be it. Just hang me and be done but don't pretend this has anything to do with crime and punishment," he said accusingly before continuing, "your definition of God is so very far from mine. Yours is fear. Mine is love." He concluded, "You must be very afraid."

He began to walk towards the noose and announced clearly for all to hear, "Let's finish this." Dowson looked on scornfully with a slight curve of his lips as the Marine sergeant helped the convict up the steps to the waiting rope, which he placed over his head as the officer waited for the captain's signal.

The preacher turned to the sergeant and said more kindly, "Leave go of me. You shall not have my death on your conscience." The sergeant released his hold as the convict turned and stared deeply into Dowson's dark eyes. He said slowly and forcefully, "May *my* God forgive you, Captain Dowson," before he crossed himself.

Dowson stiffened and his face drained of colour and for once he looked disturbed at another's words.

The condemned man turned away defiantly. His bearing was proud and dignified as he drew himself up to his full height before throwing himself off the side of the ship. He came to a halt as the rope went taut and hung from a spar out over the water, where he swung on the creaking line.

Dowson lifted his Bible aloft and as if to regain his equilibrium he shouted, "I am the law on this ship with God and right is on my side. Let this be a lesson to all of you, if you want to survive and live." He turned with a flourish and disappeared from the deck.

There were wild fearful whisperings among the prisoners before the guards moved them off deck and back to their berths. The event had alarmed even the toughest of men. No one was left in any doubt that they could easily suffer the same fate. Many wondered how much longer they had to endure the trip. By Jack's reckoning they had been at sea for a good three months.

Hours later a cry rang out across the ship and could just be heard below by the prisoners, "Land ahoy!"

***

On shore, the sun was a flaming ball of fire, which burned unforgivingly on a young lookout soldier standing wearily on the parapet of a watchtower. He wiped his brow of the beading sweat that was a constant in the scalding heat when a movement on the ocean attracted his attention. He shaded his eyes as he looked out to sea, set down his rifle and picked up his telescope. He focused on the distant spot and could see the

Aurora a few miles out in the bay. On full alert, he scrambled down the ladder and sped off passing a foot patrol of two soldiers. The young sapper shouted out as he ran past, "Ship's coming in! Round up the squads. Notify the governor."

The two soldiers picked up their pace and hurried on; they dashed across the forecourt to the lively stockade, a giant wooden structure housing battalions of men who appeared to be organising themselves into groups in readiness for the ship's arrival.

On the streets of Port Jackson people were milling. Others stared out of the windows of the dwellings close to the harbour where crowds were gathering. All were waiting to see what the latest arrival of the Aurora would bring.

***

Onboard ship, the prisoners were being hustled out of their cages and up onto the deck. As they hit the extremely warm air and the fierce dazzling glare of the sun they blinked blindly trying to adjust to the dramatic change in temperature. It was always warm and stuffy below deck but this heat was something very different.

The prisoners looked out in awe at the bustling harbour where women gutted fish, men sawed wood for boat building and the ever growing quayside crowd watched, chattering excitedly. Flying from a pole on the jetty was the Union flag.

As the Aurora docked, a soldier on horseback, Captain Bourne, with hair the colour of conkers, cantered down to the harbour. Captain Dowson and two of his officers walked down the gangplank and stepped ashore to be greeted by Bourne as he dismounted from his powerful looking dark steed and he was immediately flanked by two of his own officers.

The two captains saluted each other respectfully. It was clear they knew each other and had done this ritual a number of times before.

"Good morning, Captain Bourne."

"Good morning, Captain Dowson."

"I transfer two hundred and ninety-seven prisoners from God's care to yours. Three souls were taken to God's side on the voyage."

"I thank you, Captain."

Captain Dowson saluted his opposite number again and stepped back.

"Is there anything I need to know about any of them?"

Dowson shook his head, "No, Captain."

"Very well, carry on."

"Start bringing them down, Sergeant."

The young sergeant clicked his heels in acknowledgement, "Sir!" and stepped back onboard to unload the prisoners that had begun to file off the ship, down the gangplank to the quay whilst the two captains engaged in light chit-chat as they passed the time.

"Pleasant voyage?"

"Perfectly."

"Good. Will you dine with us this evening?"

"I'd be delighted, Captain," replied Dowson beaming broadly.

They continued with more inconsequential chatter as the prisoners began to disembark. Waiting for them was a group of armed soldiers who counted them as they set foot on dry land then organised them into groups. Many swayed where they stood in the blistering heat still feeling the movement of the ship, not used to being on dry land.

A lot of the prisoners were finding it difficult to walk having unstable legs with poor balance. Edward muttered to Jack, "I feel as if the whole world is moving. My head's reeling. Everything's wavy-like."

"I know what you mean. It's as if I'm gonna fall over." And he put his hand on Edward's shoulder as much to steady himself as well as Edward.

Captain Bourne raised his voice with an order, "Sergeant?"

"Yes, sir?"

"Take them away."

The sergeant turned towards his men as Captain Bourne remounted and moved off on his burnished black stallion.

"Right, lads! Take them up," the sergeant roared.

The soldiers manoeuvred into two groups and stood either side of the batch of convicts ready to march the still manacled prisoners through the streets following in the wake of Captain Bourne who led the way on horseback.

In the busy thoroughfares, street urchins played, women watched suspiciously from doorsteps and balconies while dogs set up a frenzied barking at the new arrivals. They passed a number of shops and advertising billboards. Jack and Edward looked around at their unfamiliar surroundings and took everything in, marvelling at the differences between England and the land they had been transported to, Australia. Jack wondered if Gipps' daughter could be one of the women observing their arrival but that thought was chased away when Port Jackson Penal colony came into view. It was set high on a hill, dominating the town, a huge settlement comprised of six separate stockades.

Inside, filthy prisoners, all in garish uniforms of yellow and black looked eagerly to see the new arrivals. Prominent among the inmates were three men wearing armbands, who appeared to stand a head above the other men as if in positions of importance. The biggest and most menacing was a thickset man in his thirties with a shock of flame coloured hair called Rust, with a pockmarked face. His two compatriots were a stocky man, Masters and his equally powerful looking friend, McQueen.

The prisoners still shackled found it difficult to walk and shuffled towards the prison. The strident voice of the sergeant blared out, "Pick those feet up." The men suitably cowed did their best but young Edward stumbled and it was Jack's hand that saved him from tumbling over. The stuttering movement caught the attention of Rust whose eyes narrowed into evil slits as he spotted Jack. He studied the boy carefully before muttering something to Masters and McQueen, who in turn scrutinised the young Dodger. Jack intent on trying to walk without losing his footing didn't notice that the eyes of Rust and his henchmen were upon him.

They entered the stockade in line and many of the new arrivals were greeted warmly by the inmates as old acquaintances were renewed. There was much calling out of welcome and some jeering as they all finally stepped inside. The soldiers drew back the stockade gate and a massive wooden bar was placed across it securing them from the outside world.

Edward gazed about him as friends greeted each other. He turned to Jack, "It's just like the first day at school, in it? Everyone seems to know each other."

"Dunno. Never went to school."

They marched on past motley groups of men engaged in card games, others playing with dice and shouting excitedly with money in their hands. Another batch were practising the shell game or thimblerig as it was often called. Edward stopped to stare but Jack pulled at his sleeve urging him on, "Don't stop. We'll likely get a beating."

"What are they doing?"

"Looks like some sort of gambling school. That last game is a con to steal money, fast hands and fingers are needed to fleece people out of what they've got."

"Don't seem much like prison to me. Maybe it won't be so bad here after all," said Edward optimistically. "At least their manacles and chains are gone."

"Maybe," said Jack and then nudged Edward to look as they passed the body of a youth hanging from a gallows. "Then again, maybe not."

They continued on until they were split into groups of ten. Jack and Edward were herded into a spartan, scruffy dormitory containing ten very primitive beds. A guard stood watching them as they entered. Once inside he bellowed his instructions, "Right! This is where you'll sleep. Each of you take a blanket and make up your bed. Soon as you're done, wait by the bed, then you're off to get your uniforms. Shape it or else."

Jack, Edward and the other prisoners obeyed the guard. They found it tough sorting out their beds with manacles on, so Jack and Edward worked together and were the first to finish.

The guard barked at them again, "Once you're kitted out with your uniform your manacles will be removed. Obey the rules, serve your time and you'll be all right. Break them and..." the guard did a cutting gesture with his hand across his throat.

***

The new intake were now all in their uniforms and had been marched to the food hall where they received their rations. The sun streamed through openings and dirt cracked window panes, showing the dust motes that floated thickly in the hot humid air revealing the drab, dusty dreariness of their environment.

At the top of the hall, stretched a long trestle table where a row of the most hardened men sat, all wearing armbands, as if they were at the head table of some official organisation. Right in the centre of them sat Rust and either side of him were Masters and McQueen. They all looked ravenous. They ate with few manners and surveyed the men in front of them as they filled their bellies, speaking sloppily in between mouthfuls.

Jack and Edward were more than delighted with their fare. Jack tucked into his soup and bread. He studied his and everyone else's vittles and nodded in approval. "Blimey, feast for a king this lot." He was so busy eating he didn't notice Rust taking more than a passing interest in him, nor did he see the eyes of Masters and McQueen running over him.

Both boys happily chomped away on their bread, wiping it around the inside of their bowls to get every last morsel. Jack patted his tummy when he'd finished. "Better than that mouldy bread and biscuits we had before."

"Aye and that skimpy slop we were fed on the Aurora," said Edward.

"We'll have to watch it or we'll get guts like a porker, if we're not careful," said Jack with a chuckle. The two boys laughed together for the first time since they had met as they felt at last they had something to laugh about.

***

The next day, the boys trooped to the food hall for their grub and settled at the same table. A group of scruffy women ambled in, giggling and chatting together. They weren't in any prison garb and wore heavy makeup with highly rouged faces and stained red lips. Their tatty clothing was provocative showing cleavage and their skirts pulled up to reveal their ankles. Some wore feathers and faded flowers in their hair, others had hats and although they were all in their teens they looked much, much older; more like women in their thirties, for the life they were living was taking its toll on their complexions; that and from being in the almost constant glare of the sun that dried and shrivelled their skin.

Another prisoner, a sixteen-year-old youth called Mason, reared up to young Edward, and Jack sensing trouble got in between them, as Mason objected, "Oi! I was 'ere before you," and with that he gave Jack a shove, pushing him on the floor.

One of the girls, who seemed to be the leader of the female gaggle called Maudie, intervened. "All right, all right." She tried to placate the aggressive Mason and said reasonably, "Come on, Mason. Leave it out. They're only boys."

Mason dwelled there a moment before shrugging and walking away, which gave Jack time to stand up. He dusted himself down as Maudie crossed to them eyeing them up and down.

"Thank you," murmured Edward politely.

"Who are you, then?" asked Maudie.

Jack piped up for both of them, "That's Edward. He doesn't say a lot. And I'm the Dodger," he said with a hint of pride in his voice.

The women came and sat at their table and Maudie introduced them all, and they each nodded back in turn at their name. "I'm Maudie, this is Nell, Effie, Kate and that one at the end, breastfeeding the kid, is Emma." She looked expectantly at them, "So, what they got you working on, then?"

"Nothin' yet," said Edward. "What you working on?"

"Our backs," said Maudie and laughed with the others at Edward's puzzled expression. "Ah, such innocence!" she exclaimed.

Just then, Mason strutted past and Edward immediately cast his eyes down to the floor.

"S'alright!" said Maudie. "You don't wanna take no notice of him. He just gets a bit funny sometimes."

"Right," said Jack as if he understood.

"Albert Rust is the one you want to worry about."

"Who's that?"

Maudie lowered her voice conspiratorially and indicated Rust with her head without looking at him. "He's the one that's in charge. The big chap with the red hair. Stay out of his way. And if he asks you to do something just do it. No questions."

Jack braved a look in Rust's direction. There was something familiar about his face. He was sure he had seen him before. "I think I know him," he muttered.

"Where from?"

"Dunno."

"Trust me, if you knew him, you'd remember. Ain't no forgetting that mean bag of..." she stopped as Jack took another look at Rust who was now gazing at Jack.

Rust held two fingers up in front of his eyes, smiled at Jack then pointed one of his fingers at Jack as if to say, 'I know you.' Jack couldn't hold his gaze and looked away nervously, feeling intimidated. He could feel bile rising into his throat and the first real fluttering of fear, since they had arrived, manifested in his stomach. He took a deep breath and focused on Edward's face instead. As if taking this as a cue, Maudie asked Edward, "So, what about you? What you in for?"

Quick as a flash Jack answered for him, "Stealing."

"Stealing what?"

"Apples," insisted Jack urging young Edward with a warning look to stay quiet.

At the top of the hall, Rust still had his eyes on Jack, boring into him. Jack felt he was being observed but he was determined not to turn around to check. He was feeling edgy and uncomfortable. Every now and then Maudie would flick her eyes to the top table. She saw Rust get up. He leaned across to Masters and said something before he walked away and left the dining hall. Maudie stiffened and sat upright. Jack noticed the change in her manner as did the others and a feeling of tension ran through them all. Jack stopped talking and he, too, sat upright and cast his eyes down. Edward looked from face to face, puzzled at the change in everyone. He was about to speak but Maudie silenced him with a finger to her lips.

Masters had started to stride down the aisles towards their table. He reached Mason and put his hand on the young man's shoulder. Mason closed his eyes in fear and struggled not to flinch at Masters' touch. It seemed he knew what to do and walked to the main door and waited there.

Masters' next target was Jack. He placed his hand on Jack's shoulder. Jack rose obediently and joined Mason at the exit. Masters looked around him and then stalked off and out through the door followed by Mason and Jack.

By now, Edward was totally bewildered and he said softly, "What's happening?"

Maudie eyed the lad sympathetically, "Best not to know. We'll just have to wait and see and hope all will be well."

3: With No Honour Among Thieves a Daring Escape Is Triggered

Jack and Mason were led through the stockade past huts and people working quietly at a variety of different jobs. They walked on until they reached a stout, thick, wooden door. All this was done in silence making both youngsters feel even more uncomfortable. Masters turned to Jack and ordered, "You, stay here."

Jack heeding Maudie's words from before did as he was told. Rust opened the door and jerked his head at Masters and Mason who both entered the room and the door was firmly closed. Jack put his ear against the door and tried to listen but the voices were muffled and indistinct. Annoyingly, he could not work out anything that was being said. He shuffled his feet nervously as he waited.

Without warning the door opened violently. Masters shouted at Mason, "Out!" He turned his eyes on Jack, "You, in!"

Jack saw Mason's face as he left. The teen looked in a state of shock. His step as he walked back had none of his earlier bravado but was hesitant and cowed. Jack followed Masters inside the large room reluctantly and the heavy door banged loudly behind him making him jump. He felt like a rat caught in a trap.

Rust sat beside a small table. He was a big man whose ruddy face was scarred. He had piercing blue eyes, which were cold and calculating. There was an uncomfortable stillness as Rust surveyed the Dodger.

Jack waited.

"Come in," said Rust in an over friendly way, which disturbed Jack and made Rust appear even more sinister as he beckoned Jack across with a seemingly amicable gesture. The feeling of being ensnared as would a fly in the sticky silken strands of a spider's web abounded. Jack felt as if he was somehow prey to this man and in danger.

Jack moved further into the room and closer to Rust at his table. "You want something to drink?" Rust asked.

Although Jack's mouth was dry he refused, "No, I'm fine, thanks." He sounded stronger and more confident than he felt.

Rust, however, brushed aside Jack's response and insisted heavily, "Course you do. Masters, get the man something to drink. Get him a man's drink." Although Rust's mouth was smiling his eyes remained icy.

Masters grinned in response and fetched a glass. He smacked it down and took a bottle filled with an amber liquid and uncorked it. He poured a large measure, turned and strolled back to Jack thrusting the glass at him, which Jack was forced to take.

"So, you liking it here?"

Jack held his ground, "Not a lot."

"Not a lot? Oh dear. You don't like the way I run things here?" He turned to Masters, "He doesn't like it, Masters."

"No... no. I..."

"Someone getting at ya?"

"No."

"Cause there's nothing worse than someone making your life a misery."

"Right," said Jack noncommittally.

"So, if they do, you just come and tell me." Rust indicated the drink, "Well, go on then. Sling it down ya!"

Jack studied it dubiously and lifted the glass hesitantly, when Rust dropped his bombshell, but still managed to sound affable. "You know, I think I know you." Jack froze. Rust pointed at the drink again, "What's the matter? Not to your taste?"

There was a sly gleam in Rust's eyes. He leaned forward putting pressure on Jack who was compelled to raise the glass to his lips. He tried to close his nostrils to the distinctive smell of raw alcohol and swallowed it down in one. He followed it with a bout of coughing as the harsh burning liquid hit his throat.

"You're The Artful Dodger, ain't ya?" Jack's face registered his shock. "Friend of Bill Sikes," said Rust with a smile but almost accusingly.

Knowing an answer was expected from him and not knowing what to say, he finally replied, "...Yeah..."

"Well, you know why I'm here, then."

"No."

"Oh, come on, Dodger. You must know. Your best pal would have told you."

"He wasn't me best pal," protested Jack.

Rust attempted to sound reasonable and leaned heavily on his words, "But, Dodger... he must have told you."

"He's dead."

"But he'd have told you before he died," insisted Rust.

"No."

"Hanged, was he?"

"Not by the law. I heard he fell off a roof an' hanged himself."

"Shame. I was hoping we'd see him out here. Weren't we, Masters?"

Masters nodded and grunted, "Right."

"Yeah, well," said Jack uncertain what to say or what was expected of him.

"Thing is, Dodger..." Rust licked his lips, "Your knowing why I'm here puts me in a very difficult predicament." He took out a pocket knife and began to clean the grime from under his nails.

"Eh?"

Rust pointed the knife at Jack as he continued, ambiguously, "Very difficult." He shook his head almost sorrowfully. "Really is."

"But I don't know," insisted Jack. "I know nothin' about you."

"He peached on me, Dodger. I was doing a job an' he peached on me. He blabbed to the law about me."

"Why'd he do that?" said Jack genuinely puzzled.

Rust lowered his voice, "Cos I was the only man he was scared of, so I reckon. Never thought he'd do anything like that though. But he did. And there's me... I mean I could have been sentenced to the morning drop. Just another job for old Jack Ketch. Terrible in it?"

"Well, he's dead now," said Jack trying to sound reasonable.

Rust sucked the air in between his teeth and adopted an almost wheedling tone, "But you see my problem? I mean, think of it from my side. It's not easy for me, Dodger... How would it look for me if anyone here found out I'd been made a fool of? That someone had dared to grass on me? You see my problem, don't ya?" He shook his head again, twisting his mouth, "What am I supposed to do when you turn up here?"

"I won't say anything," assured Jack.

Rust's tone became conciliatory as if dealing with a difficult child, "Dodger... Son... I wanna trust you. I really do. Don't think I don't wanna trust you. But..." and he sucked in another mouthful of air, "but, I gotta make sure, 'aven't I? You do see that don't ya? I gotta be safe. Safe as houses. Can't take any risks or it all comes tumbling down."

Jack unable to escape Rust's penetrating stare looked down. Rust's mouth twisted again and he slammed his hand down on the table and Jack jumped. There was an uncomfortable pause and Rust's voice took on an oily quality as he softened his tone, "I tell you what. What do we think, Masters? Can we trust him, Masters? D'you think he'd let us down?"

Masters shook his head, "He wouldn't wanna do that."

"No, course he wouldn't," said Rust pocketing his knife. "I've already sorted out Mason for you. He won't give you any more lip."

"Thanks," said Jack with temerity.

"No need to thank me, Dodger." His voice became stern, "Just do as you're told." Rust rose from his seat, walked to Jack and lightly slapped the boy's cheeks. "There'll be the odd job for you to do for me." Rust smiled cheerfully, "Always something needs doing." He took the glass and turned Jack around to face the door, "Off you go then, push off."

Jack didn't need telling twice and hurried to the door. He heard a peal of mocking laughter as the door clanged shut behind him.

***

Feeling somewhat lost without Jack, Edward went with the women to their quarters. He made himself comfortable on the edge of Maudie's bed and they chatted together. Edward felt at ease with Maudie and began to unburden himself. With Maudie's gentle questioning he talked and talked.

"What happened to your parents?" asked Maudie curiously. "You're very young."

"My dad died in an explosion on the railway. It's what he was working at. It was hard losing him. Then, it was just Mum and me. All we had was each other."

"What happened to your mum?"

"It was all right till last year. Mum hadn't been feeling too good and then she started coughing up blood. We went to the hospital and she was put in this room on her own and I was asked to leave. I didn't know what to do. Not long after, they came to find me and told me she was dead. I went into this room and there was a body. It was wrapped in a cloth and there was another piece of material on the face. I took it off and it was my mother. She was lying in this big box."

"Coffin?"

"No, she was dead... I kissed her and said goodbye. When I left the room, this woman grabbed me."

"But, why?"

"Cos I'd taken the cloth off her face. They called it a shroud."

"And that's how you ended up here?"

"Yes."

"Well, why d'you take it?"

"Cos it was all I had to remember her by. Everything else had been burned. I wouldn't give it back. She grabbed me and I lashed out... Next thing I know she had these scratches on her face. That was all."

The door opened and Jack walked in. Edward spotted his friend and waved tentatively until Jack reached his side. "Here, take this. It's all I could stash for you," and he passed Jack a piece of bread he'd hidden in his pocket.

Jack took it with thanks and chewed on it as Edward asked, "What happened?"

Effie and Nell joined them to listen, their curiosity piqued.

"Yes, tell us," said Maudie looking around at the other girls who all nodded.

"Nothing much, 'e gave me a drink."

"How much did he want for it?" asked Maudie.

"Nothing."

"Oh, he will," said Maudie knowingly.

"All he said was maybe a bit of work, you know."

"Be careful, son. Be bloody careful. Just as long as he don't have you collecting money for him."

"Why's that?"

"That's what he had Thorpie doing."

"Who's he?"

"The boy he had hanged. Didn't you see him when they brought you in?"

Edward was shocked, "Why did the soldiers let him do that?"

"Soldiers?" said Maudie scornfully. "There ain't no soldiers in here, didn't you realise that? The soldiers are on the outside. On the inside it's his lot, Rust's. There ain't no soldiers to go running to."

Jack and Edward looked crestfallen, "We've got to get out of here. I've gotta keep out of Rust's way. He'll do for me, like he did for Thorpie," said Jack.

"You can hide in here for now," offered Maudie.

Effie who had been listening asked, "Yeah, but what they gonna do after that?"

Maudie frowned, "Never thought of that." She looked from one to the other, "You can't hide in here the rest of your life."

"Yeah, well unless I do, I ain't got no life," said Jack when a thought struck him. "Has anyone ever escaped from here?"

Nell scoffed, "Oh, they've escaped all right. But, they've always come back."

"Got caught, you mean?" said Jack.

"No, just come back," said Nell. "It's not the getting away that's the trouble, it's the staying alive once you've done it."

"Why? What's it like out there?"

Maudie's face puckered up in distaste, "Wild animals. Nothing to eat. Frightening. Even if you did make it out of here you'd only come back."

"But I couldn't, could I? I got to get out," said Jack looking anxious. Edward tried to smile in sympathy but his face was frozen in worry.

The women all glanced at each other knowing the truth of Jack's words, while Jack and Edward shared a look of hopelessness.

***

Later that night, Jack and Edward were still tucked away in the women's quarters munching on some stale bread. They watched Maudie as she washed her face. Jack's expression showed he was thinking hard.

Edward looked at Jack whose face was creased in concentration, "What?" he asked. "What is it?"

Jack shook his head, "Nothin', yet." He addressed Maudie, "Do you do this every night?"

Maudie dried her face off with a rough towel and sat down at an old cracked mirror. "Most of the time unless... well, you know..." Edward and Jack looked flummoxed. Maudie continued, "Yes, well, I suppose you could say so. No different to being on the outside." She caught the glimmer in Jack's eye and justified herself, "You have to do what you have to do to get by."

"So, what got you in here?" asked Jack.

"A lovely bonnet in the Mile End Road." Maudie began to apply her makeup. She shrugged, "I just like pretty things. Can't help it, I always have."

Jack watched Maudie as she put on powder and rouge. He chewed the inside of his mouth as he thought. "Tell me, what d'you think him and me'd look like dressed like that?"

The girls stared at Jack and Maudie said with a giggle, "Why, you'd make a lovely couple of ladies. Wouldn't they, girls?"

Effie, Nell, Kate and Emma rummaged through their clothes. Kate pulled out a faded red dress with a long, tight, pointed bodice and full skirt. "This don't fit me anymore. It's too tight. Try it on. You'll need lots of petticoats and a shawl."

"I've got a couple of shawls that have got some holes in. No one'll notice at night," said Effie.

Emma pulled out a low cut empire line dress. "It was one I found in here. I wore it when I was having little 'un. Not up to the minute."

"Don't think they'll worry about that," said Maudie. "Here, put these on."

The boys studied the garments unsure what went where. The girls started giggling and began to dress them up. Maudie shushed them, "Hush up! Folks'll wonder what's going on in here."

"I can't help it," said Nell. "This is the most fun I've had in ages."

"But do it quietly," pressed Maudie. "Here, let me look at you." She turned Edward around. "We'll have to do something with your hair... anyone got a bonnet?"

"Put the shawls over your heads. Let's put some powder on yer face and pinch yer cheeks to make 'em red," said Kate.

"Come on, Jack. Your turn," said Maudie. "Hurry up!" she urged as Jack peered at himself in the cracked mirror. Effie burst into another fit of giggling.

"Don't laugh. We could all end up dead cos of this," said Maudie. The realisation of the seriousness of the situation hit home and they all fell quiet.

Emma whispered to Kate, "This could all go terribly wrong."

Maudie overheard, "Not if I have anything to do with it. Right, let's have a good look at yer." She made the boys turn around and walk towards her. "Smaller steps. Try to glide not stride. Hold yer hands just so." Maudie demonstrated and both boys copied her. "Right, you'll do. Come on let's go, before I change my mind."

The girls gathered together. Maudie lit the lanterns, in readiness, which they picked up. "Nell, you check outside." Nell nodded and disappeared out of the door as Maudie issued her last instructions. "Now, keep the light away from you, especially your faces. You stay in the middle of us."

Nell returned, "All clear."

"Come on, then." She took a deep breath, "Now or never. Let's do this."

They marched out confidently with Maudie leading the way. Jack and Edward followed behind her, side by side, with Nell and Effie bringing up the rear. They crossed the courtyard where Rust and Masters stood talking. They eyed the girls up in a perfunctory manner and hardly gave them a second look. They didn't suspect a thing.

Their footsteps echoed hollowly in the stone yard as they reached the gate. They attempted to look relaxed and although Jack and Edward were silent the other girls chattered idly to each other and / the soldier, as he opened the door. He let them through, nodding 'hello' to Maudie who flashed her most alluring smile and said, "Ta."

The gate banged shut behind them. They continued walking towards the soldiers' quarters. Maudie gestured them to come to a tree, which afforded them some cover. Jack and Edward divested themselves of the women's clothing and shawls, revealing their own clothes underneath. They scrubbed at their faces to remove the powder and rouge. Maudie gathered up the garments and stuffed them out of view amongst the undergrowth. "We'll collect them later."

Young Jack was eager to be off, "Which way do we go?"

Maudie pointed down the hill, "Any way but that way. That leads to the harbour and town."

"I remember," said Jack and Edward nodded. "Why don't you come with us?"

"Cos I've only got a year left to do. Anyway, it's not so bad here for us."

"But, what ya gonna do after that?"

"I dunno... something... pretty probably. Now, go for Christ's sake. And good luck."

The other women whispered their goodbyes and wished them good luck. Jack and Edward exchanged a glance and then began to run for their lives.

4: On the Run

Jack and Edward stumbled breathlessly through the vast wilderness of scrub to the tune of chirruping crickets that were calling happily for a mate. The creatures' twittering buzz was only interrupted by the soft thud of the boys' footsteps as they ran through the sandy soil and wild vegetation. Rambling creepers and other prickly plants stretched their shoots across the ground intending to snag and ensnare the boys' shabby attire, tearing at their shirttails and breeches. The inky blackness of night was lit by a multitude of stars, which peppered the sky ceiling.

Edward stopped to catch his breath. He was panting hard and had a sharp pain in his side. "Jack, wait!" he hissed as he bent over to ease the pain.

Jack doubled back to him, breathing raggedly, "What is it?"

"I need to stop, just for a moment. My side hurts like I've been darted with knives. Please." The boy crumpled down from the waist taking in huge gulps of air.

"We need to get as far away from this hell hole as possible. We don't want soldiers or Rust's men tracking us or..." Jack stopped midstream, "What's that?"

Carried on the gentle breeze of the forbidding dark was a sound so alien, so strange that the hairs on Jack's back and neck stood erect and in spite of the warm humid air, a tingling shiver travelled down his spine like a trickle of water.

"What?"

"That!"

A low-pitched, wheezing cry penetrated their ears in the night air. It was terrifying, like nothing they had ever heard before. Every now and then a throaty muffled growl that didn't come from a dog, or any other animal they recognised, joined in the evil rattling, coupled with slithering, scuttling and panting sounds in the bushes.

Nightmare fairy tales from Edward's childhood came to mind and he imagined an ogre or some type of fiend pursuing them. "Something's after us!" choked Edward his words sticking in his throat.

Jack attempted to calm his friend, "Nah. That's just your imagination. Your mind and ears playing tricks," but he was unable to keep the quavering fear out of his own voice.

Another high-pitched screeching joined with the demonic rumbling growls and Jack hissed, "Run!"

The boys ran wildly through the vegetation, their breathing laboured and harsh. The calls of the night, sounding like devils and demons, was interrupted by a multi-toned call as if some earthbound spirit was establishing its territory by laughing mockingly at the night.

"What's that?" asked Edward in a panic.

"Dunno and I ain't waiting to find out. Come on!"

The mournful eerie howl of dingoes joined the wild discordant screech of an owlet nightjar and reverberated around them. Jack cocked his head on one side to listen, "I don't like this. I don't like it all."

"Where's it coming from?"

"It's all around us. We need to get moving."

A tendril of a prickly creeping vine clawed at Edward's feet "Arghh!" shrieked Edward. "Something touched me!" He looked down to see his foot ensnared in some coiling vegetation. At that moment a small rat-like creature broke cover and scurried into the bush.

Both boys stopped unsure where to go and the raw animal sounds faded momentarily.

Edward, his heart still pounding as if it would jump out of his mouth, straightened up and looked heavenward. For a fleeting moment he stared in awe at the night, "Cor! See the stars, beautiful; like tiny lights punched in the sky."

A ferocious scream that dropped to a low rasping startled Jack back into flight mode.

"This ain't no time for star gazing, we got to keep moving. Ready?"

Edward nodded and the two set off again. The peculiar and spooky sounds seemed to follow and envelop them wherever they ran, which frightened them further, but spurred them onward to continue their flight, until they were so fatigued they had to stop again to catch their breath.

"We don't know where we're going," complained Edward fearfully.

Jack jerked his head back in the direction from which they'd run, "We know what's back there. We got to move forward, this way."

"But, I'm scared." Edward's bottom lip began to tremble.

"So am I," admitted Jack. "This is all new to me, too. All I know is we got to keep on the move."

"I've never heard nothing like those sounds and I keep seeing creatures skittering through the sand like nothing I've seen before. I need to stop and sleep, Jack. I know things'll look better in the morning. You go on, Jack. Leave me. Please."

"I'm not leaving you. We stick together. It's our only chance. We watch out for each other."

"But, I can't run no more." Edward sank to his knees, tears trickled down his dirt streaked cheeks, and he curled up in a foetal ball, exhausted.

Jack nodded, "It'll be all right, Edward, you'll see." He paused and looked at the still form of Edward whose breaths were coming in juddering gasps. "Okay, we stay together. We'll stop. You can sleep. My heart's thumping like I don't know what." Jack sat down next to Edward and put a protective, comforting arm around the boy, who, now, had fallen fast asleep.

As the sounds of the night grew less oppressive, Jack's heart finally slowed and stopped its relentless panicked thudding and he, too, fell into a deep and lasting sleep.

***

The first fiery rays of the rising sun began to warm Edward's face and, as it began what appeared to be its daily journey across the sky, the sound of colourful bird chatter pierced his brain. Edward was drowsy no more. He sat up letting Jack's arm fall away from him and rubbed the sleep from his eyes before scanning the vista around him. Sand, shingle and thorny shrubs abounded as far as he could see and he heard something, something different from the terrifying sounds of the night.

He turned to Jack who was still slumbering and shook him hard, "Jack, wake up."

Jack, groggy from his night's sleep, stretched and yawned noisily before realising he might attract undue attention and so stifled his bellowing sound. But, believing he'd been woken in alarm and would have to run he exclaimed sharply, "What?"

"Listen!"

Jack shook his head firmly to help him to full consciousness and reiterated, in a slightly exasperated tone, "What? What is it?"

"Can't you hear it? It's animals."

Jack focused and listened, "Sheep. That's what it is. Sheep. I heard enough of them in London, Edward. Nothing to worry about. They won't eat you."

Edward brushed a stubborn lock of hair from his eyes as his stomach began to rumble. "I'm hungry."

"So, am I. But we've got to go on."

Jack scrambled up and winced as he stood up straight, "How's your feet?"

"Sore, like I've walked barefoot a hundred miles on stony ground."

Jack extended his hand to haul Edward up and as Edward dusted himself down, brushing off the dirt debris, they heard the metallic sound of a gun being cocked behind them.

Both boys turned abruptly. The glare of the sun dazzled their eyes making them twinge painfully and partially blinded them. Jack raised his arm to shade his eyes from the glare and could just make out some shimmering shapes in the morning heat. A large man with a full rubicund face, like the harvest moon, was sitting astride a strong looking dark horse. The stranger held a rifle in his hands, which was pointed aggressively at the boys.

Standing askance and looking menacing were several Aborigines, each one holding a weapon of sorts ranging from spears and sharpened sticks, to knives. The boys froze. Their eyes stared wildly at the encircling company as the natives clustered around them curiously.

"Move forward. Let's have you," instructed the stranger. The boys swapped an anxious look and inched forward towards him, bit by bit. "Got any weapons?"

"No." Jack's voice was boldly confident; as usual, he sounded braver than he felt.

The two boys were at a complete loss as to what to do. Edward's mouth had dropped open, while Jack stood defiantly firm and flexed his small fists.

There was a silence as each weighed up the other, when one tall, muscular Aborigine burst through the other men and ran towards the white man on the horse. He pointed in the direction from where the boys had travelled. He spoke with absolute urgency and was fluent in English, "The horsemen we saw, they're looking for them!"

"Koorong, take them to your village now!" ordered the big man, without any hesitation. He addressed the boys, "I know you're from the convict camp. Go with Koorong. It's for your own sakes. Quickly now. Hurry."

As the natives moved away, Jack and Edward looked confused and appeared to dither.

"Go!"

The man's insistent command prompted the boys into action, Jack and Edward nodded to each other in agreement and ran after Koorong and another one of his men. The four disappeared into the thick bush. Two of the other Aborigines quickly and deftly destroyed all signs of the boys' tracks and footprints.

Jack stopped when he reached cover and peeped back to see four men on horseback in the distance riding slowly with trackers searching the land in the direction of the stranger. Jack needed no second bidding. He turned and ran after Edward and the two natives, who were now some way ahead.

The boys followed Koorong and under his instruction, where possible, stepped where he stepped minimising the tracks, the other native, used brushwood and prickly bindi weed to sweep away the evidence of their path. They moved quickly and stealthily. All this was done in silence.

Having travelled some distance Jack was feeling safer and bolder and asked, "If you're Koorong, who is he?"

"Jarli," said the other native.

"You both speak English."

"We learned from Mr Fred," said Koorong.

"Fred?"

"Mr Fred, the white farmer. He and his wife taught us, for many years. We work for him. They've been good to us, helped us, not like other members of your tribe."

"We don't have a tribe," said Edward. "Unless you call where we come from a tribe, like Londoners or Irish or Welsh."

Koorong snorted, "Everyone has a tribe. Like you said, it's where you're from, where you were born. Now, hush up. We need to move quietly through here. There are many creatures alerted by sound that can kill."

Edward whispered to Jack, "Like the men chasing us. But, I've seen some horrors here, creepy crawlies that look scary and huge spiders."

Jarli added, "Watch where you walk. You don't want to step on a Kapara, or Darrpa."

Edward and Jack looked at each other. Jack spoke again, "What's a Darrpa?"

"Very deadly snake, one bite and you have only minutes to live, your people call them King Browns."

Edward shivered, "And a Kapara?"

"Small black spider with a red spot on its back, again very deadly, white men call it a red back spider. Now, hush up and listen."

The two Aborigines stayed stock still. Jack and Edward did the same. Sounds of horses' hooves came thundering through the brush. Four riders passed by the thicket. Nobody moved. They could hear the raucous voices of the men as they shouted to each other while they spread out in a line to cover more ground. No one dared breathe. Edward stuffed his hand over his mouth to stifle a sneeze. They waited.

Finally, Koorong signalled to Jarli and they moved forward again this time veering off to the right where the undergrowth became more dense. There was a scuttling sound in the rocks and Edward tripped falling face forward. He put out his hands to stop himself and bit back a cry of pain as his hands caught on some bindi weed. Jack helped him up.

"They must have feet like iron to step on this stuff," said Edward commenting on the prickly, thorny weed that lurked in the sparse dry grass, which had cut his hands.

Jarli loped across, his gait was like that of a predatory animal. He grabbed Edward's hands and turned them palm up. "When we reach the village, I will put something on it to heal. Come now. It is safe to move."

The four continued on their journey through the rough country of the outback until they reached a narrow channel between a crop of rocks. The path was stony and it was hard to see what lay ahead moving as they were in single file with Koorong leading and Jarli at the rear. When they finally came through to the other side, they were on the outskirts of an Aboriginal village. A steep cliff dressed in vines and curtained vegetation rose up against a backdrop of a sparkling waterfall that cascaded into a lagoon of azure water, which even made Jack gasp at its beauty.

"Wait!" ordered Koorong. "This is for your own safety. Put your hands behind your back."

Puzzled, Edward and Jack did as was asked and Jarli tied Edward, while Koorong tied Jack's hands with some fibrous twine.

"Why are you doing this?" questioned Edward.

"Don't worry."

"I worry," said Jack. "I ain't gonna do anything. What you up to?"

"Trust us. Come on." Koorong pushed Jack ahead of him.

As they approached the village huts, men, women and children came out to stare at the two captives. The younger ones chattered excitedly in a strange tongue. One young girl giggled with her friends and pointed at them. She ran up to Edward cheekily and touched his silky blond hair, so different from her own dark curls, before running back to the other young girls and laughing some more.

Edward and Jack flinched as some of the natives prodded and poked them, feeling the muscles in their arms and muttering between each other. Edward's complexion paled and he trembled in fear. Jack, although afraid, was determined not to appear weak. He squared up to an adolescent Aboriginal who peered in his face and he stood firm without blinking until the youth snorted and moved away.

Edward whispered in a quavering tone, "Do you think they're going to eat us?"

Jack valiantly made light of it, "Nah! You wouldn't be no more than a mouthful, too much skin and bone."

A grizzled elder with long grey hair emerged to see what all the fuss was about and indicated a hut, where Koorong led Jack and Edward.

Once inside, Koorong indicated they sit. He said to Edward, "Jarli will be back with something for your hands."

"Can't do much with them tied," said Jack cheekily.

Koorong paused and with a sweeping movement took out a large knife from a leather sheath at his waist. The boys stiffened and traded a nervous look but relief flooded across their faces when he stooped behind them and cut their bonds.

"Sorry about that. Had to be done for your own safety and tribal law. I'll be back later."

Koorong left them. Jack and Edward stayed silent each uncertain about what was to befall them in this village. "You don't think they *will* eat us, do you?" said Edward.

"Why bother to try and mend your hand if they're going to kill us? They'd just chop it off, chuck it away and cook the rest of us." Edward looked alarmed. "Don't worry. It'll be okay. You'll see," said Jack, in such a way as if he was persuading himself of the truth of his statement. "Let's get some rest. We've been going for hours. We don't really know what's gonna happen."

***

The burning sun bloodied the sky a searing vivid crimson as it bled rapidly towards the horizon, which pooled with colour in an arterial splatter. The young Aborigine girl who had been fascinated by Edward's fair hair entered the boys' hut carrying two clay bowls of food, which she placed in front of them on the woven rush mat where they sat. Edward's hands had been coated with some kind of green paste in a poultice and bandaged, but his fingers and thumbs were free of constraint.

They sat cross-legged on the floor wondering what was to happen next. All whispered chatter stopped and they fell silent and looked at her. She squatted beside them and mimed eating with her hands.

Jack, feeling a lot more self-assured than Edward, was the first to speak. He patted his chest, "Me, Jack." Then he pointed to Edward, "Him, Edward... And you?"

She looked at him quizzically as he tried again, indicating himself first, "Jack... Jack." He wagged a finger at Edward, "Him, Edward... You?" He gestured towards her.

Recognition dawned in her eyes and she smiled broadly displaying a perfect set of brilliantly white teeth. She said slowly, "J a c k."

Jack nodded and grinned, "Yes, Jack. You?"

She tapped herself, "Alinta."

"Alinta. Pretty name."

Alinta pointed at Edward, "Him Edward."

Edward finally found his voice, "Just Edward."

"Just Edward," Alinta repeated.

"Edward," said Edward with a giggle.

Alinta repeated their names again.

Jack and Edward chorused, "Yes," and nodded their heads vigorously.

"Oowa." She indicated the bowls again, "Tau-wa, tau-wa."

"Eat? You want us to eat?" said Jack.

"Oowa."

Edward picked up a bowl, "What is it?"

Alinta mimed eating again and nodded her head. Jack picked up his bowl and peered at the contents. There was some sort of cooked meat in a broth with leaves and root vegetables. He lifted the bowl and drank some of the broth, wiping the moisture moustache from his lip afterwards, picked up some meat with his fingers and put it into his mouth as Edward watched Jack's reaction.

Alinta nodded, "Murrorong?"

Jack nodded and began to eat more enthusiastically, "It's good."

Seeing Jack devouring his bowl of food with relish Edward began to eat his and nodded in agreement. "It *is* good."

Alinta smiled, "Murrorong?" She patted her stomach, "Parra."

"I wish I knew what she was saying," said Edward between mouthfuls as he wiped the dribbles of potage from his chin.

"I think I get some of it," said Jack. "We know her name, Alinta. I think oowa is yes and tau-wa is eat."

"What's parra?" asked Edward. "And murrorong?"

"Parra?" said Jack quizzically.

Alinta rubbed her tummy again, "Parra."

"I think it's belly. Murrorong maybe good?"

She waited until they had finished their food, collected their bowls, smiled at them both and left the hut.

"Might not be so bad," said Jack. "Grub was all right."

"It was. I was hungry... It didn't look too pleasant."

"Better than prison grub."

"Anything's better than prison grub."

There was a rustle at the entrance and Jarli pushed through the doorway carrying some more items. He gave them each a multi-coloured rug. "Garabo. To sleep. Let's see your hands." He carefully unwrapped the leaf covered poultice, wiped away the green paste and studied the cuts. "All clean. It will be fine now. Let the air do the rest."

"Are we allowed out?" asked Jack.

"Not tonight. Rest and sleep. Tomorrow a big day."

"Why?"

"Big celebration. Welcome ceremony. You'll see."

***

As dawn began to break the Pied Butcher birds began their melodious harmonies, which were soon joined by Galahs and Cockatiels, which resulted in a less tuneful chirping chorus.

Jack and Edward had slept well through the night considering where they were. They stretched and yawned before rubbing the sleep from their eyes. Sounds of movement and chatter could be heard outside the hut when Alinta entered with clay bowls containing some kind of flatbread with a white sticky mixture.

She smiled shyly, "Edward, Jack, tau-wa."

Jack inspected the offering, "What is it?"

"Kirika." She rubbed her tummy.

"Do we eat it or rub it on our bellies?" asked Edward.

Alinta mimed eating again. "Tau-wa."

Edward tasted it, "It's sweet like honey."

"Ain't never tasted honey," said Jack and scooped some onto the bread. "Mm, it's good. Murrorong." He smiled before tucking in greedily. Edward followed suit as Alinta watched them eat with a big smile on her face.

There was quite a lot of noise outside now, with native chatter and clattering of tools and utensils. Jack peeped out and watched as men daubed some kind of body paint on the women in different styles, some with dots of different colours and others with stripes and other markings in ochre and red clay. Headdresses were being put on with bright colourful feathers, giant leaves that had been stitched together adorned the waists of the women and the beating of native drums could be heard.

"You sure they're not going to eat us? They are feeding us up," said Edward looking worried.

A strange low-pitched twanging drone that they had hadn't heard before became clearer and louder. The rumbling buzz was hauntingly soulful as if a thousand bizarrely weird animals were chorusing together to make one deeply resonating earthy vibration, which whirred and hummed. A man was sitting blowing into a long, gaily painted, tube-like instrument, which made the buzzing sound.

"Look at this!" called Jack.

Edward rose to join Jack and gazed on the scene outside. They saw Koorong putting on some sort of ceremonial dress and tried to attract his attention. Alinta took the now empty bowls and approached Koorong and gestured to the boys watching from the hut. He strolled across to them.

"What's happening?" asked Jack.

"Big ceremony to welcome you and celebrate the marriage of the young women who have come of age."

"Cor, lummy. It's a party."

"Sort of. You'll see."

"We're not expected to get painted up, are we?" asked Edward confused.

Koorong laughed and said, "No, just to be presented officially to the chief and the village."

"When can we come out?" asked Jack.

"Soon. Jarli will fetch you."

The boys watched wide-eyed as a large cooking pot on a stand was placed over a fire and an old, grinning, wizened woman with few teeth, tended it, tossing in hunks of some kind of meat from a leaf platter. The aroma drifted across to them. It smelled good. She hacked at fibrous root tubers and threw them into the mix and added a selection of leaves and small bulbs.

Edward tugged on Jack's shirt sleeve and pointed, "Look," he whispered.

Jack followed Edward's shaking finger to where Alinta stood being painted in dots and stripes. Her adolescent breasts were accentuated by some kind of braided straps that crossed her chest.

Two other young girls were being given the same treatment but sported a different design, "You don't think..." Jack stopped, "It looks like Alinta is to be wed."

"D'ya think? I mean, she ain't much older than us."

"Suppose they do stuff different over here. Those girls can't be more than fourteen."

Edward indicated another, "She don't look more than ten or eleven. Here, they're not gonna marry 'em off to us, are they?"

"Nah. We're not being painted nor nothin'."

Edward considered this and agreed, "Suppose."

Jack gazed up at the clear blue sky and the red ball of flame that grew stronger as time ticked on. "We better get back inside and wait till we're called."

They ducked back inside the hut and squatted on the rush mat. "So, we just sit and wait?"

"We wait."

***

By the time the sun had passed its height in the sky the village was alive with aboriginal music and chanting. The mass of voices outside indicated the whole village was there and the varied aromas that drifted on the breeze were making the boys' mouths water.

Koorong entered the hut, "Come, we are ready for you. To welcome you to our country and village you will be guests at the wedding."

"Who's getting yoked?" asked Jack.

Koorong looked puzzled, "Yoked?"

"Wed."

"Ah, young Alinta to Iluka. She was promised to him as an infant. His wife has died and Alinta will replace her."

"But she's just a little girl," said Edward making a face.

"It is our way, our custom. Her family have received gifts. Now, is the time for storytelling, our dreamtime, feasting, singing and dancing. Come."

Edward and Jack followed Koorong out to the clearing in the centre of the village, where people were gathered. The chief, crossed his right arm across his chest, patted it and stretched it back out in the direction of the two boys.

Jack and Edward exchanged a look and Jack mimicked the gesture back to the chief, who smiled and uttered, "Wominjeka." He indicated they should sit with Koorong and watch the proceedings. Confused but not wishing to offend they sat as asked and looked on at the spectacle before them.

***

Time passed. The sunlight had faded from the land giving way to dusk and now the cloak of night was lit by a hairless, freckled moon, which cast its silver hue on the gathering and mingled with the golden glow of the living fire where the embers fell and smouldered on the ground.

Edward was almost falling asleep except for the alien music that droned in his head. "I don't know what they're saying, do you?"

"Koorong said, it's stories all about our beginning, God, creation, our ancestors and such."

"I'm tired, after that stuff we drank, it tasted funny. My head is like it's full of straw."

"This do needs a bit of livening up, I think," said Jack.

Now, several men were doing a stamping dance and acting out some sort of hunt. One man was an animal covered in a skin and he hopped around while the others tried to catch it, which they did and the man was raised above their heads and the skin pulled off. The men shouted their words with accompanying gestures of gratitude and the tone appeared to praise someone called Baiame, which Jack assumed was their God.

One of the young men approached Jack and pulled him up to his feet wanting him to join in. Reluctant at first but much to the delight of the villagers, he tried to follow the same dancing steps of the men and then cheekily decided to have his own little bit of fun.

The men were adorned in all manner of feathers and leaves, Jack called out to Edward, "Watch! Ain't no different to pinching a gent's handkerchief..."

Jack darted behind the young man and removed a feather from his belt at his waist. He tickled the young man under the chin with it and as the young man stopped, the crowd laughed and the feather did a disappearing act, only to be produced moments later by Jack from the lap of another native. Those watching clapped in delight and Jack continued with his act, pretending to walk through the dancers and plucking items from them, which he delivered later from innocent members of the audience. It turned into quite an act and a great crowd pleaser. As the dance ended, many natives almost swamped Jack clearly clamouring for more. Koorong had to rescue him and take him back into his hut.

"That was funny, Jack," said Edward who had followed them inside. "Really funny."

"At least it woke you up. I thought you were gonna curl up and sleep where you sat."

Koorong grinned, "Funny, yes. You have made friends and admirers with your performance. Now, rest. It will soon be morning."

Jack didn't object and the boys curled up with their rugs and drifted off to sleep as the celebrations and music continued outside. The droning hum, became embedded in their brains and served to help them to fall into a relaxed dreaming state.

5: Living with the Dobles – A New Beginning?

Five days had passed in the Aboriginal village. Jack had become something of a star, with his engaging personality and pick-pocketing magic tricks, the villagers had warmed to him especially as both lads had done their best to learn some of the Awabakal language. They had managed to get by with a combination of words and mime.

The achingly bright, merciless sun had reached its peak in the sky and the boys had retired into the shelter of their hut. Edward poked at the dirt floor with a stick, making shapes and squiggles in the sand, using it as a drawing board. He cleared the images with his hand, mussing them out before starting again.

"How long do you reckon we'll be here?" he asked Jack. "Are we prisoners or what?"

"Dunno. At least we know they're not gonna eat us," said Jack with a wink.

"All right, I know," said Edward with a sheepish grin. "They're okay. Just, it's getting a bit boring stuck here, not knowing what's going on."

"Be glad those riders never caught us. We'd have been for the drop, that's for sure."

"I was thinking..."

"Yeah?"

"Poor old Gipps. He wouldn't have made it here, would he? I mean, I know it was Dowson that did for him. But, say he'd survived; do you think he'd have ever seen his daughter like he wanted?"

"Who's to know?" murmured Jack. "Gipps... nice old bloke. No harm in him, at all. Shouldn't have been on the convict ship. That Dowson, though. I'd like to get him alone and tell him what I think."

"Yeah, whack him with his Bible, the swine."

"I'd like to do more to him than that," said Jack and the two fell silent thinking about the tall, thin Irishman with the twinkle in his eye that they had regarded as a friend. A feeling of melancholy descended on the two boys until Jack slapped his leg and muttered, "Cor, love a duck! Look at us. Lucky we are to be alive and we're going on as if Jack Ketch is waiting for us outside."

Edward perked up and smiled, "Yeah, we should be glad. Hey, what's that?"

There was the sound of horse's hooves and something of a hullaballoo as the Aboriginal folk from the village gathered together.

***

Mr Fred had arrived on his dusky horse. He dismounted and looked around the assembled villagers until he spotted the village chief. "Murrorong purreung, Pirriwul."

The tribal leader stepped forward to welcome him, "Wominjeka, Mr Fred."

Fred smiled in acknowledgement and returned the welcoming words with the gesture of friendship as Koorong pushed through the crowd and crossed his arm across his chest, tapped it, and extended it to Fred.

Fred nodded, and struck his own chest in return. He spoke to Koorong, "I will take them now."

"The white boys are ready. I will fetch them."

Fred nodded in acknowledgment, "Blessings to you, Koorong."

"Jarli and I will walk to the farm with you." Koorong left Fred talking to the chief and entered the boys' hut.

He soon emerged with Jack and Edward in tow. Villagers crowded around, shaking their hands and patting them on the back. Jack and Edward beamed in happiness as they exchanged words with the tribesmen. Alinta stepped forward shyly, "Guwayu, kumbal, bingngai."

"Guwaya, tidda, Alinta. Hooroo," the boys chorused, saying their goodbyes to her before waving at other members of the tribe that surged forward wishing them well.

The boys' faces were wreathed in smiles. They looked up expectantly at Fred Doble who laughed heartily and looked bemused. "Guess I didn't have to worry about either of you. Looks like you made quite a hit." Fred turned to the chief, "Pirriwul, wunaa yaarri yarraang, junaa ngiina nyaagu gangaa."

The tribal leader smiled, nodded and raised his hand, "Oowa."

Fred mounted his horse, turned him and began to trot out of the village. The boys followed with Koorong and Jarli.

"What did Mr Fred say to the chief?" asked Jack.

"Just a farewell greeting."

"But what does it mean?" asked Edward.

"Chief, don't say goodbye, just say see you later!"

This satisfied the boys who chattered amiably together about the strange and difficult language, which they were trying hard to learn.

They passed the sparkling lagoon with its cascading waterfall, went out through the channel of rocks and into the brushland. Fred had slowed the horse to a walk and the boys were able to keep up. He turned to them, "Did you see the troopers?"

Jack affirmed, "Yes, they spread out in a line, searching the land."

"They were looking for you," said Fred.

"Thought so," said Jack.

"Why didn't you give us to them?" asked Edward.

"Nah," said Fred. "No profit in it."

They continued in silence until they reached the outskirts of the farm, which was not far from the village. Fred dismounted and clasped hands with Koorong and Jarli in appreciation. They waved and the two aboriginals returned to the village the way they had come.

Edward and Jack followed Fred now leading his horse. Jack was burning to ask questions but stayed mute not certain what to expect. As they neared the farmhouse and outbuildings they heard the bleating of thousands of sheep, which soon come into sight scattered all around the surrounding farmland.

"The troopers looked all over the farm, fair ransacked the place. Made a bad mess of the house. Mrs Doble, now she was very upset."

"Who's Mrs Doble?" asked Jack.

"My good lady wife, wonderful woman, as you'll see. Those troopers rode off to the west and came back two days later. Damned if they didn't search the place again. Had the nerve to threaten Mrs. Doble and me. But, thank the Lord, they've gone now. Won't be back. They reckon you're dead."

"That's why we stayed so long at the village?"

"That's right. I know them scoundrels, men of the law they said. Some law... I know how their minds work."

"Good job, too," said Jack. "Or we'd be gonners, both of us."

The boys followed Fred who dismounted and led his horse to a pump where there was a tin bath. He worked the handle to draw out fresh water for his stallion that drank deeply from the cool spring water. Satisfied, the horse raised its head with water dribbling down his muzzle and Fred led it to a shady post with a net of hay ready to nibble where he tied the animal before crossing to the farmhouse and striding up the steps to the wooden veranda. He called out as he opened the door, "It's only me. Got a couple of visitors for you."

"Come on in," called a cheerful voice.

The boys followed Fred into a spacious kitchen where a plump, rosy cheeked woman, with chestnut hair flecked with grey, in her thirties was scrubbing a large wooden table. She wiped her hands down her apron, put her hands on her hips and scrutinised the boys in front of her.

"Mrs Doble, my dear, these are the ones the troopers were looking for. Boys, where's your manners? Say good day to Mrs Doble."

Jack complied, "Hello, Mrs Doble."

This was followed by Edward, "Good day, Mrs Doble." He was following his instructions to the letter.

"I'm Fred Doble."

"Hello, Mr. Doble," said Jack brightly.

"It's Fred, just Fred. No ceremony here."

"They look a bit scrawny to me," said Mrs Doble. She walked around the lads and ended up back in front of them like a school ma'am inspecting her class. "When did you last eat?"

"This morning," said Jack jauntily displaying some of his impishness with a mischievous, dimpled grin.

"No. I mean food, proper food. If I know Koorong, I expect you've been living off honey and bread."

The boys shared a glance as she stooped down and said invitingly, "I've got a mutton pie in the stove. Would you like some? With gravy and all?"

"Ooh, yes, please," said Edward without hesitation. Jack just grinned in delight.

"Then get your hands washed and you can help Fred lay the table before you sit up."

The boys fought to get to the sink first and pump out the water. They giggled as the bar of carbolic soap slipped out of their fighting fingers and slid across the floor to Fred's feet. He picked it up and returned it. "Wash 'em clean, now. Don't want no sticky fingers at the table or otherwise, if you get my meaning."

"No, sir," said Jack with a mock salute.

Fred laughed. He had a deep throaty chuckle that was infectious and soon the boys were laughing along with him, not even sure what they were laughing at. The boys grabbed a rough towel from the rail on the stove and rubbed their hands dry. "Reckon that's the cleanest they've been in a couple of years," said Jack.

"Let's see," said Mrs Doble.

Both boys presented their hands palm up and the backs for her approval. She nodded and they scrambled to join Fred in setting out knives and forks before grabbing a seat around the table and waited, their mouths watering like never before, the aroma was so tantalising.

Mrs Doble laid out a steaming pie and enamel plates on which she dished up a healthy helping each. She put out a bowl of vegetables and slab of butter, while Fred cut them a slice of homemade bread, which he placed on a platter in the centre. Jack went to snatch a piece, "Nah, nah," said Fred waggling a fork. "You must mind your manners."

"Sorry," said Jack crestfallen.

"It's okay, Fred. They can help themselves. They look half starved. Go on tuck in."

The boys dived into the wholesome food with gusto. The satisfied silence while they filled their bellies was more than rewarding for Fred and Mrs Doble who set down their forks to watch them eat.

Mrs Doble nodded agreeably at Fred, "It's good to be appreciated. You eat up, lads and if you want some more just raise your hand."

Long after Fred and his wife had finished their meal the boys continued to eat as if they were ravenous dogs. Eventually, Jack wiped his mouth and piped up, "Cor, love a duck. That was grand." Mrs Doble beamed in pleasure. Jack turned to Fred, "So, how did you know we was convicts?"

"That first morning, the moment I clapped eyes on you. I knew." Jack looked puzzled and Fred went onto explain, "Your clothes and your wrists. Same as mine."

Fred pulled back his shirt cuff and showed them his wrists with livid scars that stood out against his weather browned arms. "I was one of you once. I did my seven years and I had the choice. Go home or stay. I stayed."

"You were lucky to come to our farm," said Mrs Doble.

"Aye," Fred agreed.

The boys swapped reassuring glances at this information and Jack burst out, "Mrs D. I cannot remember a better meal in me whole life."

Mrs Doble blushed in pleasure at Jack's enthusiastic compliment and looked gratifyingly towards her husband who pronounced, "Mrs Doble, my dear, you have indeed surpassed yourself."

"Great grub, wasn't it, Edward?"

Edward was busy mopping up the last of his gravy with a piece of bread and nodded vigorously.

"Say, lad. Do you want some more?"

"Thank you, sir... er Fred, no more. Thank you."

Mrs Doble smiled gently and began to clear the table as Fred rose. He took an oil lamp from the window sill, set it on the table and lit it, before sitting again. The room filled with a warm amber glow.

Fred's face took on a serious expression and he said in a low warning tone, "You know you can't go back? What are you going to do? Do you have a plan?"

"Go on," said Jack without hesitation.

"Where?" pressed Fred.

"The way we were going."

"But there's nothing there. Just bush and scrub with wild dingoes and the like." Edward and Jack traded a worried look. "I tell you what, best thing for you both is to go to bed and have a good night's sleep. I'll point you to the barn, over yonder, where you'll be comfy." He scraped back his chair, followed by the boys and moved to the front door, which he opened. The swell of thrumming cricket song assailed their ears and Fred indicated an outbuilding just yards from the farmhouse. "In there, you'll find beds made up for the two of ye. We'll see you in the morning. First, I've got Hunter to see to and then Mrs Doble and I are partial to sitting on the porch of an evening. We like our own company. So, go on, be off with you."

The boys watched as Fred strode to where his tethered horse waited patiently. He untied him and led him to a shed that was the stable. He untacked him and gave him a good rub down before ensuring Hunter had plenty of clean water, some feed to nibble and a good bedding of clean straw.

He peered at the boys through the stable door and saw Jack yawn as he walked out across the yard with Edward. They vanished inside the allotted barn, still observed by Fred who had an inscrutable smile on his face. He sighed in contentment, returned to the house, and went back inside to fetch his pipe as Mrs Doble dealt with the dishes.

Fred strolled back out, looking gratified. He settled on the wooden bench on the porch and looked up at the night sky. The scarred silver moon was just starting to wane and shone through the dim shadow of the night and the growing darkness was spattered with a multitude of stars that sprayed the heavens like tiny jewelled lights.

Fred sat back and filled his pipe with tobacco already shredded and packed the bulb tightly, he struck a match and puffed steadily until the mixture glowed and he was able to draw in the aromatic smoke. Mrs Doble, now without her apron, came and sat next to him. They sat together in comfortable silence and gazed at the pale wan moon. Mrs Doble reached across and took his arm. Fred lovingly patted her hand as she rested her head on his shoulder.

***

In the barn, the boys looked in awe at their new surroundings. Everything was spotlessly clean and smelled so fresh. There were two beds in the room with sheets, blankets and colourful, handmade patchwork counterpanes. Accompanying bedside tables stood, one by each bed and a wicker chair rested in the corner near the door. An oil lamp had been lit casting a golden honeyed blush over everything. Edward's mouth dropped agape, "Cor, this is better than I've ever seen. Proper grand."

Jack sat and bounced on one bed, "Comfy, too. Never slept on nothing like this. This must be what happiness feels like, what with Mrs D's mutton pie sticking to me ribs. Like you said, Edward. It's proper grand!"

They stepped out of their soiled tattered clothes and tossed them in a corner of the room. Jack turned out the lamp. Exhausted, they each curled up in their new beds and fell fast asleep to sleep the sleep of the innocent.

Part way through the night, Fred and Mrs Doble tiptoed to the barn and careful not to disturb the sleeping boys, they looked in on them. Mrs Doble laid out fresh, clean clothes on the chair and scooped up the dirty prison threads they had been wearing. The door creaked softly with a click and Jack stirred slightly but didn't wake. He sighed happily and settled back down, while Edward didn't move at all.

***

Fred washed himself at the pump as he prepared for bed.

"Did you see them, Fred?" asked Mrs Doble. "Like babies they are. What on earth could they have done to be sent here?"

"I don't know. It's not for us to ask. If they want to tell us, they will. Now come to bed, woman. Time for us to rest. We'll have another day of it in the morning."

"Do you think they'll stay?"

"Well, I won't tell them to go," said Fred as his wife snuggled into his strong arms.

***

Jack slept as he never had before. No more with one eye open as part of Fagin's gang never knowing when Bill Sikes would turn up or when Fagin would pull him from the filthy horse hair mattress that was his bed where the split buttons on the mattress ticking embedded themselves in his back often cutting him and making him bleed. There were no bedbugs or fleas here. Gone was the stench of urine and faeces from Newgate prison and the hulk that had been the prison ship. The journey across the ocean was but a distant memory now, but the threat of the convict camp from which they'd escaped still flooded his mind and invaded his dreams. Images of Rust's leering face mixed with that of Koorong, Alinta and Fred swirled in his mind like a tangled vision. But this night, he didn't wake in the cold sweat of fear. His dreams ran riot but somehow even in his sleep he knew they were just dreams and he felt something he had never felt in his life. He felt safe.

***

A cock crowed announcing the rising of the brilliant, burning sun. Chickens squawked as they scratched in the dirt for grubs and insects to supplement their diet of corn that had been scattered for them to forage. Bird song split the morning air and sounds of aboriginal music drifted on the wind. This together with the bleating of sheep.

Edward sat up and rubbed his eyes. "Jack... Jack, you awake?"

Jack rolled over and leaned up on his elbow. "What's the time?"

"Dunno, I never learned and anyway, there ain't no clock in here. It's morning. Early."

Jack slipped out of bed and crossed to the window. He could see men arriving for work. Mrs Doble stood dressed on the veranda with Fred who gave her a swift peck on the cheek and walked to the stable to get Hunter. He led the stallion to the barn and banged on their door, "Jack, Edward! Wakey, wakey. Time to get up and move. Mrs Doble has got your breakfast ready. Eat up and then get yourselves to the next outbuilding to help with the lambing."

Jack looked about him, "Blimey! Where's our clothes gone?"

"What's that on the chair?"

"Them's not ours. They're clean. Mrs D must have put them there for us."

Jack lifted the items up and studied them. They all looked rather big. He held them up to compare the sizes and tossed the slightly smaller items to Edward before scrambling into a faded blue cotton shirt and canvas breeches. The shirt swamped him and the breeches were much too loose at the waist. As soon as Jack let them go they dropped down and flopped over his knees. "This won't do. I need something to tie 'em up."

"Let's get across the yard and see if Mrs Doble can help. You'll have to hold them as you walk or you'll be scaring the natives," said Edward with a giggle. "And, we'd best straighten these beds first, tidy 'em up."

Jack nodded in agreement. So, they pulled up the bedcovers, making them look neater, and left the barn walking out into the dazzling but blinding sunshine that was still low in the sky. They dodged the clucking chickens that scurried around pecking at the dirt scratching for insects and more. Jack hung onto his breeches as they crossed the yard to the farmhouse and knocked politely.

"Come on in," called Mrs Doble in her warm, cheerful manner. The boys walked into the kitchen where breakfast was set out for them. "Let's have a look at you." She shook her head and tutted. "This'll never do. You sit down and have your breakfast. I'll get my needle and thread. These are Fred's old clothes. I keep a shelf of them, never know when a worker might need something. These were the smallest I could find. Now, you're in them, I can fit them. Go on, sit down and eat your fill."

Edward and Jack sat down carefully at the table. Jack looked at the spread in front of them, "Cor, I'll have a belly on me like a lard barrel at this rate. Never seen or had such fine fare."

"It's better grub than I've ever had," added Edward as they tucked into a hearty helping of cornbread, some kind of meat stew and fruit with honey.

Mrs Doble beamed as she saw them cleaning their plates with the last of the bread. "Now, do you want some more? There's plenty of bread and wild honey, if you've a mind."

Jack rubbed his tummy, "Nah, thank you. My belly is starting to pop like I'm harbouring a fugitive," said Jack with a grin.

"And me," said Edward. "I'm pogged."

"Well, I'm glad to hear it. Can't have you going hungry, now, can I? Come on, up you get. Let's see to these duds." The boys rose from the table and Mrs Doble set to, pinning, cutting and stitching. She gave them each a leather strip to tie through the loops at their middle.

"Now, that will be better," she pronounced. "I can fix some more for you while you're out, now I know your size. I'll put them in your quarters. Now, you get on out to the lambing shed and help Fred."

The boys muttered their thanks and hurried from the house back out into the heavy heat.

Work in the lambing shed, was hard but the boys were keen and willing to learn. It seemed, by all accounts that their small hands were perfect for the job in helping ewes to give birth, small enough to feel inside the sheep without damaging her.

Fred explained, "Most will give birth naturally without no help. But, you need to know the signs, so you can keep an eye on 'em. First, she might stop eating, most go off their grub. Her udder and teats will be full, may even be dripping with milk. And, you'll see two water bags from her rear end. She'll get up and sit down trying to get comfy and into the right position for labour. It's with that restless movement they might burst."

"Why does she have two?" quizzed Jack.

"Well, she has one to protect the lamb's head inside her, the other for its body. Then you can check further. Like I said, you two have got small enough hands not to damage her or cause her more pain. If you can feel the lamb's nose, then that's good. Next you need to find where the lamb's front legs are. If it's all normal she'll be okay birthing on her own."

"What if it's not?" asked Edward.

Fred mimed the actions as he described them. "If it's not coming out front legs first, then you have to pull the back legs out straight back until its hind legs and hips are out, then change the pull to downwards towards the ground behind the ewe. Here, I'll show you. Got a ewe here with a lamb in the wrong position. Okay, Edward. Follow my instructions."

Fred patiently talked Edward through the delivery. As the lamb was pulled off, Edward glowed with pride at his achievement. Fred nodded agreeably and continued, "Right, Jack. Grab a handful of straw and clean off the mess. Most important now, is to get the lamb to suckle. They need the goodness from the ewe's milk to survive. Put the little one to the ewe's teat."

Jack picked up the little scrap of a thing and tried to put the lamb to its mother. To say the lamb was stubborn was an understatement. It stuck out its feet rigidly in front of him and turned his head away. Jack brought the lamb's head around and forced it onto the dripping teat. The lamb latched on and began to suck greedily.

"Well done, both of you. It's not easy. It seems the first thing a lamb wants to do when it's born is die." The boys laughed. "You may laugh, but it's true. It's harder sometimes to get them to take their first feed than to birth them. You'll see most of the sheep have been sheared. It's cleaner and better for them when they give birth so we shear them about a month before they're due. That's the next lesson you'll have before the next lot of lambing."

Days passed and turned into months and the work was testing. Fred was tough on them but both boys knuckled down and did whatever they were asked. They became accomplished in sheep husbandry, in using the wooden wool Ferrier presses and packing the fleeces of around sixty sheep into wool bales that were then packed into jute bags. The following season they started lessons in shearing. Koorong and Jarli were adept shearers and each boy worked alongside one of them to learn the skill.

Koorong explained, "It's not just for the wool, though that's important as it brings in the money. It's for the sheep's health, as well. They'll be uncomfortable if the fleece is left to grow. Dirt will get matted in the wool and then it's useless to sell. Not only that it's easier for a lamb to find the teat on a sheared sheep. And sheared sheep take up less room in the barn," he said with a wink. "Now watch and learn."

Koorong expertly and gently tipped the sheep on its back exposing her belly and propping her shoulders between his knees for support. "Her belly should be showing and her four legs in the air. Remember the more comfortable the sheep is the less she will struggle."

Koorong demonstrated the whole procedure and then guided the boys, who were only too eager to learn. Koorong kept a watchful eye on them until he was sure they had mastered all the techniques he carefully explained. "Good, getting better," said Koorong. "Now, you just need to practice. And we'll give you plenty of chance to do that."

***

Years passed.

Jack and Edward had grown into strapping young men, although Edward seemed to be shooting up faster and taller than Jack. They'd developed strong bodies and muscles, especially with Mrs Doble providing such hearty meals. They were now used to the climate and had become an essential part of Fred's team. They learned how to pack the wool into sacks and were able to shoulder them to the waiting carts for sale in the market. No job was too big or too small for either of them.

Mrs Doble had taken her needle and thread many times to make more clothes for them, measuring them and fitting them so they had something for every occasion. They even had a chest of drawers Fred had bought at market and a cupboard in which to keep their garments. Life was good for them and their loyalty to each other and Fred, was unquestionable.

One evening after they had filled their bellies following a hard day's work, Jack and Edward were relaxing in their quarters playing cards. Edward looked around him wistfully, "Fell on our feet here, we did. If we'd stayed in that camp we'd be dead by now."

"You might not have been, but I would. I'd been marked by Rust. He would have done for me."

"Maybe. But it wouldn't have been no life, would it? Here we got everything we need. A place to live, work, friends and money."

"And the best tucker ever."

Edward patted his tummy, "You're right there. Mrs D's grub would be hard to beat."

"Still, we better get some kip. We got an early start with Koorong tomorrow."

"Yeah and I promised to get those pebbles for the game packed in a little bag for some of the kids in the village."

"Where did you get the bag from?"

"Where d'ya think?"

"Mrs D?"

"You got it. Where else?"

***

The Dobles, as was their custom, were sitting on their porch, listening to the many varied sounds of the night and watching the star filled sky in the hope of seeing a comet or shooting star when Mrs Doble, for fun, would make a wish.

"You know, seeing these lads grow up from undernourished, lean and cheeky blighters into sturdy, reliable young men fills me with joy. We weren't blessed with children but Edward and Jack have made us proud and filled a gap in my heart." Her eyes filled with tears of emotion that threatened to spill down her cheeks. "Never thought I'd say it, Fred, but we're lucky. Lucky you found them and brought them here. I look on them with such fondness."

"As do I, me dear, as do I. They're both good workers." He reached across and patted her hand and raised it to his lips and kissed it. "They've a day off tomorrow. Going hunting they said with Koorong and Jarli. They've really taken the Abos to their hearts. They've become like brothers. Crikey, Jack's nearly as brown as them. If it wasn't for his hair and slim nose, he could be one! Not many white men are privileged to see and experience what they have, learning how to track and hunt. Why... they'll be going walkabout next," he said with a chuckle.

***

The next day, Jack and Edward dressed for the village and the hunt, in light cotton shirts and trousers. They wore broad brimmed hats to shade their faces from the searing heat and walked the dirt trail that led to the village, no longer were they terrified of critters that skittered and creatures that jumped across their paths or hissed. They had learned to respect the land and everything that lived on it. They were almost native in their observations even down to chewing on eucalyptus leaves to ward off parasites. Koorong had taught them to make an infusion from the leaves that they could spread on their skin that was an excellent repellent for biting, blood sucking insects like mosquitoes and March flies.

Days with little rain and the morning sun had baked the ground solid. Dust flew up from their feet as they trudged towards the village. Jack's playful personality showed in the crinkles of his eyes with their irrepressible sparkle, to his dimpled cheeks and the jauntiness of his walk. He always had a lively spring in his step and looked as if he was about to burst with laughter, or share a joke, while Edward's more sedate manner and genteel looks had become chiselled, well defined and more manly. He had a maturity about him that belied his years but equally obvious was the camaraderie between the two, often finishing each other's sentences and instinctively knowing what the other was thinking.

As they traversed the rocky canyon Jack let out a call, which Koorong had taught him to signal their approach, "Cooee! Cooee!" His voice echoed through the channel and bounced back at him, before they heard Koorong's answering call, "Cooee."

They entered the village and children crowded around them, "Mr Jack, Mr Jack! Mr Edward!" they chorused in delight. Jack beamed and stooped down. He ruffled a little boy's hair. "How goes it, Minjarra?"

The small apple faced child grinned showing a pronounced gap between his two front teeth. "Good, Mr Jack. You have game?"

"I have indeed, come see."

Jack made his way to the shelter of a Waratah tree with its shady green foliage and mass of bright red flowers that stood almost twenty-six feet high. Around the base past the protruding tree roots the ground was hard and flat. Jack pulled out the little sackcloth bag Mrs D had made for him and poured out eleven shiny polished stones of a similar size. He spread them on the ground as the rest of the children clustered around. He selected one with a red dot painted on it, "This one I use to throw up in the air. Watch." He deftly tossed the pebble in the air, picked up one stone from the earth and caught the one he had thrown before it landed. He repeated this until all ten pebbles had been picked up and then set about picking them up two at a time. "Do you get the idea?" Jack asked.

Minjarra nodded vigorously. His eyes pleaded with Jack to take a turn. "My go, Mr Jack. My go. What game called?"

"Five stones or ten stones, depending on the number of pebbles," replied Jack.

"I got better name."

"What's that? What do you want to call them?"

"I'll call them Jacks," said Minjarra and he grinned his toothy grin.

***

The flaming blaze of the molten orange sun had begun dipping in the sky and liquefied into a shimmering haze as it married the horizon to bathe the heavens in ruddy wedded bliss.

Jack and Edward although footsore and weary, were pleasantly fatigued. The hunt had gone well. Koorong and Jarli had taken a big red and two goannas, which would feed the village for at least a month. The animal skin would be cleaned and tanned to use in ceremonial rituals or end up as a warm bed covering for when the nights became chilly. It would soon be autumn and they had lived through enough winters to appreciate the changes in temperature between day and night.

"Funny creatures, ain't they?" said Jack. "They bounce and jump like giant rabbits."

"Nothing rabbit-like about them. They be fearsome things with their boxing and kicks. One kick from them could rip your stomach out."

"True. But at least the Abos always go for one that's weak and leave the fit, healthy ones to make more."

Edward laughed, "Yeah, that's like rabbits, making young 'uns."

"And they don't take more than they need."

"Like Mr Fred said, it's respect for the land and all that live on it."

"We better put a spurt on. Mrs D will be waiting with our supper and Fred will want to hear all about it. Back to the grind tomorrow," said Jack as the two trudged their way home to the farm.

"I'll race yer!" called Edward as he sprinted off in front of Jack. "Last one back does the chores!"

Jack chuckled puckishly. Tiredness forgotten, he chased after his friend calling out, "Edward, you're a cheater but they didn't call me the Dodger for nothing. Here I come!" He sped after Edward and caught up with him on the farm's boundary. Neck and neck they raced until they reached the farmhouse where Jack skidded in a pile of fresh horse manure and tumbled down. He gasped, "Okay, you win."

Edward collapsed in giggles, "You'd best get cleaned up. I'll warn Mrs D. Hope you can get rid of the stink!"

Jack ambled back to his quarters with a good natured grin on his face, "I'll get you back, Edward. Just you wait..." As he walked into the barn he heard the crack of laughter that rose to almost hysterical merriment filtering out from the open windows of the farmhouse as Edward had obviously told the Dobles what had happened. And Jack, himself, couldn't suppress his own bubbling mirth. He bent double and laughed as he had never had before. He admitted with a gleeful shout, "Crikey, life is good!"

6: More Years Pass

The pale, watery sickle moon glimmered in the shroud of night. Ghostly clouds drifted across its face in the otherwise desolate sky. Whirring crickets thrummed with the song of life as Fred and Mrs Doble sat contentedly together on the wooden veranda as they did every night after supper.

Little was said, they had no need to chatter aimlessly but Mrs Doble could feel that there was something in the air, something unsaid. Not that Fred kept any secrets from her but she knew by the line of his mouth, the tilt of his head and the very way he breathed that he had something important to say and was working his way up to telling her. His breath poured out from him in a long drawn out sigh that was almost a whistle between his lips.

"What is it, Fred? You've been staring at the moon with that hangdog expression. It's not like you and I know it's more than tiredness, or maybe it is just that... tiredness?" She left the question hanging in the air.

She waited for him to respond but either he couldn't find the words or maybe she'd got it wrong. She tried again, changing tack slightly, "Come along, my handsome. You must be bushed. Let's both get to bed."

Fred dragged his eyes from the silver scythe of the moon that appeared to swing above as if preparing to slice through the navy darkness and his eyes lingered on his wife's gentle countenance. "Aye, I'm tired. Not as young as I was and..." He paused and sighed again even more deeply than before.

"What? What is it?" There was a flicker of alarm that flashed in her eyes but her gaze remained constant and fixed on Fred, who cast his eyes down and avoided her penetrating stare.

He took another moment before lifting his eyes to her face once more. "I've made a decision."

"Fred?" her voice wavered uncertainly as if she knew something bad was coming.

"It's time."

"Time for what?"

"I've made up my mind. I'm going to take Jack and Edward to the docks tomorrow. It's high time they saw where the wool goes. They need to see how this part of the business works."

Mrs Doble's face crumpled with dismay, "Oh, Fred. No. It's too early. Please." She sat up straight on the old wooden settle and put both her hands on Fred's face and turned him to look her directly in the eyes. "Surely not. Please... Can't we keep them for a little bit longer? They are doing so well and I do worry. What if..." she stopped and took a gulping breath.

Fred's tone dropped and became ultra-gentle, "Oh, my dearest. They must go sometime. Anyway, no one's gonna recognise them by now. They're no longer the skinny little kids we found. They're strong young men. Why Edward's a good one and a half head taller than Jack. He was a little shrimp of a lad when we first met him. They'll be safe." He took her hands away from his face, brushing her fingers tenderly with his lips before pulling her towards him and he kissed her lovingly on her forehead. "I promise you, I will look after them. Nothing bad will happen."

Mrs Doble swept away a solitary tear that had been desperate to escape her eyes. Her expression was lost and bleak. Fred rose and helped her up. He embraced her fiercely holding her tightly to his chest. The warmth of human contact proved too much and she gulped back a sob letting her tears fall freely. With his arm around her he led her into the house.

He closed the door firmly behind him shutting out what seemed now to be the treacherous night. "You get to bed and I'll bring you a lovely warm drink to help you sleep. Come on."

Mrs Doble sighed disconsolately and made her way into the bedroom. Fred looked after her with a weary but whimsical expression. His mouth turned up in a forgiving smile and he prepared a pan with some ewe's milk and took out two mugs.

Moments later he carried the mugs into the bedroom where Mrs Doble had fallen fast asleep. He placed the milk at her bedside before undressing himself and tumbled into bed beside her. Fred placed a comforting arm around her ample middle and held her close. His eyes filled with tears as he knew he was being cruel to be kind. That she adored Edward and Jack, there was no doubt. However, he knew he wasn't getting any younger and needed to teach them his ways to take some of the weight of responsibility off his shoulders. He was sure he was correct and all danger of discovery had passed. He thought to himself that everything would be all right. He perceived the threats to Jack and Edward were minimal and he needed to persuade his wife of that so that she wouldn't worry.

He lay there quietly, his eyes wide open staring up at the ceiling, knowing that sleep would be some time in coming and wondered what else he could do or say to persuade her that all would be well.

***

The delicious aroma of salted bacon, which sizzled in the pan on the range, wafted through the farmhouse. Mrs Doble wiped her hands on her pinny and pushed a strand of hair from her flushed face. She was in a quiet mood that morning and focused on preparing a hearty breakfast for them all.

Fred sat at the scrubbed table in his shirt sleeves and watched her anxiously as she went to the egg basket to select the largest of the fresh eggs she had collected that morning. Fred took another mouthful of tea before rubbing his bristly chin. He set down his mug and announced, "I'll tell them now."

Mrs Doble didn't answer. She just looked at her husband and nodded in resignation before returning to cook the breakfast.

Fred's chair grated as he pushed it back and he strode to the front door. He walked out onto the veranda and looked to see if the barn curtains were still closed. One window showed the drapes had been pulled back adjacent to Jack's bed. Knowing that Jack was always up first he stepped off the porch, walked to the barn and banged on the door. "Jack, come across now and wake Edward, will you? Breakfast's ready." Fred didn't dally, he tramped back into the house and settled himself at the table and continued to sup his tea.

Mrs Doble said nothing.

***

A few minutes later, Jack walked in yawning noisily, "Ooh pardon me," he said trying to stifle another gaping sigh that had crept up on him. Jack was now about five foot six inches tall. His skin was tanned from the weather. He sported a sparse beard and by his reckoning was now proper grown up. He had retained that rascally smile and kept that lively twinkle in his unusually large eyes with eyelashes that many women would envy. He was solidly built and strong. The hard manual farm work had honed his muscles and his biceps bulged through his shirt sleeves. There wasn't an ounce of fat on him.

"Where's Edward?" asked Fred.

"He's just coming. I left him hunting for his socks. Shouldn't be long."

Mrs Doble turned from the range, "Do you want tea, Jack?"

"Please, Mrs D."

She left the pan, moved to the table and poured Jack a piping hot mug of tea from the large earthenware teapot as Edward limped in waving a sock. "Found it!" he said with a grin. Edward had a thin fair beard and had grown a lot taller than Jack standing at six foot in his boots. He sat down, took off his unlaced boot and replaced his truant sock before tightening the cords in his footwear as Mrs Doble dispensed another mug of tea and placed it before Edward.

She smiled at him, "There you go," and she returned to crisping the bacon and laying it out on the breakfast plates with the eggs and fried bread.

"So, what are you doing today?" Fred asked Jack as he picked up his knife and fork.

"Dunno, yet," said Jack, taking a jar of chutney and putting a sizeable dollop on his plate.

"How about you, Edward?"

Edward pursed his lips as he thought, "Nothing, maybe... I thought I might go to the camp."

"Why? When you going into town, Fred?" said Jack as he began to eat.

"About the same time as you, I reckon," said Fred with a half-smile.

"What do you mean?" asked Jack curiously, stopping mid forkful and fastening his eyes on Fred.

Fred looked at both boys, his tone was measured, "You're coming with me."

Edward's face lit up in expectation, "Are we, Fred?"

Fred laid down his knife and fork, "It's about time I shouldn't wonder. When you've finished, help the young villagers to load the carts."

"Well, all right!" said Edward unable to keep the excitement out of his voice while Jack looked from one to the other with an inscrutable expression on his face. Mrs Doble turned away abruptly from the table and moved back to the stove, unaware of Jack's eyes boring into her.

"I reckon after this fine fare I'll tidy myself up. This is a special occasion," said Edward with a big grin.

"Just remember we got loading to do first," said Jack. "Don't want to mess up your best duds."

"You're right, let's eat up quick." Edward couldn't keep the excitement out of his voice and he attacked his food eagerly.

"You'll get colic or worse eating that fast," said Jack. "Remember, we share a room. I don't want your smelly after effects or complaints of belly ache," he said with a wink.

"And don't dress too smart, you don't want to attract any extra attention. The other blokes will think I pay you too much," said Fred with a half-smile.

Mrs Doble turned and looked gratefully at her husband, "Yes, you have to be careful... both of you."

Fred could see the meaning of her words was lost on Edward. He added, "We'll all take good care. Don't you worry none."

Jack's eyes showed the glimmer of understanding as he looked from one to the other, "Fred's right, Mrs D. We'll watch out for each other and that's a promise."

Mrs Doble smiled primly in an attempt to keep calm and not betray her feelings. She nodded, "Best get this lot cleared away, then. Won't have no young hands to help. Go on, be off with you."

Edward scrambled from the table and dashed out in anticipation at what he considered to be a new adventure. Jack rose more cautiously to follow him and when he was certain Edward was out of earshot he turned back. "Don't worry, Mrs D. We'll be fine. Don't think no one would recognise us now," and he nodded reassuringly before he left.

"Like Jack says, we'll be fine," said Fred as he crossed to his wife and gave her a hug. "You'll see. The time will fly past. Why don't you bake 'em something special? Some of their favourite tucker as a treat for when they come back. It'll help take your mind off things."

Mrs Doble assented with her head but she couldn't alleviate the worry that was now etched on her face and she determined to do some baking as Fred had suggested.

***

Outside, Koorong and Jarli, who were now much older, were with two younger workers. They were shouldering the wool packs and loading them into two carts. The work was heavy as each bale weighed around one hundred and ten pounds. The wool packs were crammed together, almost bursting at their tightly bound seams.

Fred sat in the driver's seat of the first cart and Jack jumped in alongside him with Koorong. Edward finished filling the second cart and took the driver's seat with the two newer farmhands and Jarli. He shook the reins and the wagon moved off behind Fred's.

The wooden wheels rolled through the dirt and brush down the track from the farm and out onto the road. Scrubland and bush stretched for miles on either side. As the carts trundled along the dusty road the odd kangaroo popped its head up at the passing activity before hopping off out of sight in the undergrowth. Colourful flocks of parakeets squawked and screamed, taking off from the branches of a Eucalyptus gum tree while pink and grey galahs delivered their high-pitched 'chet chet' song before screeching in alarm at the human disturbance.

An hour and a half later they reached the outskirts of Port Jackson. Jack marvelled at the many constructions of the town. The houses were built differently from England, "Cor, it ain't like London at all." He viewed the early settlers' homes and bush huts similar to those he'd seen in the outback and a few regal looking buildings that looked like government offices and a few traditionally styled properties that could belong in Eaton Square, London.

"Nope," said Fred. "No back streets with urchins running wild, districts filled with soot and smoke or streets flowing with slops from cramped houses. And look up... You ain't never seen a sun so warm or a sky so blue. No noise and rattle of machinery where men slog their guts out for next to nought. Here you've got a chance, a chance to make an honest, healthy living."

Jack just nodded and studied his surroundings as they drew nearer the port and dockside where several tall ships, some with three masts, others with five, and all with square sails, were anchored. Fred explained, "I see the Beejapore is in. Not a good ship, usually carries passengers. Some will be unloading grain, guano, timber and ore, and looking to take back exports from us and another that will take our fine merino wool to England."

"Why is the Beejapore bad?"

"The ship itself is one, if not, the fastest; a clipper, but when it journeyed across from Scotland in eighteen fifty-two or three it was notorious because so many people died aboard and in quarantine after its arrival."

"But why?"

"The toffs and cabin passengers lived the life of luxury, with walks on deck, fancy meals in a windowed saloon, but the poor folk in steerage were crammed in the belly of the ship with poor ventilation in foul conditions. There was little light. They were struck down with measles, which spread through steerage like wildfire. Many who died were children. It's got a bad reputation for just that reason."

Jack fell silent thinking of his own journey across with Edward on the convict ship and those who died on board. Once more, Gipps came to mind, then he remembered the preacher and his mouth set in a harsh line.

Houses and buildings had sprung up in the township and spread up from the harbour radiating out through the surrounding land. The quay was busy with carts unloading their goods. Payments were being made and bartering could be heard amongst the coarse chatter of the sailors setting foot on shore for the first time in over forty days.

Women queued to purchase spices and tea, which had arrived from the East India Company in London. Others queued for indigo dyes and cloth.

Fred jumped out of the cart followed by Jack and the others, those in Edward's cart did the same and they began the arduous task of unloading the wool bales and stacking them neatly in a place that was clearly reserved for wool merchants. As the men huffed and grunted with the exertion, some brazen women watched and tittered amongst themselves as they eyed the men's well developed muscles and lean figures. A few made lewd comments intended for the men to hear, which caused Edward's mouth to gape open and make him blush under his tanned skin.

"Do you want to know what I'm selling, sweetheart? I got the ways to take you to paradise. I mean, you can put your boots under my bed, anytime," said a redheaded female with a wink.

More doxies touted their charms on the pier, eager to engage any sailor to take back to their rooms in a working hostelry. They were heavily made up and wore colourful clothes with low cut, figure hugging bodices. They were not put off by rejection, but would make a vulgar gesture before turning on a dazzling smile to the next male they intended to ensnare.

Edward's eyes widened and his mouth dropped open again when he saw them approaching any man that took their fancy. He wiped a hand across his sweating brow as he took the last bale from his cart and he leaned against the cart, puffing lightly.

The redhead caught his eye again, "I can make you puff, dearie but you'll enjoy it far more," and she laughed riotously.

Fred saw Edward's discomfort and came to the rescue, "Save it, Rhoda, leave the lad alone. Quit your taunting. He's not for you."

Rhoda tossed her full head of ringlets and snorted derisively, "He'll be missing a treat. You know I'd make him a real man." She sashayed away seductively swaying her hips, turned her head and directed a pouting kiss at him.

Edward cast his eyes down uncertainly and chewed the inside of his cheek. Fred tried to make him feel less uncomfortable. "Don't mind Rhoda, she's all mouth. You and Jack wait over there with the others while I see the broker. Koorong and Jarli will drive the carts away." They did as Fred asked and leaned against the harbour wall observing all that was going on around them. They immersed themselves in the variety of sounds, busyness and the many assorted smells, some exotic and enticing, others sour and fetid, especially in the heat of the day, when every odour and aroma seemed much more pungent.

Jack watched Fred approach a stout man in a top hat and frock coat. They clearly knew each other and shook hands vigorously. Jack's eyes narrowed as he tried to work out what was being said as they walked to the stack of wool bales. Fred pulled out three small burlap sacks with samples of each kind of wool for sale. There were fine soft merino fleeces, much in demand, wool from Welsh mountain fat tail sheep, and long wool Romney sheep, each one ideal for a particular type of yarn. The man inspected each and Jack continued to observe the haggling that went on between them. Fred was gesticulating wildly with his hands and getting redder in the face. It seems they struck some sort of bargain and shook hands again as the man counted out cash from a wad of notes and a bag of sovereigns, which Fred recounted and pocketed. Both men appeared satisfied with the deal and Fred made his way back to Jack and Edward and the other tough farm hands.

"Right, lads... let's get into the town."

The group walked up from the grimy dockside passing traders deep in negotiation with other merchants and brokers. They ran the gamut of professional women plying their services. Edward had coloured up to the tips of his ears at their lewd suggestions and kept his head down to avoid all eye contact. Jack was bolder and cheekier often coming back at them with some smart remark as Rhoda followed them and called out, "Say, any of you want some time alone with me?"

"Nah! You girls look like trouble," retorted Jack.

"You can get me into trouble, if you've a mind," said Rhoda with a coy smile.

"Now, why would I do that when you're treating me as a sausage with feet!"

Rhoda laughed raucously and turned away, "Not heard that one before. Have a good time but remember you'd have a better one with me..." She turned away and accosted another gent coming towards her. The group moved on into the town.

The streets were getting busier and folks seemed more animated. There were shops selling all manner of items: hardware stores, clothes shops, grocers and butchers. Jack and Edward were taking it all in, not having seen anything like it for many years. The atmosphere was lively and thrilling.

British flags flew in the port, and a few soldiers in uniform were out on the streets. Edward stiffened, "Relax," whispered Fred. "You have nothing to worry about. No one is going to bother you."

A small platoon marched together down the main street on the way to the quayside. "Going to collect a consignment of convicts, no doubt," said Fred. "Come on." The farmhands and Fred continued on. Jack fearlessly trooped with the others and followed Fred up the steps into the Victoria Hotel. Edward paused and looked back at the retreating platoon with a worried expression. Jack came back and nudged him, "Come on, don't panic. Ain't nothing gonna happen to us here." Edward turned back and followed Jack into the noisy, smoky saloon.

The bar was filled with men of all types, some more well to do than others but mainly traders and merchants celebrating a good day's work. A portly man in sailor's garb was playing a squeeze box and bringing out a cheery melody, accompanied by another on a tin whistle. The tune was vaguely familiar and as Jack picked out the main part of the song he realised why it was so recognisable. "Here, ain't that the song you used to whistle all the time? It drove me mad..." he said to Edward.

Edward cocked his head on one side and listened, "Well, I never. My mother's favourite song, *This Small Violet I Plucked From Mother's Grave*. It is... it is! It was really popular at the time."

"Just as long as it doesn't get you whistling again. If something would give us away that bloody whistle would!" said Jack with a laugh.

A clutch of men at one table were playing cards. One looked up at the new arrivals, "Well, I'll be... Fred! How's tricks?"

"Just fine, Abe and you?"

"Mustn't grumble. How's the wife?"

"Just fine; thanks, Abe."

Abe returned to his cards as two more men shouted and waved at Fred, "Fred, me old cocker. Think you owe me an ale."

"I'll put one in for you, Bill," said Fred with a grin.

Two more card playing merchants hollered, "Fred Doble, you old reprobate. Time for a game?"

"Not today, Percy. I'll be across in a minute, but just to catch up. I've got a thirst on me like a desert rat."

There were more whoops and yells as folk recognised Fred. Others came up and shook his hand warmly leaving Jack and Edward visibly amused and somewhat proud at the hordes of people who knew Fred and clearly thought well of him.

Fred pushed his way through to the bar counter and ordered five ales. He nudged his way back with a tray and set it on the table where the young men sat. "There you go, fellas. Sup your ale. You've worked hard. You deserve a treat."

Jack and Edward picked up their tankards and clinked them together.

Fred noticed that Edward had fallen silent while the other two farmhands were joking and laughing with Jack. Edward had a serious expression and looked about him nervously.

"What are you thinking?" asked Fred.

"It's not like I remember," said Edward.

"Don't worry. Now, drink up, we've time for another before I order us grub."

Edward gave a cursory nod and did as he was told and began chatting with the others.

Jack stopped jawing and looked around, "Where did Koorong and Jarli go?"

"Out of town. It's not safe for them to stay here."

"But, why?" asked a puzzled Jack.

"They're black."

"But they're our friends."

"They'll come back and fetch us tomorrow."

Jack lowered his tone and said in disgust, "It's not right. They're good men. Why should it matter what colour they are?"

"Jack, you and I think alike. We're all the same under our skin. But some men, they think the Abos are inferior to the whites."

"All my eye! That's hogwash."

"We know it. But, sadly many around here hate them. They've been persecuted ever since settlers landed from the colonies. We are the intruders. Be glad we're not in Tasmania."

"Why?"

Fred took a deep breath and his voice dropped to a whisper. He scanned the bar, occasionally catching the eye of someone who recognised him and he would give them a friendly wave. "They're intent on annihilating the Aboriginal race. It's not wise to get involved in politics."

Jack's tone matched Fred's, "That sounds very much like murder to me."

"In Tassy they have something called the Sunday shoot. For sport, white men take out their guns and see how many abos they can kill. That terrible practice is spreading through the states and our communities." His eyes warned Jack to be quiet as his expression turned forbidding. "I don't like it, but you can't afford to make enemies here. Stay out of it, don't get involved. We do what we can for them, help when we can. It doesn't do to talk about it." He paused and studied Jack who had fallen silent and he could see the flame of anger beginning to burn in his eyes. "Now, Jack don't look so morose. We're supposed to be celebrating. We'll talk later, away from those who might be listening."

Jack took a swig of his ale and as Fred and the others began to joke and laugh again, he pondered on what he'd been told and his anger grew.

7: A Night on the Town

As the night went on, the Victoria Hotel became full of activity. A jolly faced man with a balding head and wearing the garb of a trader began to play the upright piano in the corner and sing. Pretty soon the man with the concertina and the other with the tin whistle joined in and they formed a trio rolling out familiar tunes that got many in the crowd singing along. The atmosphere was relaxed, one of frivolity amongst the pluming tobacco smoke and smell of stale booze and food. The floor was slippery as seaweed in places, where ale had slopped on the floor. It caused much merriment when someone slid on the wet surface.

Everything halted when an attractive woman in black button boots, long red skirt with umpteen petticoats and a black satin bodice entered the saloon. She wore a velvet hat with a large feather, fiery chestnut ringlets slipped down her back like water, she carried a reticule and her bright scarlet painted lips smiled broadly. The men stopped and stared. All chatter ended almost as if someone had put the occupants under some sort of spell. It was most unusual to see a woman in a bar. They were used to the hotel barmaids, Minnie and her sister Josie, who worked alongside their father serving ale but seeing a woman the other side of the bar where the men drank was totally against the unwritten rules of society. It was considered scandalous. Once over the initial shock, some men cat-called, others whistled trying to shame the woman into leaving.

Edgar Tucker, the burly landlord rang the big brass bell behind the counter, which clanged stridently, forcing his customers to be quiet once more, "Now, 'old up you, Larrikins. I gotta lady 'ere to entertain you lot." There were more whoops and jeers. "Not like that you, Spoonies, She's a proper singer and a lady. Give a real Victoria Hotel and gentleman's welcome to Rosie Martin."

The drinkers cheered and clapped, a little more politely this time, chinking their glasses and waited expectantly while Rosie whispered the name of a song, "Key of C please, Harry."

Edgar nodded to the jovial man on the piano. "Hit the keys, 'arry."

With a flourish Harry struck out the chords to, "I was strolling in the park one day." There was a big shout of approval and Rosie began to sing. She had a full, beautifully modulated soprano voice and paraded up and down the bar, flirting audaciously with some of the men, tickling them under their chins and batting her eyelashes at them, but being a seasoned professional, she swept away before any could make a grab for her.

Edward couldn't take his eyes off her. He had never seen anything like her before or heard anyone sing like a nightingale. "She's beautiful," he sighed.

Fred laughed, "She's a beauty all right but just take it as it's meant. Entertainment. Edgar Tucker gets all kinds of acts in from time to time, good for his business. Didn't realise there was one today. That's an extra special treat for you."

Jack eyed Rosie up and down, "She's a looker all right. Reminds me of someone I once knew." He sighed sadly with a faraway look in his eyes.

"Who's that then?" asked Fred.

"Nancy," and his expression looked lost and forlorn.

"What happened to her?" asked Edward.

"It was a very long time ago."

"Tell us," said Fred.

"Not much to tell. She was the girlfriend of Bill Sikes. He did her in," said Jack matter of factly. "There was nothing could be done. But she was always kind to us boys, me especially."

Fred didn't press him anymore as he could see her memory brought a despondent heaviness to Jack's eyes and demeanour.

Edward perked up in interest, "What happened to Bill?"

"Hanged."

That was enough for Edward, he turned his head back to watching Rosie with a soppy expression on his face. Fred gave a half grin and supped his ale, before going to the counter and ordering five meals. He took out a sovereign and paid Edgar before returning to the table where the mood had lifted and the youngsters were laughing and joking once again.

"I got rooms booked here for tonight. So, enjoy yourselves."

"What you going to do?" asked Edward.

"I'll listen to Rosie awhile and after our grub, I'll get off to bed. Here, Jack. Take charge of this. I won't give you all your wages in case you're tempted to blow the lot. Easy to get carried away in a place like this, with gambling, women and what-not." He passed Jack some coins, "There's enough there for you to have a good time."

"Thanks, Fred. Bonzer," said Jack as he shared out the money, pocketing his own.

One of the landlord's daughters, Minnie emerged carrying three plates, which she deposited on the table as Josie came with a plate of bread and butter. Fred passed the meals along the table and the accompanying farmhands put their noses down to sniff the vittles. "Smells good," said the one called Daniel, who had tight curly auburn hair and freckles to match.

"Tuck in, don't wait for us," said Fred.

Daniel looked at his brother, Bobby, "Can't do that."

"Why?"

"No tools!" he said with a laugh.

Minnie returned with two more plates, which she served to Fred and Jack as Josie handed out knives and forks to each of them and they began to eat. Little was said while they gobbled down their food with relish. It had been a long day.

Rosie Martin continued to sing and drinkers joined in when they could. She sang as many of the popular songs as she was able and as day turned to dusk she curtseyed and bowed to rapturous applause while the piano player went around the crowd with a hat and men tossed in what coins they could. She collected the cash and swept out through the door as elegantly as she had entered.

The bar became somewhat quieter but for the chink of glasses and Harry announced, "I'll just take a quick break then I'll be back to play some more." A few gents shouted out derisive comments, while others cursed and some cheered.

Fred laid down his utensils and rose. "I'll be off to my room, now. Here's your keys, two to share. Reckon you can work out who's with who. No getting into trouble. Look after each other and enjoy your night. Fred left the table and walked to the sweeping oak stairs and trundled up them. He paused at the top and looked over the balustrade on the landing. The four of them seemed to be getting on well so, with a contented smile he turned into a room and retired for the night.

***

It was some two hours later before the gaiety in the bar had died down. Jack stretched and announced, "I'm bushed. Just going to get a breath of fresh air and then I'm gonna hit the hay."

Edward nodded, "I'll come with you." He turned to the others, "Night, Daniel: night, Bobby."

The two friends, manoeuvred their way through the bar, where traders and merchants were still drinking, and onward to the door to the street. They stepped out into the shadowy night. The road was much quieter, a few sailors were rolling back towards the docks, two ladies of the night stood on a street corner trying for one last time to get a man interested enough to take back to their beds.

Jack took a deep breath and gulped in the clean air away from the eye watering smoke in the saloon and stench of stale alcohol. A merchant followed them out; he bent over in the gutter and retched regurgitating his evening meal and copious amounts of ale. The odour was stomach churningly offensive.

Jack turned to Edward, "I'm just gonna walk down the road a bit. You don't have to come with me."

"Oh, but I do. We stick together, remember?"

Jack shrugged and they ambled along in silence as they strolled away from the hotel. The doxies called out to them to taste their wares but the lads didn't engage in conversation. They just gave them a friendly wave and moved on. As they sauntered towards the track leading to the dock the sound of raised voices reached them. Along a side road, a young Aboriginal man was being shoved around by three bully boys. The thugs were pushing and spinning him from one to the other as if he were the ball in some sort of game.

"Hey, blackie. How come your palms are white and the rest of you's black?" said one fair headed man with a scar on his cheek.

"What's your name, boy?" yelled another, pushing his face into the Aboriginal's.

The third, a younger man with dark greasy hair that straddled his shoulders pretended to take pity on the young man and caught him by the shoulders to stop him falling, "Now, now, lads. Leave him be. Let him get on with his business. What's your name, son?" he said mockingly.

The young native was uncertain at this change of tone. He was unsteady on his feet and grateful to be stopped from the dizzy turning. He hesitated a moment before answering, "Ngarra."

"Ngarra!" shrieked the man. "What kind of a name's that?" The three aggressors screamed with laughter and continued to taunt him.

***

Edward and Jack had stopped. They looked on the scene in disgust, "We have to do something. We must stop this," said Jack.

"No. Just walk away." Jack just stared at Edward in disbelief. "...Look, I don't like it any more than you do. We daren't get into trouble here. It's too risky," said Edward.

"I couldn't live with myself if I did nothing," said Jack. "Take a proper look, Edward. That Abo is terrified. Why, it could be someone from the camp, Alinta's brother, anyone. If you want to go, go. I'm going to help him."

"What you gonna do? I know you're right. Oh, hell! Come on then," and the two began to walk down the road towards the affray.

***

The greasy haired tormenter, pulled out a knife, "Say, d'ya think his blood is black like 'is skin? Shall we see?" He brandished the blade in front of Ngarra's face and grinned wickedly. "So, is it red? Or is it black? Think we ought to find out, don't you?"

He continued to intimidate the native. He made a move forward with the blade waving it in the aboriginal's face when Jack called out, "What's happening here?"

The dark haired persecutor turned abruptly, "What's it to you?"

"Just thought we might join in the fun, didn't we?" he said to Edward whose expression turned to one of shock. Jack nudged him in the ribs and hissed under his breath, "Play along."

"Yeah," said Edward. "We can all have a go."

"You go find your own darkie."

"Now, that's not very friendly, is it?" said Jack moving closer. "Thought you'd like to share."

"Not in me nature, cobber. Like I said, move on unless you wanna tangle?"

Jack raised his hands as if in surrender and the others guffawed. Edward looked from one to the other. The only one with a weapon was the man Jack was trying to needle. Jack continued, "Now, that would make me mad as a cut snake. What's it worth to hand him over?"

"You got money?"

"A bit."

"Then I might take it from you and still keep the Nunga." The aggressor shifted his weight and passed his knife from hand to hand. "There's three of us and two of you... and I got the kukri..."

The other two brutes moved closer to Edward and flanked him one on each side. Edward waited until they were nearly shoulder to shoulder; he jerked his elbows back quickly, forcefully striking each villain sharply in the middle, winding them. They bent double and Edward caught hold of them by the scruff of their necks and slammed their heads together with bone crunching accuracy. They dropped like stones knocked out cold.

Jack grinned slowly and threateningly, "And now there's one of you and two of us. Fancy your chances?"

The aggressor looked at his companions who were unconscious on the floor and took in the stature of his opponents, the height of Edward and the solid build of both of them. He dithered a moment then made a decision, turned tail and fled. Jack helped up the cowering aboriginal boy, "You're all right now, mate. You're safe. What happened?"

Ngarra studied Edward and Jack's expressions, "You not going to hurt me?"

"No, we're not. We wanted to stop them attacking you," said Edward.

"But you said..."

"I know, I'm sorry. We had to do something. Where you headed?" asked Jack.

"To warn my village."

"Why?"

"They coming with gang for Sunday shoot. I must tell them."

"Which village might that be, then?" asked Jack feeling his temper rise.

"Woolloomooloo camp, north of here. I heard them talking. They saw me and trapped me. Then you came."

"Right, tell us exactly where this camp is and then you hurry back to your village, get away from here as quickly as you can. We will try and get you help."

"Yes, sir. Baiame will bless you, both."

Ngarra picked up a twig and drew, in the dirt, a rough map of his village in proximity to the port as the thugs on the ground began to stir.

"Okay, Ngarra, I have a fair idea of where you are. Now, get going and run!" urged Jack as he rubbed out the map with his foot.

Ngarra needed no second bidding. He reeled about and ran as if a pack of wild dingoes were hunting him. Edward pointed out that the ruffians were coming around, "Come on, Jack. We need to get out of here, too."

"Wait," said Jack in a whisper. "Let's see what we can learn."

"No, it's too dangerous."

"You get off if you want to, I'm going to hide out for a moment to hear what's said."

"And if they find you or see you?"

"I'll worry about that when it happens."

"Then I'm staying."

Jack scanned the area and gestured with a jerk of his head. "There's some bins over there and stacked crates. Come on." Edward and Jack scuttled over and ducked down behind them to listen. They peeped out and watched the bullies coming to and rubbing their heads. Both were bleeding.

The fair haired man with the scar checked the road around them, "Where's Charlie gone?"

"Dunno. You got a hard head, Basil," said the other. "What do we do now?"

"Reckon I'd like to get me 'ands on them two blokes."

"Would you know 'em again?"

"Dunno. Had a bit too much grog... Maybe, maybe not."

"Then, when we do, we'll sort 'em out and leave 'em as miserable as bandicoots."

"Why'd Charlie skip out on us? Where's the abo?"

"Jesus, I don't know. Let's get back."

"Arthur, you're right. We gotta shoot to plan, come on."

The vile scoundrels dusted themselves down and limped back up the road, somewhat unsteadily. Jack and Edward stayed hidden and quiet in an attempt to see which route they took. The bullies turned left at the top of the slope down a back alley and away from the town.

Jack and Edward waited until they believed the villains were well away before they stepped out of hiding. Jack nodded, "Right, let's go."

They hurried back through the streets to the Victoria Hotel. It was with relief they tumbled through the door and back into the saloon. Most people had cleared out now, and most guests had gone to bed. There were just a few drinkers and stragglers left.

Jack wandered up to the bar. "Tell me, do you know any bloke called Charlie, dark greasy hair, runs around with a man named Basil, got a scar on his cheek and Arthur?"

The landlord was tight lipped, "Who wants to know?"

"Just wondering if they're locals or from out of town. Heard they were planning some fun tomorrow."

The landlord, Edgar, leaned across the bar and his voice dropped to a whisper. "Take my advice, stay away from 'em. They're bad news. Trouble follows 'em all over. You don't want to get mixed up in any of that. Fred wouldn't like it."

Jack raised an eyebrow, "Why d'you say that?"

"Fred's a good man, true heart. The sort of fun you're talking about comes at a price and goes against everything Fred believes in, like me. Thought you'd know better."

Edward intervened, "Listen, we're no Abo haters. They're our friends. We heard what's happening. We want to do something about it. Do what's right."

"Abo lovers or haters, it's all the same. Steer clear. One righteous act won't change the world."

Jack leaned back and smiled affably, "Right, then we'll call it a night and get off to bed. Thanks, Edgar. Come on, Edward."

The two youngsters made their way up the timber staircase while the landlord looked after them thoughtfully.

***

Once inside their room, Edward turned to Jack, "What you going to do?"

"Give Ngarra's village a fighting chance."

"How do we do that?"

"We'll speak to Fred. Come on, let's hit the sack. Tomorrow will be a tough day."

"We did the right thing, didn't we?" asked Edward.

"Yes, I believe so."

"Do you think those lushy coves will come after us?"

"Dunno. With a bit of luck, we may be lucky as it was our first time in town. They ain't seen us before."

"I suppose." Edward yawned loudly and took off his shirt and trousers. He threw back the covers on the springy bed and fell in with his socks on, pummelled the bolster and shut his eyes firmly. A small smile played on his mouth, he puckered up his lips and began to whistle, "This small violet I plucked from mother's grave." He grinned even more when Jack bashed him on the head with his pillow.

***

The following morning, Fred knocked on the boys' door, "Let's be having you or you'll get nothin'. It'll be a dingoes' breakfast for you." He put his ear to the door and heard them scrambling up. He gave a quick grin and made his way downstairs to the saloon where they would be served.

Fred sat at his designated table, where he always sat, Daniel and Bobby joined him and a few minutes later, Jack and Edward scooted down the stairs. They each pulled out a chair and sat expectantly.

"Have we missed it?" asked Edward stifling a creeping yawn.

"Nope. But it looks like you both need a good wash. What did you do last night?" He pointed at Edward's shirt. "You got blood on your front."

Edward and Jack exchanged a glance. Jack lowered his voice. "We got to talk to you 'bout that."

Just then, Josie arrived carrying a large tray with five plates, piled with sausages, eggs and bacon. She set them down and went back to the kitchen. The aroma had them all salivating. Minnie soon followed with a platter of bread and butter and five mugs of tea.

"Didn't think I'd be hungry, but I am," said Daniel. "I was up half the night chucking up."

"That was the ale," said Bobby. "Kept me awake, I can tell you, with all your groaning and whingeing."

Daniel and Bobby chatted animatedly between mouthfuls of food. Fred said nothing. He studied Jack and Edward's faces. Jack tried to speak but hesitated. Fred eventually whispered, "Go on, lad, say whatever it is that's bothering you." He waggled his fork at Jack, "It's what we were talking about yesterday, isn't it? I heard rumours."

Jack licked his lips and took a sip of his tea, "Me throat's gone dry..." He took another sip and nodded. "Edward and me, we went for a walk for a bit of clean air and saw..."

"Saw what?"

Edward jumped in, "Three men..." he glanced at Jack. "They'd cornered a kid."

"Has Edgar said something?" asked Jack.

"Why? Should he?"

"I'm sure he knew these fellas and what they're planning."

Fred paused, "Eat your grub. I'll have a word with Edgar."

There was an uneasy silence while they finished their meal. Bobby and Daniel shifted uncomfortably in their seats aware that something had happened. As soon as Fred had finished eating he left the table and went to the kitchen door to find Edgar. The two were in discussion for a few minutes before he returned looking serious.

"Right, tell me what happened."

Jack and Edward gave their account of the previous evening's events. Fred sighed deeply. "You're right. It must be stopped, but it will be tough. We can't draw any attention to you. There's too many in port that agree with these activities."

"But it's wrong," said Edward.

"Yes, it is. And this is what we're going to do." He began to talk quickly in low tones as the others listened carefully.

They ate their breakfast quickly before huddling together again as Edgar joined them. They talked for an hour. Minnie and Josie were left in charge of the bar.

Fred spoke to his men. "Koorong and Jarli will collect our things from here as usual and they'll get to the outskirts of town, where it will be safer and wait for us. The farm they're headed for, is friendly and they're all sympathisers, who'll ensure Koorong and Jarli will stay out of harm's way, while they sit this out."

Edgar called through the kitchen door. Fred and his men went into the back.

Edgar spoke quickly and quietly, "As discussed, we will be joined by three more. Be sure to cover your faces. You can't be recognised. You lads must wear your hats. Remember no use of names. I got horses out back and guns. Let's give these ruffians a taste of their own medicine."

Fred nodded to Jack and Edward, "You get on ahead to the village and find Ngarra. Warn them and be sure to get them out. Go now! We'll meet you there. You know the plan."

Jack and Edward pulled on their wide brimmed slouch hats, and tugged up their rag cloths to cover their faces so all that could be seen was their eyes. Edgar passed them each a Martini Henry breech loading rifle with ammunition. The rifle slotted neatly into a leather sheath on the saddle. They were experienced riders and one of Edgar's friends had supplied them with a horse each. They mounted their steeds and set off breaking into a canter once they had left the township.

They soon reached the outback where the terrain changed dramatically from town buildings, and farmhouses to the wilds of bush and scrub. Disturbed kangaroos bounded off searching for cover as flocks of galahs lifted to the skies screaming at the intrusion of their territory.

"How much further?" asked Edward. "Are we going the right way?"

Jack shrugged, "Not sure, I hope so. Edgar's instructions were fairly clear. We keep going."

They passed a tin shack by a windmill and Jack nodded, "We're on course. There's the hut and windmill. It should be about a mile further on. Keep an eye out for three gum trees by a couple of boulders."

They cantered on and slowed to a trot as the three gumtrees came into sight. "Over there!" called Edward. He could see smoke rising from a fire. They turned their horses and passed to the left of the boulders down towards a creek, where a profusion of vegetation grew next to a thicket the other side of which, was the village.

They stopped at the edge of the camp and Jack called out "Cooee!"

One elderly man appeared from one hut but no one else came out. Jack dismounted and spoke, "We mean you no harm." He pointed to himself and Edward, "Bunji," He tapped himself, "friend." He called out, "Ngarra! Miromma."

The elderly man shouted something and Ngarra emerged from the same hut with a cattle dog. Jack pulled down his face covering. "Ngarra, please explain... it's me, Jack and Edward." He gestured to Edward who also pulled down his rag cloth face covering. Ngarra's eyes widened and he nodded. Words plummeted out of him like rocks in a landslide as he explained to the old man who they were.

The chief nodded sagely.

"Ngarra you need to get your people out of here. Men are on their way. We have friends who wish to help. Have you somewhere safe to go?"

Ngarra pointed to a rocky outcrop in the distance, "Sacred caves are there. Our women and children there already. The men are here."

"Then, you and those left, leave now and quickly. We will take your places with our friends. Stay quiet and hidden. We will deal with these bad men. Go!"

Ngarra nodded in understanding and shouted out to the village. Many men of various ages came out of huts carrying spears and sticks. They looked scared and jabbered together as they followed Ngarra's instructions and began to make their way out of the village.

Ngarra spoke carefully, "I will stay as will my father." He indicated the elderly chief.

Jack shook his head, "It will be safer for you if you all leave. I promise you we will take care of this."

Ngarra exchanged words with his father who shook his head vehemently. "He won't go."

Edward interrupted, "We're wasting precious time. Ngarra, please do as Jack says. Please," he urged. He turned to Jack, "What's the damn word for please?"

"There isn't one. No please and no thank you!"

Ngarra tried again and very reluctantly the old man finally agreed to follow the other men from his village and moved in the direction of the caves.

"You, too, Ngarra," said Edward.

"No, as I told my father, he is needed to lead our people but I will stay, I crave to know, which of those townsmen are our enemies."

Exasperated, Jack continued, "Very well. But stay hidden. Don't come out unless we tell you." He waited until the last of the Aboriginal men had disappeared from view to the caves, "Where can we hide our horses?"

"This way," Ngarra led them to a long hut near the centre of the village where there were some chickens and livestock. "In there."

Jack and Edward tethered the animals to a central post where they could nibble some hay. "Stay with the horses, Ngarra. Keep your dog with you. Do as I say. We will position ourselves. Those villains won't know what's hit them."

"What now?" said Edward, anxiously.

"Now, we wait."

8: Events at Woolloomooloo Camp

Jack, ever impatient, paced up and down the long hut rubbing his scantily bearded chin in agitation. "They can't be much longer, surely?"

"I hope not," said Edward, also getting fidgety. "I don't like to admit it, Jack, but I'm scared. I got kangaroos jumping in my stomach not butterflies. We don't know how many of them there'll be."

"Try to keep calm, Edward. You're making me jittery. Look at the facts... We should have enough fire power between us to defend ourselves and we have something else on our side."

"What's that?"

"Surprise. They won't be expecting us."

Edward chewed the inside of his mouth as was his habit when he was nervous about something. Jack scratched his neck where new bristles had sprouted and stopped pacing. He scrutinised Edward, "That's a bad habit you've got. One of these days you'll eat your own cheek."

"Sorry," murmured Edward. "You got me started on that."

"Yeah? Well, I kicked the habit. Gave me a sore mouth."

"I was just counting up, Edgar said he had three more on board."

"So?"

"So, with Fred, Edgar, Daniel and Bobby, you and me and the three we don't know that makes nine."

"It'll be enough," said Jack with more confidence than he felt. He didn't want to confess that he had reservations about the action they were about to take. "You gotta remember, they've had massacres in Tasmania, and elsewhere; whole villages wiped out by blokes such as we saw last night."

"I know."

"We heard from Edgar some colonists are beginning to do this all around the coast. It's bad news, Edward and it ain't right."

"I know."

"Then buck up and listen. Let's pray our men get here first. I don't fancy our chances with just the two of us."

Ngarra sat fussing his dog but paid attention to everything that was said.

"Not two, three," he said firmly. "I'll help."

"What's she called?" asked Jack changing the subject. "Your dog... tinko," he added in Aboriginal as the animal crossed to him wanting to be petted. Jack obliged and tickled the animal behind her ear, which set her back leg off in a frenzy of scratching, which made them chuckle.

"Koiyung, her name means fire. She's very brave. Saved me once from gwardir."

"Gwardir?"

"Brown snake with very bad temper. It raised right up to strike me, Koiyung caught it behind its head so it couldn't bite. I trapped it in a bag. Let it go later. Koiyung very brave," said Ngarra with pride.

"Ssh!" Jack raised his fingers to his lips for them to be quiet. He could hear the soft thud of horses' hooves outside. Koiyung began his fierce growling; the rumbling grew in the animal's throat, which gave Jack goose bumps. The hairs on the back of his neck stood on end, and a shiver ran down his spine.

He stealthily edged towards the entrance of the long hut and peeped out. He counted seven riders, two of which were in military uniform. He recognised Fred's physique, in spite of his face covering.

Jack lowered his hand and signalled to Edward that it was safe. He walked outside. Seven rifles were cocked, ready to fire and pointed at him.

"It's all right. He's one of us," said Fred.

The rifles were lowered as Edward and Ngarra appeared with Koiyung who began to bark and bay at them. Ngarra quietened his dog, who obeyed immediately and fell quiet, and laid down at Ngarra's feet.

"Is the village safe?" questioned Fred.

"All gone. Ngarra is the only one here," said Jack.

"Good. We've not got a lot of time. By my reckoning the renegades will be here within the next fifteen minutes. Where can we hide the horses?"

"There's some room in this long hut. Where else, Ngarra?"

"Room for three more in here. I show you another place. Come," he beckoned them to follow.

Fred, Daniel and Bobby took their steeds in with Jack and Edward's. The soldiers with Edgar and one other dismounted and followed Ngarra to another long hut, before returning to the centre of the camp where the community shelter stood and the rest of them waited.

Edgar took charge, "You all know what to do. Five of you, separate with one man to a shack." He pointed at Jack, "You with me." He gestured to Fred and Edward, "You two together. And we wait. Could be some time or we could be lucky. Our winning cards are these two." He indicated the two soldiers. "Sergeant Phillips and Private Denton, who will come out last. The private first. Right, men. Into positions."

The vigilantes scattered and followed Edgar's orders. Fred joined Edward while Edgar hunkered down with Jack. Ngarra remained close to Jack with Koiyung.

Edgar eyed Jack, "Seems I got you wrong, lad," he said. "I thought you were an Abo hater. We got enough of those. No offence meant."

"None taken," said Jack. "We've got many Aboriginal friends, noble men who've taught me a lot."

Ngarra piped up, "If it not been for Jack, I'd be dead and so would all my village by now."

Jack sighed and tried to relax, which was difficult in the circumstances. The minutes seemed to tick away painfully slowly. Each tiny sound, every whisper of wind and each unexpected creak stretched his nerve endings tighter than a poacher's snare. They waited in uncomfortable silence. The only thing to be heard was the heavy rise and fall of their juddering breathing. Jack's heartbeat pounded in his chest so loudly, he was sure Edgar could hear it thumping as if it was bursting to escape. He swallowed hard.

The wait seemed interminable. Every instant the crickets interrupted their song or the screeching cockatoos outside fell silent, Jack held his breath and listened closely. But, each time nature resumed its normal buzz and chatter, so Jack heaved a sigh of relief.

"They should be here by now," said Edgar.

"Do you think something's happened to them?"

Edgar shrugged, "If they don't come today, they'll come another." He slapped his hand forcefully across his thigh, "Dammit! These killings have to stop."

"I don't want no one to get killed."

"Nor do we, Jack. Nor do we. But history tells us different. There've been conflicts and wars between abos and settlers for more than an 'undred years. Some of the atrocities and mass slaughters were actually sanctioned by Government."

"We've had bad men, too," said Ngarra. "Daylight attacks carried out by native police with white men. Traitors to us, ones who've sided against us, standing with the white man's power for what they can get."

Edgar continued as the passion in his belly built rapidly, "In the beginning the skirmishes and killings were mainly revenge attacks for theft of food and livestock. But, we know now that this was to feed families and villages when they'd been evicted from their own lands, had their fertile growing ground stolen. It's all wrong. They were 'ere first. It's their country. We should be able to live peacefully side by side. We're all the same under our skin," added Edgar. "Take Myall Creek; that was the only time, as far as I know that justice was done successfully... once in all those years."

"Why? What happened, there?" asked Jack, glad of the distraction that Edgar had engineered.

"Twenty-eight aboriginals were massacred near Inverell, not far from here. That was the first time when whites and black African settlers were successfully prosecuted for the atrocity and it took a bucket of courage from Governor George Gipps to order a retrial, after white juries had set the perpetrators free. Settlers have been getting away with this butchery for too long, beheading children and women and worse."

"Can't imagine anything worse... Gipps? I knew someone called Gipps, once..." said Jack reflectively. They fell silent as Jack mulled over what he'd been told. "I didn't know... the extent of it... all those murders. It's sickening."

A feeling of unease filled the shack. Jack began to pace again in nervous agitation, a vein in his temple throbbed and pulsed. Edgar tried to appease him, "Don't get jumpy. You'll be no use to us. You gotta stay calm."

The more Jack tried to stem his anger the more edgy he became. Koiyung padded over to Jack who flopped onto the dirt floor despondently with his back to one of the supporting struts. He was sitting with his knees up. He took off his hat and raked his fingers through his hair. "It's all so wrong!" he exclaimed.

The dog put her head on Jack's knee and gazed deep into his eyes as some form of canine comfort. Nervous apprehension had risen to an almost unbearable level. Jack's chest tightened leaving him feeling suffocated when Koiyung, pricked up her ears and a menacing low rumbling growl rattled in her throat. The dog moved towards the entrance standing as a block to anyone who might enter. Jack sprang up, fully alert, as Ngarra warned his dog to stay quiet.

Edgar whispered, "Listen."

The sound of horses' hooves could be heard thundering towards the camp. The wait was over as six riders galloped into the village, whooping, shouting and howling like wild animals, firing their guns erratically, sending resting birds from their perches screaming into the sky.

A burning torch flew from one marauder's hand and lit the grass and straw roof of the central community hut. Greedy flames licked up the outside of the shack, guzzling on the dry wooden framework with crackling mirth, almost mocking those concealed inside.

Koiyung set up a ferocious barking and darted outside followed by Ngarra.

"There's one!" yelled a voice Jack recognised as belonging to the greasy haired lout called Charlie, who took aim, centred his sights on Ngarra and fired as Koiyung leapt in front of her master and took a bullet in the shoulder much to the glee of Charlie who hastily reloaded.

The dog yelped and fell. Bleeding and whimpering she crawled nearer Ngarra, who went to the valiant animal's side, with tears streaming down his face.

Charlie lifted his rifle to take aim again as Edgar and Jack emerged from the same hut that was starting to blaze. Smoke billowed up and caught on the wind threatening to fan the flames and spread the gluttonous, sputtering fire.

Charlie cocked his gun. Edgar spoke with cold menace, "I shouldn't do that if I were you."

"And who's to stop me?" sneered Charlie, taking aim.

"I am," said Fred coming out of another hut with Edward. Charlie hesitated. Each of Fred's crew had trained their weapons on a different thug.

Charlie curled his lip in disdain, "Four of you and six of us. You'll come off worse."

Bobby appeared from another shack, wielding a gun, "Don't think you can count, Mister."

Charlie stopped. He screamed at his fellow conspirators, "Shoot them!"

The other villains wavered as Daniel came out of his shelter followed by another armed man from a different shack. They encircled the ruffians with their rifles levelled at the bullies. Charlie yelled again, "Kill 'em!"

No one moved.

Finally, Private Denton and Sergeant Phillips materialised in their uniforms and the would-be killers gasped. "I shouldn't if I were you," said the sergeant. "Let loose one shot at us and no matter what else happens you'll be dead. Do you really want to die today?"

Charlie faltered, a bead of sweat ran from his forehead into his eyes. He shook his lank locks and snorted in fury. His finger began to squeeze the trigger, when he unexpectedly lifted the rifle in the air and fired angrily into the sky. Then he brought the rifle down sharply and aimed it at Ngarra who was weeping at the side of his injured dog.

Sergeant Phillips warned him, "Don't do it!" but Charlie's shaking finger started to pull the trigger so, Denton fired to wound him. Charlie squealed in pain and clutched his shoulder now pouring with blood as Jack sprinted protectively to Ngarra's side.

Phillips ordered, "Get going, all of you, NOW!"

Leaving Charlie, the crew of villains turned their horses and galloped hurriedly out of the camp.

Charlie snarled, "This ain't over. We'll be back. You won't always be able to keep watch to protect them. At some point you'll drop your guard and we'll be there. You wait!"

Phillips spoke again, "You're forgetting, we know who you are. We will recognise you. If anything does happen to anyone in this village you'll be arrested. All of you."

Charlie controlled his horse, one handed, heeled him and raced after his gang away from the camp.

The others watched them go. "He's right," said Phillips. "They're gone for now but we won't be able to watch them all the time."

Edgar moved swiftly, "Quickly! We must put this fire out. If the wind gets up it'll ravage the village. Ngarra?"

Ngarra was sobbing but he managed to choke out, "There's water in the creek. Buckets over there." He pointed to a stack of vessels used by the villagers to collect water. "Someone please help Koiyung."

Fred joined Jack by the side of the plucky dog. He removed his rag cloth, tied it like a tourniquet to stop the bleeding and examined the animal's injury. "It's a flesh wound, hasn't hit a main vein or artery. He'll live, as long as it doesn't get infected. It looks like the bullet passed straight through. Don't think it's hit a bone."

Jack stood up, "I'll get gum leaves and water." He hurried to a eucalyptus tree and gathered some foliage. Edward ran after the others to help collect water.

The flames from the hut were intensifying. Black smoke spiralled up in a thick column. The acrid smell caught in the back of their throats as Ngarra exclaimed, "My people will think we're done for. We have to stop the spread."

The horses in the long huts smelled the fire, becoming restless and distressed. They whinnied, pawed the ground and snorted loudly.

Fred nodded, "Agreed." He gestured to Koiyung, "Is there a flat surface somewhere we can treat her?" Ngarra picked up his beloved cattle dog and carried her swiftly inside another hut where there was a flat woven rush mat and set her down carefully. Meanwhile, Jack was busy preparing a poultice of healing paste as he'd been taught by Koorong and Jarli.

Fred collected the horses and tied them up away from the burning stench of the ruined hut. Bobby, Daniel and the soldiers tried to drown the flames and contain the fire. It was to this chaotic scene that Ngarra's father and the other male members of the tribe arrived. They immediately came to the aid of the others to help suffocate the festering furnace.

The old man searched the village with his eyes and his voice was a whisper, "Ngarra?"

Edgar reassured the elder, "Safe. Thanks to his dog," and he pointed to the shack where they were treating the heroic canine. "In there." Ngarra's father hurried inside to see his son.

An hour later, the blaze was almost out, but wood still smouldered and spindles of smoke wafted up. Edgar and Edward stamped on the remaining embers. The women and children had begun drifting back to the village. They stared in disbelief at the devastation caused to the central, communal hut used for celebrations that was now razed to the ground.

Edgar took Fred to one side, "They can't stay here. Those swine will be back. In one respect that villain was right, we can't protect them all the time. They need to move on, find somewhere else to dwell."

"What do you suggest? This is their perfect place; a place of plenty where they can hunt, fish and grow crops. If they travel further along up the creek they won't find such fertile ground."

"Maybe, I've got an idea. We can't stake out this hamlet, but we can pressure those men. Like Phillips said, we know the names of the three main offenders and I've a good idea about the others. They've been in my bar, I'm sure. If we can keep our eye on them, the threat will be less. If they know that the authorities are aware of them and their antics, it may make a difference." He called Sergeant Phillips and Private Denton across and they discussed Edgar's and the sergeant's scheme further and shook hands.

Koiyung was patched up much to the gratitude of Ngarra, "Baiame blesses you. You Ngarra's bunji."

Jack grinned. "You look after that dog. She really is a true heroine."

The compatriots mounted their horses and began to trot out of the village, exchanging friendly words with the natives who clamoured around them to show their appreciation.

Jack was the last to mount. He gave Ngarra a final wave and said, "Ngarra and Jack, bunjis,"

"Bunji," repeated Ngarra.

***

Once clear of the village the urgency disappeared from their pace. They chatted amiably amongst themselves. Fred rode alongside Edgar and said, "We'll leave you on the boundary of the town at the farm where Koorong and Jarli are meeting us. Will you be able to lead the rest of the horses back to town?"

"We'll manage," said Edgar. "Just be careful on the way back. Those rats don't know who we are but I wouldn't trust them not to come after us. They'll be as mad as a salt croc made into boots, you mark my words."

"Warning noted. Thanks, Edgar for all you did, mate."

"No thanks, needed. I'll see you all next time you're in town. I just hope me girls have managed me 'otel and customers as well as they think they can!"

Fred laughed and nodded, "They're good girls, both of 'em."

"Like your boys. Wouldn't want to tangle with any. You've trained 'em well."

A note of pride entered Fred's voice, "Aye, they'll do. Now, I best get them all back to Mrs Doble, she's gonna wonder where we've got to."

They soon reached the outlying farm on the edge of Port Jackson, where Koorong and Jarli leaned against the carts while they waited. Koorong straightened up and grinned in welcome as he saw them approach. Jarli tossed away the stem of grass he was chewing and made the gesture of friendship.

"You're late, Mr Fred. Everything all right?" said Koorong.

"Everything's fine. We'll tell you all about it on the way home. You and Jarli... you didn't have any bother out here?" he said meaningfully.

"No, Mr Fred but we did hear that some gubbahs were out for trouble."

"Trouble is right. Out at Woolloomooloo camp. Some right scurvy migaloos but we stopped it. Quite a tale to tell but don't let it reach Mrs Doble's ears."

Koorong nodded, "You have my word."

"Mine, too," said Jarli.

"Good, now let's get home. Reckon we'll be having some damn fine grub tonight."

Edgar and the others watched Fred and his men board the wagons safely. They stayed put until the drays had passed out of sight before heading back into Port Jackson.

***

Koorong and Jarli could hardly believe the story that unfolded. Both carts were alive with chatter, as each person chipped in with bits of the account. Koorong put his hand on Fred's shoulder, "Mr Fred, we're just glad you're all safe."

Jack added, "So are we. I just hope that nest of taipans slither into their own holes and leave good folk alone."

"Now, remember, not a word of this to Mrs Doble. She was worried enough about us going to town," said Fred.

"So, if she asks, why do we say we're late?" asked Jack.

"Now, I don't like lying to my missus. Just don't say nothing. Then I won't have to fib. What she don't know won't hurt her. But, if she presses us, the wheel came off a wagon and we had to wait for it to be fixed. Nothing more. Got it?"

"Got it!" said Jack. "Best tell Edward."

"He knows. We got our story straight when we were waiting at the camp." Fred wore a comfortable smile on his face, "Not far now. It'll be good to get home."

"It will and to have some of Mrs D's grub. The Victoria wasn't bad but not a patch on Mrs D's cooking."

Fred laughed and basked in the compliment, "Too right. You can tell 'er that. She'd love to hear it from you."

The carts turned off the town road and down the dirt track that led to the farm. Sheep could be heard bleating in the distance. Jack grinned, "Love that sound, better than all the singing of the Rosie Martins in this world cos it means we're nearing home." Jack looked quite emotional as he said it. "Think it's as I've never had no proper home. Not till now," and his eyes misted up. He hurriedly scrubbed at his face with his sleeve and Fred pretended not to notice.

Before the track opened out into the yard Fred let out a whistle, his signal to say that they were almost there. He could see the farmhouse in the distance and Mrs Doble sitting on the porch waiting. As soon as she heard the whistle and saw the carts she beamed so broadly it looked like she would give herself face ache. She stood up from the wooden settle, took off her apron and waved it at the menfolk as they drew nearer.

Edward stood up in his seat and waved back at her as did Fred and Jack, all grinning happily. Daniel and Bobby hopped off the carts to traipse back to their workers' homestead, a farm where they lived with family, nearly all of whom worked for Fred.

Mrs Doble moistened her lips, primped her hair and gave her cheeks a pinch, to give them a pretty blush, before stepping off the veranda and hurrying to meet the wagons. Her delight that they were all back safely was apparent. Fred handed the reins to Jack, jumped down and went to meet her. He swung her around as if she was a young lass and planted a kiss on her lips. The two walked arm in arm back to the house as Mrs D called out, "Jack, Edward! Get yourselves washed and cleaned up. I got something special for you all."

Jack and Edward drove the wagons to their holding barn, untacked the horses, fed and watered them in their stable before racing each other to their quarters, where a fresh ewer of water had been placed along with clean clothes neatly folded on the chair. There was a scuffle between them as to who would wash first, which Jack won. So, Edward stretched out on the bed, "I suppose you are my senior," said Edward. "It's only right to give way to the elderly." Jack turned around with a face full of suds, "Crikey, even your beard's turned white now!"

Jack threw a wet sponge at Edward catching him full in the face. Edward took aim and tossed it back. There ensued a tussle between the two filled with grunts and chuckles until Edward shouted, "Enough! All right, I give up."

Jack climbed off his friend that he had pinned down and returned to his ablutions when a mischievous grin widened across Edward's face; he puckered up his lips and began to whistle shrilly.

Jack tried to ignore the piercing rendition of the song he had come to dislike so intensely. He stiffened and pretended he couldn't hear by singing his own ditty over the noise until he'd finished washing, resulting in a strange cacophony of sound. "All yours," he called to Edward who bounced off the bed and took his place at the basin and jug. Jack dressed hastily and dived to the door. "See you there, Junior." He gave a cheeky wave and made his way to the farmhouse.

***

The dinner table was alive with bubbling chatter that evening. Edward recounted the events at the hotel and the charms of the singer, Rosie Martin. "Mrs D, she sang like an angel," enthused Edward, "and looked even better. Little sausage curls all down her back and a waist you could put one hand round."

"Sounds like you had a good time," said Mrs Doble with a smile. "Now, come on and eat up. I prepared all this for you. Your favourites."

"You've done us proud," said Fred with a grin. "The lads will have to come with me again, if we get this much of a welcome home."

"Can we?" asked Edward. "Will you take us again, Fred?"

Fred looked at the two expectant faces, "I don't see why not. Time you learned how to deal. All right, we'll do it again next time. This time we dealt in wool, next time it'll be sheep. Got a good breeding programme going, but now it's time to offload some surplus sheep."

"When will that be?"

"Two weeks from today. We'll have to get them ready for auction, a batch of twelve young Merinos. You can learn the rules of the market and negotiation."

Jack and Edward beamed in delight. It was something they would both look forward to and Jack added, "We'll be counting the days."

***

Later that night, long after Jack and Edward had gone to bed, Fred and Mrs Doble sat on the veranda quietly contemplating the indigo night sky. Millions of stars flecked the velvet ceiling and the moon shone full, smiling brightly and benignly down on the couple. Fred was relaxed and contented. He took Mrs Doble's hand and kissed it tenderly. "I know what you're thinking," he whispered.

"It's a mind reader, you are now, is it?"

"No, I just know you... And you had no need to worry." Mrs Doble glanced sideways at him. "No one gave them a second look. They're unrecognisable now and safe."

Mrs Doble grunted in gratification, "You still haven't said why you were so late."

"Didn't mention it cos it wasn't important."

"What happened?"

"A wheel came loose on the cart. We had to wait to get it fixed."

"Oh? And what else? I suppose you had a drink?"

"More than one if the truth be known. The boys enjoyed it, Bobby and Daniel, too."

Mrs Doble gave a non-committal, "Hmm."

"In fact, I might have another before we go in. Would you like one, my dear?"

"Why not? But, just a small one." Mrs Doble watched her husband affectionately as he rose and moved to the door. He stopped momentarily as if catching his breath and disappeared inside, returning minutes later with an ale for himself and a small sherry for his wife and sat beside her once more. "Is everything all right, Fred?" she asked tentatively.

"Everything's just fine and dandy," he smiled and took a sip of his drink.

The two sat in contented silence listening to the churring call of the nightjars and the repetitive 'oo oo' call of tawny frogmouths. These mixed together with the thrum of crickets made a nocturnal percussive melody, which was familiar and comforting. The occasional night parrot screeched but when the eerie screaming woman bird shrieked through the night sky, it silenced all other calls for a few minutes and a shiver ran down Mrs Doble's spine. She murmured, "I'll never forget Koorong's tale of the screaming woman bird as a harbinger of the spirit world. It always fills me with unease."

"It's just an old aboriginal story. Nothing more." Fred patted her hand as the usual nocturnal sounds resumed.

"I suppose so, Fred. I suppose so. It just startled me, that's all."

They continued to sit there until the moon had shifted its position appearing higher in the sky. "Ever wondered why the moon looks so different 'ere?" asked Fred.

"Don't think I've noticed."

"Yes, you must have. It's upside down here."

"What on earth do you mean?" said Mrs Doble with a laugh. "The moon's the moon the whole world over, isn't it?"

"No, I don't think so. In England, we always had a jolly faced man in the moon. Sometimes I used to think I could see his mouth move as he talked to me and he followed me wherever I went. Over here it's like the moon's flipped upside down and he has a look of alarm on his face." Fred laughed, "But, then that's just what I think."

"Perhaps the screaming woman bird has frightened him, too."

"Perhaps."

The Dobles remained outside blanketed in the warm air until Fred yawned loudly, "It's been a busy day and I'm ready for my bed. Coming?"

Mrs Doble smiled gently as she watched her husband retreat inside, her love for him clearly etched on her face. She glanced up at the moon and shook her head, "Upside down, indeed!" and she giggled to herself before rising and following him indoors.

***

In Port Jackson, Charlie and his gang were clustered around a brazier, roasting potatoes on the charcoal and swilling down ale. Charlie, flicked back his oily hair and announced to his buddies, "That big fella... I'm sure I'll know 'im again, rag cloth on 'is face or not. He's been to town before and he's sure to come again and when he does, I'll know 'im and do for 'im. And that's a promise."

9: Aftermath

Jack and Edward were in an elevated mood after the events in Port Jackson and Woolloomooloo Camp. Edward even laughed and joked about the women who had accosted him. He showed bravado retrospectively discussing it, making light of his embarrassment at the time and the bubbling fear he had felt.

Jack teased him, "Are you saying you would have taken up the offer of one of those women? Seriously?"

"Of course," said Edward unable to quite meet Jack's eyes. "I'd have been fine."

"Rather you than me. You'd likely have come back with something nasty and I don't reckon Mrs D would have liked that much."

"What do you mean?" asked Edward in surprise.

"You know... don't you?" stressed Jack with a wink before he spotted the ingenuous expression on Edward's face. He paused... "You don't? You really don't know, do you? Oh, ye Gods alive! You better get someone to explain it all to you."

Edward stared at Jack, "Tell me."

"Oh, no! I'm not going to say anything. Ask Fred," said Jack taking a comb to his thick mop of hair.

Edward coloured up, "Come on, Jack. Do a bloke a favour. Tell me what you mean," pressed Edward in his curiosity.

"Not for me to say. Thought you'd have picked up some of the ways of the world on your travels."

"Be fair, everywhere I've travelled has been with you."

"Yes, well... there is that," said Jack starting to blush.

Edward pointed an accusing finger at him, "Ah ha! You've no more idea than me. It's all bluster."

"I never said I'd done anything, but I know what's what and what goes where," said Jack defensively. "And I know the dangers..."

There was a short lull in the conversation before Edward spoke again, "Don't think I'd be comfortable asking Fred or Mrs D. Go on, tell me," he pleaded.

"Then ask Koorong or Jarli."

"Please, Jack."

"No." But then Jack saw the lost, almost desperate, expression in Edward's eyes and relented. "Oh, very well. But I'm only going to tell you once and then no more questions," said Jack as his face suffused with even more colour in spite of his deep tan.

***

Suppertime saw a subdued Edward at the dinner table. Jack chomped away on his mutton stew, his enjoyment plain to see. "By heck, Mrs D. This has got to be one of my most favourite meals."

"Even more than wonga wonga pigeon?"

Jack scratched his head as he thought, "That's a tough one. I love the bread sauce that comes with that but... Yes, mutton stew comes top. How about you, Edward?"

Edward said nothing but continued to eat his meal stoically.

"Edward?"

Edward lifted his head up sharply, "Uh? What? Sorry, I was miles away."

"I can see that," said Mrs Doble. "What were you thinking about?"

"Rosie Martin, I'll bet," said Fred with a wink.

Edward flushed and protested his denial, "Nah, you got it all wrong."

"Have I? Seems like the woman has taken your fancy. You've got the shine for her," he said with a laugh.

"Stop teasing him, Fred," said Mrs Doble. "Take no notice, Edward. Eat your supper."

Fred grinned, "You never know, the Victoria might have her back again. We'll find out at the auction. We'll get you a front row seat by the piano."

Edward gave a half smile and carried on eating his stew.

"What's on tomorrow, Fred?" asked Jack.

"I'll be riding the ranch to check the watering stations, make sure the valves are open and the sheep are getting their water."

"Are you sure you don't need us?"

"No. I'll leave word for Koorong and Jarli to start at the outer perimeter and work inwards. We'll manage fine... So, what you up to on your day off?" asked Fred.

"Going to the camp," said Jack. "I'm going to finish the toys I've been whittling for the children. Got a piece of white birch soaking. I'll get back to it after I've eaten."

"That's a grand thing to do, Jack. Is Edward going to help?"

"Edward will help me paint them. He's been mixing some colours. Jarli showed him how to make them. That's right, isn't it, Edward?"

Edward looked distracted but answered, "Uh huh. Yes, that's right."

"He'll do the dishes this evening so I can get on and finish. That's right, isn't it, Edward?"

"Yes, yes, of course..."

Mrs Doble frowned, "What's the matter, Edward? Not like you to let Jack get away with that? Edward?"

Edward felt everyone's eyes on him and instantly became more alert, "What are you saying? I wasn't really listening. Sorry."

"Didn't think so. You've just arranged to do the dishes after our food."

"Oh, what?"

Fred spoke up, "You need to pay attention. You could have agreed to anything and we'd be witnesses. You'd have to follow through, then."

"Yes," said Jack, "like giving me your pay for a week," and he winked.

"I didn't?" said Edward aghast.

"No, but you could have," said Mrs Doble primly.

"Sorry," muttered Edward embarrassed.

"Too late," said Jack with a grin. "I'm off to finish the wooden toys. If that's all right with you?" he asked Mrs Doble.

"Go on with you. I'll help Edward. Fred, take yourself and your pipe out on the porch. I'll bring you a drink," she nodded meaningfully at Fred who, taking the hint, pushed back his chair, picked up his tobacco pouch and ambled out.

Mrs Doble studied Edward's demeanour as she started to collect the dirty dishes. "Help me tidy up and then you and me are going to have a little chat. You can tell me why your shoulders are stooped like a branch heavy with fruit!"

Edward nodded and sighed. He stood up to help and the mere action of doing something as routinely mundane as clearing away the tableware made him start to feel better.

It wasn't long before they finished. Mrs Doble straightened the tablecloth and placed the lamp in the centre. She patted a seat, "Sit down. Come on, tell me what's bothering you."

Edward looked at Mrs D's expectant face and reddened, "It's embarrassing."

"Come now, you know you can tell me anything. What's the trouble?"

Edward groaned, "All right, but you must promise not to laugh." He began to repeat everything that had transpired between him and Jack, and the explanation he'd been given.

Mrs D struggled to keep a straight face but her gentle manner and understanding voice helped Edward deal with his concerns and forced her to keep the mirth out of her voice and attitude.

"Oh, Edward…"

"Thing is, Mrs D, I'm sure my mother and father would never have done anything like Jack said. I don't know what to believe."

This time, Mrs Doble was unable to prevent the smile manifesting on her face. She brushed away Edward's flaxen fringe from his forehead, "Thing is, Edward. If they hadn't, then you wouldn't be here. It's the most natural thing in the world between two people who love each other as you'll discover when you meet that special someone. Dear sweet, Edward; you should have been told this years ago…"

"But you and Fred couldn't have done it. You ain't got no kids."

"Not for want of trying. We just weren't lucky but we still have each other and we have you, Jack and the others."

"But how does Jack know all this? He's not had a girlfriend or nothing."

"Jack grew up differently from you. He was wise and old before his time. He saw what went on in the alleyways of London. He had a harsh life for a child. It's what helped him survive."

"So, it's all true?"

"Yes, and it's nothing to worry about or be ashamed of; in the right place a man and woman's love is beautiful as you'll find out. Now, no more worrying. Get yourself off and help Jack with those wooden toys. Be gone."

"Thanks, Mrs D." Edward rose and shyly planted a kiss on her plump cheek, making her gasp in surprise.

She touched her cheek fondly, where she felt the imprint of his lips. "Enough! Away with you."

Edward brightened up and grinned, "Ta, Mrs D," and he scooted out of the door and raced across to his quarters as Fred watched him in bewilderment.

Mrs Doble took a drink out to Fred as promised and settled down beside him with a happy smile playing on her lips and a twinkle in her eye.

"So, what was that all about?" asked Fred.

"You wouldn't believe it if I told you. Edward is such an innocent."

"What? Don't keep me guessing."

"Facts of life, Fred. Facts of life. Things his mother would have told him when he was older. He never had the chance. Jack gave him a crude version. I tried to be more circumspect."

"Crikey, you swallowed a dictionary? Where did you learn that word?"

"One of the books I been reading."

"Is that a polite word for something else?"

"No, I was just being careful in what I said. Didn't want to frighten the lad, Jack's already done that."

"Hmm." Fred swigged a mouthful of ale before puffing on his pipe. "Perhaps you'd like to tell me the facts of life. Don't believe no one ever told me."

Mrs D shrugged. "Give over," she said with a laugh, "if you don't know now, you never will. Let's just enjoy the rest of the evening."

As was their custom they looked up at the stars and listened to the song of the night, satisfied and happy in each other's company.

***

Jack had carved a small chicken from a piece of wood that stood on a plinth. He pushed a thin wedge that slid inside the base and the chicken would bow its head and peck at the wood. "What do you think, Edward?"

"That's grand. Let's have a go." He pressed the end and the hen tap tapped with its beak on the wood. "Really clever. The children will love it, especially Minjarra."

"I've made four. You need to start painting them. The other plaything I've done is a little man that slides up and down a pole, see?" Jack lifted it up for Edward to see. "Only done one so far. I'll make some more another time."

"You could make a load of these and sell them at market. I'm sure you'd make a fortune."

Jack chuckled, "I don't think so, don't think I could turn out enough of them."

"We could have a go at making whistles."

"Don't need to make them. We've got you!" said Jack smiling.

"Maybe for the next time. I'll help. If I can remember how they looked. I had one once, made a great noise. I used to pull out a slim stick of wood as I blew and the whistle noise would go up and down in tone. Used to drive my mother mad."

"Sounds complicated. Best leave that for now. I'll teach them how to use a nutshell or small coin instead. They can put it between two fingers at the knuckle end and blow down it. Makes a hell of a racket. Come on, let's get painting. They'll need time to dry."

The friends set to preparing their gifts for the children at the camp.

***

The following morning, they were woken early by Koorong and Jarli hammering on their door. Jack yawned noisily and hopped out of bed in his underwear to open up wondering what all the noise was about.

Koorong fell in through the entrance half carrying Jarli. "Jack, we need help." He moved Jarli inside and laid him on Jack's bed. "I couldn't make Mr Fred hear."

"He's gone out early to check the watering stations."

Edward looked at his friends, "What the hell has happened? Why is Jarli hurt?"

"Our camp, many men came shooting. They set fire to our village. Countless are dead, women, children and our elders. I escaped because I had gone to the creek to look for Minjarra."

"Is Minjarra all right?" asked Jack anxiously.

"Yes, he was with me. I found him collecting small pebbles for his game. We heard the awful noise, gunfire, screams and shouting so, we hurried back but could see we could do nothing. We hid in the thicket to watch."

"Edward, run for Mrs D. tell her what's happened."

Edward scrambled into his cotton trousers, grabbed his shirt and dashed barefoot from the barn. Jack hurriedly dressed and tried to stop the incessant bleeding spouting from Jarli's chest. Jarli was now feverish and sweating. He groaned, mumbled something and slipped in and out of consciousness.

"It looks like the bullet has gone dangerously close to his heart. It must have pierced his lung. Look!" said Jack. He pointed at the wound, which was frothing with bright red blood. "That's a sign of air in the blood."

Jarli gasped; he started to cough and splutter, then stopped and his eyes rolled back in his head as if he were lifeless.

"No, no, no!" said Jack. "We've got to keep him awake. Jarli! Jarli!" He tapped his friend's face and went to the basin and jug of water. "Try and rouse him," ordered Jack.

Koorong shouted at Jarli, "Come on. Don't go to sleep, wake up. Jarli!"

Jack grabbed a towel, soaked it in water, rung it out and handed it to Koorong. "Here. Cool him down."

Koorong was finding it hard to control his emotions, "We're like brothers. Don't let him die." Koorong began to sob.

It was to this chaotic scene that Mrs Doble arrived. She hurtled in carrying a first aid kit of sorts with Edward and flew to Jarli's side. "Oh my God. How did this happen?"

Jack swiftly explained and Mrs Doble turned to Edward, "Run back to the house, get a pan of hot water, some brandy and a sharp knife."

"Yes, Mrs D," and he raced back outside.

Mrs Doble examined the injury, signalled to Jack to help her lift Jarli forward to see his back. "The bullet's still in him. There's no exit wound. Sorry, Koorong. I heard the ruckus but thought you wanted Fred. I had no idea... Edward... Come on... Where is he?"

As if on cue, Edward burst in carrying a pan of boiling water, half a bottle of brandy and a sharp knife. He laid it on the bedside table next to Jack's bed. Mrs Doble turned to them, "This isn't going to be easy. You need to hold on to him tight!" she ordered.

Mrs Doble cut away Jarli's shirt around the bullet hole and poured some of the alcohol onto the knife and on the bloodied puncture. Jarli thrashed his head from side to side, opened his eyes wide and wailed as the brandy stung and burned.

"Can you save him?" asked Koorong.

"I don't know, I've only ever helped Fred do this once before. I'll try, but I can't promise," she bit her lip. "This is going to hurt a lot. Hold onto him."

"Just do your best. I beg you. Baiame will bless you."

"Give him something to bite on."

Jack thrust a piece of his whittling wood into Jarli's mouth. Jarli was now breathing heavily and was half awake.

Mrs D began to cut.

The cry that erupted from Jarli's belly reverberated around the room. He lost consciousness again. The birds outside flew up into the sky screeching at the tortured sound. She dipped her finger into the brandy before placing it inside the cut. "I can feel it. I don't want to push it deeper." Mrs Doble's forehead glistened with beaded sweat. Her hand shook as she tried to get some leverage on the bullet and pull it out through the wound.

No one dared breathe. Mrs D grunted with exertion and wiggled her finger drawing the metal shot forward to the surface until she could grasp it firmly between her thumb and index finger. She pulled the foreign invader clear. There was a sudden rush of blood. "Got to stop this bleeding. He's lost far too much already," she murmured. "Jack press down on it. Keep the pressure up. Edward tear up a bed sheet. Quickly." She wiped a bloody hand across her brow unwittingly daubing herself so she resembled a vicious warrior after a kill.

"What now?" asked Koorong.

"We need some of your healing paste." She glanced at Edward who was ripping strips off his bed sheet. "That'll do. Take over from Jack. Jack, go get some gum leaves."

Jack sprinted outdoors. Moments later he returned with the eucalyptus leaves and began mixing them into a paste with the hot water. He hastened to Jarli's side.

Mrs Doble nodded to Edward to release his pressure and Jack applied the thick green substance. Mrs Doble strapped the torn linen around the injured man and bound it tightly.

Jarli seemed to rally and come to; he moaned in pain as he tried to sit up.

"No, no. You must rest," said Koorong.

Jarli shook his head and said breathlessly, "Let me talk." He looked at Koorong and spoke in halting tones, "You have been like a brother. Promise me you will take care of Minjarra. He will look on you like a father. Love him as I would. Tell him I will watch over him and always love him. I'm sorry." He flopped back down exhausted and his breath came in short rattling gasps. He stopped suddenly, his mouth shaped in an 'O' for a scream that never came. Then, just as suddenly his face became tranquil again. It was no longer contorted in agony. He looked as if he was falling asleep without any worries. They all watched and waited in silence.

He gasped again and opened his eyes wide but then his face lit up. His eyes shone and he gazed in wonder around him. The others looked on in amazement and even turned around to see if anyone had walked in. Jarli appeared to study his surroundings intently as if the room was filling with people and a smile of joy grew on his face. He conversed in his own language and spoke welcoming words and an ethereal light grew brighter in the room.

Jarli reached out with his hands stretching his fingers in a tender gesture of love as if he was striving to touch someone's face before he peacefully closed his eyes.

Dust motes floated lazily in the rays of beaming sunlight that had invaded the room and an unearthly silence fell over everyone. They waited hardly daring to breathe, almost frozen in time.

Mrs Doble studied Jarli's face. She finally declared, "I don't like the look of him." She bent over him to see if she could feel his breath on her face before pressing her fingers on his neck to find a pulse.

There was none.

Her lips trembled and she tried not to cry. She shook her head slowly, her voice barely audible, "I am so sorry. I think he's gone."

"No!" exclaimed Koorong. "We must keep trying."

Mrs Doble put her hand over Jarli's heart and shook her head again, "Oh, Koorong. I'm sorry. We tried our best."

Tears began to roll down Koorong's cheeks and he slumped into the wicker chair while Jack and Edward looked on in anguish. Words tumbled from Koorong's lips, "We have been friends all our lives. He married my sister. What do I tell her? I don't even know if she is alive. And Minjarra..." He choked back a sob, "How do I tell him his father is gone?" He held his head and rocked back and fore looking completely distraught.

Jack and Edward stared at each other helplessly. Mrs Doble turned to Jack, "Get one of the carts, harness Brutus. You must get Jarli back to the camp for his burial. If the villagers have been attacked, search for survivors, help Koorong. Go now. But be very careful if those murdering thugs are about they may come after you."

"What about you?"

"Don't worry about me," said Mrs Doble grimly. "I'll send Bobby and Daniel to find Fred."

Jack hesitated, his heart was swamped with sadness as he saw Koorong take Jarli in his arms like a mother with a baby and he keened like a dingo baying at the full moon. The emotion swelled to choking point almost suffocating him but he was eager to obey Mrs D and hurried to get the horse and wagon. Once outside, where there was no one to see, his own tears of grief fell as he rushed to the stable.

Jack worked quickly, he yoked Brutus to the cart and drove it outside his quarters where Koorong and Edward waited.

Mrs Doble leaned against the barn wall, she looked defeated and despairing. Edward and Koorong went back inside and emerged minutes later, Koorong carried his comrade and laid him carefully in the dray. Edward followed with a pillow and blanket, which Koorong lovingly placed over Jarli. He eased the pillow under Jarli's head and gazed again at his dear lifelong companion's face. Koorong murmured, "Rest easy, my friend. I promise you I will look after your family as if they were mine... And I swear I will find the man who did this. He will not escape me." He turned to Edward, "He seems so serene, as if he is only sleeping," Koorong gulped and swallowed another strangled cry.

***

Brutus plodded through the farmland and into the outback until they reached the rocky outcrop and the canyon leading to the village. Jack jumped down and tethered the cart to a strong silky oak tree bright with its burnt orange flowers. Koorong and Edward moved Jarli gently and carried him between them through the canyon, past the cascading waterfall and sparkling lagoon. The beauty of the place belied what they were about to see.

Jack could smell fire and scorched wood. Thin spirals of smoke floated up into the otherwise cloudless sky. But none of them were fully prepared for the devastation they would see as they entered the heart of the village. Bodies lay scattered around the camp. Jack and Edward stopped and stared in horror at the pitiful sight of very young children brutally shot, some still in their dead mother's arms.

"Oh, no," murmured Jack as he saw Alinta curled in a foetal ball. She was bleeding from the back of her skull. He dashed to her side and lifted her head. Her eyes blinked open. She saw Jack and whispered his name before dissolving into juddering sobs. "They killed my husband, Iluka and my babies... Why?"

Jack attempted to comfort her. He spoke softly, "I don't know. They were evil men. Are you badly hurt?"

Alinta endeavoured to smile, "I played dead. Kept very still. I tried to take little breaths and waited. I thought you were them. That they'd come back." Her brave words dissolved into a whimper and she started to cry again.

"Let me see your injury. Where else are you hurt?"

"I hit my head when I fell. That's all."

Jack helped her to her feet and she scanned the gory scene around her, her eyes glazed over with the dullness of horror and disbelief. She raised a finger to her lips, "Listen, do you hear it?"

Jack focused and strained his ears. The small sound of a baby crying filtered through the oppressive air of death. "It's coming from over there."

"Oowa," said Alinta falling into her native tongue. She ran towards the sound, followed by Jack. They hurried to a hut near the centre that had somehow miraculously escaped the savage ravages of the fire. Jack dived inside. In the corner on a pile of rugs sat a young girl holding a tiny baby. Her face filled with fear when she saw a white man enter until she spotted Alinta and realised the man was Jack.

Alinta threw her arms around the young girl, "Lowanna, I thought you'd been taken."

"They took Killara. I hid under the rugs."

"Killara?" asked Jack.

"Lowanna's sister. Where? Where did they take her?"

"They said she was pretty. They were going to have some fun with her first."

"Oh, no." Jack groaned inwardly he knew what that meant. "We must find her. Stay with Lowanna. I'll be back."

Jack dashed from the hut. He searched around wildly with his eyes but all he could see were the smouldering ruins of what once had been a happy thriving village. He spotted Edward trying to help a very old man who was severely injured and bleeding profusely from two bullet wounds. Jack ran across as the old man breathed his last. Edward looked at Jack, "There was nothing I could do. Why, Jack? Why has this happened?" and he struggled to suppress the tears that coursed down his cheek. His voice cracked with emotion. "What sort of man would do this?" he still held onto the ancient tribal elder.

Jack spoke softly, "Let him go, Edward. Lay him down. We must find the survivors, gather them together over there." He indicated the remaining hut. "And we must bury the dead. Where's Koorong?"

"He's gone to fetch Jarli's body. To bring him home," he said.

"This is no home for anyone, now. Come, let's see who we can help."

Edward reluctantly left the side of the old man who had spent his last moments in his arms. As a final loving act, Edward closed the elder's eyes before rising and following Jack.

For the next hour they checked every motionless body for signs of life, looked in every hut that had escaped the torching and searched for signs of the missing girl, Killara. Koorong returned carrying Jarli. He laid him down on the ground and covered him with the blanket from the farm.

Jack and Edward moved out of the village towards the canyon where they had entered and walked around the lagoon. "It's the only place we haven't looked," he said in desperation. Edward pointed at something next to a large boulder where he could see a bundle of rags, the frayed edges of which fluttered intermittently in the gentle breeze generated by the plunging waterfall. They sped across to find the ruined body of a young girl. Her legs were splayed and her thighs encrusted with blood. The thin cotton dress she had worn was torn from her shoulders exposing her adolescent breasts.

Edward shuddered and turned away, "Is she alive?" he asked unable to look at the shockingly gruesome scene.

Jack's face contorted in pain as he stumbled towards the small, still form to feel if she had a pulse. He bent down as Edward turned back his eyes drawn to the appalling atrocity and Jack sorrowfully shook his head. "She's gone," he whispered softly.

They were alerted again to the thunder of horses' hooves and ducked down out of sight, wondering what or who was riding through the canyon to the camp. Jack peeped over the rock. He was relieved to see the familiar figure of Fred on Hunter followed by Daniel and Bobby all carrying shovels. He came out of hiding.

Fred reined in his horse, "What the hell happened?"

***

Some hours later, the group and able survivors had finally buried the dead… Mr Fred apologised to Koorong, "I'm sorry you couldn't observe all your burial rituals. I know you would like to let Jarli lie in an elevated state before cremation or internment with his possessions. You understand why it can't be done?" Koorong nodded in acknowledgement, his face full of sorrow. "And I'm sorry and ashamed of the actions of my fellow man… What will you do now?"

"There are so few of us. I don't know." Koorong studied who was left of his tribe, two young girls, a baby, a small boy and three men. "I am tempted to rebuild, start again but there are so many bad memories now it may be wiser to move on, find fresh ground."

"You are welcome to come back with us until you decide. You know you will always have a home with us."

Bobby piped up, "And us. My mother could do with the help if Alinta, Lowanna and the baby would like to stay. We have room."

"Blessings to you, all." Koorong spoke to his people. "You heard what Mr Fred said. What do you want to do?"

They dissolved into their own language. There was much shaking of heads and nodding. Jack tried to follow the conversation but could only pick out some words. Koorong turned back to Fred and the others, he made the gesture of friendship and announced, "We will return with you and decide later. I think Alinta, Lowanna and the baby will be happy to be of help to Bobby's mother."

Fred nodded, "As you wish."

They made their way to the wagon and boarded, flanked by Fred, Bobby and Daniel on horseback. As the cart set off the Aborigines looked back wistfully at the remains of their camp before turning forward to face whatever the future might bring.

***

Life for the next two weeks on the ranch went on much as before with much needed maintenance, repairing fences, checking the watering stations ensuring that the valves were open and the water for the livestock kept running. But, both Edward and Jack flamed with fury at the wanton destruction of the village and the deaths of little children who had taken both of them to their hearts and whom they had completely charmed.

Jack packed away the little wooden toys he had made. Somehow, it didn't seem right to have them on display although he kept out the little gaily painted man swinging on a pole to give to Minjarra the next time he saw him.

Suppertimes were a glum affair as if laughter and enjoyment showed a lack of respect for those who had perished in the massacre. Fred soon put them right, "Look, none of us could see this coming. None of us could have done aught about it. It's tough but we must put this tragedy behind us. The auction is on tomorrow and you are both coming with me. We got some fine Merino sheep to sell, six ewes and a ram. The money from the sale will see us through the winter to the spring. Next time it will be Romneys and Welsh fat tails. I want you to learn every inch of the business."

"But, why?"

"I need someone to rely on when I can't make market. I'm not as young or nimble as I was; so, I'm delegating some of the work to you. And if I delegate I need to know you'll be doing it right. I don't want you costing me and the missus money. Now, no more gloom. Get yourselves washed and a good night's sleep, we've an early start tomorrow."

"Is Koorong coming?"

"He'll be driving one cart and Jiemba the other."

Edward and Jack swapped an apprehensive look before rising and retiring to their quarters.

***

That night, after the lamp had been extinguished, Edward asked, "Jack? You asleep?"

"Why?"

"I've been thinking."

"Crikey, that's dangerous," joked Jack.

"What if Koorong recognises the blokes that hit his village?"

"He'll tell us."

"And then?"

"I'll know them, too." He paused and his lips twisted in determination, "I'll go after them. There'll be no escape."

10: Auctions, Market and More

Jack felt the caress of the sun's warmth on his face as it probed through the chinks in the curtains gently rousing him from slumber. He sat up and stretched, extending his arms above his head before throwing back his bed cover and padding to the window to look out. It was something he did every morning and had done since he was brought here as an escaped boy prisoner.

Edward was still fast asleep. He had the power to snooze through anything, even a severe storm with crashing thunder, sheet lightning and rain was unable to wake him. Jack often joked that if a tree fell on the barn and came through the roof, Edward would hardly stir. He'd simply turn over and continue his reverie in the land of nod.

Outside, Jack could see Koorong and Jiemba had already started. They were in the process of harnessing the horses to the wagons. Jack pulled back his curtains enabling the light to flood the room before he turned and ambled back to Edward's bed as was their morning ritual. He shook Edward's sleeping form, "Come on! Wake up!"

Edward groaned as he opened his eyes and the bright sunbeams hurt his eyes. "What time is it?"

"Time to get up," replied Jack as he began to dress.

Edward rolled over with a moan and closed his eyes again, snuggling into his pillow.

"No, you don't!" said Jack crossing to the bed and yanking off the covers. "It's a big day today, our first time at auction. Up you get!"

Edward raised his hands in surrender and finally swung his long legs out of bed. He shook his head violently so his cheeks slapped as one.

"You sound like a pig at a trough," teased Jack and caught hold of his own cheeks and loosely smacked them together. "Nearly as bad when you sleep," he observed, much to Edward's consternation. "The sounds you make... From both ends!"

Jack swilled his face quickly at the basin of water and picked up the little toy he'd made of a man on a pole and dashed out towards the house. He waved brightly at Koorong before he ventured across, "Here." He passed him the toy. "It's for Minjarra."

Koorong studied the plaything. His eyes misted up and he managed a smile, "He will love it."

Jack said no more but carried on his way to the house for breakfast.

***

There was a lot of bleating and complaining baas as the six Merino ewes and a ram were loaded. Fred already had a fine spirited ram that had proved his worth and this one was surplus to requirements. He hoped it would fetch a good price.

There wasn't the usual frivolity as the carts plodded along to Port Jackson. Conversation was brief but as they neared the port, Jack regained some of his usual lively demeanour. He paid special attention to men going about their business. His eyes were searching for the thugs they had defeated at Woolloomooloo Camp. He had a strong suspicion that one or more of them were involved in the village's annihilation and said so. "Koorong, see if you can identify any of the brutes who attacked your village. If so, point them out to me."

Koorong was draped in sadness but afforded Jack a nod of agreement while Jack and Edward continued to scan the crowds.

***

The livestock market was held close to the quay in the lower part of town, leading to it were a number of colourful stalls selling all manner of trinkets, beads and other decorative items. Female garments, scarves and other adornments hung over trestle tables under a canvas tent-like structure. Other stalls exhibited spices, vegetables and food items. The aromas were exotic and enticing. Walking through the line of stands was enough to cheer the moods of everyone. Koorong jumped down and led Brutus carefully past the line of booths, where traders shouted their wares, until the road broadened out and the pens of animals came into view.

Farmers lounged against railings chatting together near holdings of their livestock, including, pigs, sheep, cows and bullocks. The Merino sheep and ram were unloaded and driven into their enclosure and Koorong walked onto a large yard where he could turn the cart and take it back out to the docks and outlying district.

As the dray circled, Koorong stopped abruptly and gasped. Standing behind a long bench were two men. One was enticing punters to place bets on a game of thimblerig and drawing a crowd. One man deftly moved three thimbles around and lifted one to show where the dried pea was placed. He changed the cover rapidly and nimbly as men placed their bets.

The man switching the covers had long fair hair and a scar on his cheek. Koorong stared hard at him. His temple pulsed dangerously as he gritted his teeth. The man taking the money had lank greasy hair with wild eyes. He felt Koorong's eyes on him and locked him in a hardened stare before he spat pointedly into the dirt.

Koorong lowered his eyes and continued walking, leading the horse and cart. His free hand clenched tightly, the bones of his knuckles predominated and the fury boiled behind his eyes. He reached the place where Jack had penned the sheep and the others waited.

Jack sensed a transformation in Koorong. "You've seen one, haven't you?"

Koorong, nodded, "Oowa. Two of them. They're over there where I turned the cart."

"Where? Show me."

Koorong jerked his head back towards the clearing circle, "By the auction ring... I want to kill them." He stifled a cry.

"Did they see you?"

"One taking the money glared at me. He was one, Jack. He was one of the men at the camp."

Fred listened to the interchange, "Don't do anything stupid. Not now."

"But..."

"Listen to me. Leave it for now. We'll deal with it later."

Edward nudged Jack, "I'll take a walk. Go and see."

Fred lowered his voice, "Look, yes. See if it's the same blokes that were at Woolloomooloo but don't say nothing. Understand?"

Edward nodded and put his lips together and began to whistle shrilly as he walked. Jack took this as a sign that he was nervous.

Fred urged Koorong, "Do what you normally do. Take the cart and go. Jiemba will need to stay a while longer to take the shopping, after we've bought it, home. But, we will meet as usual... as planned, my friend." Koorong complied but it was apparent he was unhappy about it.

Jack added, "Listen to Fred. They won't go unpunished, I promise." Koorong appeared more satisfied and guided the wagon away.

Moments later Edward returned. "You were right, Jack. Those blokes we stopped attacking Ngarra, they're the ones doing the gambling game. Basil and Charlie. They're the ones Koorong's identified. Now what?"

"We'll have to make a plan but for now we've got an auction to attend."

***

In the central circle used as a ring, farmers clustered around as animals were brought in and paraded for inspection while the auctioneer encouraged people to bid. Jack tried to focus on the auction and selling techniques. He noted a couple of men, the same men, placing bids during the proceedings who seemed to drop out of the bidding once the goods reached a certain price. "What they up to?" Jack asked Fred.

"Well spotted," said Fred impressed. "Some farmers use shillabers, bid boosters, to try and push the price up. They're fake buyers and it's illegal. It's catching them that's tough."

"Do you do that?"

"No, the price I get will be fair. I have a reputation to uphold."

Jack continued to observe. Time went quickly and it was soon time to herd Fred's ewes into the ring. Edward ushered them in and controlled them. He displayed them to their best advantage demonstrated their health and the texture of their soft fleeces.

The bidding was strong as folks knew what a fine flock Fred possessed and his Merino wool always fetched a premium. Jack kept a sharp eye on all the bidders. He noted one farmer who moved with a swagger and had some disreputable looking associates with him. "Well, I never," murmured Jack as he spotted the thug called Arthur. "So, that means all three are here." Jack lowered his hat to shade his face and maintained his surveillance of the proceedings.

The auction was exciting and when Edward took in Fred's ram to show, the pledges went wild. Jack became so engrossed in the events he almost forgot about the prevalent danger. Such was the interest in the proceedings that more traders and bystanders came to watch. There was a roar as the hammer fell. Fred's ram had fetched a record price.

"There'll be celebrations tonight for sure," said Fred delightedly. "Now, onto the next phase. Edward, Jack come with me."

Fred pushed through the throng congratulating the purchaser on his fine deal and made his way to the auctioneer's registration table at the back to collect payment. Once the final transactions had been made and auction fees deducted Fred pocketed the balance and said, "Right, off to George Street now to the Bank of New South Wales. You can see how everything else is done. I'll keep back some money for provisions. I've a list from Mrs Doble. I daren't let her down. If ever you do this for me don't get fobbed off with payment in rum or goods to the equivalent. Only deal in hard cash. Understand?" Edward and Jack nodded. "Always double check all the paperwork. Some fly traders will try and trick you. Be prepared. A few minutes going over it all before you leave will save hours of agony later. There can be no corrections once you have left the auctioneer's table."

Edward and Jack followed Fred dodging a drove of pigs, which were being marched to the ring. They squealed and oinked as the farmer spurred them on with a stick.

They waded through the farmers and spectators and made their way to 341, George Street. It was an impressive building; all the first and ground floor windows had wooden shutters. There was an arched entrance to the main door and a short white fence fronted the building from the cobbled stoned street and pebbled pavement.

Fred strode through the arch and main door. He beckoned the hesitant Jack and Edward to accompany him. Jack swallowed hard. His shoulders stiffened and rose almost to his ears with the onset of nerves. The building looked imposing, almost threatening, as if it oozed authority by its very presence. Edward, on the other hand, had no qualms and walked straight in next to Fred who turned back, "Come on, Jack. What are you waiting for?" Jack forced a strained smile and hurried after them inside.

Fred paced across to a large desk where a teller stood. He was a thin faced man with a drooping moustache and wore round wire framed glasses. "Good day, Mr Pinch," said Fred.

Mr Pinch was engaged in writing something in a ledger, "Won't be a moment."

Jack turned to Edward and whispered, "Pinch? Did Fred say he was called Pinch?"

"I believe so, yes," Edward replied.

"Not a very trustworthy name for a bloke to be working in a bank," said Jack with a wink.

Mr Pinch finished what he was writing looked up and smiled politely at Fred, "Mr Doble. What can I do for you today, sir?"

Fred announced, "Two things. First, I wanted to introduce you to these fine young men who work for me. Jack Dawkins."

Jack acknowledged the clerk by tugging his hat, "Mr Pinch."

"And Edward Hargreaves."

Edward nodded at the banker, "Sir."

Fred continued, "From time to time they will attend to some of my banking affairs. I wanted you to meet them first-hand."

Mr Pinch was polite and Jack noted when he smiled he had what appeared to be a gold cap on one of his teeth near the front. He whispered to Edward again, "I suppose that's one way of making sure your gold don't get nicked."

Edward suppressed a laugh, which he hurriedly turned into a cough. "Excuse me," he said red faced.

Fred put a large amount of the cash from the auction on the table, which Mr Pinch deftly and quickly counted. Afterwards he filled in a slip of paper as a receipt and passed it across. Fred instructed them, "Look at the receipt make sure the figures tally with the amount you've handed over and what's written on here. See that the right amount is entered into the account book. Mr Pinch turned the ledger around for Fred to see as he completed the entry. Satisfied, Fred made his mark on the entry with his initials, bid the teller good day and they left.

Once outside the bank, Jack sighed in relief. His shoulders dropped back to their normal height. "Everything all right, Jack?" asked Fred.

"I suppose so."

"What is it?"

"I know my numbers but I can't read. Just know how to write my name, nowt else. Edward taught me that."

"Then Edward will teach you how to know my name written down. Knowing your figures. That's the important thing. You can manage that, can't you?"

"Yes, Fred."

"Then all's well. You got any problems with that, Edward?"

Edward shook his head, "All seems clear to me."

"Excellent. Now, let's get Mrs Doble's shopping and then off to the Victoria Hotel."

***

The trio spent an hour collecting various items including a bolt of blue fine cotton cloth and a roll of thicker cotton suitable for making breeches and trousers. Fred haggled with the market traders as did Jack over the price of spices, tea and fresh vegetables. They eventually had everything on the shopping list. The items were packed into the remaining cart and Jiemba set off to drive that wagon home to the farm now that Koorong had made his way to the outlying farm where he would stay until Fred and the others were ready to return.

Edward's face was flushed with excitement at revisiting the Victoria Hotel. He was hoping against hope that Rosie Martin might make another appearance there to entertain them and said so. In anticipation he began to whistle. Jack groaned.

***

By the time they reached the thriving Victoria Hotel the saloon bar was filling up rapidly with merchants, farmers and traders, many of whom warmly acknowledged Fred. Fred approached the bar and tried to winkle through to the counter to order drinks. Jack and Edward managed to grab a small table, which a rancher had vacated and who was looking much the worse for drink. He hastened quickly to the entrance presumably for some fresh air. They didn't expect him to return.

Josie was pleased to serve Fred and beamed broadly at him, "On your own today?" she asked trying to peer through the men standing at the bar.

"Not today."

"Oh, good," she said a little too quickly and then flushed red. "I'm not asking for me," she hurriedly added. "Minnie has taken quite a shine to one of your workmen."

"And who might that be?" asked Fred with a twinkle in his eye.

"Think his name's Daniel."

"Ah," said Fred. "Not with me today, next time maybe."

"So, who are you with, then?" persisted Josie, as she served another customer.

"Edward and Jack," said Fred curious to see her reaction.

"Oh," and Josie coloured up even more. She passed a frothing tankard to a burly man standing next to Fred.

"Any entertainment on tonight?" asked Fred.

"Not tonight. Just Harry playing the piano. Think there's something fixed up for the next merchant trading on the docks, a week Thursday. What can I get you?"

"Three ales please, and what's on offer for grub?"

"Usual."

Fred nodded and waited for the last ale to be poured, "Is your dad around?"

"In the kitchen."

"I'd like a word when he's got a minute," said Fred before pushing his way back through the swarm of drinkers at the bar. He made his way to the table and gave them the ale. "Seems young Minnie has taken a liking to Daniel," said Fred with a grin. "Better luck next time, lads."

Edward could hardly wait to speak, "Is Rosie Martin going to be here again?"

"Out of luck, there, too," said Fred. "Edgar has entertainment booked a week Thursday for the next wool sale. Don't know whether it'll be Rosie or not. You can ask him when he comes out to join us."

The three supped their ale in the smoke filled tavern until Jack's eyes began smarting so much he excused himself. "It's the smoke, stinging my eyes making them water. Won't be long."

He left the table and stepped outside with great relief and took a huge gulp of clean air. He blinked hard to stop his eyes from streaming, when someone tapped him on the shoulder. He turned to see Edward standing there. "What's happening?" asked Edward.

"Nothing. I couldn't breathe in there. The tobacco fumes were making my eyes burn. Takes a bit of getting used to. I'll come back inside when I feel a bit better. Is Edgar there yet?"

"Not yet. He'll be out soon enough, I expect."

"Think I'll just meander towards the quay. See if I can see those killers anywhere."

"Now, Jack. Don't do anything stupid."

"I won't. I'm just sampling the afternoon air."

"Then I'll come with you."

They set off back towards the dock and auction, which meant facing the scattered line of doxies touting their charms. One was sitting on the harbour wall. She pouted at them and winked, raising her foot and revealing her ankle. On the sole of her boot she had marked a price in chalk. She waggled her foot as bait to lure a man, any man, to her side. Jack nudged Edward, "Keep your eyes down. Don't talk to her. She'll think you're interested."

Once on the quay, Jack became more alert. "Keep on the lookout for our friends. See if they're around."

The area was still busy with farmers loading livestock. There were just a couple of auctions left and some ranchers were waiting for the final sale of three thoroughbred horses. One was an Arabian stallion from the famous bloodline of Old Hector, one of the first pedigrees to be imported into Australia, which was generating huge interest as horse racing was becoming a popular sport. Jack looked admiringly at the fine specimens waiting to be shown off in the ring.

Edward was examining the crowd. He poked Jack in the ribs, "They're over there." Jack looked where Edward had indicated and could see that Arthur had joined Basil and they were still engaged with a game of thimblerig. "Don't know where Charlie's gone," muttered Edward to no one in particular.

"I know this game," said Jack. "It's sheer trickery. If I can call them out on this then maybe the authorities will get involved."

"No, Jack. It's too dangerous. We could bring trouble on ourselves. Be sensible, please."

"We have to do something."

Edward caught hold of Jack's arm, "At least wait until we've spoken to Fred. We know they can be identified as the ones who tried to massacre Woolloomooloo Camp and know, now they murdered all our friends at the village. Come on."

Jack shook off Edward's arm. "All right. I'm just going to watch them for a while. See if I can spot their method."

Edward rolled his eyes and reluctantly followed Jack who walked towards the game. A young farmhand was pushing his way from the game. His eyes were bright with tears. He stopped Jack, "Don't go there. They're a load of cheats. I've lost all my wages. Cleaned me out. They make it look so easy."

Jack stuck out his arm to stop the youth. "How'd you like to win it back?"

"How? I got nothing left."

"Never mind. Come back with me and watch. I've got an idea."

"Jack…" said Edward warningly.

Jack turned to Edward, "Three pairs of eyes are better than two. Trust me," and he explained what he wanted them to do.

"I don't like it," said Edward.

"What's your name, mate?" asked Jack.

"William," said the lad sniffing back his tears.

"Now, listen. I know how this game works. You follow my instructions and we'll be okay."

"But I've got no money left."

"Don't worry. We have. Edward..." Jack held out his hand and Edward grudgingly took out some coins from his pocket and handed them to Jack. "You can't win this game alone. You need three of us. You can only win once and then we walk away. We watch and work out the strategy. Keep your eyes on the thimbles at all times. When the swindler stops and if he touches any of the caps, be mindful. That's when he's likely to switch the pea to another thimble. They often move it when you're distracted or getting your money out. Edward, you watch the thimble man, closely. William, keep your eyes on the covers. I'll look to see what their methods are. I'll tip you when to bet. When we get to the table pretend you went back to get some more money... You won't lose."

"If I do, it's your money I'm losing."

"You won't."

"How do you know?" asked Edward.

"Fagin taught me."

"Fagin?"

"Someone I've not thought of in years," said Jack.

"I seem to remember you telling me, once."

"No matter, now. Are you ready? When the time's right I'll hold up my fingers for either cover one, two or three from our left. Wait until then."

Edward and William nodded and they approached the table with the game where bets were being laid and they observed.

Basil looked up, "Back again?"

"I gotta try and win something back. Me mam will kill me," said William.

"Go ahead," said Basil. "Place your bet."

"I'm gonna watch a while first," said William.

"Please yourself."

Basil called out his pitch, "Roll up, roll up. Come and see if your eye is faster than my 'and. Try your luck. You could win big."

Someone in the crowd shouted, "Or not at all."

"Now, now. It's a fair game. We 'ave winners and we 'ave losers. Fancy your chances? Then place a bet."

Basil lifted a thimble to reveal a pea and then deftly and speedily switched the thimbles around. He stopped and lifted a thimble. There was the pea underneath it. "Watch again." This time he stopped and said, "Anyone want to wager?"

A farmer came forward and thrust out his money, which Arthur took. Jack's eyes narrowed and he watched closely. As the money changed hands the trickster lightly touched a thimble and switched the pea. Jack's keen eyes saw the switch, while the others were distracted. The farmer lost and took out more cash to play again.

Jack watched a few more rounds until he thought he had worked out Basil's tactics. He waited until the pot was big enough and then signalled to William to set down his bet.

"Over and round the thimble goes, where the pea is no one knows," said Basil rapidly swapping the covers.

Basil halted with his hand hovering over a thimble, the obvious one where the pea was hiding. William went to touch one cap and glanced at Jack who signalled three as Basil moved the pea to cup three and William lifted the thimble quickly to reveal it much to the shock of Basil and Arthur.

William beamed and gathered up his money.

"Do you want to try that again?" said Basil. "Give us a chance to win it back."

"No," said William. "I'm happy and he pocketed the cash and began to walk away from the table where he was stopped by Charlie who stood in front of the lad, cleaning his grimy nails with a wicked looking knife.

"Think you ought to listen to them," he said threateningly, which is when Jack stepped in.

"Let him go. He won fair and square," said Jack facing the thug. "Edward, walk William away."

Edward guided William through the crowd, while Jack stood firm. "The lad won without any cheating. Leave him be."

Other members of the throng joined in. "Yeah. Let 'im go."

"It's all right for you to win but not to lose. That seems fishy to me," said the farmer who had already lost a packet. The mass of people pressed forward; it was beginning to turn ugly.

Someone shouted, "Call the law. Let them sort it out."

Charlie dropped back, letting Jack walk after the others, while Basil and Arthur hastily packed up their game. "We'll find another pitch," hissed Basil.

Jack stopped and turned back to look and noted Charlie's evil face. The miscreant locked eyes with Jack, drew his first two fingers of his right hand across his eyes and then signalled pointing them at Jack meaning he was watching him. It was the same movement Rust had made to him in the convict camp and in spite of the day's warmth, Jack shivered.

***

William returned Edward's money and thanked them both profusely, Jack gave him a warning, "Stay away from that game and those men. It's rigged so you can't win."

"But, we did."

"Yes, and I won't be repeating it. We're all marked men. Get home to your mam. Go now."

William thanked them again and ran in the direction of the town as Edward and Jack made their way back to the hotel. Jack warned Edward, "You need to be careful now. That ruffian knows who you are and that you, with me, fleeced him."

"Only after he'd been cheating people all day. They won't be able to pitch up there again," mused Edward.

"I wouldn't count on it. Give it time. They'll be back."

"You'll have to tell Fred," said Edward.

"I will," said Jack. "When the time's right."

***

The Victoria Hotel was lively and just as busy. Harry was on the piano banging out some popular tunes and a few customers were singing along. Fred was at a larger table now and Edgar was sitting with him. Jack and Edward joined them.

"You've been a while," said Fred curiously.

"Just helping out a young lad. I'll explain later."

"What have you decided?" asked Edward eager to know what had transpired between Edgar and Fred.

"Edgar has an idea. Edgar?"

"Yes. We all know the men who threatened the camp but can't come forward as witnesses because we were masked, all of us, except for Private Denton and Sergeant Phillips. Now, with Koorong's identification we can move in on them. I knew asking the military to come with us to stop the slaughter at Woolloomooloo was wise."

"What then?" asked Jack.

"We find them," said Edgar.

"That may be difficult," said Jack.

"Why?"

"They may have moved on elsewhere after we disrupted their gambling game."

"Even if you did, they'll be back," said Edgar. "That trio are a bad lot. They'll not leave the rich pickings of Port Jackson. The important thing is to get the military involved and quickly."

"I agree," said Fred. "How do we do that?"

"Leave that to me. I'll send one of the girls to the fort. And you can tell me how you managed to beat them at their own game."

***

It was much later that evening when most of the customers at the Victoria Hotel had gone home. The usual local hardened drinkers had stayed. Harry the piano player had packed up and gone home. Fred, Jack and Edward remained at their table with Edgar, the leftovers of a meal still on the table. Josie worked the bar; her sister Minnie was nowhere to be seen. She had gone to get word to Denton and Phillips at the fort.

From outside came the sound of splintering wood, a scream and some sort of ruckus. Edgar rose and went to investigate followed by Fred. They arrived in the street to see Minnie with her bodice ripped and shawl on the ground. She was being pinned against the wall of the hotel by two men.

"Get your hands off her, now!" yelled Edgar.

One rough-neck turned around and sneered at Edgar. "And why would I want to do that?" He wore the garb of a farm worker with canvas breeches that were partially undone and a cotton shirt. His hair was tightly curled and dark. It was apparent to them what they intended to do to her.

"Because she's my daughter," Edgar bellowed.

The other fair-haired man spun around. He was clearly very drunk as he stumbled somewhat as he turned. They instantly recognised him as Basil, one of the ones wanted for the massacre at the village.

"I should do as he says," said Fred lining up with Edgar.

"Yeah?"

"Yes!" asserted Jack who had appeared in the doorway.

"You again," hissed Basil. "You're asking for trouble and I'm more than ready to give you that," said Basil slurring his words.

Jack crossed to the thug and hauled him off Minnie. "Take her inside, Edgar."

Edgar picked up her thin woollen shawl and covered his daughter's shaking shoulders. He ushered her inside leaving Jack and Fred facing the two criminals. Basil came towards Jack raising his fists. Jack swung at him and sent him sprawling. The other man once he saw Edward emerge, thought better of helping his friend, turned tail and ran. Jack and Fred dragged the dazed Basil to his feet, pulled him into the hotel and forced him into a seat in the bar where Jack restrained him.

Josie came out from behind the bar with her arm around Minnie who was still trembling. "Let me see the blackguard who did this."

Jack pulled back Basil's head, which had flopped forward. "Know him?"

"Do I know him? Oh, yes. Basil Cutler. Local troublemaker. Tries to cheat folk out of their money and possessions. Didn't think he would attack a woman, though."

"I believe it was the other bloke who went after Minnie. Basil was so drunk he decided to help," said Fred.

"Maybe. Anyway, he's a bad lot. Him and his gang."

"Then we'll just keep him here until Denton and Phillips arrive. You did manage to speak to them?" said Edgar.

"Not directly. I gave the guard on duty your message and he went to see the sergeant. When he came back he told me to expect them to call by before closing. I've no reason not to believe him."

"Then we'll keep this reprobate here until he comes."

They didn't have long to wait as Private Denton and Sergeant Phillips entered the bar in full uniform scaring the loitering drinkers who supped up and left hastily. Soon the bar was almost empty.

Edgar quickly explained events and the sergeant tried to rouse Basil. "He's too drunk to get much sense out of him. But, we can take him back and charge him with being drunk and disorderly after what he tried to do to Minnie. With Koorong's statement we'll have enough to nab him for his part in the village massacre. With a bit of luck, I suspect he might give up the others who were involved."

"I don't think he'd peach, but you never know. Those brutes tend to stick together," said Fred.

"We'll take him away. You'll need to bring Koorong to us to formally record his testimony."

Denton and Phillips tugged Basil out of the chair, where he had slumped into a stupor, and dragged him to the door. "We'll see you in the morning, then?"

"That you will," asserted Fred.

"Think we all deserve a nightcap after that," said Edgar, and he went behind the bar.

***

Outside Phillips and Denton struggled with Basil's dead weight. "It's no good, we'll never get him up the hill like this. Wait here and I'll see if I can borrow a wagon."

Phillips returned inside to speak to Fred, while Private Denton remained with the almost comatose Basil. He was unaware that he was being watched. Charlie and Arthur loitered across the street hidden from view behind some handcarts used in markets to carry goods.

Charlie growled at his companion, "We have to get him away from here. We can't run the game without him and besides, who knows what he might say? He could bring a barrel load of trouble on us both. We've got to stop him being taken."

"How do we do that? He's with the military."

"I'll soon sort that," he drew out a long sharp machete type knife. "I've got a kukri."

"Wait... you're not thinking of..." protested Arthur.

"Got any better ideas?" he snarled at Arthur, who fell silent, his face a mass of confusion. "Come on. We gotta be quick."

Reluctantly, Arthur followed Charlie out into the open. They crossed to Private Denton. Charlie grinned slyly, "Is there a problem, Private?"

Denton started. He saw the evil gleam in Charlie's eyes. Too late he saw the blade, which Charlie plunged into the soldier. Blood fountained out spraying the men and Private Denton slumped to the floor, his blood pooled mixing with the slops and vomit from drunken revellers after market.

Charlie and Arthur seized Basil and dragged him away. They grappled with his weight managing to lug him towards the now empty market area. Charlie pulled him behind some packing crates. "Stay here."

"Why? Where are you going?"

"I'm just going back to see."

"But..."

"No buts. Do what I say." Charlie left a defeated Arthur holding onto Basil, who was beginning to stir. He turned back, "If he starts to cause trouble, whack him one," and Charlie melted away into the dark creeping back to the scene of the crime.

Charlie ducked down behind the carts again and watched. He could see the still, lifeless form of Denton. As he viewed the scene, Phillips came out and rushed to the private's side. The sergeant scanned the area and Charlie remained motionless. Charlie's eyes narrowed as he spotted Fred who emerged from the hotel and hurried to Phillips before he shouted out, "Need some help here!"

Charlie's mouth twisted in fury as he recognised Fred's voice and frame from Woolloomooloo. He muttered under his breath, "I know you now, big man. I guarantee you've sealed your fate. You're a gonner." Charlie slipped away invisibly into the inky dark.

11: Aftershock

Filled with sorrow, Sergeant Phillips cradled his private's head. He felt the faint pulse in Denton's neck and stared at Fred in anguish, "He's weak but still alive. What can we do?"

Fred shouted to the others, "We've got a big problem here! Edgar!" He yelled again, "Out here, now!"

Edgar appeared. His mouth dropped open in shock and he swore softly as he rushed to them when the others came into view. "Josie, take Edward and go and get the leech. Hurry."

Josie didn't ask questions. She simply nodded and signalled to Edward, "This way. Run."

Edward and Josie dashed off into the night.

Jack scouted around the area searching for any sign of the fair haired man with the scar named Basil. He spotted something and alerted Fred with urgency in his voice, "Look here." He pointed at some bloody footprints. "I don't think Basil did this. Someone else helped get him away, two people, I think. Besides, Basil wasn't carrying any kind of knife." Jack moved further away carefully examining the ground. "But, wait! Now, I'm sure. Look! Somebody dragged Basil away. They must have stepped in Denton's blood. You can see the trail and scuffing of someone's feet being dragged through the mess."

"Jack's right," said Edgar peering at the crimson spattered path. He turned to Phillips, "Can you rouse him? Find out who did this?"

"I think we all know who's responsible," said Jack with a grimace.

"But, we need proof," growled Phillips.

"Where do the footprints lead, Jack?"

Jack followed the congealing blood smears and shouted, "Not far. It ends just down here to the right." He sped back to them. "Can't we stop the bleeding?"

"We're trying," said Edgar who had ripped off his shirt to stem the flow by applying pressure to the wound. He murmured almost to himself, "All we can do is pray."

"Bastards!" exclaimed Jack. "Ain't there nothing I can do?"

"Carry him inside," said Phillips. "Get him a shot of brandy; make him comfortable until the doctor gets here."

The three of them carried the young private inside, while Minnie went to fetch some blankets and a pillow. They prepared a makeshift bed on a long bench table. By now, Denton's skin was cold and clammy to the touch. He was shivering uncontrollably and drifting in and out of consciousness. Phillips barked, "Stay with me, Private. And that's an order. Stay with us, please," he repeated, frantically urging the young man to stay awake.

Denton groaned as blood began to seep from his lips and his eyelids flickered. Phillips demanded, "Who did this to you? Tell us. Who? Do you have a name?"

Denton's eyes fluttered open. With a monumental effort he lifted his head and tried to speak. Phillips put his ear down to the private's mouth and just managed to hear on a tortured whispered breath, "Ch... Ch... Char... ar...lie. The private coughed and his chest rattled as he gasped his last. His head lolled to one side as Phillips gritted his teeth in an attempt to stop the lump that was manifesting in his throat.

"What did he say?" asked Fred.

Phillips straightened up, his eyes clouded with emotion, his anger banishing his tears. "By God, I'll find the swine. He'll hang for this. He won't wriggle out of it. It's cold blooded murder."

"Who?" pressed Fred.

"Charlie Coombes."

"Is that what he said?"

Phillips turned to Fred, "He gave me the name Charlie. That's enough for me. They won't know he didn't say the full name. I know it was him."

"Is that right?" questioned Fred.

"Right or wrong, no one will know... or need to know."

At that moment, Edward and Josie arrived with the doctor as Minnie came out carrying a pan of hot water. Distraught, Jack shook his head, removed his hat and raked his fingers through his unruly hair. "How could this happen? How?" He began to pace back and fore.

"What next, Sergeant?" asked Edgar.

"I'll have everyone on the lookout for that killer. He's well known to us and now, he's a wanted man. Mark my words, he'll be caught."

Jack murmured to Edward, "Unless we get our hands on him first."

Edward replied softly with a warning note in his voice, "Jack."

Fred called Jack and Edward aside, "You two, get up to your room. Stay out of sight."

"But why?"

"Just in case someone recognises your names if you have to make a statement."

Edward piped up, "Surely, enough time has elapsed, now?"

"More than likely, but best be safe. We have the last words of Denton and the eye witness evidence of Edgar, Phillips and me at Woolloomooloo. That's enough. Now make yourself scarce."

Reluctantly, they retired upstairs, but kept their door slightly ajar so they could listen to some of the proceedings, downstairs.

***

The rest of the night was chaotic as police and militia arrived to speak with those who had remained in the hotel bar. After the doctor concluded his examination of Private Denton's body the undertaker was summoned. He was a thin mournful looking man with a long face and sandy hair, which befitted his occupation. He scrutinised the group and asked in a thin reedy voice, "May I ask who is taking care of this?"

Sergeant Phillips's head snapped around, "Just do it, man. You'll be paid. I'll see to that." The mortician paused seeming to accept this and took out his measure, notebook and pencil.

Edgar called Fred to one side, who was holding his blood soaked shirt; "Think you need to leave early tomorrow. I'll take care of things here."

"Is that wise?"

"It's necessary. Trust me."

"What about Koorong's testimony?"

"If it's requested, they can come to you. I'll tell them where to find you. Now, get to bed. Get some rest."

"I doubt I can sleep."

"But, you can try. I'll get Minnie to bring you one of my shirts. Mrs Doble will have a fit if she sees you in that." He indicated the saturated bloody garment. "She'll think you've gone butchering not selling sheep."

Edgar jerked his head to the stairs, "Go on up," he directed and when Fred reached the first step, Edgar turned back to the events happening in the bar and sighed despairingly knowing it was going to be a long night.

***

The atmosphere the following morning was subdued, conversation hushed, and breakfast was eaten with little relish. After the joyous excitement of the auction the evening's horrific murder had left them all numb in shock. Fred announced, "Koorong was to be here at ten but we'll make a start and walk to meet him. We have to get away. I'll settle up and meet you out front."

Fred pushed back his chair and crossed to the bar. He exchanged a few words with Edgar and handed across money for their board and lodge before returning to the table and donning his slouch hat, "Let's get going." They left the bar, their demeanour downcast, and stepped out into the town street that was slowly coming alive.

The sun had barely crossed the horizon. It blazed its scarlet fire across the burgeoning cloud filled sky, which looked oppressively ominous. It matched their mood. Gone was the clear azure blue of the heavens to be replaced by menacing, dark, rain bearing cumulous nimbus clouds rolling in from the coast.

They plodded along the dirt road away from Port Jackson towards the outlying farm where Koorong had stayed the night. The turbulent cloud cover effectively blocked the rays of the sun and stole away its warmth and light as the first drops of rain began to fall. Raindrops the size of bullets shot down and bounced on the dry dusty track, quickly turning the dirt road to a stream. Unequipped for such weather they had no option but to go on. There was little shelter in the brush and the heat baked ground was so hard that the water had trouble soaking into the earth but ran freely harassing their feet. They were soon up to their ankles in swirling fast flowing water.

"I don't like the look of this," said Fred as the rain drenched them, saturating their clothes making it difficult to walk. "Get off to the side, where it's higher," ordered Fred.

He didn't have to say it twice and they all scrambled up together. The water coursed down the road like a river, taking chunks out of the undergrowth and sending it sailing on its path. "Keep together. The speed of this could knock us off our feet. We need to link arms. It should be over soon, if we can just keep safe."

"Hope Koorong's not long," shouted Edward above the driving rain.

"I'm sure we'll see him shortly," Fred tried to placate them. "One thing, this storm should clear soon. We don't often see rain like this. Now, hang on to my arms, both of you. Stay away from the gum trees."

Ice white lightning streaked down, forking and snaking through the brooding sky. Thunder crashed overhead rumbling and growling in the wind that had gathered and had begun to gust fiercely. The rain continued to pelt down and bombarded them. They clung together, inching carefully and slowly on the newly formed bank above the flash flood, which had gouged fissures in the road. There was a splintering crack and one of the Eucalyptus gum trees was blasted by a lightning bolt, which split its trunk, cleaving the tree into two, which began to crackle and spark as it caught fire. The thick volatile syrup like sap was alight but couldn't take hold because of the heavy rain, which made the flames sizzle before they could spread and it finally petered out.

The deluge lasted no more than fifteen minutes before the wind bowled the storm clouds away further inland to dissipate in the rising heat. The three men were soaked to the skin. Jack removed his hat to shake it and looked up at the now innocent sky and the sun smiling down as if the storm had never been. "One thing's for sure," said Fred. "We'll soon dry off."

The rushing water slowed and settled as it began to seep into the ground to hide in the aquifer beneath the land and replenish the underground waterways. "Seen heavy rain before in London, but nothing like that," said Jack.

"No," agreed Edward. "That was quite scary."

"Guess we're lucky to live in sunshine most of the time, but rains like this bring beauty and their own problems," said Fred.

"What do you mean?" asked Jack.

"You'll see. Our scorched desert and brush will ignite with dazzling spot fires of white, yellow and purple wildflowers. I've seen it before. It's a spectacle to see. Mark my words as we head back we'll see the outback beginning to bloom. It's beautiful."

"Very poetic!" Edward said with a grin.

"I have my moments," Fred said laughing.

"Always smells fresh after rain," said Jack. "At least, I think so."

"I always thought it cleaned the place up in England. Cleaned off the dirt and grime," added Edward.

The three tramped on at the side of the gulley made by the water until in the distance they could see a wagon.

"Koorong!" exclaimed Edward joyfully, whose clothes were now beginning to steam. He jumped off the bank and paddled through the rapidly disappearing stream.

Jack laughed and leapt down beside him as Fred shook his head at their youthful exuberance before deciding to hop down next to them. It seemed the sudden rain storm had done something to lift their spirits. They quickened their pace to meet Koorong.

Koorong shook the reins to urge Brutus forward and the horse raised its walk to a trot as Jack and Edward ran to the wagon. Jack flopped into the back of the cart and put his hat over his face. "Think I'll take a nap in the sun on the trip back. Didn't get much shut-eye last night with everything that happened."

"Why? What happened?" asked Koorong.

"Fred will tell you," said Edward joining Jack in the back. "It's good to see you, Koorong. Think Jack's got the best idea," and he settled down beside his friend, using his hat to cover his face as Jack had done, while Fred recounted the events of the previous night to a horrified Koorong.

***

The cart rumbled on and turned off the dirt road from Port Jackson towards their homestead. On route they passed one of the several scattered and deserted settlers' dwellings in the outback. The noise of the cartwheels revolving as they ran over stones disturbed birds and other wildlife, and eyes watched them from the shack. Charlie Coombes screwed up his eyes and spat into the dirt floor as he recognised Fred and the aboriginal driving the dray. "So, the big man and the Abo are friends? We'll see about that."

"Leave it, Charlie," warned Basil. "We're both wanted for the murder of that private. Why did you have to kill him? You could have got me away without doing him in."

"Safer that way, Basil, me old mate. No witnesses."

"But there was. The private must have told before he died. Arthur said you've been fingered. We gotta lie low."

"We will. We'll take the game up the coast to the next town. But first we have a couple of loose ends to deal with." Charlie raised his rifle and set it to his eye. "Damn! Too far away. Come on. I can get them both."

"Leave me out of it. Cheating folks out of money's one thing but murder... we'll be hanged."

"No, we won't. Just do as I say. Get your gun. For starters no one will miss the Abo."

"But from what I heard he's a witness to our shoot. They'll realise that's why he's been shot. That will bring the law round our necks."

"Not if we do it right. There's just the two of them, unarmed. It'll be easy."

"But, that sergeant saw all three of us at Woolloomooloo. Those other men at the camp will know us. We didn't have our faces covered."

"Yeah, but we didn't do anything. They can't have us for that."

"Arthur said all they need is our intent and they'll put us away. I can't go back to prison again, Charlie. Last time nearly killed me. I've still got the scar Rust gave me."

"Forget about Rust. He's not the law here."

"But his fingers are far reaching. I've heard he's nobbled people outside."

"Rust ain't gonna bother you or me. So, get that straight in your head! Let's get moving. This is gonna be fun."

Reluctantly, Basil followed Charlie from the shack and shadowed him as he moved stealthily through the grass and scrub. They watched their prey as would a supreme predator after its next meal.

Charlie cocked his rifle. It was a surprisingly loud click considering they were outside. Charlie raised his rifle ready to release a bullet, which would get rid of what he described as a problem when Basil put out his hand and stopped him.

"Whassamatter?" snarled Charlie.

"Wait! I can hear something. Horses headed this way. Lots of them."

Charlie stiffened and listened. He lowered his rifle, "What the...?"

Riding towards the wagon was a platoon of soldiers led by Sergeant Phillips. He was headed straight for the cart.

"You can't take the risk now. Come on, let's get out of here. Quickly."

Charlie's lips twisted cruelly in anger, "Hold on. I wanna hear what's said."

"Don't be stupid. If they find us that'll be it. I'm going back." Basil backed off, slowly crawling back through the underbrush as Charlie edged closer. He could just pick up a few words as the militia surrounded the dray. He couldn't see the wagon only the scarlet coats of the soldiers. But words drifted on the wind.

"Came to warn you. Charlie Coombes is out to get you."

"How do you know?"

Charlie strained to hear. He caught the name Arthur and arrest warrant. That was enough for him. He reversed away gradually until he felt he could rise to his feet and ran back in the direction of the shack. His heart was thumping like a bass drum, pounding in his head. He fell in through the door of the hut and swore. "It was perfect. Had him all lined up in me sights and then they had to come along."

"Did you learn anything?" asked Basil.

"Enough to know Arthur's peached on me, probably to save his own skin. They got an arrest warrant out on us."

"What me, too?" said Basil in trepidation.

"I'd say so. Both of us for the cage and scaffold, I'd say. We'd better scarper and quick. Grab your bits. The big man will have to wait. But at least he won't be able to relax. He'll always be looking over his shoulder wondering if I'm there. That's good enough for me... for now."

The two felons picked up their few items, left their primitive dwelling and headed towards Parramatta and Windsor.

**

Phillips finished talking to Fred and advised, "I should stay away from town at the moment. According to the one we picked up, you're a marked man. They're out to get rid of witnesses from the attempt at Woolloomooloo. That means Koorong will also be in danger as he can identify those involved in his village massacre."

"Then it's just as well my men here have been initiated into how my business works. They will have to go to the market sales and auctions for me. You up to that, lads?"

Jack and Edward were now sitting up in the cart and nodded enthusiastically. "If you think we can do it, Fred, we will," affirmed Edward. "Won't we, Jack?"

"Course. You can count on us," said Jack.

"We have to continue to search the area. I understand there are some abandoned settlers' houses close by."

"Several, in fact," said Fred.

Phillips nodded and said, "Then we will move on, explore the area and look for the dwellings. Can you tell me where they start?"

Fred pointed north, "They're spread out a bit but they start over yonder about a mile away. Good luck. I hope you catch the blighters."

"We will. They've killed one of our own. They'll not escape the law." Phillips gave a fingered salute in acknowledgement and ordered his platoon, "About turn." He gestured in the direction indicated by Fred. "Walk on." The soldiers obeyed and let the dray continue on its way.

In the next couple of hours Fred's prediction came true and flowers encouraged by the rain and sun began to bloom in an impressive array of colour such as the boys had never before seen. Edward was mesmerised by the breath-taking display. Even Jack was struck by the wonder of it all. The rest of the journey passed quickly with them all enjoying and admiring the unexpected spectacular nature show.

**

Tantalising aromas surrounded Mrs Doble in her kitchen as she busied herself baking some sweet treats to follow her carefully prepared wonga, wonga pigeon, of which Jack was particularly fond so she was surprised when she heard the familiar "Cooee" call outside. She glanced at the kitchen clock, wiped her floury hands on her apron and tried to make herself look more presentable by fluffing up her hair, pinching her cheeks and moistening her lips before dashing outside. Delighted to see the cart on the drive in the distance, she waved madly and answered back with her own, "Cooee!" She waited until the wagon drew nearer and ran out to meet them.

Mrs Doble studied their faces and could sense something serious had happened, "What's wrong?"

"Let's get inside and we'll tell you. Did you have the rains here?"

"No, nothing. Why?"

"We got caught up in flash flood. Scared Edward half to death."

"And me," added Jack.

"Where are Daniel and Bobby?" asked Fred.

"In the gathering shed packing wool bales."

"Jack run there, tell them to stop and come up to the house. We have to get them prepared. Mrs Doble would you be kind enough to make us all some tea? Come on, Edward." Mrs Doble began to walk back flanked by Fred and Edward. Koorong hesitated uncertainly. Fred stopped and looked back, "You, too, Koorong. Come indoors."

"I'll see to Brutus, first."

112

Koorong drove the cart to the stabling barn and untacked Brutus, giving him fresh hay and water. He joined, Jack and the others in the yard and followed them into the house looking uncomfortable.

***

They all sat around the scrubbed pine table, except for Koorong who hung back leaning against a kitchen cupboard. Mrs Doble spoke softly, "Come on, Koorong. Take a seat. You belong here as much as anyone else."

Koorong sat as Mrs Doble prepared tea for them all. She dished up a plate of snacks before sitting down herself to listen to what Fred had to say. He explained the events as they happened, as best he could, with a few interjections from Jack and Edward. Mrs Doble was dumbfounded and Bobby and Daniel looked both horrified and shocked. Fred continued, "So that's how it is. We are all marked men. We will have to watch our backs and cannot afford to be careless with these men on the loose. Now, I'll understand if any of you want to leave and work elsewhere where you will feel safer. I won't stop you."

Fred scrutinised each and every single one of them around the table. Koorong was the first to speak. "You have always been kind to me, treated me fair, allowed me into your home and taught me much. Why would I turn my back on you now? Where would I go? Minjarra and I are proud to call you friends, bunji. I will stand with you."

Jack was next to speak, "I'm with Koorong. This is the only proper home I've known. I'm not going anywhere."

"Nor me," agreed Edward.

Bobby and Daniel shared a look of agreement, "No way; we're not nongs. We'll be sticking around for any tick of the clock."

Fred nodded and smiled, satisfied. He added, "I'll understand if any of you change your mind. Now, let's have that brew."

Mrs Doble obliged and poured the tea for everyone but her eyes betrayed her thoughts. Jack could see that she was worried.

***

Later that night as Edward and Jack were getting ready for bed Jack asked, "Why do you think Mrs D looked so troubled?"

"Wouldn't you be? Fred, all of us, are going to be nervous. Mrs D cares about everyone. She's bound to be concerned."

"I suppose you're right. I just thought there may have been more to it." With that he climbed into bed and settled down leaving Edward to turn down the lamp and stumble across in the dark to his bed.

***

In the Dobles' bedroom silver ribbons of moonlight streamed through the chinks in the curtain and pooled on the floor. Mrs Doble turned restlessly in the bed. Her eyes were wide open as she struggled to get to sleep, "Fred? Are you awake?" Fred grunted and rolled over. "Fred?"

He leaned up on his elbow, the invading light from the gibbous moon partially illuminated his face giving him an odd-spectre like look. "What's the matter?"

"Fred, I'm worried."

"Aren't we all?"

"No, seriously," she sighed heavily as if her forthcoming words would cause pain. "I don't want you to return to Port Jackson."

"But, our livelihood is dependent on trade at the port."

"I don't care. I care more about you. Let someone else deal with it," she pleaded. "I'm afraid... It's a long trip to the town on a lonely road where anything might happen and now those murderers are after you, who knows what could occur." Her last few words came out as a sob.

"Hey, there, there," said Fred reassuringly drawing her into his arms. "I've already set things in motion. I'm not getting any younger and the aches and pains of old age are catching up with me. The lads will be doing more for me now they understand the business. So, don't you worry none."

Mrs Doble snuggled into Fred's strong arms and her juddering sobs levelled off and she seemed a little appeased. "Promise me, Fred. Promise me you'll not go to the port again, please."

Fred held his wife tightly and let out a soft breath that gently caressed her face, "If that's what you want. It can be arranged. But we will have to go into town at some point. We can't be prisoners in our own home. I have affairs to settle, we have goods to buy but I will promise you that I will not undertake any unnecessary journeys to the port. There, does that satisfy you?"

Mrs Doble sniffed and whispered, "I suppose it'll have to do."

"Now, close your eyes and let's get some sleep. It's been a hell of a day." They cuddled up together but Mrs Doble's eyes remained wide open even after Fred had drifted off into a snoring sleep.

***

The following morning, everyone was on edge. This continued through the next few weeks. No one did anything alone. When it came to patrolling the farm and checking watering stations they worked in pairs or threes and carried firearms and other weapons at the insistence of Fred, always on the lookout for any strange person or unexplained activity.

The next market day loomed. Jack and Edward prepared to visit the port on Fred's behalf and were instructed carefully by Fred on what not, as well as what, to do and what was expected of them. Both Jack and Edward were confident that they could carry out Fred's wishes and do the best for the farm.

Edward and Jack set off with Koorong followed by Daniel and Bobby in the next cart. Jack had been given money for their stay at the Victoria and was determined they would to do their very utmost for Fred. At the same time, he was looking forward to a night out in the port while at the ranch Mrs Doble waited anxiously for their safe return.

***

The following day, Mrs Doble was hanging out her washing when she heard the rumble of the cart wheels and the familiar "Cooee!" call announcing the workers' return. She ran joyfully towards the porch, "Fred! Fred, they're back."

Fred in his rolled up shirt sleeves, sucking on his pipe, emerged from the house beaming and called back, "Cooee!" He turned to his wife who had joined him on the porch, "See, I told you it would be all right."

They welcomed them back delighted to hear all about their trip and celebrated the sale of the wool bales as they appeared to have done extraordinarily well.

"Jack's a great bargain maker," said Edward enthusiastically. "We got our patter off pat, Jack would draw them in I would display the quality and Jack would do the final deal, while I got the next lot ready. Worked a treat... Even Mr Pinch at the bank remembered us."

"Sounds like you did a grand job. You'll become experts in no time. Thank you." Both young men beamed with pride before going into the kitchen to have the welcome home feast Mrs D had prepared.

***

Many months passed and things became more relaxed. Fred stopped looking over his shoulder. Even Mrs Doble lost that harried, careworn look that had lived on her face since the death of Private Denton. Jack and Edward believed something must have happened to Charlie Coombes and his cronies or they had travelled far enough away so as not to cause them any more trouble. So, the threat, which had hung over their heads, seemed to be diminished, although Jack never took anything for granted.

It was a few weeks later that Fred joined them on their next trip to Port Jackson. There were items to get for Mrs D and Fred wanted to buy a few sows at auction. Koorong was to remain behind, as was Bobby and Daniel who were preparing a pen and housing for the expected pigs.

The journey to the port was lively and full of chatter, with Edward even breaking out into song. "It's a damn sight better than your whistling," teased Jack.

"Why don't you join in? You know the songs as well as I do."

"What? And have Brutus rearing up and galloping off to get away from my keening," exclaimed Jack.

"Yes, spare us that," said Fred with a laugh.

The wagon lumbered on towards the port. On the outlying district, other carts came into view and many people on foot, all heading for the markets and auction. The usually quiet road turned into a busy thoroughfare. Some people were almost skipping their way to the quay.

Fred and his lads, as he called them, were comfortably relaxed. No one was paying attention to them and they were not scouring the faces of those around them. They didn't see the saturnine face of Charlie Coombes glowering from the side of the road, his hat pulled down low over his face.

***

Charlie squinted at the dray; a flicker of recognition registered in his eyes, he hardly dared breathe but murmured almost imperceptibly, "The big man." He resolved to watch and follow them, all be it discreetly. He was carrying a wool blanket bedroll, wrapped in a horse-shoe shaped small knapsack covered in waterproof canvas and had a bundle of plant material tied with twine.

Charlie Coombes was determined to be careful. He was out for revenge. Vengeance was the fire that stoked his belly and gave him purpose. A chilling grin crept on his face. Still keeping his head down, he hurried after the wagon without anyone noticing him. He knew his appearance had altered somewhat. His straggly lank and greasy hair had been cropped. He sported a fearsome scar that ran the length of his right cheek, drawing the skin down tightly from his drooping right eye like the trailing chain of a monocle.

So far he had evaded capture and fully intended to keep his freedom. He shadowed the cart and watched it rattle across the cobbles to the Victoria Hotel, where they took the wagon around the back to the stable block. Charlie continued to observe from a safe distance and saw the big man and his companions enter the hotel. "So, that's where they're staying," he murmured under his breath. But now, now he needed to find Arthur. He didn't forgive anyone who peached on him. He'd be back for the big man, later.

Charlie slunk away and wandered down town to the less respectable side of Port Jackson where thieves and scoundrels abounded. He was convinced it was where he would find Arthur and use him to his advantage. A mocking laugh escaped him that turned into a deep belly guffaw. His eyes lit with delight at the thought of what he was going to do.

12: Plots and Retribution

Charlie slipped down a side street to a tavern known to him and where he expected to find Arthur. He managed to avoid the recklessly bold women who solicited his attention except for one red headed doxy, who was particularly persistent. "Come on, dearie, I'm all yours for two bob, or a fourpenny knee trembler, if you like."

Charlie decided he'd had enough of her pleading and caught her by the throat with his gloved hand, "If I want something, I'll ask for it or maybe I'll even take it. Understand?"

"All right, all right," she said her voice choking with fear. As he released her his hat slipped off and she saw the full extent of his scar and stifled a scream. Charlie grabbed his hat from where it fell and thrust it back on his head, pulling it low over his face. Shaken, the woman scurried away to find a new patch to work from.

Charlie swore and spat into the dirt before he sped to 'The Captain's Wife' and sidled into the public bar. He purchased a tankard of ale and located to a corner table. His eyes darted around the busy area. He spotted a number of people he knew and a couple of old associates, but there was no sign of Arthur. He decided he would bide his time before approaching one of those he knew and he waited until the chosen miscreant, a lanky man with an acne scarred face and thin lips, had in Charlie's eyes, consumed a sufficient amount of alcohol.

The rogue, who answered to the name of Wilfred, staggered to a seat and sat down with a thump and swallowed down the dregs of his snifter. He looked glassy eyed and was dribbling a little.

Charlie made his move. He dragged his chair across and straddled it facing the felon. "Hello, Wilf," he said with a rasp.

Wilf blinked twice and stared hard, "What the...? Charlie? That you? Thought you were dead..."

"Very much alive, Wilf. Contrary to what you've 'eard."

"Wouldn't have thought you'd be safe 'ere. Yer a wanted man. Not safe for no one with you, neither."

"Need your 'elp, Wilf. Then I'll disappear out of your life."

"What is it?" Wilf screwed up his eyes and attempted to focus on Charlie's face, before shuddering, "Crikey. What happened to you?"

"Caught the wrong end of a knife in Windsor. The bloke that did it, is in the ground now. Dead as a clat." Charlie took out a small knife, removed his gloves and deliberately began to clean under his fingernails. "Now, you gonna help me, Wilf? Or not?"

"Depends."

"On what?"

"What it is."

"Just want to catch up with a couple of blokes, nothing bad."

"Who?"

"Seen anythin' of Arthur?"

"'Arf a brain Arfur? Nah. Not lately."

"Why's that?"

"Heard he'd been caged."

"We talkin' 'bout the same man?"

"Yeah." Wilf hiccupped before he slumped forward and his eyes closed.

Charlie swore under his breath and spat on the floor. He glanced up. His good eye narrowed as he caught sight of a familiar person entering the tavern. It was Arthur.

Charlie grinned humourlessly and returned his chair to its original place and watched as Arthur greeted a few customers before skulking towards the bar. Charlie pulled down his hat and waited.

Arthur pushed through the rabble to the bar and ordered a drink, banging his coins down on the wooden counter. Charlie crept up beside him. "Hello, Arthur. I was just told you'd been nabbed."

"Charlie!" Arthur swallowed uncomfortably. "Heard you'd been done in," he added nervously.

"Not me, just laid low, kept quiet. Thought it time to come home, see me old mates."

"Looks like we were both wrong, then."

"Looks like it," said Charlie spitting again. "So, what's the jabber?"

Arthur shrugged. He looked about him shiftily, "Not a lot. How's Basil?"

"Settled in Windsor. Got himself a woman, got wed."

Arthur bit his lip, "No one to run the game, then?"

"Not at the moment." He paused, "Need your help."

"Why? What's up?"

"I see the big man's in town."

"Big man?"

"The Abo lover, Fred Doble. It's time his number was called. He's in town. I'm gonna make it my business he don't leave, or if he do, he won't last long and you're gonna help me."

"Listen, Charlie... I don't think..."

Charlie grabbed his wrist, "You owe me. You're gonna help, whether you want to or not."

Arthur's eyes looked panicked. He stared Charlie directly in the face and gasped, "What happened to you? Your eye..."

"A little difference of opinion in Windsor. Don't worry none. The other bloke's dead and in the ground. That's when I decided it was time to come home to... friends, like you. You are my friend, aren't you, Arthur?"

Arthur licked his lips, "Course. D'ya need to ask?"

"Good. Then get me another drink and I'll tell you what I want you to do." Charlie left Arthur at the bar and returned to his table. He replaced his gloves and uncovered his bundle of plant material. He took an empty snuff box from his pocket and removed a distinctive dried spiny seed pod, opened it, shook the seeds out, and secreted some in the snuff box, before covering the bundle of dried angel trumpet plants and tying it back to his bedroll.

Arthur hesitantly crossed to Charlie carrying two ales. He sat nervously; a twitch had begun pulsing in his cheek. "So, what you been doin' all this time? Couldn't have kept up thimblerig with Basil dropping out. He was the man, sharp, nimble of finger, best at the game."

Charlie nodded, "He was the best all right. Did it for a while until he got swish'd. Mind you, the woman's a looker. I'll grant him that."

"So, 'ow did you make your way?"

Charlie frowned and took a swig of his drink, "Got into a new line of work, Arthur. Couldn't believe it when I 'eard you'd gone bad."

"Me? Nah. I wouldn't get involved with the law, wouldn't tell 'em anything. You know me."

"I thought I did, Arthur. I thought I did. Just telling you what I've heard. Word has it you'd been boned and that's when you went bad."

"Not me, mate. I swore I knew nothin' I ain't given nothin' away."

"Then how come you're walking about?"

Arthur shrugged, "Dunno. Must 'ave believed me."

"Well, Arthur, me old mate. If you are me mate... You're gonna have to prove it to me. I got a job for you to do."

Arthur flinched, "Yeah, yeah. Course. Anything. What do you want?" his eyes darted around shiftily.

"Well, see 'ere. I can't move around as freely as I'd like, so I want you to do a little chore for me."

Arthur looked alarmed and forced a strained smile, "Course."

"Glad you said that. I'd hate to come looking for you if you refused. You'd be watching yer back forever, never knowing when I was going to pop up or if it was the day you'd breathe yer last. Wouldn't let an old mate down, now, would yer?"

Arthur tried to smile again but it came out more of a grimace. He mumbled through gritted teeth, "What do you want?"

"Remember the big man? From Woolloomooloo? Course you do... He's staying at The Victoria Hotel. You need to go there and take these." He passed Arthur the snuff box. "In there are angel trumpet seeds. I don't care how you do it but get them into his grub somehow. Make sure he eats them. Then walk away."

"What do they do?"

"You don't need to know that. Just get it done."

"How am I supposed to do that? It's impossible," Arthur protested.

"I'm sure you'll think of something, then get back here. I expect he'll only be there overnight. You'll need to nobble him tonight or tomorrow morning."

"And what if I can't?" pleaded Arthur.

"I don't accept no excuses. You 'ave to prove your loyalty and friendship to me... or..."

"Or...?" said Arthur fearfully.

"There'll be no more tomorrows for you," said Charlie with dark finality.

**

Arthur scurried away from the tavern in turmoil. He didn't know what to do. Charlie quickly followed as unobtrusively as possible and watched where his old friend went. If the man went to the law he knew he'd have to get out of sight. If he went to the hotel then he just might do as he was told. Not that it mattered, Arthur was going to die anyway. Charlie wanted to laugh but managed to contain the loud guffaw that threatened to erupt. He scanned the road, busy with people. Mollishers waiting to seduce any naive bloke that crossed their path, pedlars trading in trinkets and sweetmeats, and farmers hoping to buy and sell livestock.

Charlie watched as Arthur hurried up the road to the Victoria Hotel and swore as he almost bumped headfirst into the big man emerging from the hotel with two others. He waited to see what Arthur would do. Arthur entered the hotel. Charlie hung around for a while to see if he came out. He didn't. So, Charlie decided to tail the big man and see what he did.

Fred appeared carefree as he walked around the market towards the auction ring with Jack and Edward. He greeted people, acknowledging them with a friendly word and stopped to chat at length with those he had not seen in a long while before they registered with the auctioneer and moved on to inspect the animals on offer, assessing their health and profitability.

**

Inside the hotel some hardened drinkers had gathered. No one took any notice of Arthur as he made his way to the bar. "Josie? An ale, please."

Josie looked up in surprise, "On the wrong side of town, aren't you? What you doing in here?"

Arthur licked his lips nervously and whispered, "Josie, I'm in trouble."

Josie frowned, "I want nothing to do with you or any of your cronies."

"You don't understand. I ain't been in any kind of trouble since Charlie left. I'm not about to start now."

"Why? What's happened?"

"He's back. Charlie's back and threatening to do me in unless I do what he says."

"I don't know..." said Josie uncertainly.

"I just need to keep out of his way. He can't know I'm here. Can I hide away somewhere? Please?"

Josie looked doubtful, "Go to the law. He's a wanted man. Then you'll be safe."

"He's got eyes everywhere. I can't be seen talking to anyone or I'll be dead. I'm scared he might come in here."

Josie looked about the bar, "There's nowhere you can sit that you won't be seen."

"What about your kitchen?"

Josie looked hesitant, "I don't know about that..."

"Please, Josie."

"If father finds out he'll kill me," she said passing him his ale.

"He won't. And if you don't help me, I'm a dead man. Do you want that on your conscience?"

"No, of course not."

"Then help me."

"Isn't there somewhere else you can go?"

"No. Charlie knows where I live, my family and places I go. He wouldn't think of looking here. It's my only chance. Then you can get a message to the law... to that sergeant who helped me before." He could see Josie was weakening. "Please."

"How long you gonna be here?"

"I don't know... a while... just till the light goes. I can keep out of sight more easily in the dark."

"It's against my better judgement... but..."

"But?"

"Follow me."

"What about Edgar and Minnie?"

"Father's gone to market and the auction. Minnie is with him. It's just me at the moment. Come on." Josie stepped out from behind the bar and walked briskly to the kitchen followed by Arthur, who scanned the scullery and saw the oven cooking pies and stew simmering on the stove. Josie picked up a stool and took him to the walk in larder. "In here. At the end of the pantry there's a space by the steps leading down to the cellar, you can hide there. Here's a stool you can sit on. Don't filch any grub. I'll get you something later, when it's cooked."

"How do I know your sister or father won't find me?"

"Minnie doesn't like the dark, she won't go in the cellar. Father will be out front serving drinks and chatting to guests. He's got friends staying. One bloke he hasn't seen in a long time. No more questions, make yourself scarce."

Arthur took the stool and walked to the back of the pantry where it was dark. The steps leading down looked ominous. But he knew he had no time to be scared. He had to work out how he was going to do this and realised it would be difficult. He sat on the stool and took out the snuff box and opened it. He sniffed the seeds, they were fragrant and looked harmless enough. Surely someone would notice if they were in food being eaten? He tried to reason with himself. Perhaps he should go to the law? Give Charlie up? Charlie had always terrorised and bullied him. If he did this, would he ever be free? Could he believe Charlie when he said he'd leave him be if he did this one thing? Arthur was more than aware that Charlie was not a man of his word. Arthur swore. He convinced himself he'd do it and make his escape. He'd be all right, surely? But, if that was the case, why did he feel that somehow he was signing his own death warrant?

Arthur fingered the seeds. If he could crush them somehow, they were more likely to be ingested. He began to look around the pantry for anything that would help him reduce the seeds to powder. On the lower shelf there were various implements. Arthur picked up a pestle and mortar that had been used for crushing spices. He picked it up and tipped the seeds inside and got to work, grinding and crushing the peppercorn size seeds. He worked on them until he had a fine powder and filled the snuff box with it and looked for another receptacle in which to put the remainder. Then, he sat and waited.

***

Fred and worker chaps, as he called them, were each munching on a hot baked potato with salt cooked in a brazier by one of the vendors at the market. Edward was huffing and puffing with the steaming spud that was almost too hot to handle. He blew hard on his, wrapped in paper, and tried to take another bite, "I can't eat this, yet. It's much too hot." He glanced at Fred who seemed to be chomping quite happily on the roasted vegetable. "You must have the jaws of a volcano. Doesn't it burn your mouth?" asked Edward.

"Used to it. I like everything piping hot, my tea, my stew, everything."

"I need a drink to cool my mouth down. I'm sure I've blistered it."

"Me, too," said Jack. "I've taken the skin off the roof of my mouth. I can't eat it that hot. Don't know how you do it, Fred. I like my grub warm not scalding."

Fred laughed and took another huge bite while the lads shook their heads in amusement. They made their way to the auction ring as the swine they were interested in were due for sale.

Jack kept his eye out for any shill bidders, so he knew who to watch when it came to Fred's turn to buy. He spotted two such men, who looked like farmers and nudged Edward. "See the bloke with the straw hat and whiskers?" Edward nodded. "You watch him. When our parcel comes up, get close and warn him off. I'll do the same with that stocky fella, yonder." He pointed out another thickset labourer with a balding head and beard.

They moved around the ring into position as the drift of young sows entered the circle and bidding started. Jack sidled right up to the hefty man and whispered, "I don't think you should bet on this lot, if I were you."

"And why's that?" growled the man.

"Cos I know your game and unless you want the law on you, keep your bids to yourself."

The man turned and faced Jack, "And who's gonna stop me?"

"I will... Just take my advice and leave it. I don't like shills, nor do my mates."

The man glanced about him and saw an officer approaching the ring. He scowled and muttered, "Just this lot?"

"Just this lot," affirmed Jack. "You can do what you like with the rest."

The shill nodded and muttered reluctantly, "Agreed."

Jack watched the auction with interest and noted that Edward had also stopped the other shillaber from interfering in the sale.

Fred was delighted. The bidding went far better than expected. There was one other in the race, who finally dropped out and Fred won the bid. He shook hands excitedly with those around him and when Jack and Edward returned to his side, he slapped them on the back in appreciation. They made their way to the auctioneer's table and paid up, making arrangements to pen them up until the morning in the animal compound, close by. Fred beamed, "Right, chaps. Let's get to the Victoria and have a drink and a bite to eat. I reckon there's a plate of stew with my name on it."

***

The night at the Victoria was riotous. It was as busy as ever and the atmosphere was light and free. Fred was surprised at how much he'd been missed. Jack and Edward were bemused as traders and farmers engaged him in conversation and drink after drink was bought for him.

Jack turned to Edward, "Looks like Fred's gonna be a while. Can't see him joining us for supper, can you?"

Edward smiled and shook his head, "Nah. Think we'd best eat and get up timber hill, don't you think?"

Jack grinned as Edgar came and sat next to Fred and they began to laugh. "Now, Edgar's here, we'll have no chance. I'll order at the bar. What do you fancy?"

"I'll have some pie. You?"

"The same. Reckon we'll leave the stew for Fred, if he ever gets around to eating, I'll tell Minnie," said Jack with a laugh.

He strolled to the bar and had a word with Minnie who nodded. "I'll just tell Josie." She slipped out to the kitchen where Josie was dealing with the orders.

***

The kitchen was hot and steamy with vegetables bubbling and meat cooking. Josie was dishing up two plates of food when Minnie entered. "Two pies, Josie for Jack and Edward."

"What about Fred?"

"He's busy drinking and gossiping. Jack says to save him a portion of stew. Remember he likes it really hot. But he's not ready for it yet."

"Lucky you said that. There's only enough left for one or two. I'll keep it back. Tell Jack I'll be out with their grub. Take these plates out to table six."

Minnie picked up the two hot plates and exited the kitchen as Josie began to serve up two pies and mash with gravy. Josie grabbed a tray, set down the cutlery and prepared meals and left as Arthur crept out from the pantry. He had heard everything.

He knew he hadn't got much time. With a trembling hand he opened the snuff box and tipped the contents into the rest of the stew bubbling on the range. He was breathing heavily like a hog on heat and droplets of sweat pearled on his face. He gave the stew a stir until he believed the powder had dissolved before moving stealthily to the back door just as Josie returned to the kitchen. Arthur started guiltily.

"Arthur, you going now?"

"I think I'll be okay, now it's dark."

"Okay. Don't you want something to eat before you go? I can let you have a little stew, if you like? I've just got to keep one portion back."

"No," said Arthur a little too quickly. "No... thank you. I need to get away. Thanks, Josie."

"When you can, tell the law. Now hurry before anyone sees you."

Arthur slunk out of the kitchen into the pressing dark and Josie bolted the door after him.

Arthur moved quietly down the street towards 'The Captain's Wife' and tried to calm his laboured breathing and still his racing heart that thundered in his chest. The bar was still full and a few drunks lay collapsed in their seats with heads on the tables. Arthur's eyes searched the area and spied Charlie exactly where he had left him.

Arthur paused hesitantly wondering whether he should turn tail and run. It was as if Charlie was imbued with a sixth sense and could feel Arthur's eyes on him. He glanced up and locked his gaze onto Arthur before he beckoned him across. Arthur swallowed hard and wiped his now dripping hands down his coat and moved towards the table.

"Have you done it?" rasped Charlie. Arthur nodded and bit his lip. "Don't look so worried. We'll be all right now. Let me get you a drink."

"Nah... thanks. I'd best get back."

"If you're sure?" Arthur nodded again and a droplet of sweat fell from his face and splashed on the table. "Right. Must 'ave tested you. Tell you what. Meet me 'ere, tomorrow at eleven. I might 'ave another little job for you."

The vein in Arthur's face began to pulse again and he bit his lip, "Okay, Charlie. See you tomorrow." Arthur turned and hurtled out into the street. He leaned against the pub wall and took a deep breath. He was still shaking and moved off into the alley that led to his poky shack. As he walked, his step became less hurried although his heart continued hammering violently as the blood was pumped round his body and rushed to his head. The sound in his ears was almost deafening. He feared his heart was about to rise to his mouth and jump out. He forced himself to breathe more steadily and continued down the alley into a side street unaware that Charlie had sneaked out of the inn and was following at a discreet distance.

Arthur steadied his breathing as he neared his small shack. He looked about him fretfully and turned to scour the darkness behind him. Charlie slipped into the shadows and waited. As Arthur started to open his front door, Charlie came swiftly from behind, put his hand over Arthur's mouth and with his other hand, drew a knife across his old friend's throat and cut deep, slicing the carotid artery. Blood gushed out covering Charlie's fingers. Charlie snarled, "Won't go bad on me again, Arthur. Justice has been done." He let Arthur's body fall to the floor, where he lay twitching as his life force ebbed away. Charlie struggled to stifle the giggle that rose so readily to his lips and he skulked away into the night to wash his hands of Arthur's blood. He wasn't going to hang around and had achieved what he had set out to do. He walked up the side street back to the alley and afforded himself a loud hoot of triumphant laughter.

***

The following morning Fred settled up with Edgar and turned down the breakfast on offer, "Think I had a few too many ales last night. My guts are feeling a bit queasy."

"I'm not surprised," said Edward with a grin. "You sank enough liquor for all of us put together."

"I'm surprised you're even standing," added Jack. "I couldn't have consumed that much, ever."

"Well, it was a special occasion. I had a good time. It can't have helped me eating so late either. Come on, finish your breakfast and let's collect those pigs."

Jack and Edward ate up and quickly followed Fred from the bar after he'd said his goodbyes and they returned to the market. On route they noticed an excessive amount of activity in the streets and alleys in the poorest part of town. Fred stopped a bystander, "What's happening? Something up?"

The man looked shocked, "Just found Arthur Wilkins. He 'ad his throat cut last night. Right at 'is front door. Poor bloke bled to death."

"Arthur? Did he used to go about with Charlie Coombes?"

"That's the one."

Fred's expression became grim, "Come on, chaps. Let's get the pigs and head home. I don't much like the idea of hanging around here."

***

The journey back in the wagon was uneventful apart from trying to keep the pigs contained. Fred had made a wire cage, which sat in the back and Edward travelled leaning against the door to the pen to keep it closed. Each time one of the animals passed urine, it seeped out and soaked Edward's trousers. He complained loudly, "How about Jack taking over and me sitting up front for a while?"

"No point in us both getting soaked and giving Mrs D an extra wash load," said Jack cheekily. "Don't expect Fred would want that stink next to him either."

"Jack's right," said Fred. "You better just sit it out; you can change and scrub up at home. Besides, my guts are playing up; that stench will only turn my stomach."

So, Edward suffered the rest of the journey uncomfortably and specially to irritate Jack, he began to whistle.

***

Mrs Doble was sitting on the porch waiting for their return.

Koorong had got the pig pen ready next to the chicken coop. He had laid out vegetables for them to forage and filled a trough with clean water. They both heard Jack calling out, "Cooee!"

Koorong immediately responded and Mrs Doble went to greet the cart. Jack and Edward unloaded the pigs and got them into their pen as Fred jumped down. "You all right?" asked Mrs D. "You don't look too well."

"I'm okay, just got a bit of guts ache that's all."

"Too much drink and not enough to eat," she said.

"You could be right. I did have quite a bit last night."

"Fred, you know that's no good for your digestion. I'll go and make you a powder. That will help and some of Koorong's special tea."

Fred followed his wife inside. He was starting to see double and could see flashing lights out of the corner of his eyes. "Think I'll just have a bit of a lie down. I'll see you all at supper." He talked to himself as he made his way to the bedroom but he wasn't making any sense. It was as if his mind was wandering back to his prison days as his speech became garbled and he talked of chains and keys. Mrs D's face filled with concern but she let her husband go. Rest would be the best thing of that she was sure.

***

That evening, Fred didn't come out for supper. Mrs Doble and the others ate together. She questioned Jack and Edward, "How could you let him get into this state?"

"It wasn't intentional, Mrs D" said Edward. "We went up to bed before Fred, he was having a grand time in the bar so we left him to it. We didn't know he'd drunk so much until morning when he was off his grub."

The door to the kitchen opened and Fred staggered out looking pale and sweaty. "I'm gonna sit on the porch a while. I need some air. Too stuffy in here."

Jack nudged Edward, "Come on. We'd best get to bed. Thanks for supper, Mrs D." They both scrambled up and left for their quarters as Fred stumbled out to the porch and flopped onto the settle. He gazed at the stars, as Mrs Doble came and sat next to him. "Why on earth have you done this to yourself?" she reprimanded. "I thought you'd know better."

"I'm sorry, m'dear. It won't happen again. I'm paying for it now. Maybe a snifter of brandy will help settle it. Do you want one?"

Mrs Doble nodded her head, "Maybe, a small one." She sighed languidly and watched Fred lurch indoors and shook her head.

Fred came back out carrying two glasses and passed her one, "Never seen the sky look purple before. I swear I can see faces in the dark, Jiemba and Jarli."

Mrs D stared at her husband, "You can't have. They're both dead."

"I know, but they look alive to me. There's bubbles and baubles flying around. Can't you see them?"

Mrs Doble peered into the darkness straining her eyes, but all that was visible to her were the amorous clouds that kissed the stars and embraced the waning moon. "You certainly had a bellyful," she said with a laugh and rested her head on his shoulder, closing her eyes. "Long time since I heard you being so poetic," she sighed.

Fred patted her hand and his eyes moved rapidly back and fore taking in all the weird and wonderful things he was seeing.

They sat together like young lovers immersing themselves in each other and the romantic night. Mrs Doble didn't see the bloodied froth in the corners of his mouth. She was blind to his lips turning blue and his sudden contorted expression.

***

Edward and Jack had turned in for the night and both drifted into a sonorous sleep, happily content with their bellies full and the spreading warmth of a last drink soothing their dreaming minds.

A piercing scream shattered the comfortable peace of the night. Jack stirred and leaned up on his elbow, "Edward! Did you hear that?"

"I heard something," said Edward sleepily. The scream was followed by an unearthly wail and both young men jumped out of bed and ran out towards the house. Mrs Doble was on the porch rocking back and fore whimpering mournfully next to Fred who was slumped in a heap on the floor, motionless where he had fallen from the wooden settle.

"My God. Oh, my God," Mrs Doble repeated over and over.

Edward knelt down by Fred as Jack asked, "What happened?"

"Fred, oh Fred. My God..." her words choked in her throat.

Edward listened to Fred putting his ear close to him and then he felt for a pulse in his neck. His voice was urgent, "He's not breathing." Edward rolled Fred onto his back and stared at the liquid that had escaped his cyanosed lips.

Mrs Doble's tears flowed freely, "He just fell down. He was saying all sorts of strange things like he was delirious. He was seeing things."

Edward's face crumpled into despair, "He's dead."

"No! No! he can't be... Fred!" She embraced her husband and supported his head in her lap murmuring his name softly, over and over again. "Fred, wake up. Wake up, please. He can't be dead. We must be able to do something." She looked pleadingly at Jack and Edward. "Help him, please."

Edward took a cushion from the wooden seat and placed Fred's head on it gently.

Jack took Mrs Doble's hands and said softly as he lifted her up, "Let him go, Mrs D. Fred's gone." She fell sobbing into Jack's strong embrace. Edward rose and wrapped his arms around Mrs Doble and the three of them clung together as if their lives depended on it in absolute grief and sorrow.

13: Funereal Days

The next few days were fraught and spent in gloomy contemplation. Mrs Doble didn't have any time to brood as she was busy making arrangements to bury her beloved Fred. It was a simple affair to be attended by a few. She explained around the kitchen table to Jack and Edward, "I know Koorong would like us to follow some of his tribal customs but I can't have Fred elevated on a bed on sticks until all that's left are his bones. He would be there for the vultures to pick at and eat." She shuddered, "The minister from Port Jackson is coming to say a few words and Fred will be buried in a place that he loved, here on this farm."

"I thought Koorong was gathering those that are left from his village?" said Jack.

"He is. I am allowing him to build a sacred fire and blow the herbal smoke through the farmhouse. I will leave all the doors and windows open for him to do that. It will cleanse the place of any bad spirits or luck and help speed the passage of Fred's soul to the afterlife that is their belief. He will never say Fred's name again. You must respect that."

"But why?" asked Edward.

"They believe saying his name will disturb his spirit. It is vital for the rebirth of his soul to drive it onto his next life. Fred would appreciate that. We will allow this... for Koorong. He will organise that side of things. I will prepare a table of refreshments for the mourners. It will have to be in the barn not the house. Danny and Bobby are making a box for Fred's body to rest in and I am asking you both to find the perfect spot where he can be buried."

Jack nodded, "Leave it with us, Mrs D. We'll dig a grave and make sure it's deep enough that no dingoes can dig it up."

"What time is this all happening?" asked Edward.

"Tomorrow at two in the afternoon. It will give the preacher time to get here. We can't have Fred's body lying around in this heat. Best he's buried sooner than later." She stood up from the table, "Now, is there anything you want to put in the casket with him?"

"Like what?" asked Edward.

"Anything of significance, anything that meant something to him. The aboriginals like to place items in the coffin for him to take on his journey." Jack went to interrupt and she waved her hand to quiet him. "I know, I know. We are not aborigines but Fred had enough respect for the people as you do. They are our friends. He would want us to afford them this as a parting gift."

Jack noticed that apart from Mrs D's obvious turmoil and distress that she had a steely glint in her eye that he had not seen before. He could perceive she would have her way and it was not something he would argue with and said carefully, "Then his pipe and baccy would be important and his brandy." Mrs Doble assented with a nod and looked at Edward to see if he had anything more to add.

"Pipe and tobacco are useless without a light. I'd put in his tinderbox and his favourite glass for his snifter."

"Done," said Mrs D her eyes glistening with tears. "I will put in his best shirt," her voice began to crack, "and…" She stopped, unable to say anymore as her emotions waved over her like the rising swell of the ocean rushing towards the shore. Jack stood and embraced her tightly as she complained in a strangled voice, "Don't be nice to me… Please."

He didn't let go. Edward joined him and they held her until her sobs diminished into quivering gasps of air. "Mrs D, don't you worry none. Me and Jack'll look after you. We promise. Won't we, Jack?"

Jack's soothing words came out like melted butter, "Of course. Fred would want us to. We'll take care of you. I guarantee it."

Mrs Doble disentangled herself from them and wiped away the salt tears that had streaked her face. "I can't let you do that. Off you go, find a good spot for him. Go on. I have some serious thinking to do." She took out her hankie from her apron pocket and blew her nose hard. "Go on. Be off with you."

Jack and Edward were disinclined to leave her in her charged emotional state but she shooed them away. They respected her wishes, even though they were torn between comforting her and carrying out her request, and so, in quiet agreement they left the farmhouse to find Fred's final resting place.

Jack looked around the yard. It was almost as if he was seeing the place for the first time and with new eyes. He studied the chicken coop that he and Edward had repaired and filled with all the many devices they had invented to encourage the chickens to forage. There were rocks with hollows where they had hidden grain, a wire netting grid in which they'd inserted green leaves for them to peck, small piles of pebbles that concealed other foodstuffs; all were things to make life more interesting for the hens, to stimulate them, keep them laying and kept them scurrying around their pen until the hatch was opened to let them roam free. Jack had even devised the door with a mechanism that the birds could work themselves to open. He sniffed hard to stop himself crying and turned his face to the honeyed warmth of the sun.

Edward looked sideways at him, "What you thinking?"

Jack gulped and forced out his words determined his voice would not crack, "Fred… and all he taught us." He indicated the fowls, "Remember when we first came?"

"Do I ever? Never thought I'd have been lambing and shearing sheep."

"Me neither. Thought I'd be returning to me old life, in some way. Just trying to survive."

They continued in silence passing their quarters that had developed from sparse furnishings of just two beds and now looked like a real home. They moved on past the outbuildings and into the pasture where the brilliant sun had risen in the vibrant cerulean sky with just a few wisps of clouds that looked like combed angel hair. Edward and Jack gazed at the land that stretched before them scattered with sheep grazing contentedly. An occasional vibrating bleat of an ewe calling to her lamb added to the tranquillity of the scene. Eucalyptus trees edged the skyline and they strolled towards them almost reverently.

Once there, they stood in the shade of the greenery where the ground was mottled with molten golden nuggets of sunlight as it shimmered through the leaves. Jack slid down the smooth trunk of one tree and sat facing the bucolic view that stretched before him. Edward slumped down beside him and not a word was said as they appreciated the spread of the farmland before them.

Jack took off his hat and scratched his head batting at a lazy fly that had decided to worry him and Edward sighed with a mixture of melancholy and whimsical calm. He was the first to break the placid stillness. "It's beautiful. I don't think I've ever really studied the land before."

Jack replaced his hat, "It's perfect. If you were to stay somewhere forever, where better than this?"

Edward nodded, "Fred would love this." His mouth suddenly contorted in grief, "Why did he have to die? Why?"

Jack shrugged, "His heart just gave out. Stopped beating. Mrs D said he'd had signs of it before. He'd always put it down to indigestion."

"What do you think's going to happen?"

"Don't know. But we best be prepared. Mrs D can't manage the place alone. She could sell up and have a comfortable life in the town," said Jack.

"Or she may carry on and us with her?"

"It's possible."

"Anything's possible."

They sat for a few minutes more surveying the scenic view until Jack slapped his leg and stood brushing off the leaves and grass that had stuck to his trousers. He stretched out his hand to Edward and heaved him up, "Then we're agreed? This is the spot?"

Edward pursed his lips, "It is. Best get back, get a couple of shovels and start digging."

"I'll see if Mrs D wants to take a look. See if she'll give her approval."

"Right," Edward dusted himself off and the two walked back to the farm in quiet reflection. Neither of them knew what was to happen and Jack resolved wordlessly that he would be prepared.

As they reached the farmhouse they saw that Koorong had gathered the surviving members of his village who waited in the yard. They were in some sort of discussion as Jack and Edward went to the silo that housed their tools and selected a couple of picks and spades before returning to the house and stepping onto the veranda, "Mrs D?" called Jack.

Mrs Doble came into view and eyed her workers, "Yes?" Her eyes were red and puffy from crying. Her bearing seemed to have shrunk and Jack thought she looked lost. No longer standing proud with her shoulders back she looked hunched and defeated. Her eyes had lost their keen awareness together with the glint he'd seen earlier and now appeared milky and unseeing.

"Do you want to come and check the place we've found?" asked Jack tentatively.

She nodded, "I'd like to see where he'll be. Is it far?"

"Not at all. Come with us," said Jack softly.

She stepped off the porch and followed them through the yard and out to the open countryside. They led her to the avenue of gum trees that overlooked the expanse of grazing land now covered in sheep. She took a deep breath and tried to swallow the new lump that was manifesting in her throat. Her eyes misted as she struggled with repressed tears and she murmured, "I didn't think I could cry anymore. This is wonderful. I knew you'd find the ideal spot." She scanned the outlook committing every detail to her memory, every blade of grass that swished and rippled in the breeze, each tree and shrub that graced the landscape and the fresh smell of eucalyptus with the sounds of the sheep and birdsong drifting on the warm draughts of air. "Perfect. I'll get back to meet the minister. Do you need any help?"

Edward shook his head, "Me and Jack will manage. We'll see you at the farm."

They stood and watched her make her way back. Her usually bright confident steps had diminished to little more than a shuffle and Jack felt his heart drop despondently.

Edward continued, "She'll never be the same. She's broken. I swear it."

"Aye, you're right. Come on, let's get this done."

They began to work with the pickaxes to break the solid ground and winkle the soil free before they could begin to dig what would be Fred's last resting place.

***

In spite of the developing heat Mrs Doble sat on the porch in her bombazine black widow's weeds. A hat with a black lace front covered her face and hid the damage that her tears had done to her complexion. She carried a fresh dainty handkerchief to dab at any eye that threatened to spill tears. All of the windows to the property were wide open and the doors propped back with flat irons.

Koorong waited with the cart as Daniel and Bobby, shouldered with some difficulty, the home made coffin with Fred's body to Koorong's wagon and loaded it. At the end of the drive, two horse pulled coaches plodded down the track to the farm. Mrs Doble rose ready to greet the minister and guests.

The preacher in his full regalia, clutching his Bible was in the first carriage along with Edgar, Josie and Minnie. The second housed a few more of Fred's friends from the port. The news of his death had travelled to the fort and Sergeant Phillips trooped behind the wagons with several members of his platoon. They halted in the yard outside the farmhouse. The sergeant saluted Mrs Doble and he said simply, "So sorry for your loss. Fred was a good man."

"Yes, he was. Thank you for coming."

The minister, a stout man with a bald head, alighted and mopped at his face with a large white crumpled cotton handkerchief. He spoke quietly to Mrs Doble and she seemed to accept what he said with a nod.

The small solemn party of attendees began to walk towards Fred's final resting place. The cart with his casket rumbled along the track to the pasture and gum trees where Jack and Edward waited. The preacher and mourners with heads bowed, gathered around the open grave as Bobby and Daniel with Jack and Edward's help, lifted the coffin from the dray. Using ropes, they eased it carefully into the pit as the minister, Reverend Wells, began to intone a prayer before reading a short excerpt from the book of Job chapter nineteen verses twenty-five to twenty-seven. He followed this with reading Psalm thirty-nine, which ended.

Hear my prayer, Lord,
listen to my cry for help;
do not be deaf to my weeping.
I dwell with you as a foreigner,
a stranger, as all my ancestors were.
Look away from me, that I may enjoy life again
before I depart and am no more."

The mourners reflected on the words that resonated with every single one of them and bowed their heads in silent prayer before Edgar stepped forward and said a few words extolling Fred's character and loyalty as a friend. Edward sniffed and wiped his arm across his eyes before putting up his hand. The minister engaged his eyes and nodded.

"Fred gave me the only home I knew after my mother died. He expected us to work hard but he paid us for that and he also brought us joy with his sense of fun. I just wanted to say that I will miss him."

Jack looked uncomfortable with this open admission from Edward; he cast his eyes down and took a deep breath to quell his rising emotion. Once back in control he glanced up and the minister signalled to him to toss a spade full of earth over the casket.

The reverend blessed the coffin and all those in attendance before the funeral party processed back to the farm leaving Jack and Edward to fill in the grave. After several shovelfuls Jack stopped, leaned on the handle and gazed over the sweeping vista.

Edward stopped, "What is it?"

Jack looked wistfully at the stretching pasture and swathes of wind grass that rippled in the warm breeze as fluidly as running water; its silky fronds curved and bent with the wind as if bowing in deference to Fred. "I was just thinking, this might be one of the last times we can enjoy the serenity of this land. We might never see the sheep grazing here again or run free without any cares in this place."

Edward shaded his eyes from the growing flare of orange that coloured the sky and dazzled him. "We don't know that," he said defensively.

"I do," said Jack forlornly. "We're on our own now. I just have this feeling." He said no more but continued to fill in the trench. Edward bit the inside of his cheek, a habit he hadn't fully broken. The two friends finally filled the void and the remaining earth was piled dome-like on top, so the grave was clearly marked.

"It needs a cross," said Edward. "A marker to show where he lies."

Jack wiped his arm across his face. They were both sweating profusely. Jack felt a strange comfort in the scratch of the fabric against his weather browned face and blotted the excess moisture that continued to leak at an alarming rate. "I believe Bobby has that in hand. We'll come back later and fix it in the ground. Now, let's get back to the farm."

Weary from digging in such unrelenting heat they plodded back, drained of emotion, their shoulders drooped as if under sentence of death. There was no spring in their step, no joy in their demeanour. They returned in silence out of reverence to Fred who had given them purpose in life and now Jack felt that he had none.

As they neared the farm he lifted his head and his nimble mind continued to work and plan for an uncertain future. They stopped when they reached the yard. They could see Koorong with a few Aboriginal friends and villagers who were fanning aromatic smoke from fires of native leaves in through the open doors and windows. Koorong took a thickly compressed bunch of white sage and lit it. As it began to burn, he blew out the living flame so that it smouldered producing wisps of cleansing smoke and entered the house.

Jack and Edward watched for a moment before venturing into the barn where Mrs Doble had prepared some light refreshments for the mourners to talk and exchange humorous anecdotes about Fred and reminisce about his many qualities. Her manner was stiff and awkward as she conversed with those she didn't really know. Her politeness hid her sadness, which became more apparent when she spoke to Daniel and Bobby's family.

As soon as she saw Jack and Edward, her face suffused with colour and she tapped a spoon on the trestle table to attract attention before speaking, "I'd like to thank you all for coming. Fred would be proud to know that he has such fine and loyal friends. Life here has never been easy but Fred made it what it is. This is hard for me but I have to tell you what I feel." She hesitated in an effort to calm herself and suppressed the tremor in her voice. "Without him I cannot see a future here and I wanted... I needed to tell all of you, together, that I have made a decision." She paused again, took a deep breath and licked her lips before taking a sip of water. She smiled nervously and apologised, "I'm not used to making speeches and my mouth has gone dry like the desert. My lips are sticking to my teeth, forgive me, please." She took another long draught and inhaled deeply, "I have decided to return to England." Her voice cracked and she coughed. Everyone waited until she had recovered sufficiently to continue. Mrs D drew herself up to her full height, "Please don't try and dissuade me. I still have family in England, a brother and three sisters as well as many nephews, nieces and cousins. I don't want to end my life here never seeing them again and dying alone. I know this will come as a shock to many of you but I've made up my mind to return and I trust that you will show consideration for my wishes and decision. That's all." She just managed to control the sob in her voice and hold back the flood of tears waiting to be undammed and released. "Please eat and drink your fill. Now, if you'll excuse me." Mrs Doble left the barn to return to the house.

The mourners appeared stunned by the announcement and whispered quietly amongst themselves. Jack and Edward swapped concerned looks as their greatest fears had come to pass. Jack knew from now on everything would change.

***

It was an hour later that Jack and Edward waved off the funeral party who were returning to Port Jackson with Reverend Wells. Jack and Edward remained subdued and turned to Bobby. "Is the cross ready?"

Bobby nodded, "I'll just get it. It will do until something better can be made."

Jack murmured, "I don't think Fred would worry. He'd be happy with anything." Jack waited quietly until Bobby returned from the workshop with a crude wooden cross that was bound with leather strips tying the crosspiece to the main shaft, and passed it to Jack.

Jack acknowledged Bobby with a smile of acceptance and taking the marker and a mallet he retraced his path to the grave. He went alone. He needed to think.

He ambled slowly in the late afternoon warmth of the sun as if on a carefree country stroll while he ordered his thoughts. Crickets thrummed and joined together in musical harmony with the high-pitched chet chet song of the galahs that flocked to roost in the line of gum trees above the meadow. The fiery setting sun surrounded Jack as he walked on towards the skyline making it seem as if he was marching into an inferno.

Jack stood for a brief moment at Fred's graveside as if he was compelled to say something but instead he focused on hammering in the rough cross to mark where Fred's body lay. Each strike of the mallet brought forward a grunt as he exerted his strength and energy in making the cross secure. He didn't want it tumbling over in brisk winds and rotting on the ground. In view of that he collected some stones and rocks and packed them around the base of the cross.

Now, Jack was alone the unspent tears were allowed to run in rivulets down his cheek. He didn't sob or wail but stared at the mound of earth that housed Fred's cadaver. He was comforted by the fact that no one could hear or see him. He removed his slouch hat and sat under the gum tree staring at the burial pile. His voice when he spoke was shaky, "Well, Fred, I couldn't say ought with everyone 'ere. Not cos I don't care cos I do. You gave me so much more than a job and a place to sleep. You gave me the next best thing to a family, something I never had and I want to thank you for that. It's sad that you've left us and now Mrs D wants to up sticks and go back to England. Can't say I blame her. But I will miss her and her mutton pies and all she's done for me. That's it really. Don't know what I'll do now, maybe find another farm to work on. You've given me the skills to do that. I just wanted this little talk to tell you how I'm thinking. I'm not one for sharing me feelings, never 'ave been. I'm proud to have known you and learned from you. You are someone I'll never forget."

Jack scrambled up, brushed away the last of his tears and returned his hat to his head. He took another long look at the burial mound, "Goodbye, old friend." He turned away and retraced his steps back to the farm.

***

A few days passed as Mrs Doble packed up her clothes into two small bags and other considered essential items and memories went into a sturdy trunk, which were loaded onto one of the carts. Jack and Edward waited outside for her to come out. She stepped onto the porch where she and Fred had sat together night after night and sighed heavily before stepping into the yard. She turned and looked back at the house as if consigning the whole place to her memory. Taking another deep breath, she climbed into the wagon, helped by Edward and sat next to Jack holding the reins and as Edward sat the other side of her Jack made one final plea, "Why not stay?"

Mrs D shook her head, "I want to go back home. I want to die in England."

"Are you certain, Mrs D?"

Not trusting herself to speak she smiled and nodded primly. Jack flicked the reins and the dray drawn by Brutus moved forward and through the yard. Mrs Doble turned for the last time, looking back on her old life and drinking in the memories that liquefied in her mind. Most of the journey towards Port Jackson was spent quietly but as they reached the outskirts of the town Mrs D spoke again. "I need to stop off in Ramsgate Street. There's a company there going to settle my affairs with the farm and whatnot. I'd like you to wait."

"Sure thing, Mrs D," said Edward.

Jack's face was furrowed in a frown as he struggled with his thoughts as he knew, in his heart, what was going to happen. He was determined not to let his despondency get the better of him for his last goodbyes. He knew his future would be unsettled. He would be homeless and jobless again. However, he believed that he and Edward would go forward together and he had some ideas of what they could do.

They circled into Ramsgate Street. The hefty wheels rumbled on the cobbles like a drum major beating out a regular rhythm as if heralding some key announcement. All that was missing was a trumpet fanfare and ceremony. The sky today was unusually gloomy. Weighty grey clouds clumped together masking the sun and customary azure sky, "Getting me ready for England's weather," joked Mrs Doble for want of something better to say. Jack wanted to remark that it matched his sombre mood but something choked the words in his throat so he said nothing.

"Over there!" Mrs Doble pointed at a large building. "Stop there. I won't be too long." Jack dutifully drove the wagon to pause outside the building, which had a fancy sign that Jack couldn't read.

Edward scanned the structure and quietly read the wooden placard in front of the construction. "Bowkett and Bessant Lawyers," before murmuring to Jack, "what are we going to do?" There was hopelessness in his voice.

"We'll survive," said Jack confidently, not wishing to depress Edward. "This is a big old place. I won't get caught this time. I'll teach you the tricks of the trade from my old life. We'll get by. We can travel the roads and through the towns. We may find legitimate work on route. You never know. If not, I know how to earn a penny or two."

"Where will we sleep tonight?" said Edward, his face crumpled in misery.

"We can sell this cart, and Brutus. That'll buy us a few days."

"We should take it back to the farm."

Jack's tone was firm, "We'll sell it."

They sat and waited quietly as the minutes ticked by, each adrift on their own sea of thoughts. Edward was about to speak again when Mrs Doble came out of the building and walked purposefully towards the dray. Edward jumped down and helped her aboard.

"There's a boat next week. I will stay in a hotel until then."

"You could always come back to the farm for now," said Edward hopefully.

"No. I've said my goodbyes. I won't return to the farm again," said Mrs Doble resolutely.

Jack shook the reins again and Brutus plodded on. "Where to, Mrs D?"

"Shepherds Crook Hotel on London Road."

"I know it." Jack redirected the wagon and Brutus and they made their way to the very pleasant, very English, genteel hotel and pulled up outside. Edward hopped down and helped Mrs D out. He collected her bags, which she picked up and wiggled the trunk to the edge of the cart to lift out.

"Oh no, you don't," said Mrs D. "Let me check myself in and you find somewhere safe for the cart. There's a coaching yard at the back, if I remember properly. The Ostler can look after my trunk. The least I can do is give you a treat before we part company. I can't promise your favourite Wonga, Wonga pigeon or mutton pie but they do an excellent English high tea here, from what I remember. Go on. I'll meet you inside in the tea garden."

"What about the weather?" said Edward looking up.

"It'll be fine. Look, the clouds are already dispersing; there's enough blue showing now to make a sailor's pair of trousers. That means the sun is coming out and it will be another fine day tomorrow." Mrs Doble made her way along a short tree lined path to the foyer and reception area. Jack clicked an instruction to Brutus and the faithful horse clip-clopped around to the stabling and coach yard at the back of the hotel.

Fifteen minutes later the three of them were seated around a pine table graced with a fresh, brightly coloured blue gingham cloth with a fine lace overlay. Set on the table was a plate piled high with assorted bread rolls and sandwiches, another laden with a variety of cakes and Mrs D was pouring them each a cup of tea from a dainty teapot into fine porcelain cups.

Jack and Edward were eagerly devouring the snacks on display and showing clear enjoyment of the feast in front of them. Jack bit hungrily into an egg and cress sandwich and used his finger to scoop the oozing soft mashed egg that had dribbled onto his chin into his mouth. "What will you do back in England?" he asked between mouthfuls.

"I'll visit my brother and sisters, if they are still alive, and I have other family that I've yet to meet. You've both grown up and must find your own lives." She leaned down and retrieved her bag from the floor, opened it and took out a large envelope, and removed a document, which she passed to Jack with a smile. "This document gives you both the farm. It's yours now."

Jack went to interrupt, "But…"

Mrs D silenced him with a wave of her hand, "It's been planned for a while now. I have plenty of money to see my life through. Fred wanted it and so do I. My Fred was very fond of you both. Now, you can have the start in life that he never had."

Jack's mouth gaped open in shock. He threw the paper down got up and ran out.

Mrs Doble called after him, "Jack! What's wrong?"

Edward picked up the document, "Jack!" and ran after his friend.

Jack sped down the road into Main Street and stopped at the next corner trying to catch his breath. He punched a wall hard, bruising and bloodying his knuckles just as Edward caught up with him.

"Jack! What's the matter?"

"What did they do that for?" he said as he rubbed his cut fist and became extremely angry. "No one never gave me nothin'. What did they do that for?" The anguish in his voice was plain to hear.

"Jack, they're good people. They want us to be happy," said Edward gently.

"Nah! They want something. No one gives you something for nothin'."

"But…"

"I'm a thief. Always been a thief. I don't want handouts from nobody. If I want something I takes it. Bloody people. Spoil everything, they do."

Edward is bewildered, "Why are you so angry, Dodger?"

"You wouldn't understand." Jack's face turned red with anger. His eyes were smarting as he tried not to cry.

Edward pressed Jack in a stern tone, "What have you been doing?" Jack said nothing but looked down shamefaced. "Jack, what have you done?"

Jack looked up and murmured softly in almost a whimper, "I don't know what to do."

Mystified, Edward asked, "What about?"

"I've been nicking off them for years."

"What?" Edward was flabbergasted.

"I was getting a wedge for us when we were old enough to come back to the port. What am I gonna do?"

"You been stealin' from Fred and Mrs D?"

"Yeah, a bob or two here and there. I saved it, Edward. Nothing to spend it on at the farm. What shall I do?"

"Nothing. If you say anything you'll ruin it all." Edward engaged Jack's eyes and spoke steadily and quietly, "Nothing. Just leave it. It's for the best." Jack began to calm down. His breathing became more even. Edward continued, "This time, you don't have to nick it." He held up the document with its red wax seal. "It's all ours, Dodger."

Jack gave Edward one of his lopsided grins, "At least we won't have to eat mutton pie no more."

Edward grinned back, "I wonder what beef tastes like?"

"Yeah. We can find out, can't we?" Edward nodded and Jack blinked back his tears. "Come on, let's go back."

They turned and made their way back to the hotel where a worried Mrs Doble was standing out in the street. She held out her welcoming arms and Jack snuggled into her. "I'm sorry."

Mrs Doble stroked his head, and murmured soothingly, "It's all right, Jack. All a bit overwhelming, I know. Come now. Let's go and finish that tea."

14: Goodbyes and New Beginnings

Jack and Edward remained in the best side of town with Mrs Doble in Port Jackson until it was time for her to board the ship and set sail. The pair only had what they stood up in and had to make a trip to the market to purchase a few items to keep themselves looking presentable as the Shepherd's Crook Hotel was an establishment that was more upmarket than they had been used to frequenting with Fred.

The three days passed rapidly, filled with accompanying Mrs D to visit friends and acquaintances to say her goodbyes. Jack and Edward made a quick return to the Victoria Hotel and reconnected with Edgar and his daughters promising to return the next time they were in town. They escorted Mrs Doble to the shipping office to purchase her ticket and overheard her say she was travelling first class at which they exchanged a look of surprise but did not comment. Jack knew if ever he returned to England, although he felt that would be unlikely, unless he wanted to be hung that he would have to travel in steerage. They watched her register and left her heavy trunk for luggage handlers and porters to load now that the boat had taken delivery of its supplies for the long journey back to England.

A variety of people were gathered on the quayside as Jack pulled up with the wagon. Jack marvelled at some of the gentlemen and ladies elegantly dressed that waited to board. Ladies in lace, using parasols to shade their faces from the sun and wearing delicate gloves, holding pretty, petite hankies that they could put to their noses to offset some of the offensive pungent smells at the harbour. There were other more ordinary looking, hard working types bunched together, standing behind a stout rope to separate them from the monied passengers who were also waiting to embark.

Jack and Edward jumped down and helped Mrs D from the wagon. Jack secured the dray to an iron ring used for mooring on the dock while Edward collected her luggage. They embraced her for the very last time warmly, feeling her love run through them both, right to their bones. Jack had a quick thought that this was what mother love must have felt like. She finally disentangled herself, "Now, we must say goodbye. Be strong, both of you. Don't make this harder than it is." She paused and inhaled deeply to steady herself and make her words clear. "You have a bright future ahead of you. I promise you that." She studied them again as if committing their features to memory.

She brushed a lock of Jack's stubborn hair away from his eyes and gently caressed Edward's face sprouting with bristles. "I will always think of you as my boys."

Edward rubbed at a stray tear that had somehow dodged being blinked back. He picked up her two bags and passed them to her, sniffing vigorously. Jack didn't trust himself to look at Edward but watched Mrs D start for the gangplank where a sailor stood welcoming those who came aboard. She stopped, turned and came back to them and said quietly, "Another thing… It's been more than enough years since your escape and you came to us. No one will be looking for you now. No one. As far as the law goes you don't exist. You're free." Jack and Edward traded looks. Jack noted that Edward's mouth had gaped open as if he was catching flies and Jack was none too certain that he wasn't doing the same but Mrs D hadn't finished. She had another ton of feathers to drop on their heads. "The very last thing I want you to do, is to see Mr Bessant at Bowkett and Bessant. Do you remember where that is?"

"The lawyers? Yes, I remember," said Edward looking bewildered.

Mr Bessant wanted to see you after I'd gone. Go there today. This will be the last thing you do for me." She set down her bags and gave them another hug, holding tightly to them both and was afraid to speak but she managed to whisper softly, "Be happy." With that she dropped her arms, retrieved her luggage and glided to the gang plank where she was ushered up by the sailor. She didn't stop and she didn't look back. Jack and Edward watched her walk, her proud bearing accentuated by the fine clothes, which they had never seen her wear before that seemed to set her apart from them and their class.

They stood transfixed until she disappeared out of sight and remained there for some minutes, motionless and quiet, staring at the ship until Edward finally came to as if brought out from a trance. "Come on, we best get over there now and obey her last wishes." Jack remained stock-still hardly daring to breathe. "Jack!"

The insistent tone in Edward's voice seemed to wake him from his standing slumber and he shook himself. "Yes, of course. We'll do what's right." The two of them untied the cart and turned it around to make their way back to the solicitors' office.

***

The wagon rolled forward driven gingerly up the slope to the road. The regular beat of the wheels boomed as they resounded and rattled when they met the complaining cobbles punctuating their mood and indicative of time passing. They passed through the less salubrious part of town and entered the more exclusive neighbourhood. Bowkett and Bessant's office was ahead. Jack stopped opposite the white stucco building where they both alighted. They stood there a few minutes studying the place in order to gather the courage to enter. Any place of authority made them both nervous.

Jack was the first one to move, "Come on, let's go in and get it over with." He walked with more confidence than he felt and opened the door. Edward quickly followed. They entered a small, dingy hallway that belied the outside of the construction, which had stout wooden doors leading off and a staircase with wrought iron bannisters. Jack was confused, "Where do we go?"

Edward studied the signs on the doors, "Over here." He pointed to the name, Bessant, "Must be this one." He knocked politely and opened the door to a small outer office, which housed a heavy mahogany desk in front of a tall cupboard. The bureau had piles of papers sitting either side of a clerk, almost boxing him in. He appeared to be a tall, thin older man with spindly arms. He wore a yellowing shabby powdered wig that was favoured by the judiciary of the day.

Jack was reminded of some kind of insect as the man, with his twig-like hands, wielded a quill pen that scratched across parchment document he was working on. The desk had a name plate, which meant nothing to Jack but read, 'Mr Spanner – Clerk'. Jack cleared his throat and the man lifted up his jaundiced eyes and questioned, "Yes, gentlemen? Can I help you?" His voice was oily and the words slithered from him like a snake with a slight hiss.

Jack's voice was controlled and even, "Can we see Mr Bessant please?"

An eager look lit, almost ferally, in the man's cobra hooded eyes, "You would be Mr Dawkins and Mr Hargreaves," he said nodding as if to make them affirm their identity.

Edward responded with a puzzled, "Yes," while Jack was silenced and now looked uncomfortable.

"You are expected," he announced with an insipid smile. Spanner rose and his legs were as skeletal as the rest of him. He stepped out from behind his desk; his boots clicked like crab claws on the hard, tiled floor and he rapped on a door leading to an inner office.

A voice within called, "Enter."

Spanner went inside and the sound of fevered, excited whispering could be heard but the words were not discernible. Jack and Edward waited until the clerk materialised. His jaded complexion now had some colour and his lizard grin appeared to welcome them. "Please go in. Mr Bessant is waiting for you."

Jack tried to shrug off his misgivings about the insectile manner of the clerk and cautiously followed Edward into the office's inner sanctum. The difference in the two rooms and men was remarkable. Mr Bessant was as short as Spanner was tall. He was portly with a cherubic face and a healthy bloom to his cheeks. He had a pleasant demeanour and engagingly expressive face. His gold rimmed spectacles gave him an owl-like wisdom filled appearance. The wig of his profession was smart, neat and white, almost giving him an angelic halo in the bright, clean impressive chamber where sunlight's fingers reached in through the window and tickled Bessant's face. Book shelves were ordered and filled with erudite weighty tomes, and the highly polished desk gleamed in the afternoon. He stood against his desk and held out his hands in welcome and firmly clasped Jack's left and Edward's right wrists. His voice when he spoke was resonant and earnest, his attitude congenial; he seemed delighted to see them, "Ah, Mr Jack and Mr Edward. Thank you for coming so promptly." A merry twinkle glimmered in his eye as he asked, "Now, I am wondering, which is which?" he looked from one to the other as would a mother bird surveying her nest of chicks.

"I'm Jack."

Bessant nodded affably. He indicated two smart, plum velvet covered chairs and cordially invited them to sit, "Please be seated, gentlemen." The deference in his tone was in sharp contrast to anyone else they had ever spoken to or met. Edward visibly relaxed at this unexpected respectful note in his voice and took a chair. Jack also sat. but on the edge of his seat. They faced Mr Bessant who returned to his side of the desk, opened a drawer and removed a file. He peered at it before looking at them over the tops of his glasses and smiled amiably. "This is it. Now, I have instructions from Mr Fred Doble concerning your futures. Mrs Doble has I believe, informed you of the transfer of the sheep farm to your good selves?" he beamed at them again seeming delighted at their good fortune.

Edward responded cordially, "She has, thank you, kindly."

"She has not, because she never knew, informed you of Mr Fred's interest in gold."

"Gold?" said Jack in surprise.

"Yes, Mr Jack. Gold." Jack and Edward exchanged a look of wonder. "Have you ever heard of a town north of here called Bathurst?" Jack and Edward shook their heads. "Remember the name, Bathurst. Last year there was talk of gold found on the outskirts of Bathurst. Mr Fred sent one of his aboriginal friends to check the location who had a friend in the Waradjuri tribe who confirmed that gold was indeed there, but no white man had discovered it. Fred instructed me to purchase, on his behalf, many acres of land in that area, which, as per my instructions, I did. Earlier this year gold was discovered in quantity on the land. It was discovered after Mr Fred spread some anonymous rumours in a few bars around town; now, many colonists are arriving here. You will be very rich. The government of New South Wales paid Mr Fred ten thousand pounds." Mr Bessant paused. He clearly enjoyed the stunned expressions on both clients' faces and the fact he'd rendered them speechless. He continued, "What? I hear you ask. What has this to do with us?" He wagged his finger at them, "And I say, what a very good question. And I will answer it in the following manner. Everything!" Jack and Edward traded another look of stunned disbelief. "It is all yours, Mr Edward. Mr Fred has given it all to you! Or rather he transferred it all into your name." Mr Bessant could barely keep his hands still with the excitement of what he was imparting. He seemed to love the drama of the situation and built on it. He removed a sheet of paper from the file. "I have taken the liberty of opening a client account at my bank in your name. This is the current balance."

With a flourish like a magician performing a difficult but spellbinding trick he made the announcement. All that was missing was the percussive roll of drums. "A little under twenty-two thousand at the moment and it will increase considerably."

Edward's voice was barely a whisper, "But why? Why did he do it? I don't understand."

Bessant's smile grew broader and his elation was apparent. He paused so that the full effect of his words would put them even more in awe of the news, if that was at all possible. His tone became measured and reasoned, "Mr Edward, you were, or I should say, are, Mr Fred's grandson."

Jack's jaw fell slack and his eyes almost popped as Edward murmured, "His..."

"Grandson! Yes!" said Bessant with glee.

Jack had been listening carefully but still couldn't reconcile himself with this information, "How do you know?"

"Let us suppose that when Mr Fred left England, he left behind a wife and daughter. That said, the then Mrs Fred, did not wish any communication with him owing to his bigamy with the current Mrs Fred."

"Bigamy?" Edward's voice was shocked.

"That was the reason for his transportation. Bigamy. A couple of years later he learned that Mrs Fred had died and that his daughter had married a Mr Benjamin Hargreaves. Is that correct? Mr Benjamin Hargreaves was the name of your father?"

"Yes," Edward was in such a daze he could only answer monosyllabically.

"And they moved around owing to his work with the railway?"

"Yes."

"Mr Fred wanted to send money but we could not find a permanent address. We then found out that Benjamin Hargreaves had been killed in an accident on the railway and that his daughter had died of consumption. Is that correct?"

"Yes."

"Mr Fred had no idea that he had a grandchild until you mentioned your father's work and the manner of both their deaths. What was your mother's given name?"

"Rachel."

"Quad erat demonstrandum! The son of Benjamin and Rachel Hargreaves is you, Mr Edward. Mr Fred's grandson! Did your mother ever tell you her maiden name?"

"No."

"It was Doble."

"Why did he never tell me?" Edward's eyes had grown brighter.

"Because of the present Mrs Fred. He did not want to upset the applecart, so to speak." Mr Bessant then turned his eyes on Jack. "Mr Jack, Fred looked on you both as his sons. Mrs Doble and he were never blessed. Whenever Mr Fred came into town we would meet. He always spoke highly of *his boys*."

Edward shook his head trying to grasp everything he'd been told while Jack just stood there looking astonished. Edward managed to mumble, "But... he never said..."

Mr Bessant chuckled. It was a warm throaty sound. "You don't understand, do you? It was because you made Mrs Fred happy. And he was happy because she was happy. It's that simple." He flapped his arms about, "I know, I know. It's a lot to take in." He beamed at the dumbfounded pair, picked up a small brass hand bell and rang it looking towards the door, which opened almost immediately.

Mr Spanner's head swivelled around the opening and he asked, "Now?"

"Now," asserted Mr Bessant who couldn't look more pleased than if he'd been showered in gold. Spanner retracted his head leaving the door ajar.

"This calls for a celebration. A drink together, gentlemen, if I might humbly suggest and then I need you to sign some papers." His fingers played with his cuffs as Spanner came in holding a tray with a decanter and four glasses. "A little port wine, gentlemen." Spanner poured from the decanter and passed the glasses around. "I miss Fred. We were old friends from way back. We were shipped over here together."

"What? You were transported?" said Jack in amazement.

"But you're a lawyer," added Edward.

Bessant chuckled, "Obviously not a very clever one." He looked around them again, threw his head back and laughed uproariously, so much so, everyone joined in.

Jack and Edward sipped the full bodied warming liquid, which was not yet to their taste, having never before consumed it. But, by the end of the glass a nod of appreciation passed between the two.

Mr Bessant signalled to Spanner to replenish the glasses while he took out various documents. He passed them to Edward to read who in turn handed them to Jack who pretended to review the subject matter and passed them back.

Mr Bessant indicated where they should both sign. Edward added his signature first and gave the pen to Jack who scrawled his name and returned the pen to Mr Bessant who smiled beatifically at them both. "Well, young sirs. That I believe concludes our business for today. Do you have the transfer documents in your possession?" Edward nodded. "Then all is well. Do remember to call in from time to time and if there is anything I can help you with, be assured that I am here at your convenience just as I always was for Mr. Fred."

Mr Spanner indicated the decanter, which he lifted in his bony hand, "One more before you leave? After all it is a very special day," he said servilely in his reedy voice.

Mr Bessant sighed serenely, "Of course. One more won't hurt. After all, it's not every day a client of mine comes into a fortune."

Spanner scuttled with a tip tap of his boots across the floor to them to refill the glasses. Jack was reminded of a spider whose rapid sudden movements on the silken strands of a web would terrorise a tangled trapped fly. He gave an involuntary shiver, which he hurriedly turned into a toast, lifting up his port, "To Edward and his great good fortune, grandson of Mr Fred." Edward couldn't prevent the grin spreading across his face and Mr Bessant joined in joyfully. Mr Spanner lifted his glass in his bony knotted fingers and put it to his slit of a mouth. They drained their glasses and Jack and Edward left the office, stepped out into the fresh air feeling slightly tipsy.

Jack giggled as he slipped before climbing up to take the reins. Edward clambered up the other side. They were both grinning like lunatics scarcely able to believe what had just transpired. "Did you see?" asked Edward joyfully.

"What?" asked Jack as he flicked the reins and urged Brutus forward. "Mrs D."

"What about her?"

"In all the years we lived with them. I never once heard Fred call her by her first name."

"Why? What is it? She's always just been Mrs D."

"Her signature..." He paused to keep Jack in suspense.

"What? Don't tease."

"Ellen. Her name is Ellen Doble.'

"Ellen Doble," repeated Jack. "That's a lovely name."

"It is, isn't it?"

They plodded along the road and turned the corner into main street and started moving through the less wholesome part of town where two men brawled outside a bar. The boys looked across as three drunkards fell out of a bar on the street and began to jeer at the men who were so full of ale they couldn't have hit a wall let alone each other. They slipped into the road and lay there looking dizzy. The three inebriates roared with laughter. They didn't give Edward or Jack a second glance but Jack's blood ran cold as he recognised the flame red hair of Rust, and his minions, Masters and McQueen. Jack gulped, turned his head and focused on the road ahead. The smile had fled his face. He took a sidelong look at Edward who was oblivious to the three roughnecks' identities. And, as they cleared the bar Jack urged Brutus into a trot. Edward was still eulogising about the surprising news they had received.

"That Mr Bessant was a jolly bloke," said Edward. "Very pleasant. Mind you... he would be if he was Fred's friend. Wonder why he didn't come to the funeral?"

"Too busy, I guess."

"Hmm. I expect so. What did you think of the other one, the clerk, Mr Spanner?"

"Didn't like him. He gave me the creeps."

"He was a bit strange in appearance. Can't condemn a man for that."

"No and I've met worse."

"Like who?"

"Bill Sikes and Rust. Did you see back there?"

"What? The fight?"

"Yes, the men who were cheering."

"Didn't take any notice."

"That's just as well," said Jack.

"Why?"

"It was Rust and his henchmen. They're out now. Must have served their time."

Edward looked alarmed, "Did he see us?"

"He did and he didn't bat an eyelid. He didn't know either of us. Mr D was right. No one will know us now."

***

Back in Mr Bessant's office, the lawyer sat with a silly smile on his face still supping port. Spanner entered and sprawled in the chair opposite holding a glass.

"I think, Mr Spanner that went rather well," said Bessant looking pleased.

"I agree, Mr Bessant," said Spanner as he took another swig. His chameleon-like eyes pivoted slyly before he pronounced, "Peasants and lummoxes are two words that spring to mind when describing Mr Dawkins and his friend."

"Very apt, Mr Spanner." He sighed contentedly, "You know, I love dealing in probate. There is so much money to be made."

Spanner gave another gaping grin, "Some more port, Mr Bessant?"

"If you please."

Spanner rose and tipped up the decanter filling both glasses once more. He rubbed his insectile hands together in smugness before picking up his drink and holding it aloft, "To us and peasants and lummoxes," and he guffawed.

"This is the big one that we've been waiting for. We can retire in less than six months. But we must be careful. They won't be so lenient with us this time."

"They can't prove anything. We've given them more money than they could have dreamed of. And why retire? The gold keeps coming in and we keep paying them a little and we keep getting richer. I like it!"

"To us, Mr Spanner."

"Yes, to us, Mr Bessant."

"However, we must be vigilant this time. Not as before, my dear Spanner."

"You will never let me forget, will you?"

"Simply a reminder. We would not be here were it not for you."

"I promise you I will never again probate a will whilst the testator is still alive. Is that good enough for you?"

"I would have thought, in general, that was a sound rule of thumb. Also, this time do not give the widow her estate until the husband has passed. When she asks him to explain the paucity of her inheritance he should not be alive to tell her that lawyers have embezzled the rest. But look on the bright side. Fred Doble is definitely dead. Happy days, Mr Spanner. Happy days." They chinked glasses once more and Mr Bessant afforded himself another riotous laugh.

***

The journey back to the farm was made in a state of euphoria. Edward was looking happier than he had ever been in his life, while Jack, although pleased, was more thoughtful. He shook his head to clear his mind of the drink that seemed to have given him some type of brain fog.

"Just think, Jack. We can do anything. Anything we like. We will be sitting pretty for the rest of our lives." Edward smiled serenely and sighed in satisfaction.

"I am thinking; and having the farm is more than we could ever have hoped for. But the gold is yours, Edward. Not mine and the farm must continue to pay its way. We have to consider how that will work. I'm thinking now, there's no Mrs D to welcome us back with a feast fit for a king. We've got to work out how to look after ourselves and the farm."

Edward glanced across. "I shouldn't worry. I've got enough to get us a cook and cleaner. We have Koorong and Minjarra and there's Daniel and Bobby."

"They will continue to work for us, for sure. But we have to figure out some kind of plan. If only I hadn't drunk so much port wine."

Edward laughed and said, "And there's more where that came from. I shall go into town and get our supplies including some of that ruby delight. I'll have a word with Edgar and see if he can recommend someone to help in the house. You wait and see. It's the beginning of a new era for us."

Jack grinned, "As you wish. Like you said, you can do anything now." Jack urged Brutus into a trot and concentrated on the track ahead while his mind began to try and make sense of everything that had happened and what his next move would be.

Back at the farm, Jack and Edward sat at the scrubbed pine table. The fire on the range had gone out, "First things first," said Jack taking charge. "We need to get this lit and make ourselves a pot of tea. Check the larder and you can make a list of what we will need. Then we should call a meeting with Koorong and the others. The farm still has to survive, we have sheep to feed and look after. We can't do it alone."

"Agreed. What's the plan?"

"I'm still figuring that out. I'll keep thinking while I clear the ashes, you get the wood. Let's get this lit and have some grub to soak up that drink."

***

The following morning, Jack and Edward convened a meeting between themselves and their workers, "So you see, the farm is now ours. We want to assure you that nothing work wise will change. We still want you all to work here and we will pay you the same as our boss but with a few other changes. Edward and I will be moving into the farmhouse. We hope to get some help with looking after the place and feeding us otherwise I reckon we'll all starve." Everyone around the table chuckled at this. "Koorong, the main body of your villagers who work here can stay in the dormitory barn, if you want and you and Minjarra will take over what was our quarters. It'll be more comfortable for you both."

Edward chipped in, "We are proposing that once things are settled, however long that will take, that we will run the farm on a different footing. The time will come that, you Koorong, and Daniel and Bobby will take over the day to day running of the farm. You'll be responsible for everything and it will run on a profit shared basis." There was a gasp from the boys. "We will all have an equal stake in the place. So, the farm will run well whether we are here or not. It is an incentive for you to make it work as you will, in effect, be working for yourselves. I will get the papers drawn up properly and you will all have contracts so that should anything happen to either one of us the farm will go on as our boss would have wanted. This is a chance to grow and for you all to benefit from our good fortune and to make the place bigger and better than ever. It won't happen at once but it will happen."

"Also," interjected Jack, "there has to be trust and I know I can trust all of you. When you go to the port markets and auctions it will be the responsibility of Daniel and Bobby to play fair with Koorong. As you know, he won't be able to spend time there as it's not safe for him. Any questions?"

The assembled group sat in stunned amazement. Bobby was the first to speak. He stood up and shook everyone's hand. "We're all going to be partners. It's a great day for all of us. Thank you, Jack, Edward. No one has ever done anything like this for me before."

"And no one had done anything like this for us either," said Jack. "It's all thanks to... well, you know who."

"Right. Let's get out there and get to work. There's shearing to be done and wool to be packed. We've a busy season ahead."

The workers left the table with smiles on their faces as big as was imaginable. They went out chattering excitedly and Edward and Jack grinned and shook hands. "That was the right thing to do," said Edward. "It was a great idea of yours, Jack. And now I must get to town. We need provisions and someone to 'do' for us."

Jack nodded, "I'll check on the flock on the far side and get them back for shearing. The Merino are already penned. See you later." He put on his slouch hat and left the house. Things had changed so fast he needed more time to think and he could do that best alone. Something else was bothering him and brewing in his mind. He just needed to work out what it was and then he would act on it.

15: Future Plans

Changes were happening fast at the farm and life was as busy as ever but much more enjoyable now the team were working for themselves. They were all more driven to do their very best. On one of his many trips to Port Jackson Edward had hired a live in cook come housekeeper, Miss Delia Bonnet, a plump spinster, in her mid-forties, with a pleasant homely face who relished looking after the team. She was pleased to be retained by them, as her previous employer, an elderly bachelor, had recently died and she had come highly recommended by Edgar. Her name suited her well as she was given to wearing an old fashioned cotton mop cap edged with lace, underneath which she tucked her hair that was loosely encased in a bun, which was prone to releasing tendrils of grey hair that stuck to her skin when she cooked at the range.

"Pleased to welcome you, Miss Bonnet," said Jack when he greeted her. "I reckon if you hadn't come along we'd have all died of starvation."

"Oh, go on with you! I'm sure you would have managed somehow. I can give you lessons in cookery, if you've a mind. Not that I want to put myself out of a job, but there will be a few occasions when I will have to step away from the farm. Not for more than two or three days, just enough time to visit my brother and his family. Mr Edward said it would be all right," said Miss Bonnet seeing Jack's look of consternation.

"And so, it shall," agreed Jack. "Tell me, where do you hail from with a voice like that?"

"Ah, we were originally from South Wales."

"And moved here to New South Wales?" Jack said with a twinkle in his eye.

"Aye. You'd think I'd have lost my accent the years I've been here but no, it still comes out, especially when I get cross or I read aloud. Do you like poetry, Mr Jack?"

"Never tried it. Does it taste nice?"

Miss Bonnet laughed, "You are a one. Mr Edward said you were a joker."

"Let me get your bag and I'll show you your room and the kitchen."

"That would be lovely, so it would. Thank you."

***

Edward had come good on his promise about relieving the past tedium of mutton pie, although it had always tasted good, and for the first time in their lives the young men

147

sampled beef. It was as succulent and delicious as they had both hoped, especially when Miss Bonnet cooked it encased in pastry and it was well-seasoned with mustard. There was much more variety in her cooking and evening meals were full of lively conversation.

Miss Bonnet had an engaging personality with a jolly manner. She especially enjoyed the back chat she got from Jack, who would tease her about wishing he was twenty years older and he'd make an honest woman of her. She was someone who talked in pictures and had a strong Welsh lilt to her voice, which they learned came from her parents long since passed who had travelled to Australia in search of a better life. The farmhouse was kept spotless, the table scrubbed every day and Jack commented, "Everything's fresh and clean but you, Miss B, you're not obsessive about it, like plumping up the cushions as soon as we stand up, like they do at the Shepherd's Crook."

"That's because I know how annoying that kind of fastidious behaviour can be."

"And how do you know that?"

"My sister-in-law." Miss Bonnet sighed long-sufferingly, "I love her dearly but she's so blooming house proud, she even puts paper underneath the cuckoo clock."

Jack roared with laughter. He believed things couldn't get any better. They were getting a name for themselves around the town and people seemed to want to make their acquaintance of which Jack was always suspicious, while Edward was more than happy to make new friends.

It was Edward who suggested that they bought a more suitable carriage for their new standing in society.

"But what's wrong with the cart?" asked Jack.

"It's fine for work and transporting goods but not for arriving as guests to dinner or going out on the town."

"But we don't get invited to dinner," protested Jack.

"Nor will we unless we address our manner of dress and mode of transport. We'll take the wagon into Port Jackson tomorrow and you can drive it back. I am going to purchase something more impressive."

Jack shrugged, "It's your money, Edward. Do what you wish. I'm fine with Brutus and the dray."

"Just you wait and see what I come back with. I know you'll be pleased and enjoy it."

"Very well. We're taking wool to the market and getting supplies tomorrow. You can do your private shopping then."

***

The following morning in Port Jackson the wool bales were unloaded and stacked in their designated spot. Jack waited to meet the merchant, while Bobby and Daniel remained with him. Filled with enthusiasm Edward left the quay and went off into the town. The dockside was busier than usual as a passenger ship had docked and Jack watched the travellers disembarking with interest.

Three young ladies waited for their luggage with whom he presumed was their mother, or some other relative who was fussing around them unnecessarily. They were attractive wenches with wasp waists that caught the eyes of the young men who were not averse to staring at the beauties. The girls basked in the attention from them and tossed them an occasional smile, tilting their heads to the side and eyeing them flirtatiously. The young women chattered excitedly amongst themselves occasionally peeking at the men mischievously and giggling while the older lady reprimanded them. The girls huddled together whispering frenziedly and while the older lady was engaged with one of the porters one of them was pushed forward by the others.

She smiled coquettishly at Jack as she approached him, fluttering her eyelashes. The other girls giggled some more. "Excuse me, sir. I wondered if you could tell us the way to the Shepherd's Crook Hotel? And where we might get someone to help transport us and our luggage."

Jack touched his hat deferentially. His dimpled cheeky smile transformed his face and he looked positively handsome. "I can certainly direct you to the hotel. It's in London Road and if you walk up the slope from the quay you should be able to find a carriage to take you there. I shall be going along there myself after I have concluded my business."

"Oh? How lucky. Maybe you could offer us a seat on your mode of transport?" She eyed him coyly.

"Unfortunately, no. I have some matters to attend to before returning to wait for my partner to come back and then we will be along."

"Such a pity! Maybe we will see you later, in the tea garden, perhaps? I hear it is an excellent place."

"Maybe, Miss...?"

"Miss Lennox, Ruby Lennox. Those are my sisters."

Jack glanced back at them and they each gave him a small wave just as the older lady returned shaking her parasol at the girls.

"And that's my Aunt Mary!"

"Miss Ruby Lennox," boomed her aunt's voice. "Come here at once!" Ruby bowed her head and gave Jack a beaming smile before fleeing back to her aunt's side.

Daniel and Bobby sidled up to Jack, "What did she want?"

"Help with their luggage and a ride to the hotel."

"Did you say, yes?"

"No, just maybe. I think I'm seeing them later... Do you fancy helping me out, lads? I can't manage all three," said Jack with a grin.

"That's four with mother," said Bobby cheekily.

"That's their aunt," corrected Jack.

Just then the merchant arrived and Jack began bargaining with the man. The deal was done swiftly and Jack counted and pocketed the money. The three of them boarded the wagon to make their way to the bank. They passed the gaggle of women stepping into a carriage and pair. Ruby caught Jack's eye and gave him a sneaky wave but her hand was slapped down by her aunt.

***

Mr Pinch acknowledged Jack with a raised hand as he approached the teller and removed the money received for the wool. Jack peeled off some notes and passed them to Daniel and Bobby and found himself repeating the same words that Mr Fred had said to him when he first came to the port. "I won't give you all your wages in case you're tempted to blow the lot. Easy to get carried away here with gambling, women and what-not."

Bobby grinned and said, "You sound like Fred. Don't worry. We'll be fine. We've learned from our previous mistakes, haven't we, Daniel?"

Daniel affirmed with a nod, "You can give us the rest at the farm. Put the profit into the farm account."

Jack finished completing the numbers on his deposit form with Mr Pinch, checked the ledger and showed the account to Daniel and Bobby who nodded in satisfaction. "Right, well I'll see you at the Tea Garden, then?"

"Not for us," said Bobby. "We're off to the Victoria."

"Yes, seeing Minnie and Josie, if they can get an hour or two off."

"Have fun. You realise you're leaving me with three very attractive young ladies?"

"You'll manage. Mind you I'd be wary of the aunt. Think she might end up beating you about the head with her parasol," said Daniel with a laugh.

"I hope she'll be well tucked up in bed by the time I get there... maybe a complimentary sherry will help her to sleep," joked Jack. "Besides, I have to get back to meet Edward. I may see you later, if not, tomorrow at ten. You better take the wagon and stable it at the Victoria. I can ride back with Edward if he's managed to buy something else."

The boys slapped Jack on the back and left the bank larking about playfully and laughing. Jack waited for Mr Pinch to make an entry in Jack's personal bank book and glanced around the bank. He was interested to see Mr Bessant in deep conversation at the counter with another clerk. Jack watched covertly, and his eyes narrowed as the spindly figure of Spanner scuttled through the door, his coat tails flapping like the carapace of a beetle preparing to fly. They exchanged a few words and Spanner passed Bessant a sheet of paper, which the lawyer perused and signed before he beamed benignly at his clerk who was looking thrilled. Bessant folded up the document and secreted it in his inside coat pocket, patted it and the two turned to leave together chuckling, oblivious that they were being watched.

Jack leaned over the counter to Mr Pinch, "Mr Pinch, those two men over there," he indicated the duo as they went out through the door.

Mr Pinch peered over his owl-like frames to see who Jack meant, "Ah! Mr Bessant and Mr Spanner. Two of the bank's best customers."

"Really?"

"Why? Do you know them?"

"I believe Mr Edward does," lied Jack glibly.

Mr Pinch gave one of his rare smiles; his gold tooth flashed in the sunlight. "I understand one of their many investments has born fruition. It has been quite the talk of the bank."

Jack assimilated this knowledge and nodded affably, "Good luck, eh? Interesting. Do you happen to know what investment?"

"Mr Pinch thought for a moment and pursed his lips making him look even more owl-like. "I'm not absolutely certain but I think it was something to do with gold."

Jack gave a half smile, "Yes, gold is a big subject in the bars and markets. Well done them," he said glibly. "I believe Bathurst is particularly popular at the moment for prospector's claims."

Mr Pinch nodded vigorously, "Yes, I have heard that said and I'm not sure but that may have been mentioned by Mr Bessant in passing."

"Really?"

"I shouldn't say anymore, not without all the facts. It's not good to gossip." Mr Pinch passed Jack his bank book for him to check.

Jack examined the figures, "Thank you, Mr Pinch. See you next time." The teller smiled affably and returned to sorting through a pile of files.

***

Jack was absorbed in his own thoughts as he made his way back to the quay from the bank. He enjoyed the walk even though the sun was now at its height and the temperature had risen considerably. He passed some of the more fancy properties with carriages that sat waiting on the drive to do their owners' bidding. He moved on into Main Street that led to the docks where doxies waited for gentlemen. He smiled at some who called out his name but wouldn't be drawn into any conversation. As he reached the slope he heard a shrill whistle and someone shouted, "Jack!"

Jack glanced around and saw a fine, impressive open two horse carriage with Edward holding the reins. Jack crossed to greet his friend.

"Isn't this something, Jack?" Edward grinned with pride. "It's ours to use whenever either of us wants to."

Jack walked around the vehicle; he checked the chassis, undercarriage and running gear, particularly examining the wheels and axles. He paid attention to the straps that rested around the horses' haunches that were attached to the shafts of the carriage before looking at the harnesses and then finally at the horses themselves. They were two beautifully turned out chestnuts with a white blaze on their noses. They looked like twins. Jack gave a nod of approval and clambered up next to Edward who merely grinned.

Edward turned the carriage and urged the steeds into a trot and they left the quayside, travelled through the main body of the town and proceeded to an outlying district with distinctive and palatial properties. Jack gazed about him and frowned, "Where we going, Edward?"

"It won't be long now," said Edward with a fixed grin on his face.

"But, I got girls waiting for me at the Shepherd's Crook." Edward's smile deepened and he flicked the reins spurring on the steeds as Jack looked about him.

The road widened and Edward slowed the horses to a walk when they reached a fancy stone wall and a pair of intricately ornate but sturdy gates. Edward jumped down and undid the latch and pushed the gates open. He was amused by Jack's bewildered expression as he climbed back onboard and turned the carriage driving it through the gates and up the extensive drive.

"What are you doing?" asked Jack, a note of panic entering his voice. "Come on, let's get out of here before we get nicked."

Edward took no notice of his friend but pulled up before the sweeping steps that led to a pillared front door. He jumped down and sat on the steps and raised his arms, "Do you like it, Dodger?"

"What?"

"The house. Cos it's ours!"

Jack alighted and sat next to Edward, "You're barmy."

"It's ours, Jack. I bought it for us... or rather we bought it together. I signed a document at the lawyers that made us partners in everything. Everything split straight down the middle, the money coming in, the lot!" Jack sat looking stunned. His jaw had dropped open to a wide unbelieving 'O'. Edward put his fingers under Jack's chin and closed Jack's gaping mouth. "I would never have made it without you, Jack. You looked after me, right at the start, all the way through everything. You have always been at my side." Edward looked reflective and gave an amused snort. "My mum said I would live like a king and now I'm going to. And you with me. We're going to live better than we could have ever imagined." He removed a large key from his jacket pocket, "Want to look inside?" Edward scrambled up and mounted the steps. He inserted the key in the lock turned it and pushed it wide open. "Jack?"

Jack was still sitting looking dazed. He hurriedly wiped the wet skin under his eyes before darting up and following Edward inside. He turned around in the large imposing hallway, with its marble pillars and an inspiring curved oak staircase such as Jack had never before seen. A decorative plaster frieze ran around the top of the walls and above them was an elaborate ceiling rose, which in itself was a work of art, from which hung a lavish unlit candle chandelier. "Come and see, I'll give you the grand tour." He glanced at Jack, "I should shut your mouth if I were you, you never know what might fly into it!" jested Edward. "It's ours, honest. Yours and mine."

The downstairs was grand by any standard and expansive. Several rooms ran off from the hallway and a corridor led down to a large kitchen where there were a series of labelled bells on a long panel. Bright copper pans and kitchen utensils hung from a rack, "Do you think Miss Bonnet will like this? This is a mansion to make any housekeeper proud."

Jack was unable to speak as he stared around him in disbelief. His tour of the house was a blur. The décor was opulent, the furniture sumptuous. There were so many reception rooms, Jack lost count; each one was given their official names by Edward as he ushered Jack through them, the dining room, drawing room, library and study to mention a few.

Upstairs was equally luxurious; there were several bedrooms with rich brocade curtains and four poster beds. "I can see you wondering how I managed it?"

"I don't understand."

"I had help, I bought this place awhile back after I got my inheritance. It was partly furnished and the rest I did. What do you think?"

"I ain't never been in anything like this in me life," said Jack in his common cockney accent, which always came out much stronger when he was annoyed or surprised. "And it's ours?"

"It is."

"What about the farm?"

"That's something to talk about but we have enough from Fred's gold investments to keep us comfortable for the rest of our lives. We should maintain our interest in the farm, but let the others run with it. Like you've said they'll have an incentive to keep it going, working for themselves and we can check on it from time to time."

Jack marvelled at this news, the vastness of the space and Ruby Lennox and her sisters went right out of his head. "So, no hotel for us tonight?"

"No, you can pick your bedroom and tomorrow you can collect your things together with Miss Bonnet. Now, let's go and get something to eat."

***

That night Jack went to bed in his new surroundings in something of a happy daze. He was finding it hard to believe everything that had transpired. Things like this never happened to people like him but he knew his future was assured thanks to Edward. However, something still niggled him and he finally fell asleep with a million thoughts rambling through the trellis of his mind.

Jack fell into a fitful sleep that drifted into deep slumber. His eyes moved rapidly from side to side as if viewing a countryside scene from a carriage. Mr Fred's face zoomed in and out of focus with Mrs D wagging her finger at him and laughing. Bill Sikes leered and waved his cudgel that was covered in blood and human tissue, while Fagin whispered Jack's deepest fears, "It's back to Newgate for you, Dodger where Jack Ketch is waiting. I'll see you in Hell." But his dream quickly changed from a confused jumble of people and places to an image of Spanner with his needle arms speedily weaving. They were like overworked spinnerets making a gigantic spider's lace threaded trap. His face was a skull and his eyes shone red as he feverishly strived to complete the sticky snare. At the top of the netting was a fat onyx glossy spider with its eight eyes watching him and Dodger saw his face reflected in every one of them. The head of the arachnid became the round jolly face of Bessant. His fangs dripped port wine and he loomed closer looking evilly menacing, his cherubic face was more villainous than angelic. The creature scuttled towards him brandishing its front legs as if to parcel him up in a deadly cocoon. His mouth gaped open and his fangs were poised ready to bite. Jack woke with a start.

He was soaked in perspiration and leapt from his bed trying to shake off the remnants of his nightmare. He rushed to the window and pulled back the heavy drapes that had served to keep the room in inky blackness. A silver river of moonlight flooded across the room brightly illuminating his chamber.

Jack gulped, in an attempt to soothe his taut nerves, and stared at the night sky just as a shooting star fleetingly grazed the heavens. He heard Fred's voice, "Make a wish, Jack. That's what Mrs D would do." And suddenly, as if being guided from beyond he knew what he had to do.

Jack dressed swiftly. He tiptoed from his room but didn't know why as he and Edward were the only ones in the house and Edward was in a room much further along the landing. Nevertheless he didn't want to disturb him or give him cause for alarm. So, like the thief he always claimed to be, he crept from the house into the muffled night where a few clouds scudded and occasionally masked the ghostly face of the moon.

It was a good night for a walk. He became more alert with each step he took. The elite part of town, he was in, was quiet and still. He moved on, stepping swiftly through the normally busy area close to the docks, which was hushed now as reprobates and drunks had returned home from their favoured hostelries to sleep off their night of booze. The air was comfortably balmy and Jack picked up his step as he moved nearer to the business quarter.

The white stucco building of Bowkett and Bessant came into view. After a quick look around, he silently stepped towards the premises. There was no one to see and no one to hear as he removed his whittling knife that he always carried and edged closer to the entrance.

He stooped down and holding the door firmly, he pushed the blade into the small crevice that housed the latch. He slid the tool up until it met the lock and exerted pressure on the door at exactly the same time as he flattened the catch mechanism, which clicked and opened. Jack stepped inside and closed the door softly.

The dawn was just about to break and the rising sun was stretching out its paintbrush bristle rays and washing the sky a deep crimson as the birds awoke from sleep and began to chirrup to herald in the beginning of a new day. Jack studied the doors from the foyer and silently stepped to Bessant's outer office. He fiddled with the fastener and entered just as a radiant beam of light burst through the window. It was as if a stage had been lit for a play and Jack grinned.

***

Mr Bessant left his modest house, locked his front door and placed the key in his pocket, which he patted, a habit he'd developed whenever he secreted something inside his coat. He strolled to his work place basking in the rising heat, singing a little ditty to himself. The few clouds that had been present overnight had sailed away leaving a beautiful sapphire ceiling. The fragrance of blossoms native to the area, and in full bloom, wafted through the air as bees busy pollenating the flowers hummed. Mr Bessant tipped his hat to a young lady on her way to market. "It's a delightful day, don't you think?"

The young lady smiled in agreement and went on her way. Bessant talked to himself, as he approached his offices, "Couldn't be better. Ah me!" he sighed. "My ship has certainly come in and about time," he chortled to himself.

Bessant removed his keys and put his hand on the knob of the door, which opened a fraction. Bessant frowned, he pushed the door to the foyer with his finger while remaining firmly outside and peeped in. A quick scan of the area showed there was no one lurking there so he entered, calling, "Is someone there? Mr Spanner?" There was no response so he came right into the hallway and closed the door firmly behind him. He waited and listened... The place was silent and still. Feeling a little more confident he advanced to his outer office door and opened it. It was empty. Bessant heaved a sigh of relief and waddled to his own chamber and entered to see Jack sitting behind his desk and in his chair.

The shock of seeing someone there drained the colour from his face. "Oh my God!" He then adopted a righteous tone and demanded, "What are you doing here?"

"Good morning, Mr Bessant," said Jack in a matter-of-fact voice.

"How did you get in here?"

"The door was open."

"No, it wasn't!" retorted Bessant as his eyes flicked to the papers on his desk and then he spotted the safe door was also open. "You've opened my safe," he said accusingly.

"Not me, mate. It was already open," said Jack calmly without a hint of menace in his tone.

Bessant scurried to the safe and knelt down removing a handful of files in a large folder. He waved them at Jack. "You've been through Mr Hargreaves' files," he said indignantly.

Jack murmured coolly, "Just looking after a friend." He scrutinised Bessant's expression and his eyes didn't waver or blink but fastened onto him like a predator stalking its prey.

A whimper like a wounded puppy slipped from Bessant's lips as he collapsed into a chair, letting the folder drop to the floor. "Oh, God. Oh, no. So, you know everything?"

Jack's grin was hawkish, "Just about." He paused for full effect and with a sterner edge to his voice asked, "So, what you gonna do now, Mr Bessant?" His cockney vernacular became even stronger and he raised an eyebrow waiting for Mr Bessant to reply.

Bessant's voice became wheedling in his pleading, "Please don't go to the law. Please. You know what they'll do."

Jack's voice remained coolly calm, "Don't think any of us wants a hanging. As I said, what you gonna do?"

Mr Bessant was now very flustered and went from being an unearthly pale colour to becoming redder and redder in the face. His voice became more high-pitched as he attempted to adopt a conciliatory tone and persuade Jack that he would make recompense. He began to blabber, "I'll pay it all back. Everything. Today! Immediately. Now."

"Well, that's a start," Jack's eyes did not deviate from Bessant's face.

"If I write a promissory note, now and change the gold payments to Mr Edward, will that suffice?"

Jack appeared to consider this assurance carefully. He locked eyes with Bessant and saw the fear flickering in the solicitor's gaze. Bessant appeared unable to move as if he was struck by moonlight and pinioned to his seat. He looked as if he wasn't breathing.

Jack finally spoke, "Yeah. That will do, for now."

"Thank you, Mr Jack. Oh, thank you, thank you," Bessant gushed. He was now sweating profusely and looked as if he was about to cry.

Jack's voice became coldly authoritative, "You'll continue to look after Edward and you'll charge him the correct fees for doing so. I don't want him to know of our little chat. But, Mr Bessant, if you make any mistakes at all, and I mean any, I will bring in the law and then, Gawd help you."

Those words seemed to charge Mr Bessant with fevered energy. He instantly snatched up pen and paper to write the note, while Jack helped himself to a glass of port. Jack watched Bessant write as he sipped his drink. All that could be heard in the office was the sound of the pen moving on the paper, which Bessant signed with a flourish. Jack downed the rest of the rich ruby liquid in his glass.

Bessant handed Jack the paper, which Jack appeared to study. Jack then picked up the folder of Edward's files, which Bessant had let fall to the floor. Jack tucked it under his arm. "I'll keep this, just in case," Jack warned.

Bessant was unable to stop himself from stuttering out, "How... how did you know?"

"Never trusted lawyers, no how. You said you were lagged and I trusted you even less. I thought you were up to something. There's a lot of money involved. Big temptation for someone who's not quite on the right side of the law. What with that and rumours I'd heard of your very good fortune at the bank... Well, it was no surprise to me."

Jack strolled to the door and turned. He waved the note at the defeated man who sat puffing miserably in the chair. "I'll give this to Edward and I will say that you made a mistake."

"Thank you, Mr Dawkins. Thank you. And thank you for giving me another chance." He was effusive in his gratitude.

"It's good to know you'll be doing right by us. Never had no lawyer in my pocket before. It feels good." Bessant forced a smile; his face was now dripping with moisture and scarlet with shame. Jack put his hand on the door and stopped. He looked back at the plump man who seemed to have shrunk further into the seat. His self-importance had diminished, "You asked me how I knew... I didn't know nothing."

"But you told..."

"I didn't tell you nothing. I always thought you lawyers were clever, but you, Mr Bessant... You told me everything. Everything I never knew. And everything I needed to know to be absolutely sure of your trickery. That's because you forgot something, didn't you?"

Bessant looked confused, "What?"

"I can't read," said Jack with a laugh.

"But you signed the original papers... you looked at them."

"I've learned how to write me name all right, but Edward does the reading. If you were such a great friend of Mr Fred he'd have told you that. And another thing, you never came to his funeral, a good enough friend would have turned up to pay his respects." Jack smiled in gratification as Bessant closed his eyes in despair and dropped his head into his hands.

Jack touched his hat and was gone.

16: Settling Down to the Loving Winds of Change

Jack was taking some time to get used to his new plush surroundings and the lifestyle that accompanied the move to town. While Edward seemed more accepting and managed to fit in very well, Jack found it hard to relax. He was used to hard work and now so much of the labour on the farm had been drafted out to Bobby, Daniel and Koorong that Jack found himself wondering how to spend his time. He felt guilty if he wasn't up and busy. It was not in his nature to lie about and do nothing. For lambing and shearing Jack ensured he was on hand. Market and auction days he blossomed. He loved the haggling over prices and driving a good bargain but when he was at the mansion house he was given to going out on the town, which seemed to him to be a mindless occupation and one he had difficulty getting used to but he felt he had to do something. For that reason, he had purchased a fine palomino mare with a golden honey coat and long snowy white mane. It was a beautiful creature, versatile with great manoeuvrability and endurance. Jack called her Bonnie and while Edward had taken to using the carriage and pair, Jack would ride Bonnie, especially if he was going out alone.

One such evening, when the light had been squeezed from the sky and left the pinky tinged spectre-like misty grey of dusk, Jack stepped out from a rowdy bar into the dusty street, where music filtered into the night air. The moon battled through the encroaching cloud and darkness as Jack, who was slightly tipsy, untethered his horse, mounted her and set off into the night.

Bonnie trotted through Main Street and into Sutherland Road. He wasn't certain where he was heading but just wanted to ride and clear his foggy head from the surfeit of alcohol. The further he travelled the clearer his head became and the more squalid the road ahead appeared.

Jack sniffed distastefully as the stench of stale beer and bodily fluids that mingled in the air assailed his nose. He slowed Bonnie to a walk and passed men who were lying drunk in doorways wearing a mantle of hopelessness and desolation. Fights spilled out from the bars. Men and women quarrelled with no dignity or modesty not caring about themselves or each other. Jack moved on from the seedy thoroughfare towards a church whose spire stretched towards the moon like a beacon in the foetid air.

As he approached the house of worship he heard the sound of a piano playing, not the rough tinkling that prevailed in the inns of the back streets nor the modern tunes that could be enjoyed in the entertainment put on in more respectable establishments. This was like something he had never before heard. A melodious strain of hauntingly beautiful harmonious music that captured his heart and mind. The soft fluted notes beckoned him forward and he found himself inexplicably drawn to the sound.

Jack stopped and dismounted, and as if in some magical trance began to walk towards the arched wooden door, so drawn was he, by the poignant composition. His expression was one of awe. He was lost in the mood of the sonata. He didn't know what it was but it made him lost for words and Jack never ran out of anything to say. He leaned against the heavily carved door with its elaborate iron hangings, put his ear to the wood and listened carefully. The enchanting musical work of art was mesmerising and he just had to see who was playing the piano with such a light and expressive touch. He opened the latch and stepped inside.

The church was bathed in golden rose fairy-tale candlelight. The flames flickered and elfin shadows stretched and danced in the corners near the stone pulpit where a petite, graceful young woman was seated at a piano; her fine, elegant fingers, dextrously nimble, picked out a poignant unforgettable melody.

Transfixed, Jack was transported into a world of imagination and through the piece of music he envisaged a small craft floating effortlessly on a gently rippling lake in shimmering silver moonlight. He was further enchanted by the image of the young woman in front of him with her lustrous spangled ringlets catching the soothing mellow glow of the candles. Her unblemished skin was like fine porcelain. Her eyes were closed as she played, swaying rapturously as she lived and felt the music. Her cheeks had an attractive blush, which belied the heat and strength of the sun. Jack was totally captivated. He had never heard or seen such beauty in his entire young life. He gasped aloud as he realised this, such was the impact of the mystical music and the angelic countenance of the young woman that he listened to; he became aware that he'd been holding his breath as if it prevented the image before him from dissolving. He quietly closed the church door and continued to watch and listen to this exquisite young lady and her music.

She finished the concerto and held the moment of completion of the final chords, which resonated around the building, until it became perfectly still. Only then did she close the piano lid and rise. She suddenly became aware that she was being watched and turned to see Jack standing there as if hypnotised. Her full sensuous lips parted in surprise and she moistened them with her tongue. Jack felt compelled to step towards her but could not speak. It was as if he was under some kind of spell.

Her voice that was as perfect and vibrantly alive as a bubbling mountain stream broke the reverent silence, "Hello. How long have you been here?"

"Play some more, please," Jack pleaded.

"No, I'm sorry, I can't. I am late as it is. I have to go home and put the children to bed."

Jack looked crestfallen and just managed a soft, "Oh."

The church door opened and a swarthy man in his thirties wearing the livery of a manservant entered the church. He disregarded Jack and announced, "Your carriage is here, Miss Martel."

"Thank you, Toby."

With that the manservant left, leaving the door ajar and Miss Martel glided past Jack. Her fragrant perfume pervaded his nostrils as she stepped past. She was light on her feet and Jack believed he had never seen such perfection in a woman.

Before she reached the door, he somehow found his voice and managed to say with an appreciative sigh, "That was beautiful."

She stopped and turned with a smile that melted Jack's heart, "Why, thank you."

They stood like that for a few seconds before Miss Martel continued to the door where she stopped again and turned to study Jack, "I will be practising again tomorrow night."

"In here?"

"Yes. Will you be here?"

"Yes."

"Goodnight Mr...?"

"Dawkins, Jack Dawkins."

"Goodnight, Mr Dawkins." Her voice was silky like cream.

"Goodnight, Miss Martel."

Jack watched her leave in wonderment before coming out of his charmed stupor and he followed her out into the now very special night. He stood outside the church door to see her enter a smart carriage, where Toby waited holding the reins to two matching horses. Her delicate floral scent lingered in the air and Jack remained there watching until the carriage trotted out of sight.

"Miss Martel," Jack said with a sigh breathing longing in his voice. He finally started to walk towards his horse, Bonnie. There was a skip in his step as he ran the last few steps and he punched the air in delight. "Tomorrow night," he said to his mount. "Tomorrow night, Bonnie."

Jack's ride back to the mansion was a blur. He ignored the drunks in the street; he didn't hear the doxies shouting his name, or stop to stare at the ruffians brawling outside the many sleazy hostelries. He cantered through the rough side of town and entered the very fashionable area and made his way to the mansion where he galloped up the sweeping drive before he subdued Bonnie to a trot and steered her towards the stable block.

He untacked his mare, still wearing a broad grin that refused to leave his face. He brushed Bonnie down, checked her feed and water, gave her a net of hay to nibble and settled her for the night humming part of the tune he'd heard Miss Martel play that he could remember. He rushed around to the front, dashed up the steps and dived in through the front door. He met Miss Bonnet on his way in who smiled cheerily at him. "Mr Jack, I've kept you back some supper. It's in the kitchen keeping warm. I'll see you later. I'm just off to meet a friend. Good night."

"Night, Miss B." Jack practically sang the words.

Miss Bonnet laughed. "My, my, you're in a good mood, tonight!"

Jack caught hold of her and whirled her around as if in a country dance before planting a kiss on her cheek and setting her down, "That I am, Miss B. Have yourself a good night out. I'll see you later." Jack lunged past her and swung on the bannisters at the bottom of the stairs before jumping off humming loudly.

Miss Bonnet shook her head and beamed at his unusual good humour and left the house. Jack whizzed through to the kitchen and set himself a place at the table and took out his supper warming in the oven. He sniffed in the delicious aroma and murmured "Mmm..." before he sat down to devour the tender stewed steak casserole with a good helping of buttery mashed potato.

Well trained by Mrs D he cleared away his plate and utensils, washed and dried them before putting them away. Still humming he went off to find Edward, who was enjoying a glass of port in the drawing room. Jack bubbled in grinning from ear to ear.

"Someone's in a good mood."

"Wait till I tell you. You won't believe it."

"Why? What's happened? I thought you were just going out for a drink?"

"I was, I did. It was meant to be. I was supposed to go out and I was supposed to pass that church on my way home."

"Church?"

"Church. Edward, it was beautiful. Magnificent."

"The church?"

"No, Edward, although yes, the place was pretty special; it was lit with candles an' all. The music was like nothin' I've ever heard. Beautiful. And she was the most divine creature I've ever laid eyes on. Beautiful. Did I tell you, she was beautiful?"

"Yes, I think you just have."

"Well, she was. There's no other word. She was beautiful and I'm seeing her tomorrow."

"You are?"

"I am. She was so dainty, so petite, so demure and educated not like me. Her voice was like... like... whispering grass... coated with honey and cream." Edward looked amused and allowed Jack to continue. "Oh, Edward, I'm seeing her tomorrow."

"I know."

"S'funny... The last time I was in a church, I was on a job for Fagin. I nicked the silver off the altar cos Fagin had a buyer." Jack looked up as he remembered the episode. "I seems to remember I made a few bob that night. Oh, Edward... Did I tell you she was beautiful?"

Edward laughed enjoying Jack's exuberance, "Yes, I think you mentioned it... a few times... So, when am I going to meet her, Dodger?"

"I dunno... Soon, maybe."

"You sound just like me when I mooned over Rosie Martin."

"Rosie Martin? Rosie Martin couldn't hold a candle to her. She is but a shadow compared to a bright living flame." Jack sighed. "Miss Martel. Miss Martel." And he held his hand over his heart and began to sway to the inner tune in his head as he hummed more of the music from the chapel. "Ye Gods! She's an angel sent from above and I... I can't wait for tomorrow night."

Jack poured himself a glass of ruby wine and flopped into a chair. He raised his glass, "To Miss Martel, music and tomorrow night!"

***

Jack could hardly sleep that night. He was more excited than he could ever recall. He was almost wishing the night away so that the day would come more quickly. He leaned back on his duck down pillow, folded his arms behind his head and sighed dreamily. He concocted and imagined many varied scenarios in his head of what seeing her again would be like and what he would say, then as he recreated in his mind their first meeting in the church a thought struck him. 'Could she be married? No, no... she was Miss Martel that's what the manservant had called her... But then again, sometimes servants addressed young ladies as 'Miss' even though they weren't and she did say she had to get home to put the children to bed.' His face puckered in a frown... 'Children... that would change things. Maybe she was just being polite thinking I would return purely for the music?' Oh, Lord... he needed answers. Then again, how could he question her so personally?

Jack sighed again; this time in melancholy. 'This friendship could be over before it has even begun... Should I cut my losses now and avoid disappointment? Why does the thought of not seeing her again or getting to know her better fill me with such dismay? What would Mr Fred say?' He knew the answer to that. He could almost hear Fred's voice in his ear, "If you don't ask, you don't get. You'll never be happy if you spend the rest of your life wondering what if... In fact, if I hadn't listened to my heart I would have been stuck in a loveless marriage and never had the rich life I had with Mrs D. You gotta try, lad... You gotta try..." And with Fred's voice echoing in his brain Jack finally floated away on a sea of dreams as if he were on a boat in the moonlight where the haunting music wrapped him up in a blanket of harmonious sleepiness, soothing him to slumber.

***

Jack woke early and waited for the enthusiastic sun to bounce up from the horizon. He had drawn back the drapes and waited for the slatted pattern from the shutters to stencil the floor of his bedroom and opened the window and covers blinking in the bright light.

The day was perfect. Parakeets squawked and galahs chattered. They seemed as eager as Jack to welcome the new dawn. Outside was fresh and untainted as the early morning dew accentuated the fragrances of the budding and blossoming shrubs and plants, whose scents hung in the air. Sharp blades of grass were dressed in crystal droplets that punctuated each cutting edge revealing the lurking jewelled doily webs that should have lain hidden to trap unwary insects and flies. Jack felt his heart was bursting with the joy of being alive.

Remnants of his dreams came into his head, together with memories of Mrs Doble whose last instructions to him were to be happy and with that thought in mind, Jack decided to make himself look as presentable and respectable as he possibly could. He would try to ignore the devil that sat on his shoulder telling him he wasn't good enough and was striving for something unattainable.

The day passed excruciatingly slowly. Jack had a bath and scrubbed himself all over, removing the grime of a week's work. He laid out his best clothes and like a fop around town fussed over what to wear. Finally, he settled on his Sunday best outfit, never yet seen in church but reserved for special occasions as he wasn't a congregant.

He took a collarless white starched shirt that Edward had bought him at a Gent's outfitters and selected a stiff, collar and laid it on his bed. He opened his door, walked along the landing to the top of the stairs and shouted, "Edward! Edward!"

Miss Bonnet looked up and called, "Mr Jack, you've got a bell on every tooth, so you have."

"Sorry. It's just I need help."

"Why? What's wrong? Anyone would think you were dying. Besides, you're wasting your breath. Mr Edward went out about half an hour ago."

"Oh, what? Now, what am I going to do?"

"What is it?"

Jack lifted up the collar he was still holding and asked, "How do you fasten this thing to the shirt?"

"Haven't you got any studs?"

"Studs? Not sure, maybe. They're a pretty new invention. I've never worn one of these things before."

"Find the studs and I'll help you. Or you could go out collarless…"

"I suppose. I just wanted to look me best."

"I expect Mr Edward has some in his room."

"I can't go in there rummaging around. I don't want to nick 'em."

"I'm sure he'll understand as long as you tell him and put them back, after. Go on, hurry up."

Reluctantly, Jack ambled across the landing to Edward's room and knocked politely, calling Edward's name as he opened the door. He took a cursory look around the neat and ordered room and strode to a dresser by the window. On top was a pot, which contained six studs. He selected two and left quickly closing the door quietly behind him.

"I've got two," he called out to Miss Bonnet before running down the stairs carrying the collar.

"Right! Now, let's see." She examined the collar and studs. "One should be short for the back and one long for the front. You've got two short ones."

"Won't that work?"

"Take this one back and get a longer one for the front. And hurry up!"

Jack ran up the stairs two at a time and dashed back into Edward's room, returned the short one to the dish and selected a longer one with a mother of pearl front. He raced back down jumping the last two steps.

"Mr Jack!" reprimanded Miss Bonnet. "You'll do yourself or someone else an injury, so you will."

"Nah. It's just a few steps."

"Now, turn around and I'll fasten the back." She deftly attached the back of the stiff collar to his shirt before moving around to the front. "You could do with getting a manservant to do this. Heaven knows the place could do with one. The company would be good, too. It's a big house. Now, hold still and stop wriggling." She attached the front of the collar but Jack immediately put his fingers between it and his neck and the stud flew off and rolled under the hall table, "Uffern a darn!"

"What does that mean?" said Jack on his hands and knees crawling under the table to reach the wayward stud.

"Hell and darn. My swearing in Welsh is very good and no one knows what I'm saying so, I can say what I like," said Miss Bonnet with a smile.

"Got it!" said Jack holding it up as if it were some kind of prize. He stood up and passed it to her. "Reckon you could teach me a few words. They could come in useful."

Miss Bonnet fiddled with the fastener once more. "Now, don't go sticking your fingers between your neck and the collar. Leave it be."

"But, it's uncomfortable," Jack protested.

"Leave it," she said in a low, threatening tone through gritted teeth.

Jack didn't argue. "No, ma'am."

"Now, I'll be off and don't go quarrelling with your collar stud again!" she warned.

Jack laughed almost popping the rogue stud once more. "I'll try, but I don't fancy me chances." Miss Bonnet shook her head despairingly and left.

Jack walked sedately up the stairs and back to his chamber. Afraid to turn, he looked straight in front of him moving awkwardly to his room as if he were carrying a bucket of water on his head. Once inside he sat down with a bump on the bed and the mischievous fastener exploded out again. Jack groaned, "This'll never do. She'll think I'm some sort of simpleton if I walk about like this." Jack removed his shirt and undid the back stud. "I need more practice," he mumbled to himself. He took off the collar and replaced it in its pigskin box and donned his shirt again. Collarless it was more comfortable. Jack took the ill-disciplined studs and returned them to the pot in Edward's room.

Jack flopped on his back and lay on his bed staring at the ceiling. He glanced at the Ormorlu clock sitting on his chest of drawers and was glad Mrs Doble had taught him how to tell the time and not just the o'clocks, which he'd known before.

He sighed heavily and allowed himself to imagine how the evening would go and his head began to nod and his eyelids drooped. He forced them open again but the strain was too great and he floated away into a dreamless sleep.

Jack turned over feeling relaxed and happy when he became aware that night had come. "Oh, what!" he yelled in irritation and leapt off the bed. He lit his lamp and studied the time. It was with huge relief he saw that he was not too late to get to the church. He grabbed his coat, dashed from his chamber and raced down the stairs almost knocking Edward off his feet who was just entering.

"Thought you'd be gone by now," mused Edward.

"I have... I am," yelled Jack as he fled out of the door and left Edward looking nonplussed.

Jack hastened down the steps and ran around to the stables to get Bonnie. He saddled her quickly, tacked her up, vaulted onto her back, kicked her in the flanks and urged her out on the road, through the town towards the church where he hopped off and tethered her before tiptoeing inside the minster.

He slipped inside the candlelit temple and sat in a pew near the font and piano where Miss Martel had just sat and was already lost in her recital of Beethoven's Waldstein Sonata. The feeling she generated with her playing was breath-taking, Jack thought. The pace of the piece altered from fast to slow and her impressive rapid left hand runs, which crossed over her right together with the pedal trill, high melody and repetition of its sweet theme reminded Jack of daybreak when birds awoke and sang in lively chirruping triumph at the dawn of another magnificent day of life to live. Jack wondered how she wasn't out of breath such was her performance that he could only sit and listen in awe.

A second theme reappeared, which transported Jack to thoughts of beautiful dance-like music, which then dropped away to fine delicate piano music that seemed to die away but unexpectedly travelled into a dazzling performance that ended in a rush of grandeur. Her head dropped and her hands remained resting lightly on the keys before she arose and turned to see Jack standing there with a look of wonder on his face. He felt he should do something and had stood up and now seeing her lovely face the applause he intended to give her left him transfixed as she crossed towards him.

"Good evening, Mr Dawkins."

Jack was momentarily stuck for words as his voice would not come but as she neared him he eventually managed to murmur, "Good evening, Miss Martel."

She waited for him to say something else but when he didn't, she prompted, "Did you like it?"

Jack cleared his throat before saying emphatically, "I should say so."

"How long have you liked Beethoven?"

"Who?"

"The music," she said with a laugh.

"Oh, was that Beethoven last night? And today?" Miss Martel nodded looking amused. "In that case, I've loved his music since yesterday." She giggled delightedly, her sausage curls bobbed with her laugh.

Toby, the manservant from the previous night opened the church door and entered. He saw Jack and frowned, "Your carriage is here, Miss Martel."

"Thank you, Toby. I will be along in a moment." He assented with his head, threw one last look at Jack and then left.

"Do you have to put the children to bed?"

"I do." Miss Martel began walking towards the door when a thought appeared to strike her. She turned back and looked Jack directly in the eyes. "I'm having luncheon at The Mansfield Hotel tomorrow."

"That's nice," said Jack for want of something better to say.

"The girls will be with their father. I shall be dining alone."

"Yes, well... it's good to be alone sometimes."

"I don't like eating alone."

"Oh, I see. Well, could I buy you luncheon, Miss Martel?"

"That would be uncommonly generous of you. I will be there at one, Mr Dawkins."

"So, will I." said Jack with a lopsided grin as he watched her glide out through the door.

He stood there awhile before collapsing back into a pew in stunned disbelief. 'Luncheon! Have I just agreed to take her to luncheon?' The inane grin remained on his face until the candles began to sputter and the shadows grew heavier. Jack realised it was time to leave. Reluctantly, he stood up and walked to the door almost afraid that the whole conversation had been in his head. But no, he knew it hadn't and he found it difficult to believe that someone as refined as Miss Martel was prepared to spend time with him. But she had suggested it and he wasn't going to question the rights and wrongs of it. Jack determined he would be there a fraction earlier. There was so much he wanted to know about her. Maybe, just maybe, he would be able to ask her some of his most burning questions, but now, now it was time to return home. He couldn't wait to tell Edward all about his evening and just maybe tomorrow he'd succeed in managing to fasten his collar to his shirt if he could bear the chafing. The Mansfield Hotel, he knew, was one frequented by the wealthy and very imposing. Jack hoped he would fit in there and determined that he would.

17: Luncheon and More

The day began brightly as the sun flirted with the few fluff balls of clouds that were playing in the azure sky. Jack bounded out of bed with hope in his eyes and flung open the curtains and shutters allowing the brazen flaming globe to burn through the glass claiming the room as its own. Jack opened the window and inhaled deeply allowing the seductive warmth to bathe his skin and he beamed happily as he viewed the glorious day. Today would be a good day, he was certain of it. He remembered Mrs D saying that life was what you made it and Jack convinced himself that he would make it good. After all, he had an appointment with a beautiful lady. All he had to do was turn up.

Today, Bobby would be driving to market expecting to meet Jack at the quay. This was one day he would take off and entrust the deal on the wool bales to be done by Edward. But he had to tell him first. With that in mind he dressed hurriedly and dashed downstairs to the breakfast room where Edward was already seated and Miss Bonnet was serving a mouth-watering breakfast of everything that Jack enjoyed. Jack sped towards his seat.

Edward eyed him up and down, "Got dressed in a bit of a rush, did you?"

"Why? What's wrong?"

"You look like you've escaped from some woman's cupboard because the husband has arrived home and you had to dress in the dark," said Edward with a laugh.

"What?"

"Your shirt and waistcoat are misbuttoned."

Jack glanced down and grinned, "Got my mind on other things," he said as he undid his chemise and vest and lined the buttons up correctly with their fastenings. "Edward, I need to ask you something."

"What's that?"

"I'm having luncheon with Miss Martel and wondered if you could do the deal with the wool merchant today?"

"But, you always do it. You usually get the best price," said Edward.

"It'll be just this once, please."

"Bobby can manage it, I'm sure."

"It's best if one of us is there. Will you?"

Edward studied his friend's face and relented, "I suppose. Say, you're not going to make a habit of it, are you? No one is as confident as you at doing business."

"I promise you, it'll just be this one time. Can I count on you?"

Edward grinned back, "Oh, go on then."

"Thanks, Edward. You're a real mate." Jack sat down and helped himself to some crispy bacon and eggs, with fried potatoes and bread.

Miss Bonnet smiled in satisfaction at their obvious enjoyment of her food and left the young men to their breakfast.

"So, tell me all about it," said Edward in between mouthfuls. "Meeting Miss Martel again?"

"Got it in one."

"Where are you going with her?"

"Mansfield Hotel. In their restaurant."

Edward whistled long and low, "That's a swanky place. Very smart."

"You ever been there?"

"A couple of times. They have great food but it's expensive... The staff are helpful as you will see." Jack nodded appreciatively. "I thought you would want to meet Koorong's family? Relatives from the same tribe north of here are coming to the ranch today. They are talking of relocating and rebuilding the village camp. You did say that after the sale you would return to meet them."

"Oh, no. I completely forgot. It went right out of my head. All I can think about is..."

"Miss Martel, I know."

"I'm gonna have to make this right... Do I have time to get back to the farm and then here for luncheon?"

"In a word, no."

"No... yes, you're right. I'll go back afterwards. So, I may not be back tonight."

"Better let Miss Bonnet know."

"Yes, don't want to raise her Welsh gander, as she's warned me before." Jack took a bite of his bread with the yolk of his egg, which burst and dribbled all down his chin and front."

Edward glanced at his friend, with an amused grin. "You'll have to get changed again."

"Why?" Edward indicated Jack's clothing.

Jack looked down and groaned, "Oh, what? I don't have another vest."

"You can borrow one of mine," said Edward with a laugh.

"I'll see if Miss B can get it out."

"Finish your breakfast first. Looks like you'll need it, you've got an action packed day."

***

Miss Bonnet tutted as she scoured the dried egg yolk off Jack's, waistcoat, "Duw, Duw! There's a slop, you are. As mucky as a pig in mud."

"Will it come off?"

"I've scraped off most of it. Now, I need my brush and soap. See if I can get rid of the rest. I'll put it on the guard to dry. Check it in an hour."

167

"What about me shirt?"

"Take it off and I'll wash it. Don't you have another?"

"Somewhere..."

"Then, I suggest you find it. Go on. Don't dally here watching me."

"Right!" Jack left Miss Bonnet in the kitchen and went back to his room. He peered in his mirror and rubbed at his chin that was harbouring blobs of yellow egg yolk in his apology of a beard. He made a decision. "This has got to come off." Jack knew it wouldn't do if something dribbled on his chin at luncheon and stuck in his paltry whiskers but clean-shaven he would feel it and be able to mop it away with a napkin. He just hoped he could make himself presentable in time and not end up with razor cuts that wouldn't stop bleeding as he hadn't shaved in a long time.

***

Jack arrived at the Mansfield Hotel fifteen minutes early. He looked immaculate now he was smooth skinned, without a cut in sight, wearing his freshly laundered frilled white shirt, with a mustard cravat, light tan breeches, tall leather black boots and the fitted brown light wool frock coat of a gentleman and top hat such as the merchants wore, which reminded Jack of his days as the artful dodger when he would wear such head gear. It was great for hiding things!

The waiter, tall and slim with an intelligent face and limpid blue eyes, approached him and took his hat. "Yes, sir? Can I help you?" His voice was rich and pleasant, his tone was polite.

"I'd like a table for two, please. I am expecting a lady to join me."

"Certainly, sir... Mr...?"

"Dawkins, Jack Dawkins."

"Step this way, Mr Dawkins."

Jack followed the man into the restaurant and seated him at a table by the window, which overlooked a rose garden and expansive lawn that made Jack wonder how it kept so lush and green. Jack knew that he and Edward could do with some kind of help for the mansion grounds that were too big for them to manage.

Jack gazed around the fancily furnished establishment with its marble tables and large ornate mirrors, which made the place appear twice the size. There were unlit lamps, which hung from the ceiling leaving Jack to imagine what the brasserie would look like at night and how long it would take to lower and light all the lamps.

"May I bring sir a drink while you wait?" asked the ever genteel waiter.

"Yes, thank you. And you are?"

"Atwill, sir. At your service. What would you like?"

Jack wanted to say that the gentleman's name suited him, his occupation being a server but believed it would be rude to say so. He dithered slightly, not knowing the correct type of beverage to order in such a smart place. "Um, an ale will be fine, Atwill. Thank you."

Atwill bowed slightly and walked away giving Jack time to gaze longer at his plush surroundings. He spotted another gentleman sitting alone who was sipping something in a goblet. Atwill soon returned and placed a glass of beer in front of him. "Your drink, sir."

"Thank you."

"Will there be anything else, sir?"

"Um, what grub have you got, then?"

"I'll fetch you a menu, sir."

Jack looked around at the other tables with a few occupied by couples enjoying their meals. There was one other waiter on duty who seemed to be attending to the other side of the restaurant. Jack's eyes became fixed on the door and he watched as a woman arrived and made her way to where the single gentleman was seated. Jack observed him as the man rose to greet her. He gave her a short bow and helped her into her seat before resuming his own chair just as Atwill returned.

"Here you are, sir." He started to pass Jack the menu.

"Er… could you read it to me?" The waiter looked perplexed so Jack explained, "I forgot me specs."

Atwill appeared unfazed by the request and calmly recited the bill of fare to him, as Jack tried to memorise the list of options. Atwill left his side to attend to another table as Jack saw Miss Martel entering. Mimicking the actions of the gentleman he'd noted, he rose, bowed slightly and pulled out a chair for her and helped her into her seat before sitting himself back down.

She had on a beige cotton dress with a blue flower print and big blue sash that highlighted her tiny waist. Jack thought he could possibly hold her waist in one hand, it was so small. The dress sported the popular puffed leg of mutton sleeves that tapered from the elbow. The skirt fountained out with an abundance of petticoats. She wore an elegantly adorned hat, fine lace gloves and carried a reticule.

"Thank you, Mr Dawkins," said Miss Martel with a shy smile. Her burnished copper ringlets bounced enchantingly as she spoke and moved her head. "The skirts of these dresses are indeed difficult to deal with at times. A gentleman's help is always warranted and appreciated. Jack flushed with pleasure in that he had done the right thing.

Atwill crossed to their table carrying a menu. "May I get you a drink, madam?"

"Yes, thank you. I will have a dry sherry, please." Miss Martel carefully removed her fine lace gloves and placed them with her reticule on an adjacent chair while she viewed the glorious garden outside the window.

"I'll have one of those as well," said Jack.

Atwill nodded graciously and passed Jack the menu, which he opened upside down. Atwill leaned forward and unobtrusively turned the menu the right way up without Miss Martel noticing.

"What would you like to eat?" asked Jack.

Miss Martel pulled her eyes away from the shrubs and flowers and smiled brightly at him. She had the most perfect lips, thought Jack as he leaned back in his seat and itemised the dishes he recalled. "Fish in white wine sauce. Fillet of beef and Navarin of lamb all served with seasonal vegetables of the day." He looked expectantly at her.

"Um… I'll have the lamb, please."

"Me, too," said Jack returning the menu to Atwill who wrote down the order before clearing away the excess cutlery and left discreetly. Unusually, for someone so quick witted, Jack was stuck for words and they both went to speak together and laughed, "After you," said Jack.

"No, you first. After all, you are my host," said Miss Martel with a tilt of her head.

Jack gave one of his crooked grins and said, "Nice here, innit?" He then remonstrated with himself in his head at saying something so bland and daft.

"It is. I can only afford to eat here once in a blue moon." Miss Martel spoke with candour.

"Yeah? Stylish, innit?" Jack paused, looking uncomfortable. He cursed himself for his lack of clever conversation and suppressed a heavy sigh.

Miss Martel appraised the young man sitting opposite her and asked gently, "May I enquire into your means of employment, Mr Dawkins?" and smiled sweetly moistening her lips. Jack looked at her, fascinated by her mouth. So, she repeated her question, "What is it that you do for a living?"

"My... Oh, I have a half share in a sheep farm."

"Really? Then, you are a colonist?"

Jack looked horrified, "A colonist? Me? Naah, Miss Martel." He spoke truthfully, "I was sent here as a convict. I was lagged."

"Lagged?" she questioned, unfamiliar with the term.

"Transported."

"How long ago?"

"Fourteen or fifteen years ago, now."

"Then you must have only been..."

"I were an ankle biter. A nipper," said Jack with complete honesty.

"But, that's awful!"

Atwill set down the two sherries and a basket of bread.

"Thank you," said Miss Martel with a charming smile.

"Thanks," uttered Jack copying her. Atwill bowed deferentially and left leaving Jack to ask the one question that had been burning inside him for so long, "Where's your husband today?"

"My husband?" she replied looking surprised.

"Yeah, you said your kids were with their father today."

"But, I'm not married."

"Oh?"

"They are not my girls. I am their governess."

"But, I thought..."

"Mr Dawkins, had I been married with children and a husband I would not be lunching here with you today."

Jack considered her words carefully and had to confess to himself that her response delighted him. He grinned, "No, I suppose not."

Not in the least bit affronted but rather amused, Miss Martel went onto explain, "I came here from England, with the captain and his children, nearly a year ago. The captain works in the garrison near the stockade and I teach his daughters. He comes home after work every evening and looks after his girls for a couple of hours, which is when I go to the church to practise the piano." She pursed her lips in order to prevent the escape of a giggle.

It was at that moment that Atwill arrived carrying a tray with two plates of food. He set it before them serving Amy first.

"Oh! This looks very good," she said savouring the flavoursome aroma that rose from the steaming plate before her with caramelised onions, garlic, herbs and anchovies surrounding tender chunks of lamb together with seasonal vegetables and turnips. "I just love French cooking." She picked up her cutlery and Jack watched which utensils she used and how she held them. He adjusted his knife from its pen grip to hold the handle in the palm of his hand and his index finger rested on the top of the blade and he began to eat with relish, nodding approvingly.

Little was said during the meal apart from when Atwill returned to ask if everything was okay. Jack nodded enthusiastically but couldn't speak with his mouth full of food but Amy put down her utensils and patted her mouth before agreeing, "It's delicious. Thank you."

"Thank you, madam." Atwill smiled pleasantly and bowed before retreating.

They continued with the meal in silence until Jack scooped up the last bite, set down his cutlery, leaned back in his chair and patted his belly, "That was proper grand. A feast fit for a king." He was tempted to belch in appreciation but managed to swallow the burp. He waited until Miss Martel had consumed her repast and she replaced her utensils daintily on her plate, lining them up together. Jack hastily adjusted his own plate and did the same.

As silent as a phantom, Atwill reappeared to clear the dishes and asked, "Would you like to look at the dessert menu?"

"Please," said Jack. Atwill nodded as he removed the empty plates and returned with the menu and passed it to Jack, who in turn handed it to Miss Martel, "I'll let the lady choose."

"Very good, sir."

Miss Martel perused the list of items, "There are some of my favourites on here, "Snowdon Pudding, Almond pudding, Little Quinomie cakes, ooh and Kisses," at which Jack caught her eye, she blushed and dropped her head.

Atwill stood with his pencil poised on his order pad, "What would madam like?"

"It all sounds lovely, but I think I'll have Almond pudding."

"And for you, sir?"

"I'll have the same. Although, I'm actually quite full. But I can always make room for something sweet."

Atwill bobbed and returned to the kitchen.

"This is a real treat for me," said Miss Martel. She smiled and continued, "Mr Dawkins, do tell me about your farm and what you do there." She smiled expectantly, her lips parted in anticipation to react to whatever she was told or to say something.

Jack cleared his throat and began to explain the workings of the farm, lambing, shearing and packing wool. He felt more comfortable talking about something he knew well and by the time the puddings arrived Jack was far more at ease. He found himself chatting about Koorong, Edward, Daniel and Bobby. All the time Miss Martel listened carefully, nodding her head in understanding or stopping him to ask a question.

"I never knew there were so many different types of wool and what garments their yarn would be used for," she said. "I thought a sheep was a sheep and that was it. I would be most interested to see your farm one day, if that would be permitted?"

Jack studied her expression to see if she was mocking him, but could only see sincerity in her eyes. He pursed his lips, "Of course. It would be my pleasure to show you," and grinned lopsidedly at her.

Atwill like a shadow, arrived with a pot of coffee for them both. "Perhaps you would like to have your coffee in the lounge or in the garden?"

"No, no. Here will be fine," said Miss Martel quickly. She glanced across at Jack. "The mid-day sun is a little too hot for me to sit out and the lounge with those sumptuous cushioned seats are so deep I have trouble sitting with any kind of dignity... if that's all right with you?"

Jack nodded, "Fine here," he said to Atwill. "Thank you."

"As you wish, sir," Atwill said. "Shall I pour?"

"Please," said Jack.

Atwill poured the coffee with finesse and like a wraith vaporised into the background leaving them to chatter animatedly together. Atwill stood back and watched the couple. He couldn't help but smile at their obvious delight in each other's company. On hearing Miss Martel saying it was time to leave he made out their bill and on Jack's signal brought it to the table.

"I really must go soon. But thank you. I have had a lovely time," Miss Martel said with honesty.

Atwill handed Jack the bill, which meant nothing to him. He understood numbers but not words and the way it was written was unfamiliar to him. He stared at it before reaching into his pocket and pulling out a roll of notes. He looked questioningly at Atwill with one arched eyebrow. So, when Miss Martel leaned across to retrieve her reticule and gloves from the chair Atwill coughed as she sat up and he looked out of the window as if something had caught his eye. Miss Martel, her curiosity piqued, turned to see what he was looking at. At that moment Atwill quickly put three fingers up to Jack and winked. Miss Martel turned back to see Jack peeling off three notes. He placed them on the silver platter and handed it to Atwill who bowed again, "Thank you, sir," and he slipped back to stand at the opposite wall of the room.

Miss Martel made to rise. Jack stood immediately and held the chair pulling it back for her, giving her room to adjust her dress as Atwill returned with Jack's hat. Jack murmured his thanks and as they turned to leave Jack looked back at Atwill and mouthed 'thank you.'

They entered the street. Miss Martel extended her hand to Jack and thanked him again. "I really did have a wonderful time, Mr Dawkins. Thank you."

"No, thank you, Miss Martel. I enjoyed your company, but please call me Jack."

"Jack," she said his name thoughtfully as if savouring the sound of his name. "I meant what I said in the restaurant, I really would love to see your farm sometime and of course your town house. They both sound intriguing. And if I am to call you Jack, then you are to address me as Amy."

"Is that your name? Amy? What a beautiful name."

"Thank you, Mr Dawkins," she corrected herself, "Jack."

"Miss Martel, I mean, Amy would you like to join me for luncheon again?"

"I would be honoured. I shall be playing at the church again if you care to listen to some more Beethoven."

"I'd be delighted," said Jack grinning like a buffoon.

"Then I will look forward to it. And now I must bid you goodbye. I see my carriage has arrived." Jack glanced towards the road and saw Toby sitting waiting patiently holding the reins. He looked sideways at Jack and then looked away again distastefully. Jack made a point of giving him a friendly wave before strolling back down the street whistling part of one of the tunes he had heard Miss Martel play that he'd remembered.

He stopped on the corner and watched the tawny stallions pulling her carriage trot past and waited until it disappeared out of sight. He looked at his pocket watch and started to run. He knew he had to return to the house, get Bonnie and ride onto the farm as he had promised Koorong.

***

Jack soon cleared his head on the hard ride back to the ranch, not that he felt drunk except perhaps on happiness. He could swear that he had never felt like this in his life before and he couldn't wait for another trip to the church to listen to Amy Martel play some more of her music that she loved.

Amy... Her name was Amy. He'd never met anyone called Amy. It suited her. It was just perfect, like her. All these ribbons of memories flowed, twisted, knotted and curled as they ambled and tied bows in the fabric of his mind.

As he raced through the outback he indulged himself in wishes and dreams of what could be. But then, he told himself off. What could he expect? A rough uneducated ex-convict. Why would he dare to think that she would ever be interested in him romantically? The thought was ludicrous. She was a governess; he was just a thief and now a farmer. She was learned; he knew nothing. She was knowledgeable; he was not. She was accomplished; all he knew was sheep and thieving. She could play the piano like an angel, he could whittle bits of wood. No, it would be impossible. There was no comparison and slowly his ecstatic flowering hope began to wilt away.

***

Jack slowed Bonnie to a walk as he approached the track leading to the farmhouse when the familiar but still alien sound of Aboriginal music wafted on the breeze. There seemed to be some sort of celebration taking place as other musical instruments joined the droning, vibrating buzz. There were a variety of sticks being tapped together producing different notes in a percussive melodic beat. The music reached a crescendo as Jack clattered into the clearing. He saw Koorong in the yard with the surviving aborigines from the massacre. They sat together with the visiting tribe, a mixture of men and women and an illustrious chief in his full regalia. Jack waited and watched as they finished playing their traditional celebratory music before he rode into the yard.

173

Minjarra was happily playing 'jacks' with a small group of children. As soon as he saw Jack riding towards them, he jumped up and ran to him. "Mr Jack, Mr Jack!" Jack dismounted and Minjarra threw his arms around Jack, "Mr Jack, some magic please. Please, Mr Jack," he pleaded.

Jack delivered his wonky impish smile and promised, "Of course, Minjarra. Just give me a few moments and I'll be back." He crossed to Koorong and was introduced to the chief.

Koorong gave the welcome gesture replicated by Jack and he broke into his own language to talk to the chief before turning and explaining, "We have decided to return to the village. Rebuild and start again with our cousins, who are being squeezed out of their own camp. Many white men are stealing their land and attacking their people, picking them off one by one. As you know we have a paradise close to this farm. It has everything we need. It calls to us. Now, the welcome ceremony is over we are planning to show them to the village straightaway. Of course, I will still work for you and maybe some of the others will become part of your workforce, too?"

Jack smiled, "I'm sure we can accommodate more help. May I have permission to accompany you? I would like to see the village again and hear of your plans."

Koorong nodded his head agreeably, "Of course, Mr Jack. I have already told Chief Jandamarra of our friendship. He was sceptical and suspicious at first as he has only met bad white men. He was planning revolution against marauding white men in his area. I have told him of our history together and of your benefactor," Koorong didn't mention Fred's name. "He had many interesting things to say. Things I know will anger you but explain much."

Jack looked puzzled, "Koorong what are you saying?"

"Come. Journey with us to the village and I will let him tell you in his own words."

Jack took Bonnie to the stables to give her a deserved rest, food and water. He ran back across the yard to where the tribesmen and women gathered and were preparing to leave. Minjarra hurried to Jack's side and slipped his hand in his, "Mr Jack, magic, please."

Jack smiled at the lad, "I will, I promise. Can you wait until we reach the village? I will do some then."

Minjarra nodded and grinned his toothy grin, "I'll wait. But you must do." He let go of Jack's hand and ran back to his cousins and the other children to gather his game of five stones.

The group of indigenous people waited while Koorong collected a wagon drawn by Brutus and the children and women climbed in the back, while Daniel brought the other dray and the remaining men climbed in. Jack was sandwiched between Koorong and Chief Jandamarra.

The two carts trundled through the yard and out onto the road. Unexpectedly, the aborigines burst into joyous song. Musically, it was a song of hope, optimism and love. Jack felt uplifted and inspired and couldn't prevent a smile from growing on his lips. He sighed, 'Oh, how I love this place; more than the fashionable town mansion that is so difficult to maintain; more than anything else. Here I felt free, uninhibited and I love not only the land and my work but the people and Koorong are a huge part of that.' Those were Jack's thoughts as they travelled through the countryside and passed the different flocks and breeds of sheep he had so carefully reared under Fred's instruction.

They began the trek to Koorong's old village and the chief began to talk, clearly translated by Koorong. Jack was amazed and Koorong was right, he grew angry.

18: Truth Will Always Out

Koorong's cousins and family hailed from north of Port Jackson. Chief Jandamarra, whose eyes flashed with fire, had an incredible story to tell as Koorong translated. "White men have continued to move down the coast and steal the best land." His tone became more vehement as his tale unfolded. "They disrespected our way of life, abused the newly acquired stolen ground, harvested the riches the earth offered. But, not content with that they raped the land," his voice contained a choked sob, "to the extent that nothing would grow. They plundered our rivers and slaughtered wildlife, taking more than they needed out of greed, leaving nothing for our people." He beat his hand against his chest as if to still his beating heart, "They accuse us of stupidity but it is the whites who are inferior, who lack intelligence. We have always followed a disciplined lifestyle and have a culture to honour the earth and know the scarcity of nature's treasures." He shook his head in sorrow, "We demand that all live in harmony with our land as hunters and gatherers. The white man's constant destruction of the forests, clearing of the yams and all other vegetation from waterways is more than foolish. It is brazenly selfish. Both of those are our main food source, this act of stupidity has to be stopped at any cost. Who can blame us for striking back and not showing surprise when colonists fall sick from malnutrition and starvation after they've destroyed the primary food sources. It is their own fault."

The chief spoke eloquently. He was a passionate communicator making his feelings very clear that he neither trusted nor liked white men. Koorong was fluent in translation and showed no apology for what was being said and Jack expected none.

The chief continued, interpreted by Koorong, "I know my cousin here, admires and respects you, Mr Jack. He has told me much of what you have done for his people. But I believe you are a rarity amongst white men."

Jack listened and murmured sympathetically as he was well aware of the actions of the kind of white men that Koorong had defined. What he was not prepared for was what followed as Koorong described what else had been happening. The chief now sat silently, his face a picture of sadness.

"You said there was more," said Jack expectantly.

Koorong nodded and took up the rest of the story himself. "Chief Jandamarra is one man prepared to fight back. It didn't work. And men who joined him in the battle who spoke up louder and fought harder, men who were willing to wage war on the white man to keep their rights were dying. Not just the ones who were arrested and executed for retaliating against the authorities but other members of the same tribe who were innocent of any crime; they were falling ill on a mass scale."

Jack looked up, "How? If not in battle, what? In illness? Or more of those terrible massacres we have seen here?"

"Despite opposition, the Sunday Shoot has continued throughout the country, but this is worse." Jack's right eyebrow raised in question as Koorong enlightened Jack, further. "Murder, Mr Jack. Murder. Your benefactor was murdered."

The jump to Fred's death was shocking. "What? No, it was a heart attack... wasn't it?" Doubt had crept into Jack's voice.

"No. It was premeditated, planned, cold blooded murder." Koorong's voice cracked with emotion. "There is a man, we all know him, a very bad man. You call him a bye-blow, and he has a group of other evil doers who work with him. He has boasted in the towns how he has successfully killed in retribution and can do it to order and in such a way that it will look like heart failure. A man who wants rid of his wife, a woman who desires her husband dead, someone who wishes to purge himself of an enemy... He will do it for a price. He cites the death of our previous employer by name, who he nicknamed 'the big man', as a prime example of what he could do. Anyone who wants to be free of someone can contact him and he will do away with their irritation... his words... anyone with a score to settle can hire him to do the job."

"What man? How?"

"He's nothing more than a paid assassin," said Koorong bitterly.

"For Gawd's sake, Koorong. Who are you talking about?"

"He calls himself Charlie..." He spat out the name with venom.

"Charlie Coombes?"

"That's the badger."

"He's a wrong 'un, I know. But, how? How did he manage it?"

"Poison, Mr Jack."

"Poison?"

"This bye-blow has made it his business to learn all about nature's deadliest plants and what they can do to someone."

"But, how could he have poisoned him?"

Koorong shrugged, "Dunno. But he did. Rumour had it, he got someone else to do it. And then he dinged the chiv. So, there were no witnesses, no lag to peach on him."

Jack could feel his rage grow and blood rushed to his face. The thought that someone had deliberately taken Fred's life affected him far more strongly than he could ever have imagined. "He was the nearest thing to a father I've known," Jack whispered as his eyes smarted with tears of anger. He swallowed hard. "How did he manage a mass poisoning to kill the tribes' people? I don't see how. Aborigines are clever when it comes to nature. Heck... when I think of all you've taught me."

"Don't believe we know everything about the natural world. This brute has made it his business to learn even more. He built fires of oleander, which gave off toxic fumes, killing women and children. Stores of vegetables and fruits were infiltrated and deadly ingredients added of death cherries, yellow pop flower seeds, poison sedge, fire bush seed pods and more. Even the pips of innocent fruits like apples have been used, ground into a powder and mixed with flour."

"I don't understand. How did they get into the stores?"

"Not all aborigines are good, Mr Jack. There are bad ones in our race, too, and they helped him achieve his goals. A few of our people worked with him and his cronies. They were paid well. Those that were caught were dealt with. It is a very sad time for our people, which is why we want to start again, here."

The countryside scene ahead became misted through Jack's eyes, as he tried to restrain the tears that were ready to fall. As they neared the village and approached the narrow outcrop of rocks with its canyon that led to the old camp, Koorong hopped down from the wagon and secured Brutus to a eucalyptus tree before ushering the chief down and everyone from the back.

Jack's mind was working wildly and recklessly as he wondered what best to do. He was determined that Charlie Coombes would pay for what he had done. But he didn't know where to find the man or if he was even in the area. He knew for official retribution he would need more than the chief's word.

The mid-afternoon sun was showering its cleansing rays across the land and washing their faces in warmth but Jack felt the stubborn flow of ice in his veins that refused to flee as his fury festered in his body and fermented into his bones. Jack swore an oath to himself that he would make it his goal to get justice for Fred and said so, without mentioning Fred's name. Koorong heard and nodded agreement.

As the other cart drew up and unloaded its human cargo Jack turned to Koorong, "Do you have any proof? Real proof that can be used against this vile specimen of humanity?"

Koorong shook his head, "All we have is mainly rumour and hearsay, except..."

"What?"

"There have been wholesale mass poisonings of our people in Bathurst. Using chemicals widely obtainable on sheep farms, like we have. You and I both know these substances are freely available."

"I can't believe it," Jack gasped in disbelief.

"And one other thing. The captain of a small garrison near Windsor had employed some ex-convicts as cooks. One of them was Charlie Coombes."

"But, how? There was a warrant out for his arrest over Denton's murder."

"I don't know. They believe he'd changed his name. It was much later when he was recognised and fled. But that's not it. There is more."

"Tell me."

"Part way through one meal the captain began to feel ill. He was violently sick and couldn't face the rest of his food. He put it down for his dog to eat. The dog died."

"That's as good as any proof, surely? Do they know who cooked it?"

"The next meal that was served was taken to the camp doctor by the captain. The medical man discovered it was laced with a combination of Moreton chestnut seeds and Angel Trumpet seeds."

"What's that?"

"The first is a black bean that grows in moist soil by river banks and mountain sides, its seeds are highly toxic. The Angel Trumpet seeds are quite fragrant and belie the damage they can do."

"So?"

"Those are the seeds that can mimic a heart attack."

Jack fell silent. Koorong gathered his people together and Daniel came to Jack's side. "Do we wait here or go with them?"

"We go with them."

Koorong led the way through the canyon, past the glittering waterfall and shimmering lagoon, and into the remnants of the old village.

Koorong stopped and surveyed his old village, clearly filled with emotion. Jack, too, felt a wave of nostalgia flood through him. In his head, he imagined the children playing, the people who welcomed him in the past who were now no more. He looked around at what was left amongst the good huts and the burnt out ones whose straw roofs had been destroyed. He half expected the ghosts from the past to appear and run through the camp.

Koorong stepped forward and addressed his cousins. "This is a place of beauty. A haven. It has everything we need. The lagoon fulfils our water needs. The river that feeds it is blessed by Baiame and provides fish for us to catch. The land is lush and green we can grow what we need. The crops we had left and not reaped have seeded. The birds of the land have benefitted and we will profit from that. There is an abundance of wildlife that we can work with in harmony."

Jack spoke up, "I will give you some sheep for your own flock to use as you wish and I will help you to rebuild the village with whatever materials you need."

"And I, too," announced Daniel standing shoulder to shoulder with Jack.

"I will hope to persuade Chief Jandamarra that we are not all evil. That we can live in peace side by side. You have my word."

Koorong translated all that Jack and Daniel had said and the chief nodded wisely. Suddenly, there was optimism in the air. Jack could feel it. It was good to be hopeful to try and create a place of safety and accord.

Jack turned to Koorong, "It's unlikely that those renegade white men will revisit this place. You should feel protected here and safe. Let's make a start. What do you need?"

As Koorong listed materials Minjarra crept up to steal Jack away, and with a shrug, Jack joined the children at play.

***

The next few days were more than busy. Apart from running the farm, Jack spent his days ferrying goods along to the new village and helping to restructure the camp. In the town Jack had made out that the materials were for farm repairs and no one suspected anything different, which both Koorong and Jack felt was wise. The less people knew about it, the better.

With rebuilding in progress Jack was unable to get away to the church to hear Amy play and he prayed she would not think badly of him. He made up his mind to persuade Edward to get a message to her, in case she had forgotten him. As he returned to the mansion to fetch a few more items of clothing he met Miss Bonnet on her way out. "Why? Mr Jack! You have been something of a stranger these last few days, so you have. I have missed you."

"As I have missed your wonderful cooking, Miss B."

"You could turn any woman's head with flattery like that. Will you be home for supper tonight?"

Jack grinned his crooked smile, "Not tonight. No. But I will be back home from tomorrow and things will get back to some kind of normality."

"I'm glad to hear it. Can I do anything for you?"

"Nope. Just here to collect some clothes. Farm repairs are taking their toll on my normal dress."

"You should be wearing your old work clothes not your best bib and tucker!"

"I know, I know. Is Mr Edward at home?"

"He is, indeed. In the drawing room."

"Thanks, Miss B," said Jack bombing past her into the house.

Miss B shook her head in an amused fashion and walked down the drive towards the town.

Jack skidded along the polished corridor to the drawing room and dived inside, "Edward?"

Edward turned from the Tantalus where he was pouring himself a glass of port, "Jack. It's good to see you. I have missed your company. Miss B isn't half as accommodating as when you are around. How are things at the camp?"

"Almost done. One more day should do it. I will select some sheep as I promised to give them as a gift from us and then you must come and see what we have done."

"I most certainly will. It will be good to see the village again and meet Koorong's cousins."

"Edward, I have a favour to ask you."

"Of course, anything... What is it?"

"I need you to get a message to Miss Martel for me, please. She is unaware that I have been working and I don't want her to think I am no longer pleased to see her. Can you do that?"

"Certainly, just tell me where and when and what you want me to say."

"Most nights she's at St. Mary's church from six in the evening, practising the piano."

"Where is it?"

"Right at the bottom of Sutherland Road. You can't miss it."

"Believe me, I can miss anything." Edward saw Jack's look of consternation and laughed. "Don't worry. I'll find it. What do you want me to say?"

"Explain to her that I have been busy with work. She should understand and ask her if she can meet me at The Mansfield Hotel at one o'clock the day after tomorrow. I have already booked a table."

"Tuesday?"

"Yes. That's usually her afternoon off."

"Consider it done. And now, my friend, how about a glass of port before your ride back?"

"Thank you, but no. I need to get back and get things finished. I can't leave Bobby and Daniel to complete things on their own."

"I'm sure they are more than capable but as you wish."

"Thank you. You will go, won't you? Tonight? Promise me."

Edward laughed again. "Don't worry so much. It will be done."

"Thanks, Edward and now I really must be going. I'll see you in two days. But you'll see Miss Martel first... won't you?"

"Go on. Be off with you," said Edward with a wry grin.

Jack smiled and dashed from the room.

***

True to his word, Edward took the carriage and pair and made his way from the mansion to the less salubrious part of town where women touted for business and drunks rolled and brawled in the streets. He passed quickly through that seedy area and into Sutherland Road. The horses clip-clopped their way to the bottom where St. Mary's Church stood. It was five minutes past six. Edward stopped outside and heard the heavenly music playing. He jumped down after securing his horses and carriage and crept inside the candle-lit church.

He settled himself in a pew at the back and listened to the enchanting music. Jack had been right. She had a fine hand and played beautifully. Momentarily, he lost himself in the classical piece being played and watched as she performed for no one but her own satisfaction. Edward could well see why the dainty and petite Miss Martel appeared to have captured Jack's heart.

The time passed quickly and as she completed the sonata and held her fingers on the keys, as was her habit, Edward rose and began to applaud while walking from the back of the church towards the piano at the font. "Bravo!"

"Jack?" The eager smile faded from Miss Martel's lips as she saw a tall, fair headed stranger approaching her.

"Miss Martel, that was wonderful."

"I'm sorry. Do I know you?"

"My apologies. I am Edward Hargreaves, at your service," he said clicking his heels.

"Edward... Hargreaves? Why, you must be Jack's friend and partner?"

"One and the same."

"How is Jack... er Mr Dawkins? Is he well?"

"He's just fine. He asked me to bring you a message as he has been tied up with business at the farm and didn't want you to think he'd forgotten you."

Amy Martel blushed a deep crimson, dropped her eyes to the floor and was for a moment stuck for something to say. She raised her head and tried to speak. It came out as a squeak so she cleared her throat and started again. "You said you had a message?"

"Um, yes," said Edward temporarily mesmerised by her beauty. "Sorry... yes... he asked if you would meet him at the Mansfield Hotel Tuesday... er the day after tomorrow."

"At what time, sir?"

"He said one o'clock. Will you be there? He intimated that Tuesday was your day off..."

"Yes, Mr Hargreaves. Tuesday is indeed my afternoon off and yes, I will be there."

They were interrupted by the arrival of Toby who entered and announced, "Miss Martel, your carriage is waiting."

"Thank you, Toby. I will be there shortly."

Toby looked sideways at Edward with a look of bewilderment. He bowed politely and left.

Miss Martel hesitated slightly and added, "Please convey my best wishes to Mr Dawkins and let him know that I will be delighted to join him at one. Thank you." She swept from the church with poise, her head held high and Edward looked after her in amazement. He shook his head almost in disbelief and said to himself, "Jack's really found himself a special lady."

***

Jack had chosen six young Romney ewes and a ram. He loaded them with Daniel's help ready to take to the village. They passed through the farm boundaries and into the bush. Jack never stopped marvelling at the sounds that could be heard. The bird song chatter, their alarm calls interspersed with the gentle hush of the wind, and the bleating of sheep calling to their lambs.

As they travelled, he studied the landscape with renewed interest. Tufts of pheasant tail grass waved in the warm breeze. Its beautiful arching dark green leaves swayed gracefully when the wind sighed. They were just beginning to turn an attractive copper threaded with gold and bronze, which Jack knew would remain through winter and, like an artist's brush, paint the land with colourful hues. The seasons were so different here and he loved it. He didn't miss the smoke and grimy smut of London or the back street squalor he had known as 'home'. He knew that when summer returned this grass would be topped with airy arching sprays of rosy flowers that would hang down almost kissing the ground. Jack's heart filled with love for the farm and he realised he much preferred it to the fine house in town, a novelty at first but now... now he knew it was where he wanted to be. But he also knew unless something changed he would never leave his friend, Edward and would live with him wherever he wanted to reside.

Daniel and Jack enjoyed the easy silence between them. They knew each other well enough. There was no necessity for idle banter so when Daniel broke the moment Jack listened. "You know, mate, we all miss your daily input into the farm. It's a great thing you're doing for all of us and it is serving a purpose but..."

"But?"

"Will you ever come back full-time?"

"Never say never but at the moment it seems unlikely."

Daniel, shrugged, "Pity. Understandable, but a pity nonetheless."

Brutus plodded on and each rumbling turn of the wheel punctuated the sudden change in mood, which was now more wistful and melancholic.

Once they arrived at the rocks, which defined the passage through to the village, they secured the cart and Brutus, who was left to nibble at the vegetation under the gum trees, and unloaded the sheep to drive them through the rocky passageway to the camp.

Jack stood at the edge and became quite emotional at the sight of the settlement now filled with people, children playing and women weaving rush matting using some of the very grasses he had admired on route, threading colour into the light green reeds that were the strong base of the rugs. Chief Jandamarra stepped out with Koorong to receive the gift of the sheep and a look of mutual respect passed between them.

Jack was invited into the newly repaired communal hut, while Koorong and Daniel ushered the sheep safely to the pen Koorong and others had made. The chief bade Jack to sit while an appealingly pretty girl, served him some traditional fare of flatbread and wild honey, which Jack received graciously.

Koorong and Daniel entered the hut and joined Jack, each receiving the same repast. The young girl approached Daniel shyly and smiled timidly lighting her face with serene joy. She patted her chest, "Kirra," and looked questioningly at Daniel. She repeated the gesture and her name, "Kirra."

Daniel broke into a freckled grin, indicated himself, "Daniel."

"Daniel," reiterated Kirra.

Jack looked at Daniel and Kirra and was aware of a spark of chemistry between them. Koorong noticed it, too and frowned.

Kirra was more than attentive to the visiting young men. Koorong, unable to stop himself, rose and took the girl to one side and spoke roughly to her. Daniel whispered to Jack, "What's going on?"

Jack spoke quietly, "I think she is in trouble for paying you so much attention."

"But, why?"

"Isn't it obvious? You are not one of them."

Daniel snorted, "Then, we best be getting back. I can't watch her being taken to task because of me."

"Sit tight, Daniel. We have to wait until the chief gives us leave to go. Swallow your misgivings. They are our friends. Treat them as such. I don't have to tell you. Remember Minnie."

Daniel remained seated but it was clear he was unhappy about Kirra's reprimand. The rest of the celebration passed peacefully and when the chief rose, Jack and Daniel did the same. They made the gesture of friendship. Jack shook Koorong's hand and murmured, "Don't be so hard on the girl. Daniel knows nothing can come of it." Koorong nodded and the young men turned to leave but when Daniel looked back to say goodbye he caught Kirra's eye and Jack again could see the attraction between them.

Jack and Daniel made their way through the gorge and back to the wagon where Brutus waited. Jack untethered the horse. They boarded, and began the journey back to the farm. Jack looked across at Daniel whose freckled face was stuck in a frown. "It won't work, Daniel. Put her out of your head. I expect she's already promised to someone."

"Why? Why not?"

"One thing, you don't know her. Second, her family would never permit it. Koorong would never allow it. You are too different."

Daniel appeared to accept Jack's wisdom but was pensive for the rest of the journey and Jack began to worry that Daniel wouldn't listen to him. He sighed heavily as his mind ran riot. 'Who am I to dictate when I, himself, am so different from Amy? We are from two different worlds like Kirra and Daniel. Jack decided he would stay out of it but prayed Daniel would see sense.

***

Finally, Tuesday arrived and Jack made his way to the Mansfield Hotel. Atwill stood at the desk of the restaurant ready to admit guests. "Mr Dawkins, how good to see you again. I have reserved the same table as before, overlooking the rose garden. I trust that is in order?"

"It most certainly is," said Jack passing Atwill his hat, which was placed on the coat stand by the entrance desk.

Atwill led the way to the table carrying the menu. He pulled out the chair for Jack. "Does sir have his spectacles today?"

Jack patted the pockets of his frock coat and let out an expletive, "Darn... No. Forgotten them again."

"Will sir require me to read the menu?"

Jack thought for a moment and asked, "What would you recommend, Atwill?"

"Sir, the chicken in white wine and cream sauce is delicious. It's what I would choose," said Atwill kindly. Jack nodded. "And what would you like to drink?"

"I'll have a dry sherry, please, Atwill," said Jack remembering the drink of Amy's choice from last time.

"Very well, sir." Atwill bowed.

"Before you go, last time Miss Martel mentioned a pudding called 'Kisses' what is it?"

"They are little cakes made of meringue with fresh fruit and cream. Three to a serving. Called kisses because they are so sweet."

"Thank you, Atwill."

He bowed and melted away as Jack viewed the exquisite garden once more. He noted that there was a young couple seated there enjoying a pot of coffee or something similar and he observed the gentleman's actions. In truth, he was becoming a little nervous as he waited for Amy to arrive.

Atwill returned with his drink and Jack studied his pocket watch with a puckered brow. It was five minutes past one. The devil on his shoulder began to whisper in his ear, 'She's late. She's never late. She was very punctual last time. Maybe she's changed her mind? Maybe she's not coming.' Jack twisted his hands anxiously and began to gnaw the inside of his cheek, a habit he believed he'd successfully stopped. He winced as he bit the tender part of his inner buccal cavity. At that moment he saw Amy arriving and Atwill led her to the table. The pain in his cheek forgotten, Jack rose to greet her and pulled out her chair for her to adjust her dress before sitting.

"I am so sorry to be late. Please forgive me," she said quietly. "One of the girls fell and I had to bandage her knee before I left. The family are going away for a little while. I do hope I haven't kept you waiting too long?"

"Not at all."

Atwill waited for her to be seated, "May I get you a drink, Miss...?"

"Martel and yes, a dry sherry would be perfect. Thank you."

Atwill again dissolved into the background and then returned with her drink and a menu.

"Have you decided what you want?" asked Amy as she studied the bill of fare.

"I'm taking Atwill's recommendation of the chicken in white wine and cream sauce."

"Mmm. It sounds most appetising. I think I will have the same." Atwill bowed deferentially and left.

Jack smiled, "You got my message, then?"

"Yes, and met your dear friend Mr Hargreaves. He explained that you had been busy at the farm and couldn't get away."

"I wanted to come and hear you play again. I was sorry to have missed your practising."

Amy flushed with pleasure, "And I am looking forward to introducing you to some more of my favourite pieces."

"And I am looking forward to hearing them," said Jack giving her another dimpled smile.

"Might I enquire what you were so busy with at the farm? Were you shearing or lambing? Have I missed some important part of the country calendar? Remember you promised to show me the ranch. I will hold you to that."

"I also said I'd show you the mansion in the town. But I know you have little time to yourself."

"But, I have. Both today, tomorrow, and Friday. The captain is taking his daughters to visit their aunt. I have three whole days to do as I wish. And, I took the liberty of cancelling my carriage believing that you might escort me home, instead."

Now, it was Jack's turn to colour up. He could hardly believe his ears and almost said so but stopped himself in time. "But, of course. It will be my pleasure." He just hoped he was saying the right thing and using the correct words. This was all so new to him.

"Then that's settled. After we have eaten you can take me to your fine town house and give me the grand tour."

Atwill arrived carrying a tray set with plates covered by a silver dome and side bowls of vegetables and set them out on the table. He stood at the side of them and lifted both covers at the same time revealing the dishes underneath. Jack couldn't help but be impressed and believed that Atwill had done this especially for him. He left them to enjoy their meal.

Amy smiled in delight, "This is a good choice. Quite mouth-watering. Do tell me, what was it that kept you so occupied at the farm?"

Jack didn't know why but he found himself telling Amy about everything that had happened. She listened sympathetically and in awe. Jack continued, "Please don't repeat any of this. The last thing we want is for men to come and shoot up the camp again."

"I won't breathe a word. You have my promise. But, what you have told me is horrific and what of Daniel and Kirra? Are they never to be allowed to meet? It's so romantic like Shakespeare's tale of Romeo and Juliet."

Jack nodded agreeably, although he hadn't a clue what she was talking about. The devil on his shoulder piped up again, 'You are ignorant and uneducated, what do you know of Romeo and Juliet or William Shakespeare?' He sighed despairingly.

"Have I said something wrong?"

"No, I was just thinking, I know nothing of the story of Romeo and Juliet. Perhaps you would care to enlighten me?" he admitted with complete honesty.

Amy smiled at him, "But of course. I'd be delighted," and she began to impart the story of the play.

Jack listened spellbound and when she had finished his eyes were moist with tears. "That is so terribly sad. And it sounds just like..."

"What?"

"Nothing... but it could be a prophesy for Daniel and Kirra." And he thought to himself 'or of Amy Martel and me, Jack Dawkins.'

Atwill appeared as if by magic to clear the dishes and asked if they wanted a dessert.

Amy nodded enthusiastically, "The almond pudding was delightful last time but I think I might try something different. Jack?" She paused as she perused the dessert menu that Atwill had brought.

"I thought I would like the kisses, if they are still on the menu?"

Atwill nodded, "They are indeed, sir. And for you, Miss Martel?"

Amy blushed, "I believe I would like kisses, too."

Atwill assented, "An excellent choice. Who doesn't enjoy kisses?" said Atwill before vanishing again leaving Jack and Amy looking slightly uncomfortable. Amy broke the embarrassed silence with a delicious giggle. "Why, I do think Atwill has us marked down as a courting couple. How silly."

Jack mustered a laugh thinking it wasn't silly at all but his deep desire. The devil popped up again, 'Now, you can put that thought right out of your head.' Then, the angel on his other shoulder twittered, 'Go on... say something witty, something funny... "Miss Martel, Amy..."

"Yes?"

"I can't think of anything entertaining to say."

Amy looked at him in surprise, "I don't think we need to talk. After all, our kisses have arrived." She coloured up again.

They were saved further mortification by Atwill placing the sweets in front of them. That was when Amy unable to contain herself, laughed. Her giggle was so infectious that Jack laughed, too, although he didn't know why; but the merriment released the nervous tension and conversation flowed smoothly once more.

The rest of the meal passed pleasantly, Atwill brought the bill but this time he had circled the total amount and underlined it. He passed it to Jack who understood, happily paid the money and passed an extra note to Atwill. "Thank you for your excellent service."

Atwill, touched by Jack's generosity, bowed, "Thank you, sir. I hope to see you both again soon," and gave him his hat.

The youngsters left the restaurant and Jack helped Amy into the carriage and drove her to the town house. They turned into the sweeping drive. "The house is up ahead."

Jack pulled up in front of the stone steps. He jumped down and helped Amy from the carriage. They walked up to the front door and Jack suddenly became aware of the state of the outside. There were a couple of empty bottles on the terrace. The grass was overgrown and the garden unkempt with weeds and out of control undergrowth. Amy stopped and looked around. She didn't comment and Jack felt a twinge of shame at the neglected grounds.

He opened the door to admit her and she paused in the impressive hallway, which was to his relief, clean and tidy, except for a cushion that had tumbled on the floor, from the hall settle. "Well? What do you think?"

"It's lovely," she said spinning around and taking in the décor.

"Only lovely? It's fantastic!"

"No, it really is lovely." Amy picked up the cushion and replaced it on the wooden settle and sat. She beamed at Jack, "Well, I am ready for the grand tour."

"Well, all right!" Jack's enthusiasm was infectious and plain to see. "Today the house, tomorrow the farm. Er... that's if you have the time?"

"Why, yes and even if I didn't I would make time, for you." Jack could hardly restrain his delight. He bit the inside of his cheek again, fearing he had said too much. Amy raised her hand, which he took and helped her to her feet. This time the devil on his shoulder said nothing.

19: Romance Flowers

Amy was excited to be visiting the farm she had heard so much about. As Jack turned the carriage from the road to the track with fields either side he pointed out the boundaries of the ranch. "This is the start of the spread, which stretches for many miles. Some of the land is just scrub and sand used as a buffer zone between us and the local natives, but much of it is fertile ground and meadow pastures perfect for the sheep to graze."

"I've never seen so many sheep. Which are your prized Merino ones?"

Jack smiled at Amy's enthusiasm and answered her questions as fully as he could. "They are sturdy adaptable foragers with a creamy thick fleece of tightly crimped hair. Their wool is highly prized. Basically, there are four types of Merino that do well in this climate. They are easily spotted with the folds of wool around their faces and are creamy in colour."

Amy clapped her hands delightedly as she spotted a flock. "There, over there! Are those Merinos?"

"You're a quick learner! They are, indeed."

"Only because I have such an excellent teacher. Which are the Romneys? No, no... let me guess... They are similar in size, well-muscled, with a uniform heavy fleece, some of them have little hats of wool on their heads, which sets them apart, wide heads, with black noses and hooves. You see I do listen!"

"We'll have you lambing next!" said Jack with a laugh. "You have the ideal hands for it."

"From Governess to shepherdess... I would like that," she said with a shy smile. "You explain everything so clearly and when you speak you smile. I like that, too..." Amy trailed off as if fearing she had said too much.

Jack was pleasantly surprised at her genuine interest and her exuberance was irresistibly catching. "Okay, test time now... you are doing so well... what about the fat tails."

"Easy" said Amy with relish. "They have fat tails and hindquarters! Some of them have pretty black muzzles and black floppy ears like..." She glanced about her, "Those over there!"

Jack was enchanted by her obvious curiosity and she continued to ask questions as they rattled on down the track. "In about half a mile we should see the drive to the farmhouse. From here as far as you can see, is our land. Edward's and mine."

Amy said nothing, she was stunned into silence and appeared to revel in all that Jack was showing her, which pleased Jack even more than he could have imagined. The carriage turned into the drive and soon the yard and farmhouse came into view with all the out buildings and barns. Outside one barn was Brutus harnessed to a cart.

"Ooh! Is this it?" exclaimed Amy. She was like a small child at Christmas with a new toy.

"It is. It's where Fred Doble and his wife gave us shelter, work and a new life."

Koorong emerged from his and Edward's old quarters carrying some items together with Minjarra, which they loaded into the back of the cart. He gave Jack a friendly wave and strode across to them, followed by Minjarra, as Jack helped Amy from the carriage.

"You are leaving?" said Jack.

"Yes. Returning to the village. Just taking our last few items."

"This is Miss Martel, an acquaintance of mine."

"Happy to meet you, Miss Martel," said Koorong with the gesture of friendship.

Amy looked to Jack in bewilderment and saw Jack give the same signal to Koorong. She imitated the movement and smiled in greeting, "Pleased to meet you... Koorong, isn't it? I have heard much about you."

Minjarra tugged Amy's skirt, "I am Minjarra, Miss pretty lady."

Amy bent down and ruffled Minjarra's wild curly hair. "Hello, Minjarra. I have heard all about you, too. You like to play games, do you not?"

"Yes, Jack's."

"Jack's?"

"Five or ten stones. I call it Jack's," he grinned his toothy grin. "Wanna play?"

Amy laughed, "Perhaps later. If you are around?"

Minjarra looked sad, "We go now. Won't be here to play."

"Well, we can't have that, can we?" said Amy. "Let's step onto the porch and I'll give you a game."

Koorong looked at his nephew and said something in Awabakal. Amy looked questioningly. Koorong explained, "I told him not to bother you, Miss Martel. I'm sorry."

"Don't be. I'm sure we have time for one game. Yes?"

Minjarra nodded fiercely and Amy sat on the wooden settle in the porch with the boy. He took his precious pouch of stones and they began to play in the intervening space between them while Jack looked on in admiration. He observed how gentle she was with the child and seemed genuinely interested in him and what he had to say. Jack admitted to himself that Miss Amy Martel was constantly surprising him.

***

The sun had risen to its height in the deep cerulean sky. Koorong and Minjarra had left the farm and Amy had been given a full tour of the dwelling and accompanying barns. She appeared impressed with everything. They retreated inside the farmhouse to escape the glaring heat where Jack set about making some refreshment. He found tea in one of the cupboards and the larder contained some tinned goods. There was milk in a jug left by Koorong together with fresh bread and butter. The salt chest contained some pork joints and strips of bacon. Jack announced, "Before the chickens all vanish to the village, I'll check for some newly laid eggs."

"Oh, do let me come with you. I would love to collect some fresh eggs." Her face was earnest in expression and Jack was reminded of how she might have looked as a little girl.

"Let's take the egg basket." They walked out together to the hen coop and Jack opened up the nesting box to reveal three large brown-shelled eggs. He passed Amy the basket and allowed her to collect them and put them in the basket.

"They're still warm!" she exclaimed.

"Better search around. They often lay in bushes and on the ground, in fact anywhere that takes their fancy."

Amy squealed in delight as she spotted one that had rolled towards the water trough and put it with the others. They found two more and made their way back to the house. "This is better than hide and go seek," she said merrily.

Once inside, Jack lit the range and put the kettle on to boil. "I was planning on going to the village tomorrow, if you want to come? Koorong will be back later to collect the pigs. The chooks will have to wait collection until after my visit."

"I would love to... But how can we do that? Don't you have to get back to Port Jackson?"

Jack shook his head, "Only to take you home. Otherwise I would remain here until after my visit to the camp."

Amy gestured upstairs, "You have three bedrooms, do you not?"

"Yes," said Jack uncertain what she was intending.

"Then you can sleep in your old room and I can take one of the others and we can return to town together tomorrow."

"But, won't you be missed?"

"There's no one at home except for the servants. I told you, I have three days to do as I wish and I wish to stay here and go to see the camp tomorrow. If that's all right with you?"

"Fine by me but what about your needs and night clothes?"

"I assume there is soap and water?"

"Yes, and there are items of clothing that have been left by Mrs D... although, they will bury you! Mrs D was a very ample woman."

"Then, I will manage. And together we can cook up a feast with what we have here. It will be fun. I have never done anything like this before."

"Nor I," admitted Jack.

"I have to say... and I hope you don't mind... I loved your house in the town but I like it better here, Jack. This place... the countryside... it's beautiful."

Jack beamed as he looked around the familiar kitchen, "I've some good memories here, with Fred and Mrs D, but Edward chose the house in town."

Amy studied Jack's face closely but Jack was unable to read the meaning of her expression.

A silence descended on them.

"Why don't you show me, which room I can use?"

Jack nodded, "This way." They went up the wooden stairs and Jack took Amy to what was the Dobles' room. He opened the blanket box, which contained items left behind by Mrs D. He gave a lopsided dimpled grin. "Couldn't bring myself to chuck them out. Seems it was the right thing to do."

Amy rummaged through the chest and pulled out a long white cotton night shirt. This will do fine. Now, let's get cooking. I'll race you downstairs."

"That's not fair. I'll never get past your dress. It will take up the whole width of the stairs!" said Jack cheekily.

"Why do you think I said I'd race you?" said Amy with an impish look, before she lifted her skirts and dashed out of the door leaving Jack looking bemused. He waited a moment and then threw back his head and laughed and laughed.

***

That evening Jack found himself sitting on the wooden settle on the porch with Amy next to him. They looked up at the night sky with its myriad of glittering stars and watched in wonder as a shooting star grazed the heavens on a path to earth. Amy whispered, "It's beautiful."

"Fred and Mrs D would sit here night after night watching the magic of the heavens," murmured Jack. "Every time they saw a shooting star or the trail of a meteor or comet, Mrs D would make a wish."

"Did they come true?"

"Dunno. Never told us what she wished for. Fred used to say it sent her to bed happy. Look! Look!" cried Jack as another shimmering trail sparked across the midnight blue of the velvet night sky. "Make a wish! Quickly, before the shower fades."

Amy closed her eyes tightly and pursed her full dewy lips and softly murmured, "I wish... I wish..." and she went inside her head to complete her silent wish.

Jack wondered what it was. "What did you wish for?"

"I can't tell you that. It won't come true. Did you make one?"

"No. I left that wishing star all for you. I'll take the next one."

They sat quietly contemplating the navy heavens and at that moment Jack fully understood why Fred and Mrs D enjoyed sitting together on the porch every night. It truly was blissful.

***

The next day, Jack opened his eyes and for a moment wondered where he was. He looked around his old room in the farmhouse and smiled before extending his arms up in a satisfying stretch and then he remembered... Amy was in the Dobles' old bedroom and his smile broadened. He pushed back the handmade patchwork coverlet and ambled to the window and pulled back the curtains.

The vermilion sky heralded the emergence of the dawn. He watched spellbound as the colour morphed into a more gentle cinnabar with swathes of nutmeg before the sun drowned the pigment in a yellow buttery blaze of glory as it rose in the sky.

Jack sighed, he had missed this place and the mornings. It almost seemed as if he was observing nature for the very first time. He splashed his face with water and rubbed his emery chin with its budding whiskers unable to stop grinning. Salt and tooth powder still sat in a pot on his tallboy. He scrubbed at his teeth and swished his mouth around to freshen it up and wondered if Amy had everything she needed.

He dressed swiftly and brushed his unruly hair into some kind of order before inspecting himself in the mirror. With his untrained eye he believed he'd do! He left his room quietly and made his way downstairs and was surprised to see that Amy was already up and she had buttered bread, cut into fingers and had water boiling on the range for the rest of the eggs they had collected yesterday.

"Good morning!"

"Morning to you, too," said Amy. "Sit yourself down. Tea's made and breakfast will be just a few minutes."

Jack sat, still unable to believe what he was seeing. "Did you find everything you needed?" he asked.

"Yes, there were plenty of things left that I could use, so I managed. I must say I am really looking forward to going to the village. It will be lovely to see Koorong and Minjarra again. I do believe he is quite a bright boy. He could learn so much if schooling was available for him. It is such a shame there is nothing here."

Amy chattered on about her feelings regarding the importance of education and the devil popped up on Jack's shoulder again, 'Education is important to her. What will she say when she finds out you have none?'

Amy served the eggs and sat herself. "This is a rare treat for me. I haven't done anything in the kitchen since I left England. I have been watching the cook at the house and itching to try and create some of the meals I've seen prepared. But, it is frowned upon for me to mix with the other servants. So, this is an absolute joy. Thank you, so much."

Jack nodded and was a little stumped as what to say so he began to eat his breakfast and allowed Amy to talk for the two of them. He had never seen her so animated and natural. It pleased and amused him that the initial stiff formality of what was considered respectable conversation had vanished. Of course, they had had their moments before but this was the third day they were spending together and she was much more at ease in Jack's company than she had ever been previously.

Breakfast over, Jack insisted on clearing up and washing the dishes. He shooed Amy out onto the porch to wait for him, which she was happy to do. She watched the chickens scurrying around and scratching in the yard. By the time Jack emerged Amy had christened every hen with a name to suit its personality. She pointed at a white hen strutting around with feathers growing down its legs, "See, that one there! That's Spats!"

"Spats?"

"Yes. The height of fashion for chooks just like feathered gaiters." Jack looked amused. Amy pointed to another with a fluffy head, "That's Hattie and that black one is Liquorice." Jack shook his head amused and listened as she identified every chicken in the yard.

Jack brought the carriage and pair around to the front yard and they set off. Amy had settled into a contented, peaceful quietness. She looked about her, avidly drinking in the views the landscape offered. Jack pointed out Fred's final resting place and she nodded appreciatively at the exceptional vista. "Jack, it's beautiful. I'm so glad you let me see it."

The carriage stopped short at the gorge, which led to the camp. "I did wonder whether we'd get here in a carriage and pair. It's not the best terrain for this. Sorry, if the ride was a bit rough."

"Don't apologise. I've loved every minute of it," said Amy with sincerity. Jack helped her down. "I'm not really best dressed for this. I should have donned some of Mrs D's work clothes or maybe borrowed yours," she said with a laugh as her skirt snagged on the spines of a spiky blue devil plant. Amy gathered her skirt and held it before her as she negotiated the narrow passage. She gasped in delight when she saw the cool rippling lagoon and tumbling waterfall. Here the vegetation was fertile and lush. The sunlight dappled through the bushes and trees. It was an oasis in the outback.

As Jack entered the camp, the children came running towards him and crowded around. Minjarra sprinted towards him and tucked his hand in his. "Mr Jack! Mr Jack! We're going to play Weet Weet. You play too!" Jack laughed and allowed himself to be carried across towards the clearing in front of the communal hut. The children had a play stick, a small club-like object, which they would take turns at throwing. The one who threw it the furthest was the winner. Amy noticed his easy rapport with the children and how he interacted with them. He genuinely seemed to be enjoying himself with them and they clearly adored him. She seemed quite moved by this.

The little girls gazed in awe at Amy and were riveted by her dress as they danced around her. The young women were fascinated by her. They couldn't resist touching her dress and her hands comparing her silky fair skin to their own. Jack looked back at Amy between throws of the kangaroo rat play stick with a fixed grin on his face.

A young mother carrying a small baby came out from the communal hut with Koorong and the chief. She crossed to Amy and stared at her wide-eyed. Amy put out her arms to hold the baby and the young woman relinquished her bundle without question. Amy smiled in delight and the young mother stroked and felt the material of Amy's dress, her face an expression of wonder.

Koorong introduced Amy to the chief who acknowledged her politely and said something in Awabakal. Amy asked, "What did he say?"

"He understands you are a woman of learning and wondered if you would like to come into the communal hut for our history telling."

"History telling?"

"We pass down our ancestors' stories of how we came to be and much more in the form of storytelling. I have been given the honour to give the lesson this morning. You would be most welcome."

Amy beamed. "Why, I would be delighted. I will sit with the children and learn with them as I know nothing of your culture and would deem it a privilege, although sitting in this," she indicated her dress, "will be difficult. So, I may stand behind them."

Koorong recounted Amy's words to the chief who nodded sagely and said something else. Amy looked questioningly at Koorong.

"The chief says that education is the key to understanding each other. That maybe you will impart that knowledge to your people. Come, let us go in."

Amy passed the tiny infant back to his mother, lifted her skirts and entered the hut. Koorong clapped his hands and the children stopped their game and ran to Koorong who ushered them inside followed by Jack.

The children sat cross-legged in rows and Amy stood behind them to be joined by Jack. The chief sat facing them and Koorong stepped into the space at the front and began his story of the creation. He was kind enough to translate the words into English after each section and Amy listened intently.

"Bee-rook-born was the first man and he had a wife. They lived in a beautiful place that had much food. Baiame, the creator, told them they could eat anything they wanted but not to touch the honey from the Yarran tree or evil would come to them. The wife was tempted and took honey from the tree. There appeared a black winged bat called Narahdarn. Narahdarn is the symbol of death. So, Bee-rook-born's wife brought death to the world."

Amy turned to Jack and whispered, "It is not so different from our own story of the creation... fascinating."

"We are no different from them apart from the colour of our skin. If we are cut we both bleed and our blood is red. If we are hurt we cry and if we have fun we both laugh. Basically, we are the same. But they have more understanding and respect for the land than any white man. It makes me ashamed what my own kind have done to them. They are my friends."

Amy looked at Jack with new eyes, "You speak so much truth. Shakespeare himself couldn't have said it better."

Jack looked bemused, "I have no idea what you are talking about."

"You will. As I told you the story of Romeo and Juliet I will also tell you the tale of the Merchant of Venice and you will see how what you have said has been relevant through all history."

Jack raised an eyebrow and turned back to watch the rest of the lesson, which was being performed with actions by some of the younger men. They listened closely to the rest of the instruction with almost an air of reverence.

The instruction hour passed quite quickly and the children fled the tent in glee, eager to continue their games outside.

Jack addressed Koorong, "It is time for me to take Miss Martel back to Port Jackson. Thank you for your warm welcome. When you collect the chooks be careful with them as each and every one of them now has a name." It was Koorong's turn to look nonplussed. Jack continued, "Miss Martel has christened them all." They all laughed together.

***

During the carriage drive back Amy was quietly thoughtful. Jack glanced across, "Have I said something to upset you?"

"Not at all. I was just thinking."

"What?"

"How strange it is that Koorong's story of the beginning of the earth is so like ours of Adam and Eve in the Garden of Eden. It is almost identical. Very strange."

"Yes, I suppose it is."

"Jack, I loved it out there. Do you know, I was always afraid of the natives. Stories I'd heard. They are not fearsome at all."

"I've known Koorong and others like him for many years. They're all right."

Amy sighed and they continued the journey in silence when Amy decided to snuggle into Jack's arm and he flushed with pleasure. She sighed again. "I really am going to miss being here."

"How do you mean?" said Jack wondering what she would say.

"The captain is returning to England with the girls and me with them."

The devil popped up on Jack's shoulder once more and whispered, 'See, she's not for you.' Jack cleared his throat almost afraid to ask, "When?"

"Next week."

His response was accepting and matter of fact, "Fair enough."

Surprised, Amy sat up straight and pulled away from him, "What did you say?"

"I said, fair enough."

Her eyes misted over, "I thought you would be upset."

"What's the point in being upset? Don't change nothing. We've had a great time. I'll always remember it."

Amy's face crumpled despondently. It was clear that she didn't know whether to say anymore, but came to a decision that forced her to speak. "I was thinking that Edward could manage the house and the farm and you might come back to England... with me."

"And risk the morning drop? No thanks," said Jack definitively.

"What's the morning drop?" asked Amy confused.

"Don't tell me you ain't never been to a hanging?"

"A hanging?"

Jack turned his head and looked at her, "I'm a lifer. If I go back, they'll hang me."

"But you were only a child... a small boy..."

"That's the law for you." Jack shrugged, resignedly, "But, I ain't gonna risk it."

Amy couldn't hide her disappointment, but was equally adamant in her reply, "No you must not."

Feeling there was no more to say they continued travelling in silence but now there was space between them, a void, not just physically in the carriage, but mentally, too. The voice in Jack's head mocked him and laughed, 'You're not good enough for her. Never will be. Best cut your losses and say goodbye.'

But then the angel spoke, 'Let her go, but have one last drink before she leaves. Surely, that can't hurt?'

***

That night Edward and Jack sat on the terrace at the mansion together enjoying a glass of port wine. Jack was unusually but understandably melancholy and Edward could see he was visibly upset by the news he'd divulged of Miss Martel's imminent departure. Unable to bear the burgeoning sadness surrounding his friend he dared to ask, "Why didn't you ask her to stay, Dodger?"

"And do what? She ain't a bangtail or doxie or a maid. What could she do here?" said Jack hopelessly.

Edward paused momentarily and then suggested, "Then, why don't you marry her?"

"Bleeding marry her?" He snorted in derision. "She's class, a swank. She don't want me. She wants a toff. You make me laugh, Edward. Her kind's not for the likes of me. She needs a real man about town, one who can read and write, who knows about music and Shakespeare. What do I know? Nothing."

"So, what you going to do?"

"Dunno. I honestly don't know. I'm seeing her tomorrow night. I'll bring her back here after piano practice for a farewell drink and say goodbye. She's assisting the captain to clear the house and help the kids pack so I won't see her after that she'll be too busy."

"But..."

"There ain't no ifs and there ain't no buts. It'll be done and that's that."

Edward could see there was nothing to be gained by arguing. Jack could be stubborn at the best of times and it seemed his mind was more than made up. He watched his friend sadly as he poured himself another glass of port. It was going to be a long night.

20: Formal Resolutions

Jack had dressed in his finest attire and suffered the stiff collar that he'd fought so hard to attach. Now, he had his own box of studs and no longer had to borrow Edward's and he had to admit he was getting better at dressing more like a gentleman although he was happier in his work clothes. He made up his mind that he would try and look more comfortable to make his final goodbye to Amy perfect. He would not be unhappy or press her on anything. They had reached such a fine understanding at the farm that he didn't want to spoil those happy memories. Edward had made him question his thinking but the devil in his head made it perfectly plain that she was not for him and he determined he would temper his behaviour and attitude to reflect this.

With these thoughts tussling in his mind he waited quietly in the church for Amy to arrive. He had got there early not wanting to disturb her final piano practice by walking in after she had begun and he made up his mind to be the best version of himself that he could possibly be. He even slapped his own hand away as he was tempted to ease the tight stiff collar away from his neck. He swore softly under his breath and decided that he would suffer wearing his best togs to let Amy have a good last impression of him.

He did not have long to wait as just a few minutes later she glided in and sat at the piano and lifted the lid. She glanced at him and smiled shyly and he was once more fascinated by her dainty appearance and the way she wrinkled her nose when she smiled. He returned her smile and held his breath while he waited for her to perform.

She lifted the lid and ran her fingers down the keys to warm up before stopping and settling. Then, she began. She played the first piece he had ever heard her play when he was initially drawn to the church by the haunting melody composed by whom he now knew was Beethoven. He remembered her saying it was called The Moonlight Sonata and once more Jack was transported to another world imagining sailing on the gentle ripples of a lake in a boat bathed in silver ribbons of light. The voices in his head stilled their chatter and he lost himself in the music just as Amy did when she played.

All too soon the sonata ended and Jack filled with emotion, stood and applauded. Amy turned as if to drink in his admiration of her. She rose and asked, "Do you remember that melody?"

Jack nodded, "Of course, it's the first one I heard you play and it's beautiful. I have to admit it is my favourite. Everything you play is beautiful but that one... That one gets me right here," and he hammered his hand against his heart in his chest.

"I shall be sad to go, and sad to leave such an agreeable instrument behind. Who knows when I will be able to play again?"

"Let's not think about that now. Come. We will spend our last night together and be happy."

"I don't think I will ever be happy again," said Amy as she followed Jack from the church.

The drive to the mansion was swift and silent as both of them contemplated their future. The carriage stopped at the stone steps and Jack helped Amy from the carriage. They entered the magnificent building and walked into the vestibule.

Amy gasped and looked in disbelief at the grand piano that sat in the hallway. Jack was quick to speak, "It's paid for. I didn't nick it, honest."

Amy floated towards it and sat on the plush, padded stool and raised the lid of the grand to test the notes. She beamed at Jack and began to play The Moonlight Sonata yet again. She smiled at Jack and said quietly, "Because it's your favourite and I want you to remember this." Jack smiled and listened.

As she came to the close of the first movement she studied Jack's face again and mouthed nodding her head, "Yes."

Jack mouthed back, puzzled, "What?"

Amy stopped playing and looked at him. "My answer is yes. I will." Jack looked befuddled. Amy repeated, "I said, 'yes'. I will stay. I will be Mrs Jack Dawkins." Jack looked shocked. "You were going to ask me to marry you, weren't you?"

"Er... Um... I think so... Yes, yes. YES!"

Amy smiled in relief and pleasure that her boldness had paid off. She sat down and began to play again, this time it was Mendelssohn's Wedding March and she giggled.

Jack raced to the foot of the grand staircase and yelled, "Edward! Edward!" The urgency in Jack's voice brought Edward out onto the landing. Jack shouted again joyfully, "Edward, she's gonna stay. We're getting married." He did a strange little jig around the foyer and could not stop grinning. "Edward, we're getting wed!"

Edward beamed with happiness, while Amy looked bemused having believed that she and Jack were alone. "I am so pleased," said Edward staring down from the landing.

"Come down and congratulate us," demanded Jack.

Edward ran down the stairs, walked towardss Amy, took her hand and kissed it, "Miss Martel, I am delighted to hear that you and Jack are betrothed."

"Why, thank you, Mr Hargreaves."

"And, Mr Dawkins, Jack..." said Edward and stopped.

"What? Edward, tell me, what do you think?" pressed Jack.

"I think... I think..." Edward teased.

"Edward?"

"I think it is wonderful news and it's about time!" He clasped his friend in an affectionate hug. "I shall fetch some champagne, we must celebrate this news in style." Edward disappeared along the corridor towards the kitchen and wine cellar while Jack escorted Amy to the drawing room where she sat on a sofa and patted the seat next to her, "Come and sit with me, Jack. Your friend is really very pleasant. I can see he is important to you."

"Edward is the very best of men," agreed Jack. "He is like my brother."

"I understand that."

"But?"

"Here I am consenting to marry you and yet, I know very little about you, Jack. I don't even know how old you are or when your birthday is."

"I don't neither."

"Don't what?"

"I don't know when my birthday is. I've never had a birthday. So, I don't know how old I am."

Edward entered with champagne and three glasses; he had just caught the end of the conversation. He set out the glasses and opened the bottle, which exploded with a pop. The cork flew up and Amy giggled as Edward poured and explained to Amy, "I know I am younger than Jack. I asked him to share my birthday but he refused. He foolishly thought it would take something away from me."

"Then Jack can share mine." She laughed as she received her glass and raised it in celebration. "There is sound reasoning behind the offer, Mr Hargreaves." She grinned and added, "Sharing mine means he will never forget it!"

They all laughed together and Jack asked, "So, when is it?"

"The first day of January."

"Sounds good. There! I have a birthday at last. The first day of a new year and a new beginning for me."

"For us!" corrected Amy.

"For us," repeated Jack.

"I'll drink to that," said Edward raising his glass. "The first day of January. To Jack and Amy."

Jack and Amy chorused together, "To us!"

And Jack added, "To us all! And now, please let me release this darn collar that's impaled on my shirt, as long as you don't mind?" he turned to look at Amy who laughed and nodded. Jack immediately set down his glass and fiddled with the stud, which pinged and flew across the floor.

***

That night it was later than usual when Amy returned to the captain's house. She wore the flush of love in her cheeks and there was a glow in her eyes, indeed in her whole demeanour. She breezed in through the front door and leaned against it closing her eyes and sighing with heart fluttering longing.

She was surprised when the door to the library opened and the captain came out. He strode towards her. His tone was clipped, "Miss Martel, you are very late this evening. Do not forget we have to prepare the house and pack things up before our departure. I am expecting you to help the girls with completing the packing of their trunks."

"And I will, sir."

"I'm glad to hear it. I fear this farmer has turned your head somewhat. I shall be glad when we leave and you will be out of his clutches."

"But, sir…"

"What? What is it?"

Amy took a deep breath, "I will not be going with you."

"What do you mean?"

She spoke firmly, "I am not leaving. I have agreed to become Mr Dawkins' wife."

"But, you hardly know the man!"

"I know enough. He's kind and thoughtful and more honest than anyone I have ever met." Indignation burned in Amy's eyes.

"A farmer!" the captain snorted derisively. "A manual labourer. Think how you will be wasting your life."

"Or enriching it," said Amy quietly.

"I made a promise to your family that I would look after you. What about my girls? They adore you."

"And I them. Surely, they would not deny me this chance of happiness?"

"And if it doesn't work out?"

"It will," said Amy with growing confidence. "But, if it doesn't there will be other boats home to England. Please, sir… Understand that I have to do this. I have to follow my heart."

The captain relented, "Of course, I understand. I was in love once, too. You do love him, don't you?"

"More than words can say."

"My own wife's family were against her marrying me. They despised the fact I was in the military. We had a good life until the good Lord, in his wisdom took her from us."

"I never knew."

"Why would you? I never talked about it. Emily and I eloped, we struggled to gain her parents' acceptance. It was hard but they embraced us eventually." The captain studied Amy's face and relented. He sighed heavily, "Very well. I can see your mind is made up and I have known you to be a wilful creature since you were a child. But promise me you will break the news to my children gently. They will miss you, I know."

"Then I have your blessing?"

"I wouldn't put it quite like that. But I accept your decision."

"I will still help with the house and packing and if you return for another term of duty. I would be happy to see you."

The captain bowed stiffly, "And I, you. Tell me, how will you manage?"

"We will manage fine. I will be well provided for. He has even bought me a grand piano."

"Then, he must indeed love you, too." The captain's tone had changed noticeably.

"He does, I know what's in his heart."

"Then, there's no more to be said. Good night, Miss Martel." The captain retreated into the library and Amy ascended the stairs to her room with renewed life and a spring in her step."

**

The next three weeks passed like a whirlwind. Amy said her tearful goodbyes to the captain and his daughters. They attended the church to hear the reading of the banns and Amy moved into the mansion into her own room at Miss Bonnet's instruction. "It will be bad luck to see the groom on the night before your wedding. We will have to hide you away. So, you'd best take the room farthest away from Mr Jack's, so you should."

Amy blushed, "There's no argument from me. I am hoping that with Edward as Jack's best man and giving me away and you as my matron of honour that one of you or both will be able to act as a witness?"

"Mr Edward will have enough to do, whereas I will gladly be at your disposal, but the law tells us that you need two. There will be no family in attendance so it will be a very small wedding party."

Amy's expression changed to one of alarm. Then who will we get as another witness?"

"Now, Miss Amy don't you worry none," said Miss Bonnet. "In my last employment there was a young girl, Dora Wicks and she, I know, will welcome the opportunity. She's a nice lass. I will ask her along, if you've a mind?"

"Please do. That will be one less thing to worry about. I know Jack was thinking of either Daniel or Bobby but they will be tied up at the farm especially as they're lambing. And sadly, Koorong would not be permitted. The law is so foolish, so yes, please ask your friend. I will be eternally grateful."

"Consider it done. And now... you... what will you wear?"

"I thought something simple; one of my day gowns...?"

Miss B clicked her tongue, "No, no, no! Indeed, to goodness. I never heard such a thing. It is your wedding day. You must look the part. It must be every young girl's dream. It was always mine although I was never lucky enough to find a beau."

"But Mr Jack..."

"You leave Mr Jack to me."

Miss Bonnet left Amy and strode to the drawing room, where Edward and Jack were enjoying a glass of port. "Mr Jack!" she announced drawing herself up to her full height of five foot three and she looked formidable.

"Miss B?" said Jack looking startled. "What can I do for you?"

"It's not what you can do for me, but what you can do for Miss Amy."

"Why? What does she need?"

"A dress, Mr Jack. A dress. You cannot expect her to get married on the most special day of her life in a day gown. She needs to look and feel like a princess. She needs a veil... that's traditional and it's no good you telling me her day dress will do, it won't."

"Very well..."

"I am not going to argue..."

"Very well..."

"I insist!"

"Miss B, you are not listening. I said 'yes.' Get her whatever she wants, whatever she desires, just leave me out of it. I know nothing of weddings or etiquette."

"That, Mr Jack is more than obvious. So, I have your permission?"

"Of course. Whatever it takes."

Miss Bonnet swept from the room leaving Jack looking after her as Edward struggled not to laugh. As the door closed Edward burst into laughter. "I never knew she could be such a tyrant. Woe betide the man that crosses her," said Edward. "But... she is right. Amy should have whatever she wants on her special day. And what about you, Jack? What will you wear?"

"No fuss for me. I'll have no airs and graces. What you see is what you get."

Edward laughed again, "I'll smarten you up, Jack. You may not want to look like a traditional toff but I'll make you look presentable for your wedding day. You will accompany me to my tailor. I am, after all, giving away the bride and have a double duty as your best man."

Jack considered this for a moment and nodded, "You're right, Edward. At least I should look presentable. Make the appointment."

***

Miss Bonnet, it seemed, was not only a demon in the kitchen and an amazing housekeeper, although she complained the house was bigger than she was used to and she could do with much more help, but she was a proficient seamstress, too, which was just as well. Alterations were needed to the white lace bridal dress that they had purchased in a lady's outfitter in Port Jackson. It was a delicate lace and silk dress that was embellished with tiny seed pearls on the bodice that was tight fitting but with a demure high, neatly frilled neckline that rose to her chin. The silk came to a V under the lace overlay and the lace extended over the arms of the sleeves to the elbow. The rest of the satin silk sleeve was like a second skin and came to a point on the back of her hand. The waist was cinched in and streamed generously over her slim hips, grazing the floor at the front and extending into a sweeping train at the back. Amy's waist was so tiny that Miss B had to take her needle and make the necessary alterations. The veil flowed from a crown of flowers encrusted with small pearls and trailed down her back to the floor.

At her final fitting with Miss Bonnet, Amy looked stunning. She turned to view herself in the full length mirror. Miss B nodded approvingly, "Miss Amy, you look like a princess from a fairy tale; every little girl's dream."

"Will I do? Do you think Jack will like it?"

"If he doesn't, I'll box his ears, so I will. Have no fear, he will remember how you look on this day, forever. It will be imprinted on his heart," and a single tear trickled down her cheek.

"Oh, Miss Bonnet!" cried Amy in dismay.

"Tis nothing. A bit of smuts in my eye from squinting so much and sewing in candlelight. That's all. Now, out of that finery and I'll hang it up to keep the silk wrinkle free." She helped Amy out of her dress and reminded her, "I'll be there to make sure the train walks with you and now, once I've helped you redress, leave me be to attend to mine. I have to shorten the hem. It won't do for me to trip up behind you as you walk down the aisle."

"I can't thank you enough, Miss B. I only wish my mother could see me."

"I expect she will be there, looking down on you... and your father. You will make them both proud, I'm sure." Amy blushed and her eyes glittered brightly. "If you don't think me being rude, what happened?"

Amy cast her eyes down, "They both died of consumption. My brother joined the military when we were left as orphans. My sister married a gentleman. I lived with them for a while and continued in education to become a governess. I wanted to be self-sufficient. It seems it was the correct decision otherwise I would never have come here, tutored the captain's children or met Jack."

"No, I expect not. Now, I need to know has Edward ordered your flowers?"

"I believe so."

"Good. That's one less thing for me to worry about. Now, get yourself off and leave me to do what I need."

***

The wedding day finally arrived. The Mansfield Hotel was booked. Edward had driven the carriage with Jack dressed smartly in high fashion, courtesy of Edward's tailor, and he entered the church to wait, growing more and more nervous with anticipation, while Edward returned to the house to collect Amy, Miss Bonnet and Dora Wickes. Dora was waiting in the hallway. She was a big bosomed girl with poorly dyed fluffy blonde hair but a pretty enough face. She was wearing her Sunday best clothes. She gazed in awe as Amy glided down the magnificent staircase followed by Miss Bonnet dressed in her own bronze satin matron styled dress with a high neck and bronze overlay of lace with a cape and smock effect and fitted sleeves. She had a bonnet adorned with bronze lace and controlled Amy's train as she stepped behind her.

Once in the foyer, Dora retrieved the bouquet of white lilies from the top of the grand piano and passed them to Amy. Miss B had a smaller posy of locally grown flowers. There was a single cream rose buttonhole remaining for Dora, which Miss B carefully attached.

"Will I do?" Amy asked.

"Do?" said Miss Bonnet. "Why, you will more than do. My dear child, you look beautiful. Now, let me adjust your veil. You must keep your face covered until after you have said your vows. Here, let me pull it down. I will be on hand to help with putting it back and Dora can hold my bouquet. Are you ready?"

Amy nodded, "I am as ready as I'll ever be."

"Sure? Speak now, if you want to change your mind."

"No, I love Jack. He's the kindest man I have ever met. He makes me happy."

Miss Bonnet assented, "Then, all's well so it is."

Just then Edward opened the door. He stood transfixed for a moment before coming to, and announced, "Ladies, your carriage awaits. Miss Martel, allow me." He opened the door and the odd collection of people trooped out after them. "I must say, Miss Martel... Amy. You look... breath-taking. Jack is a lucky man."

***

Inside the church Jack waited nervously. He was dressed in new clothes, which were fashionable but not traditional groom wear. The vicar stood in his official raiment clutching a Bible. An elderly man with shoulder length silver hair sat at the piano clothed all in black. He kept his eye on the church door until it swung open and then he struck up The Wedding March.

Dry mouthed, Jack swallowed hard and turned his head. His eyes lit with love as he saw a vision in white gliding down the aisle on Edward's arm. The breath caught in his throat and he felt his whole body tremble. Amy reached his side and he gazed at her through her gauze veil. He whispered, "You look beautiful."

Amy smiled serenely. She turned and passed her flowers to Miss Bonnet who had become pink cheeked and misty eyed before focusing on the minister and the words he had to say. Jack tried to pay attention to the vicar's words but found them echoing in his head seeming to have no meaning until he came to the serious part of making their vows.

Amy spoke clearly and engagingly, while Jack could hardly get his words out. He appeared entranced by Amy's loveliness, which had quite literally taken his breath away. A prod in the back from Miss Bonnet spurred him to focus and he finally responded with the right word in the right places and all too soon the cleric pronounced them man and wife. Jack sighed in relief and could not stop the spread of a ridiculous grin on his face. Miss Bonnet passed both bouquets to Dora and helped Amy lift and adjust the veil from her sweet face. She retrieved Amy's lilies and passed them back to her and attended to Amy's train as the bride and groom left the church to the pianist playing The Bridal Chorus by Wagner.

As they hit the bright sunlight the couple were showered with rice, thrown by Josie and Minnie who shouted out their congratulations and applauded. They curtseyed before Amy, "Sorry we can't stop, we have to get back to work." They turned to Jack,

"We just wanted to make sure you'd gone through with it," said Minnie with a laugh.

"We must get back to the bar, Father sends his felicitations. Well done, both of you," said Josie and the sisters left hurriedly for the Victoria.

Miss Bonnet prompted Amy, "Right now, Mrs Dawkins. The next wedding tradition to be observed..."

"What's that?" asked Amy.

"Time to throw your bouquet. As you reach the carriage door throw it behind you."

"They're so lovely, I hardly want to lose them but then, tradition is tradition!" Amy closed her eyes and tossed it over her head. There was a gasp as it landed in Dora Wicks' hands. She beamed, "Ain't never had that happen before. Thank you."

Edward ran up to the carriage, "Congratulations, Mr and Mrs Dawkins."

"Thank you, Mr Hargreaves," said Amy. "And thank you, Miss Wicks for being a witness...I... we are much obliged to you."

"It were a real pleasure, I love weddings and catching the flowers is thanks enough."

Jack smiled, "Miss Wicks, will you join us for the wedding grub? You'll be more than welcome."

"Oh, please do, Miss Wicks. We are eating at Mansfield's. It's where Mr Dawkins took me for our first luncheon."

Dora beamed delightedly, "Oh, yes please. I would love it." She clutched the bouquet of flowers and in that moment she looked not only charming but like a young girl who had been given the best surprise in the world.

Edward grinned, "Then that's settled. I shall be happy to accompany both you and Miss Bonnet to the restaurant."

Edward extended his arms and the ladies tucked their hands in his elbows and made their way to one hired carriage, which had waited and set off for the hotel. Jack took the second carriage and helped his wife into it before climbing aboard to drive to the venue. Jack's broad but lopsided smile seemed fixed on his face and nothing could dim the light in his eyes.

The two carriages trotted through the town towards the hotel, which was incredibly busy that day, but there again, as Amy remarked, it was a Saturday. The small wedding party entered the Mansfield and made their way to their table courteously led there by Atwill.

Everyone visibly relaxed. The restaurant was filled with the polite chatter of well-dressed colonists, who had an air of superiority about them. One or two turned to stare at the arrivals, others ignored them and another couple looked at them in a demeaning fashion before returning to their own inconsequential conversation.

On the table in a silver bucket embossed with the restaurant's name sat an opened bottle of champagne and crystal flutes. Atwill took the bottle and after they were seated he poured them each a glass. Dora giggled as the bubbles tickled her nose when she raised it up to Edward's first toast of the young couple. She sipped the drink and hiccupped. She glanced around looking embarrassed and put her other hand to her mouth. Amy smiled gently and whispered, "I hiccupped, the first time I tasted champagne, too."

Dora looked gratefully at Amy, and whispered back, "I ain't never been in no place like this before neither. I'll never forget this. Thank you."

"No, thank you, Miss Wicks. We couldn't have got married without you."

"I don't know about that."

"You certainly made it easier for us. Thank you."

"No, I loved it. I wasn't doing nothing anyway."

Atwill leaned across to Jack and handed him the menu, revealing convict scars on his wrists, which Jack noted. He passed the bill of fare to Amy. "I will leave the choice of food to my wife. After all, she chose me as her husband, so she must know her onions."

Everyone laughed and Amy handed the bill of fare back to Atwill. "I have no need of the menu. We shall have the Navarin of lamb. I can vouch that it is delicious."

Jack nodded sagely in agreement and Atwill smiled broadly, "Yes, ma'am," before disappearing with their order.

"Miss Wicks, tell me, is today your day off?"

Dora looked down self-consciously, "No, ma'am. I don't have no work at the moment."

Jack caught Amy's eye and she nodded encouragingly at him, "Miss Wicks, are you looking for employment?"

Dora looked up and murmured quietly, "Yes, I am. But there's not much about at the moment."

"Then this must be a lucky day for us all. Would you consider working for Mrs Dawkins?"

"Doing what?" said Dora in surprise.

"As a lady's maid?"

Dora gulped, "Oh, yes please."

"Then that's settled. Miss Wicks welcome to the household."

Miss Bonnet looked as delighted as if she herself had been promoted and honoured. She patted Dora's hand and murmured, "I can promise you, Dora, you will love it. They are fine people."

***

On the other side of the restaurant was a table of colonists and one man in particular was being extremely loud. He totally humiliated his waiter who had brushed against his arm while he was taking a sip of his drink and the liquid spilled down his chin and front. He remonstrated rudely against the poor waiter who didn't know what to do and kept apologising. Jack watched as Atwill walked across and tried to soothe matters but ended up being lambasted himself. Jack could see Atwill trying to be civil but the man was having none of it and demanded to see the owner. Atwill retreated to the kitchen and another gent approached the table to speak to the person criticising the service at the top of his voice.

Atwill emerged from the kitchen and walked to Jack's table and apologised for the disturbance. "No need for that," said Jack. "The man's got no manners. We were just about to make another toast to Miss Wicks who is coming into my wife's employ. Could we have another bottle of champagne, please, Atwill?"

"Certainly, sir," said Atwill deferentially and melted back to the wine cellar.

The rest of the wedding celebration went beautifully and while Jack paid the bill, Edward led Miss Bonnet and Miss Wicks out to the carriage and helped them inside. Jack soon emerged with Amy and assisted her into her seat, while Miss Bonnet fussed over her train and Jack stepped up into the driver's seat.

Jack was just about to shake the reins and click an instruction to the horses when Atwill came chasing out of the restaurant. Jack saw him approach, "What's the matter? Tip not big enough or have I forgotten something?"

"No, I er... I don't know how to say this..."

Jack looked puzzled and jumped down taking Atwill to one side, "Come on, man. I've seen your scars," Jack gestured to Atwill's wrists. "You can trust me. Spit it out."

"I've seen yours, too. That's why I'm talking to you. Got any work?"

"You got a job."

"They're all colonists. Stuck up bastards."

"What were you lagged for?"

"I got caught."

Jack laughed impishly, looked Atwill up and down. "You're a big enough bloke... Can you drive a pair?"

"Yes, sir."

"Do they owe you money in there?"

"Got paid this morning."

"Dump your apron and climb up..."

"Yes, sir."

Atwill climbed onto the carriage and took the reins. "If you work for me, you call me Jack. No ceremony here."

"Yes, Jack."

Amy looked questioningly at Jack. "I'll tell you later. Jack looked inside the carriage and laughed. "Blimey! With your dress, there's no room in here for me." Jack climbed up alongside Atwill. "Take us home, Atwill. I will show you the way."

Atwill's face creased into a smile. He flicked the reins and the horses trotted off towards the mansion.

***

That evening celebrations continued with much merriment. Amy retired first with Dora who helped her out of her regalia and took her dress away and hung it up in her boudoir. "Oh, Miss Amy it's beautiful... you're beautiful."

Amy smiled. "Why thank you, Dora. You're very kind."

"No, Miss Amy 'tis you and Mr Jack who are kind to give me this position."

"And let us hope we will have a friendship to go with it."

Dora bobbed a curtsy, "Oh, I do hope so, Miss Amy. I do hope so."

Dora helped Amy out of her corset and into her night attire before unbraiding Amy's hair. She took a brush and began to comb through Amy's lustrous locks.

"Thank you, Dora. I'll see you in the morning. Good night."

"Night, ma'am."

Amy sat on her stool in front of the mirror in her virginal white silk nightdress and whispered, "Mrs Jack Dawkins," and sighed.

21: One Year Later

The year had passed quickly. There had been much happiness in the household and life had gone on as before but more joyously as friendships between them all had blossomed. The household was much more like a family than how the colonists lived in their self-important grandeur. There was a marked difference between the settlers' assumed superiority and the way they treated their servants. In fact, surprisingly even Miss Bonnet and Atwill had struck up an excellent rapport with each other, which made the running of the house so much easier, although Miss Bonnet still complained that she needed more help. But the biggest news of all was that Amy had fallen pregnant just a few months after their wedding much to the delight of everyone and her due date was imminent.

They were sitting together at supper but Amy was unable to manage more than a spoonful of Miss Bonnet's famous and tasty Welsh stew known as cawl and pronounced cowl. Amy doubled over and groaned. Jack was immediately attentive, "My love, Amy... are you all right?" He was conscious of the fact that Amy's pregnancy had not been easy for her and that several times during her confinement she had been ordered to stay in bed and rest as she had suffered with intermittent bleeding. The doctor had diagnosed placenta previa and insisted that she take care. Jack was careful to observe this. With Miss B's and Dora's attention, Amy thrived. As Amy groaned, once more, Jack asked again, "Amy? What is it?"

"I have a pain and my stomach is cramping."

"Is the baby coming?"

Amy winced as another contraction took hold, "I think so. I have had a regular dull ache most of the day but now the discomfort is much sharper and getting more regular. Arrrgh!" Amy doubled over again.

"Dora, run for the doctor. Go quickly now." Dora jumped up and hurried from the room. "Miss B, help me to get Amy upstairs."

Jack and Miss Bonnet helped Amy from her seat and assisted her from the room to go upstairs. Every so often Amy would try and stifle her cry of agony. Miss B turned to Jack. "I'll take her from here. You go away, get yourself back downstairs. This is women's work."

Amy gave another wailing whimper. Jack's face contorted with worry and Miss B shooed him away as she opened the bedroom door. "Go! Go now, if you want to be useful get some water onto boil; the doctor will need it. Hurry."

Jack fled downstairs to do Miss Bonnet's bidding but his hands were shaking and he was all of a dither. He managed to fill two large pans and set them on the range to heat. He paced around the kitchen rubbing his chin and biting his lip.

Atwill walked in, "Let me do this, Jack. You get into the library with Mr Edward. Go on."

Jack nodded, appreciating the fact that someone else had taken charge. He hurried along the passage and as he reached the foyer, Dora burst in with the doctor. "This way, Doctor," Dora ushered the doctor to the stairs and they went up together as a shriek of agony ripped from the bedroom and echoed down to the hall. Jack stood trembling in the vestibule and watched Dora come scurrying back down the stairs. She noted Jack's anxious face and ran towards the kitchen. Moments later, Atwill came striding down the passage and took Jack firmly by the arm and led him away to the library.

Edward had poured a drink and thrust the glass at Jack as he entered. Jack took it and sat with a thud onto the wing back chair that was placed by the window overlooking the garden. Atwill exchanged a look with Edward who then provided Atwill with a drink and the three sat nervously, uncertain what to say.

Edward was the first to speak, "Amy will be fine, Jack. Stop fretting. Women give birth all the time; otherwise we wouldn't none of us be here today! She has the best medical help money can buy. Dora and Miss B are in attendance. What could go wrong?"

"I suppose." Jack licked his lips and downed his drink in one and coughed as the burning liquid caught him in the back of his throat and he was reminded of when Rust forced him to take a drink as a child. He shuddered.

Another plaintive cry tore through the house. Jack rose and walked to the window becoming aware that the garden had been neglected. He made up his mind there and then to find someone who could do that kind of work; after all, his son or daughter would need a garden to play in while growing up.

Edward poured them all another drink as another pitiful howl was heard. Suddenly, there was the unmistakeable sound of a baby crying. Jack held his breath and Edward nodded encouragingly as a smile manifested on his face. The library door burst open and a flustered but delighted Dora burst in. They all rose and stood in anticipation.

"Oh, Mr Jack. It's a boy. You have a little boy."

Edward and Atwill stepped forward beaming and pumped Jack's hand vigorously, congratulating him while all Jack could do was grin inanely.

"Don't you want to see them?" asked Dora with a smile as she watched the antics of the men.

"You mean... Can I?" he said incredulously. Jack couldn't contain his excitement.

"Come on, Mr Jack," said Dora gently. She led the way from the room to the bedroom. Cheers from downstairs reverberated across the landing as Dora opened the door.

Miss Bonnet was hurriedly clearing away the blood stained sheet as the doctor was putting on his coat. Amy was sitting up in bed holding the now swaddled and cleaned baby. The doctor spoke confidentially, "Don't tire her. They don't call it labour for nothing," he joked. "You have a fine son with a lusty pair of lungs. But, your wife needs to take things easily. Also, I shouldn't try for another child, be happy with one. Mrs Dawkins is very small pelvically, after her problems in gravidity and the difficult delivery it will not be wise to pursue another pregnancy." He studied Jack's concerned expression. "You shouldn't worry. They will both be fine. Your son is a good weight. He's a strong boy. Now, I'd best be on my way. I will visit again tomorrow and bring my bill."

"Thank you, Doctor Long," said Amy.

Jack seemed to be struck dumb and just acknowledged the doctor with a nod. The door closed quietly and Jack moved towards the bed. He sat in a chair provided by Dora and gazed with love and admiration at Amy. He was still totally stuck for words. Amy smiled and turned the bundle around for him to see. His eyes filled up and he choked back a sob letting the tears run freely down his face. He continued sitting gazing at Amy and their son. He was completely captivated by the immensity of everything. It seemed almost too much to bear and Amy stretched out her hand to her husband, which he grasped gratefully and held tightly.

Slowly, Jack rose and leaned over the pair. His lips tenderly brushed his wife's forehead that was flushed and sweaty from the exertion of birth. Jack put his hand out to his infant son in awe of the perfect little fingers and nails and as he stroked the baby's diminutive dimpled knuckles, his child curled his tiny hand around Jack's finger and clasped it forcefully. Jack gasped in delight at this magical moment and grinned lopsidedly at Amy.

"Aren't you going to say anything?" asked Amy quietly.

Jack took his eyes away from his son's face and fixed them on his wife. He retrieved his finger and let out a whoop of joy and danced around the room in a crazy skipping caper. Amy's eyes widened in amusement and she laughed as he fell back into the seat and took her hand again and kissed it.

***

Following doctor's orders and at Miss Bonnet's insistence, Jack left Amy to rest. With a feeling of euphoria, he raced back down the stairs. He never believed he could feel so happy, so complete. He dived into the library where Atwill and Edward were raising their glasses and toasted Jack as soon as he entered.

The words tumbled from him like a rolling landslip as he described his newly born son, whose strong grasp and perfect features had enchanted him so. Edward had never seen Jack so animated. He, too, was filled with emotion and slapped his friend on his back. Atwill smiled and poured them all another drink as Edward announced, "To Jack, Amy and the baby and indeed to all of us, for good fortune, wealth, health and happiness!" The three men lifted their glasses and chinked them together. There was no doubt amongst them that the bottle would be finished that night.

Jack murmured softly, "I want to do something good, something for someone else."

"To earn your place in heaven?" asked Edward wryly.

"No, to do the right thing. Edward we must talk."

***

Jack adjusted to fatherhood quite rapidly and enjoyed sharing parental duties as much as he was allowed by Miss Bonnet, who always seemed to be on hand to take the baby out for a stroll and although never having been a mother herself she seemed well versed in baby care. For this reason, Jack and Amy decided to abduct their son from the house and take a ride in the carriage to the farm. Jack was anxious to see Koorong and let him know what he and Edward had decided.

The just risen sun shone brightly casting a soft rosy hue on the house and the road. Outside, its starfish rays filled the sky with brilliance and warmth. It was another flawless day that demanded travel and exploration. Jack and Amy, who was now fully recovered, escaped with their son, Tom, and had left the mansion before anyone else had risen and thus got away from the clutches of Miss B before anyone could stop them. They felt like naughty giggling children on a wild adventure that brought them both joy and laughter. As they approached the town where the road neared the quay, there was a flurry of activity from other early risers who were setting up their wares to trade with arriving ships. Here the road from the port spread in three directions and Jack shook the reins to lead the horses to the one that led to the countryside. The carriage turned and took the road to the outback and trail to the farm.

The journey was steady as the carriage rolled from the road and onto the dusty track. Jack was lost in his own world while Amy cuddled her son in the carriage and took advantage of its movement with its soporific rumbling drone to catch up on some much needed sleep while the baby slumbered in her arms.

Jack reflected on his life and his harsh beginnings that had led him to something he had never believed possible. The devil on his shoulder jumped up to wrangle with him once more. It raised its voice to him again, warning him that things were too good to be true that he didn't deserve the blessings bestowed on him. His face clouded with concern and in spite of the growing heat, he shivered.

"Snap out of it, Jack," he told himself. "All this self-doubt does no good. Just be happy to be lucky for once." He nodded as his temporary worry cloud lifted. He began to count his blessings instead and realised he had much to be thankful for. It was just what he needed to silence his fears. His cheeky smile returned together with a twinkle in his eye and he pushed the horses into a merry trot, breathed in the fresh country air and sighed with contentment and love as he enjoyed his surroundings.

He watched as kangaroos popped up their heads to see which travellers had disturbed them from their grazing and flocks of galahs flew from their perches with their squawking cries. Their grey and pink plumage drew a swathe of colour across the sky and the whoosh of their wings lifted his spirits still further. He felt a pang of nostalgia wave through him for his old life on the farm with Fred and Mrs D when things were uncomplicated but happy. Now, he was more than happy but had responsibilities; responsibilities he would take seriously.

***

Amy sat on the wooden settle on the porch nursing the baby as Jack conversed with Koorong. After skating around polite pleasantries Jack's tone became more serious, "Koorong, I needed to see you. But, firstly, I wanted to introduce you to my son."

Koorong studied the infant in Amy's arms who let out a hearty bawling complaint and he smiled, "He is a fine boy." Tom wailed again, his mouth puckering and sucking, searching for sustenance as he nuzzled into Amy's chest. Koorong laughed, "He has a strong cry. Not to be ignored."

Jack smiled and his tone grew more serious, "There's another matter I want to discuss."

"I'm listening."

"This farm. We want you to have it."

Koorong's face clouded with an emotion that Jack could not quite read. He sighed deeply, "How can you give me what is rightfully mine?" He paused; "Jack, you are my friend, I don't want to be at odds with you but this is and always has been my land and my people's land. The white man took it and now you want to give it back?" His eyes searched Jack's face.

"I thought you would be pleased," a subdued Jack said quietly.

"I do not doubt that you meant well. Just as your benefactor did by giving me work on the farm, which you continued but..."

Amy intervened and added, "Koorong, we make a lot of money from the wool in Sydney. In spite of the profit share agreement that is currently in place, Jack and Edward wanted you to have *all* the money for your people. For you to control it. To have it all. He and Edward would step aside. How you treat Bobby and Daniel will be up to you. You will take charge of the whole enterprise and the profit."

Koorong looked amazed at the generous offer. There was a slight hesitation and then he beamed at them both. "That I can accept. And Baiame blesses you very much. The white law does not allow me to hold land anyway for I am Aboriginal."

"And you should be proud to be so... Law or no law, it will all be done legally, have no fear. Even if we remain as figureheads the entire business will be yours for your people."

Koorong nodded. "Mr Jack you are an honourable man, as was Mrs Doble's husband. I have no words but to ask if you will all come to the village? It has grown much. Our chief and elders will want to greet your son."

Jack nodded and Amy uttered, "But, of course. It will be our privilege. Tell me, will Minjarra be there?"

"He will. And I know he will be more than happy to see both of you. Minjarra is growing fast and will soon be initiated into manhood. He sees Jack as an uncle."

"And Minjarra will be as a big brother to our Tom. You, Koorong will be uncle and friend to him, too, as you were a friend to me," said Jack.

"I would be honoured," said Koorong clearly moved by Jack's suggestion.

"Then that's settled," said Jack and he shook Koorong's hand while Amy looked on with pride. "And now, I would like to pay my respects to the grave, yonder. We will then be delighted to accompany you to the village."

***

Jack removed his hat and stood with his head bowed at Fred's graveside, while Koorong waited with Amy and Tom further back in the line of trees. Amy could hear Jack's voice but not discern what he was saying.

"Mr Fred, you gave me and Edward a life. Edward was your proper grandson, but I was not your blood; yet, you treated me as you did Edward. I thank you for that and I hope you understand what I have done and why I done it. Me and Edward have made a promise; we will find that murdering skunk who did for you. Yes, Fred. We found out you was done in. Poisoned. And I will get the bloke back. I know who it is, just we ain't got no proof. But, I won't forget. I never will. I won't forget nothin'." Jack's voice had dropped to a whisper. "You will be avenged. I'll see to that." Jack remained there awhile as if saying a prayer to himself. Then, he replaced his hat and pulled it forward to shade his teared-up eyes. He walked back purposefully passing his wife and Koorong, and strode to the waiting carriage where he climbed aboard to wait for Amy and Koorong to catch up.

Amy dived inside to feed Tom in privacy as Koorong stepped up to sit beside Jack at the reins. Jack clicked his instruction to the horses who trotted off on the trail to the rocky canyon that hid the way to the village. The layered rock strata varied in hues of vermillion red and fuchsia pink. When the sun hit the tiers, it gave the impression of a chasm ablaze with molten lava, a gorge of fire. Jack stopped the coach and secured it in the shade. He helped his wife and child from the carriage. They followed Koorong through the canyon.

As they reached the outskirts of the camp, laughing children came running. Minjarra saw the arrivals and gave a whoop of glee and raced towards Jack who swung the boy around much to his delight. There was much nodding and smiling as everyone crowded around anxious to greet Jack and Amy and keen to see the new arrival, who took little notice of all the fuss.

The young woman who had brought her child to see Amy on her first visit emerged from a hut and smiled broadly stretching out her arms to Amy's small bundle. Without hesitation Amy relinquished her son into the woman's arms who continued grinning and talking in Awabakal. Amy asked Koorong, "What is she saying?"

"She says, you have a healthy baby who will grow into a fine young man. It is Baiame's wish."

Amy smiled back and made the gesture of friendship she had learned from Jack. The woman blessed the child and passed Tom back. Amy asked Koorong, "What of her son?"

"Yindi? He is fine and growing rapidly. In fact, here he is."

The toddler waddled from the hut in search of his mother. His thumb firmly placed in his mouth. His mother scooped him up to show Amy, who beamed and patted her heart and young Tom to indicate mother love. She turned to Koorong again as Jack was in discussion with the chief who seemed pleased and patted Jack on the back. "Tell me, Koorong, what does Yindi mean?"

"In some tribes it just means boy but here, in our language it means sun as in the sky."

"That's lovely. And does the child have a sunny disposition?"

Koorong nodded, "Like no other. He never sulks and rarely complains. He is like his namesake the sun and will one day rule the tribe. He is the chief's youngest, favoured by Baiame to one day be our leader."

"Before the chief's older sons?" quizzed Amy.

"I should say his only son. Yindi has many sisters, tribal law dictates that they cannot rule."

"So, what if something happens to the chief before Yindi comes of age?"

"We have a caretaker leader, from the elders."

"Like a committee?"

"I not know that word."

Amy thought to explain, "Like a counsel... People work together... a team."

"A team, yes."

"Ah, I understand." Amy nodded. "That's good thinking, very democratic."

"Democratic? Another new word," said Koorong questioningly.

"It means things are discussed and agreed. Everyone has a say."

"I listen. I learn. You are a good teacher."

Amy couldn't help but look pleased. "It was my job. I used to love it."

"Used to love what?" asked Jack as he came to Amy's side.

"Teaching. Mrs Dawkins loved to teach," explained Koorong.

"She teaches me all the time," said Jack sincerely. "She'll do the same for Tom. I know it."

"Then, you will be a good team," said Koorong with a grin.

"And now we must be getting back. Miss B will be worried. She frets whenever we take Tom out. I don't believe she thinks we can look after him quite as well as she does."

Koorong laughed, "We have women like that here."

"Never underestimate a mother's love," Amy chided. "Otherwise, none of you would have grown as strong as you have."

Koorong nodded in agreement, "There is truth in what you say."

Jack fell silent, as sadness clouded his eyes. Finally, he whispered gently, "Come, we must return."

Amy bade Koorong goodbye and followed Jack. Koorong murmured, "Blessings on you, Jack and your family." As he uttered those words a bird shrieked and flew up from the bush.

***

Jack was thoughtful on the way home. He had no doubt that he and Edward had done the right thing and this gave him great comfort. He felt so much better after his visit to the village and longed to retain that feeling. But Amy's words had settled on him like a heavy mantle. Everyone he knew had enjoyed the love of a mother or father, or both. It was something he had never known. He made up his mind that Tom would never have this feeling. He would be brought up in love from both his mother and father and give Tom the self-esteem he needed to succeed in this tough world.

He knew that one day he would find the monster known as Charlie Coombes and justice would be done. He kept reminding himself of this fact lest he should forget but he knew he wouldn't forget. Not ever. Planning his revenge kept him occupied for the entire journey but didn't shake off the coiling snake of unexplained fear that writhed inside him.

***

On their return the fuss and attention they received from Miss B was both humbling and annoying. It was humbling to know that someone cared so much but annoying that they should be subjected to the sort of parental questioning reserved for families. Fortunately, Amy with her quiet diplomacy soothed Miss Bonnet's sharp complaints and obeyed her orders to rest. Miss B took charge and Amy gratefully retreated to her room.

She lay on her bed for a while but itched to have her corset loosened as she couldn't quite get comfortable so, she was forced to rise to look for Dora. She was about to ring the bell to summon her when she glanced out of her window into the gardens and saw Edward and Dora sitting together under a tree, laughing together at something Edward had said. Amy continued to watch and a smile grew on her face. She observed the way they looked at each other; how they leaned in towards each other as they spoke and that they mirrored each other's movements. It was obvious to Amy that the friendship between Edward and Dora was more than platonic. Amy couldn't stop the delight from manifesting in her face and spreading through her body. Her corset discomfort forgotten she decided to find Jack, there and then, and tell him what she had intuited.

Amy giggled and slipped out from her room and travelled down the stairs and along the corridor into the library where Jack was sitting lost in thought appearing to look out of the window but really not seeing anything.

"Can you see them?" asked Amy as she entered.

"Who?" asked Jack distractedly.

Amy groaned lightly in exasperation and pointed into the garden, "Edward and Dora."

Jack looked out of the window, "Yes. What about them?"

"Oh, Jack. Don't you see it? You men can be so blind sometimes."

"What?"

"Look at them! I mean really look! Wouldn't it be wonderful if they were together? Like us… married."

"Married! What? Oh, my love. That is so very…"

"Romantic?"

"Fanciful. They haven't known each other very long."

"We didn't know each other very long either," said Amy with a wry smile and she arched her eyebrow quizzically just as Jack had done many times before.

"But that was different," Jack reasoned. "He cannot yet feel the love that I feel for you."

Amy gasped and love filled her eyes, "Oh, Jack. You always surprise me."

"Surprise you? How? I don't understand."

"Jack…" She shook her head. "That is the first time that you have ever mentioned love."

Jack looked aghast, "No. It's not… it can't be… is it?"

Amy nodded, "It is." She moved into his arms and nestled against him and sighed. Her eyes becoming moist with tears of joy.

Jack held onto her tightly and whispered, "If Edward feels just a little of what I feel, he will be a happy man." He lowered his face to hers and kissed her tenderly, he felt the wet salt tears on her face and stopped. He leaned back and wiped his fingers underneath her eyes, "Why, Amy you're crying. Have I upset you?"

"No. Oh, no. You have made me happy. Very happy, indeed."

***

The next few months were tumultuous with Jack and Edward discussing future plans. They sat in the library and Jack broached the subject, "Edward, Amy and I have noticed that you and Dora…"

"Yes?"

"Seem to be getting close."

Edward nodded, "Dora is a delightful girl. Of that there's no doubt. She's good company, makes me laugh and more importantly laughs at my jokes." Edward's face grew serious, "What are you trying to say, Jack?"

"I want you to be happy, like me. I had thought…"

"Yes?"

"Maybe you and Dora would be a good match?"

"You mean, get married?"

"In a word, yes."

Edward fell silent for a moment and then his face broke into a grin, "Why not? We all get on. Dora does make me happy but do you think she would have me?"

"I don't doubt it. From conversations Amy has had with her, Dora is quite smitten with you."

"In that case, why not? I pressured you and saw what you did not, so how can I ignore what you and Amy have noticed? Let's get everyone in here."

"What now?"

"Now! There is no time like the present and you have fired me up with enthusiasm. I will ask her now."

"But I think the ladies have retired."

"Then, we will just wake them up. But what if she says, no?" His face crumpled up with despair, "What if she doesn't want me? How will we live afterwards? The awkwardness. I couldn't bear it."

Jack shook his head in amusement, "Edward, trust me. She will say, yes. I'm sure."

"Then, I'll do it now before I change my mind. Come on, let's rouse the household. Gather everyone here. Must make sure we have champagne on hand, if she says yes. I'll run and get it and the glasses. Jack, ring the dinner gong, get everyone here, now!"

Jack leapt up from his seat with his lopsided grin as Edward fled to get the best glasses and champagne. Jack took a deep breath and dashed to the hallway. He waited until Edward emerged from the passage carrying a heavy tray. He watched Edward disappear to the library and then picked up the stick and hammered on the metal surface making as much noise as possible. He shouted at the top of his voice, "Wakey, wakey! Everybody up."

Atwill was the first from his room, "What's the matter? Is there a fire?"

"Atwill, get to the library now!" he bashed the cymbal disc even harder. Amy was next with baby Tom who had started to cry followed by Miss Bonnet and Dora all in their nightgowns and mop caps. "To the library, now, everyone. Hurry."

"Jack?" demanded a concerned Amy. But, Jack avoided any questioning by hastening to the library while the ladies chittered in alarm as they made their way downstairs and followed Jack to the library.

Soon they were all gathered in the library and looked at each other in puzzlement and embarrassment. Edward was nowhere to be seen. Jack sat with an inscrutable smile on his face when Edward flung back the curtain stepped out and walked towards Dora, he got down on one knee, took her hand and asked, "Dora, Miss Wicks, will you do me the honour of becoming my wife?"

Dora gasped, then blushed, and then stuttered, "I... I... don't know www...what t... t... to say."

"Say, yes," whispered Amy, her eyes shining with happiness.

Miss Bonnet simpered and fluttered her eyelashes, "Oh my... Oh my..." She kept repeating those two words, over and over.

Dora pulled Edward to his feet and beamed whispering, "Yes. Yes, I will. Oh, yes." And everyone cheered. Dora looked down shyly, "Just remember I don't normally look like this... I really am..."

"Beautiful," finished Edward and swung her around in his arms as Atwill popped a champagne cork and poured the champagne. He passed the glasses around and everyone chattered excitedly. He even managed a wink to Miss Bonnet who flushed with colour as he whispered something in her ear.

Celebrations continued until two bottles had been emptied and the ladies retired in the afterglow of delight. Jack turned to Atwill and asked, "Tell me, what did you say to Miss Bonnet to make her blush so?"

Atwill grinned and replied, "I told her that if she'd a mind, I'd like to keep her bed as warm for her as her roast beef warms our stomachs!"

Jack and Edward roared with laughter.

22: The Killing of Dreams by Harsh Reality

There was huge excitement in the mansion with the prospect of another wedding to happen in the household and this time Edward vowed it would all be done properly with appropriate attention to detail and so would take time to plan. He wanted to enjoy it and for it to be absolutely perfect. In the meantime, there was a Christening to organise as Miss Bonnet had been agitating about the correct time for Tom's baptism, which apparently was, according to tradition, already far too late. Miss Bonnet insisted that the child should not be walking. Tom was already pulling himself up on the furniture and trying to stand. At the moment he couldn't do it unaided but Miss B, decreed he would soon be toddling therefore the ceremony needed to be done now.

The church and the minister were booked. It was to be a small but simple ceremony with Edward and Atwill as Godfathers and Dora as Godmother. Miss B flapped around like a clucking mother hen ensuring her brood were all dressed correctly and that Tom looked perfect in his Christening gown although Jack complained that it made him look too much like a girl especially with his long dark locks. Miss B had often commented, "With hair and eyelashes like that he's far too pretty to be a boy, so he is! He's going to be a little heartbreaker when he grows up. I am sure of it."

***

The day arrived and the ceremony passed without a hitch. Tom didn't cry. The only one that blubbered was Miss B. She soaked two hankies, her own and Atwill's. Everyone was in excellent spirits as they left the church.

Atwill pulled away in the two horse carriage with Miss B sitting up front next to him. The carriage had been tastefully decorated for the Christening. Edward and Dora sat facing Amy and Jack with little Tom.

Jack kissed his wife tenderly and gazed at his small son. "Let's get back home to celebrate the baptism of our son. We have friends, good grub that Miss B has lovingly prepared and drink enough for everyone. We will have a proper celebration."

Amy moved in closer to Jack as she cuddled her son and sighed in contentment. "I don't think I have ever felt happier. It is all more than I could ever have wished."

***

A scream of agony reverberated around the shadier part of town at the bottom of Main Street. Rust with his flame red hair and pockmarked skin was standing outside the Leather Bar, scrutinising the road in both directions. He picked at his teeth and an evil grin slid across his face as there was a thundering crash and the sound of shattered glass coming from inside the bar.

McQueen square faced, powerfully built with bulging muscles and the mean looking, brutish, stocky Masters came skulking out of the bar. Masters shook his right hand and rubbed his sore and bloody knuckles. They both swaggered towards Rust whose eyes had narrowed to slits as he continued to survey the road. "I 'eard the glass. Give you some trouble did he?"

Masters revealed his bloodied, grazed knuckles and growled, "Just a little. But I guarantee he won't next time. I've already rearranged his nose. He won't want it flattened anymore." Masters guffawed scathingly and passed Rust a wad of money.

"Is it all there?"

"Every penny. He knows protection costs. I mean, this place is full of convicts. It's not safe, is it? Anything could 'appen. After all, he don't want his place wrecked, do he?" Masters grinned ruthlessly revealing his stained, broken teeth and chortled callously.

The thugs sauntered arrogantly along the dusty road laughing raucously, jostling and ribbing each other. They stepped back as the two horse carriage driven by Atwill turned into the street and rumbled past. Rust peered inside at Jack and Amy laughing together happily with Edward and Dora. They looked the epitome of joy.

Rust spat into the dirt and wiped his mouth on his frayed sleeve. "Damn colonists. Who do they think they are?" he stood with his arms akimbo and glared at them as they travelled past oblivious to the attention thrust upon them by the ruffians. Rust grimaced and ordered, "Masters, find out who they are."

***

The Christening party arrived back at the mansion and adjourned to the drawing room where a fine spread had been laid out and champagne waited. Miss B fussed around ensuring everyone had plates and serviettes. Amy delighted them with a rendition of Beethoven at the piano and chatter ranged from the proposed wedding plans to attending a naming ceremony for Tom in the village at the request of Koorong. It was the happiest Jack had ever felt and he felt his heart would burst.

One by one the household retired leaving Jack and Amy to settle their son to sleep before turning into bed themselves. Amy snuggled into Jack's arms and smiled as she listened to his easy breathing as he fell asleep.

Amy lay there thinking of her life at the mansion and how good things were for them all. Amy was looking forward to a welcome home dinner for the captain and his daughters who had returned to Port Jackson for a six-month term of duty. He had invited her and Jack to dinner the following evening. She recalled her pleasure in Jack's acceptance of the invitation but knew he had said yes purely because he had recognised her desire to visit and reacquaint herself with the captain and his children. Amy smiled as she remembered Atwill's lessons in dining etiquette that both Jack and Edward had attended after they had married. Jack had learned quickly and she was proud of that and proud of his agreement to wear formal dinner attire. He had looked so handsome at his fitting at Edward's tailor. Amy closed her eyes and drifted off into a peaceful sleep secure in the knowledge that all was well and she was filled with hope for the future.

Outside in the stables the horses were restless. They stamped their feet and whinnied and a neighbour's dog began to bark, which turned into a howl. It was a lonely, mournful sound that cut through the humid night air but no one in the mansion stirred, as two figures crept around the grounds and house. One man walked through the garden to the windows of the drawing room where a lamp had been left burning and envious eyes peered in at the debris left behind by the party.

***

Amy stepped in front of Jack and adjusted his cravat, "Thank you for making the effort. You know it means a lot to me."

Jack grinned cheekily, "Well, I am wearing my best bib and tucker." He paraded around the room striking various poses. "How do I look?"

"Like a gentleman."

"Not like a colonist?"

"No, not a colonist. They are stuck up prigs from what I've seen."

"Couldn't agree more. Let's hope your captain approves."

"I'm sure he will."

"In spite of my accent?"

"It's not that bad. It's part of you. I find it endearing."

"Do you, now?"

"I do." Amy batted him on his nose and Jack took her into his arms and held her close. He sniffed her hair, "You always smell so good, fragrant and fresh."

"I smell good? I hope I look good, too?" Amy gave a twirl in her evening gown.

"Seems to me, Mrs Dawkins that you are fishing."

"Fishing?"

"Fishing for compliments!"

Amy blushed, "Get on with you. It took you long enough to mention the word love."

"Love is not just a word."

"No, it is much more than that but still it took you long enough to say it," repeated Amy.

Jack grinned. "It did, didn't it? But I shall make it up to you, my love. There you go that's one mention you weren't expecting today."

Amy laughed, "Jack Dawkins, you are incorrigible. I doubt we'd be wed if I hadn't said anything."

Jack screwed up his face and whistled between his lips, "Reckon you're right. But it don't matter no how. We're wed and happy. We are happy, aren't we?"

"Very. And now, I will fetch Tom to say goodnight."

Amy glided from the room and returned moments later. She set Tom on the floor in front of the fire. "Watch him carefully, I just need to speak to Miss Bonnet." She left leaving the door ajar.

Jack sat in the wing back chair and watched his son crawl to the chaise longue to pull himself up. He stood unsteadily holding onto the seat and Jack encouraged him, "Come on, my son, come to me." Jack patted his lap and urged him again, "Come on, little chap. Walk to your dad. There's a good boy. You can do it." Jack continued to egg him on making reassuring noises. The little one held out his arms and let go of the seat. He tottered a few steps and landed on his bottom with a bump and stuck his dimpled fist in his mouth and began to suck.

Jack was in awe and could barely contain his excitement. "That's it. Who's a clever boy?" He waited as the child attempted to stand again this time, unaided. Tom pushed himself up with his hands and wobbled before collapsing on the floor again. Jack rose and scooped him up. He sat with him on his knee, praising the child before lowering his voice, "Tom, you have a blooming wonderful mum and you got two parents that love you. I never knew my mum and dad. For a long time, I was known as a foundling. That's another name for orphan. I was abandoned, see. Left on the steps of a workhouse. That ain't going to happen to you. You will have the life I never knew. With a mum and a dad. You won't be cold. You will never want for grub. You won't have to sleep with rats and fleas. You won't get beaten and you won't have to nick things that don't belong to you. And you certainly won't have to fear the law. You won't never have to be afraid. I sometimes listen to your mum singing as you go to sleep. All I ever heard was rain, dogs barking and the snores and farts of Fagin and the gang. You will have a good life, my precious little son, the very best. I'll see to that. Now, don't you go telling no one that I was ever afraid cos I'm the Artful Dodger. And Artful Dodgers ain't never afraid." Jack held his little boy tightly and kissed the top of his head. "You're like a little cherub, you are and you're loved, really loved." He stopped as his voice caught with emotion and he sat cuddling his little son, his heart bursting with pride and affection.

Amy stood outside the door, listening. She had heard everything Jack had said and was overcome with emotion as tears filled her eyes. She hurriedly wiped them away with her gloved hand and floated in smiling radiantly. "Time to get this little boy back to the nursery." She walked to the bell pull and rang.

Miss Bonnet hurried in and took Tom from Amy's arms, "Now, don't you worry none. Little 'un will be as safe as houses with me. You go and enjoy yourselves it's not often you get to go out alone. Make the most of it. Atwill is bringing the carriage around. You have a good time and I want to hear all about it in the morning."

"You will, Miss B," said Amy with a laugh. "I will bore you with all the details, what we had for dinner, what music was played, everything." Amy picked up her cape and Jack placed it around her shoulders. They both gave Tom a kiss before Miss Bonnet raised Tom's little hand to wave at them as they left the room and went out of the door.

***

The clock struck ten and its chimes echoed through the house. Edward and Dora were sitting in the drawing room enjoying a nightcap as they finalised their wedding plans. Dora was sporting a beautiful diamond ring. She looked proudly at her left hand, "I have never owned anything so lovely as this or been so happy in all my life. I cannot believe everything that has come to pass in such a short time."

"Nor I, Dora, my love. We have been well and truly blessed. Let us pray we will be lucky like Jack and Amy to have our lives made complete and have our own little one, a playmate for Tom."

"Oh, I do hope so. And now I really must get to bed. I have promised to visit the dressmaker tomorrow. For another fitting."

Dora rose and Edward stood politely, took her hand and kissed it gently, "Until tomorrow, Miss Wicks, soon to be Mrs Hargreaves."

She gazed long into his eyes before removing her hand and walking to the door when she heard the sound of glass shattering and the splintering of wood. "Whatever's that?"

Edward was instantly alert, "I don't like the sound of that. Dora get yourself upstairs now and quickly. Hide behind the curtains, in a wardrobe... anywhere. Stay there and don't come out until I tell you."

Dora hurried up the stairs and slipped behind the window drapes on the landing gathering the bulk of her dress to ensure she was completely hidden. She could just see onto the landing and stairs through a chink in the curtains.

Edward waited until she was clear and tiptoed to the door and carefully opened it. He saw three thugs creeping up the stairs wielding knives. One of them turned and looked back. Edward's heart froze in horror as he recognised the ugly, cruel face of Rust with his bush of flame red hair, who now pulled up a scarf to hide his identity.

Edward glanced about him for a weapon of some sort and wondered if he had time to get to the kitchen and get himself some sort of blade but knew if he moved he would be spotted, but he needed something. He looked at the fire irons in the hearth and picked up a poker as the men disappeared along the landing.

***

There was a wailing cry from upstairs as the thugs entered the nursery. Rust scrawled something on the wall before he grabbed Tom savagely from his crib and they came out to be faced by Miss B who had been woken by Tom's plaintive cry and who was now screaming enough to burst his lungs.

"Just what do you think you're doing?" questioned Miss Bonnet. "Put that child back at once," she ordered.

The miscreants stopped momentarily before breaking out into hysterical laughter as they saw the diminutive Welsh woman in her night gown and mop cap holding out her arms for the baby. "Give him to me," she demanded. "Now!"

Rust snarled and walked up to her holding the infant, invading her space and rasped, "Why? What you gonna do?" He shoved her hard with his free hand and sent her sprawling. He laughed and commanded his men, "Let's get out of here, quick!" He turned and began to walk across the landing to the stairs. Filled with fury Miss B leapt up and jumped on Rust's back and began beating him about the head. Rust recoiled, turned and threw her off. She went flying down the stairs and landed with a sickening crunch at the bottom. Her body was twisted awkwardly and blood pooled around her head and neck, which was clearly broken.

"Let's get out of here," said Masters.

"No, you don't!" roared Edward stepping out from the drawing room brandishing the poker. "Give him to me."

Rust yelled, "McQueen! Take the kid and go." He thrust the red faced screaming infant at McQueen. "I'll deal with this. Masters, grab him!"

Masters stepped forward and Edward raised the poker as he tried to strike the fiend but Masters sliced his arm with his kukri almost severing Edward's hand. Edward screamed in agony and dropped the poker. Rust stepped behind Edward, caught him around the neck and viciously drew his blade across Edward's throat, slicing through his carotid artery. Blood fountained out as Edward slumped to the floor. "Right, let's scarper before anyone else sees us." They ran out of the front door without looking back.

Dora had seen it all but remained hidden behind the drapes, too terrified to move and was now whimpering like a tortured animal.

***

One hour later, Jack and Amy had left the captain's table promising to return with the baby to show him. The evening had been a great success and Atwill had been well fed in the kitchen eating the same food as the invited guests. He was now driving the carriage back to the mansion. Amy nestled her head on Jack's shoulder and murmured, "Thank you. It was a lovely evening, wasn't it? Aren't you glad you came?"

"If you're happy. Then I'm happy. I suppose we ought to have him back at some point, show him where you live and that our Miss B is just as good a cook as what we had tonight. Then he'd know you were being looked after."

"He knows. I told him enough times."

The carriage turned in through the gates and up the extensive drive and stopped at the stone steps. Jack got out and helped Amy down. "Night, Atwill."

"Goodnight, Jack, Mrs Dawkins."

"Goodnight, Mr Atwill," said Amy with a contented smile.

Atwill flicked the reins to take the horses to the stables and settle them as Amy and Jack began to ascend the steps.

Jack halted and a suspicious frown appeared on his face as he saw the front door was slightly ajar. Instantly alert he raised his hand and ordered, "Wait here."

Jack pushed open the door with one finger and stepped into the dark hallway. He saw the light burning in the drawing room and another coming from a room upstairs. A feeling of cold disquiet surged through him making the hairs on the back of his neck rise up like taunted snakes.

Amy stood on the steps outside the open door and peered in. Jack felt his way towards the stairs trying to adjust his eyes to the dark and called out, "Edward!" He skidded in something, slipped and fell landing on the floor with a bump and put his hand in something sticky. He smelt an almost forgotten smell from his childhood of coppery blood. He rose and walked into something soft and stopped.

Amy pushed the door open wider but Jack instructed, "Don't come in. Wait there, please."

"Jack, are you all right? What's happened?"

"Oh, Christ!"

"Jack?"

"Stay there!" The silver moonlight released from its cloud cover filtered through the open door and Jack could see two bodies. "Amy, fetch Atwill, now. Hurry!"

Jack marched to the drawing room and picked up the still burning lamp and hurried back to the hallway and set it down. He turned over Edward's body and held back his cry of horror as he saw his friend's throat had been slashed and his hand almost amputated. "Edward!" Sadness gripped him; he rose and saw another broken body. It was that of Miss Bonnet and Jack bit his knuckles to stop himself from crying aloud.

Fear raged through him, "Oh, no... Tom!" Jack raced up the stairs to the nursery and dived in through the door to see that the crib was empty. "NOOOOO!" A terrible cry erupted from the pit of his belly and reverberated around the room. He looked at the wall that was smeared with blood and words were scrawled over it.

Jack dashed back downstairs uncertain what to do. He sat at his friend's side cradling Edward's head, with tears streaming down his face as Amy and Atwill entered. Amy looked on in shock at Edward's corpse. Atwill dashed to the side of Miss Bonnet to see if she was breathing. He tried to lift her up and hugged the spinster to him, holding her tightly and rocking with sorrow, a faint mewling coming from him.

Jack gazed up at his wife in pain, "The baby's gone."

"What?"

"Tom, he's gone."

Amy hurtled to the stairs and flew up them like a woman demented. She threw open the nursery door and searched about the room crying inconsolably. Then she read the writing on the wall and fled back down the stairs, sobbing.

"Them words, what they say?" asked Jack but Amy was so distraught with grief she couldn't speak. Atwill laid Miss Bonnet back down carefully and went up to the nursery. He shouted down from the landing, "Jack, it says, bring £5,000 to Jacob's Creek tomorrow night at ten. Come alone or the kid dies."

Amy howled like a she-wolf baying at the moon, which dissolved into hiccupping sobs so that she could scarcely breathe.

Atwill heard another sorrow filled groan coming from behind the window drapes. He crossed quickly and flung them back to reveal Dora who crumpled to the floor in a heap. Atwill helped her up onto a chaise-longue in the upstairs hallway as Dora spoke. "Edward made me hide. If I hadn't, they'd have killed me, too," she sobbed. "They weren't going to leave no witnesses."

Amy struggled to compose herself and went up to see Dora and sat next to her on the seat. She tried to speak but the words stuck in her throat and just wouldn't come out.

Jack mounted the stairs and asked Dora gently, "What happened?" Dora sat with tears streaming down her face so Jack asked again and Amy took Dora's hand. "Dora, what happened?"

"Mr Edward... is he...?"

"Sorry, Dora. There's no easy way of saying this...Edward's dead."

"Oh, no! He tried to stop them. So, did Miss B... Please say he's not dead," and she began to cry in anguish and twiddled her engagement ring.

"Dora you must tell us what happened."

Dora strived to talk between sobs, "We were in the drawing room, I was just going upstairs to bed when we heard this almighty noise, glass breaking and wood smashing. Mr Edward told me to go upstairs and hide. I hid here behind the curtains but I could see what was going on through a small gap. Three men came up the stairs with black scarves over their faces. They had big knives. Tom was asleep. They went into the nursery and snatched him but he started to cry and that woke Miss Bonnet. She challenged them demanding they give her the baby. The big one just shoved her but Miss B was having none of it. She jumped on the man's back and started hitting him and he flung her off and threw her down the stairs. I heard her land. Horrible it was. That's when I heard Edward. He'd come out and he went for them. I could hear Tom yelling like I've never heard before and grunts and other noises. I know they'd hit Edward but I hoped he wasn't dead, just unconscious or something. I stayed where I was. I didn't dare move. Edward told me to hide." She began weeping again.

"Amy whispered, what are we going to do, Jack?"

"They've said what they want. We've no choice but to do it."

"But what about the bodies? Shouldn't we call the police?"

"No. They won't hurt the baby, not if we do it right. Atwill, are the horses untacked yet?"

"No, I was just taking them to the stables when Mrs Dawkins called me."

"Get the carriage back out front, then saddle a horse and tie it on the back. You can help me get Edward into it and Miss B."

"Right," Atwill left speedily.

Jack turned to Amy, "I'll take him back to the farm. I'll bury Edward with his grandfather, Miss B, too."

Dora began to wail again in utter despair. Amy put her arms around her, "Can you tell us anything about the men, anything at all?"

"I didn't see their faces. But the big one who was giving the orders had bright red hair."

Jack's mouth turned into a hard line, "I know exactly who that is. Dora, look after Mrs Dawkins. Amy, I'll be back here tomorrow. Don't talk to no one. No police nor nothing like that."

"But..."

"No buts. Do as I ask. Please."

"All right."

"Now, is there a bag handy?"

Amy nodded, "In the kitchen hanging up behind the pantry door."

Jack hurried down the passageway to the kitchen and found the bag. He went upstairs with it and disappeared into Edward's room. Moments later he emerged with a well-padded bag and ran down the stairs.

"Come on, Atwill." He turned to Amy, "Lock all the doors."

"What about the windows? One of them's smashed."

"Close the wooden shutters, all of them, light the lamps and sit tight. Don't go out anywhere. It will have to do until we can get it fixed."

Atwill opened the front door and helped Jack carry Edward and then Miss B's body out to the carriage. Lastly, Jack picked up the bag and tied it to the pommel of his saddled horse that was behind the vehicle.

Inside, Edward was on one seat, Jack on the other and Miss B lay on the floor together with a shovel. Atwill climbed up front, flicked the reins and the carriage took off down the drive at a dangerous pace until Jack called out, "Drive slower, we don't want to attract no attention. We can pick up speed once we're on the road to the farm."

The carriage slowed and Jack stared despairingly at Edward's body. "Why, oh why, Lord? Why did this have to happen?" Jack lowered his head as if in prayer but was lost in the realm of desolation.

***

Atwill's face was grim. He stifled a roar of anger, "I'd only just got started to calling her Delia; in private, of course. She was a winsome lass with a good heart. I had hoped..." He trailed off.

Jack lifted his head in the heavy gloom that had pervaded. "I'd forgotten she was called Delia. I only ever heard Edgar call her once by her first name. She was always Miss B to me."

"She was a brave woman. From what Dora said she put her life on the line without a minute's hesitation."

"She did," said Jack morosely. "And Edward, too. They were both loyal and true. Friends to the end. They didn't deserve this," he said bitterly.

"What you gonna do?"

"Once I got Tom safe, there'll be a reckoning, make no doubt about it."

"You said you know the man."

"Pretty sure I do. And the murderer's beef is with me and no one else."

"Well, I got issues with him now..."

"Leave it with me, Atwill. I'll make sure we both have satisfaction."

The carriage rumbled on and Jack picked up Edward's limp hand and silent tears rushed forth. He wiped them away on the sleeve of his coat and looked at himself, "Crikey... didn't even 'ave time to change," he murmured. "I got something at the farm. Get out of this dog's dinner."

For the rest of the journey Jack stared stonily ahead and his anger grew.

***

At the farm, Jack hurriedly changed out of his evening wear and into his old work garb. He chucked the items that were now stained with Edward's blood into a heap and hurried back to the carriage, instructing Atwill to go towards the line of trees where Fred was buried.

226

The first dim streak of a rosy dawn was beginning to break reviving the flowers in the grassy meadow from their night's slumber. The gentle glow of spreading warmth was in opposition to the harsh reality of the night's events. Atwill and Jack removed both bodies and lay them side by side. Jack grabbed the shovel. He picked the spot next to Fred's grave and began to dig. Each spade of earth was accompanied with a grunt. Jack needed the physical exertion to temper his mood but all it did was harden his resolve.

Atwill, cloaked in his own despondency, looked at Jack anxiously also feeling his pain, "I'll do that, Jack," he said quietly.

"No, this is something I must do."

"Then let me at least dig Delia's grave."

Jack paused to wipe his sweating brow and nodded. Atwill went to the outlying shed and took another tool passing two aboriginal men on horseback who greeted him. Atwill exchanged a few words and pointed to Jack before joining him to dig.

The aborigines rode over and stared at Edward's body. They were filled with their own grief for they had known Edward and his gentle nature. One of them rode off at speed, while the other stayed to help.

***

Jack leaned on his shovel and stared unhappily at the three mounds each with their crude crosses erected. Atwill, Koorong and a number of other aborigines were gathered around the burial site. Jack turned to Atwill, "Take the carriage, head back and look after the women. Untie my horse and leave him with me." Atwill nodded. "Tell me, do you have your pocket watch? I don't have mine."

"I do."

"Let me lend it. Does it keep to time?"

"It does. I put it right by the town clock every day." Atwill removed it from inside his jacket and passed it to Jack. Jack checked the time and placed it in his own pocket.

"Go now. Drive carefully and be safe. Clear up the mess in the hall and Tom's room. Make sure the place looks as it usually does."

"What do I tell Miss Bonnet's brother?"

"Nothing yet. We will have to work something out. Now go."

Atwill shook the reins and the horses trotted off back down the dusty track. Jack watched until he was out of sight and then he and Koorong spoke together. Koorong patted Jack on the back and he mounted his horse and galloped off away from the farm. The sun had now risen to its full height in the clear blue sky. Jack thought that on such a day as this it should be raining. The heavens should be weeping for the loss of innocence and the good. He rode his horse hard towards Jacob's Creek. It would be a long day and night.

***

The scarred silver face of the moon shone unusually brightly in the dense dark of evening at Jacob's Creek. Stars freckled the ceiling twinkling lustrously in the shadowed blackness. Jack waited astride his horse in the scrub at the edge of the creek facing a

227

thickly wooded area. He listened to the music of the stream as it rippled through the vegetation with the occasional splash of a fish jumping and croak of a frog. Crickets trilled and night birds called from their territories warning others to keep out while others chittered to attract a mate.

Jack waited. He removed Atwill's watch and looked at the time. It was two minutes to ten. Jack closed it, returned it to his pocket and urged his horse to step out from cover and walk to the river bank. Off to his right there was a movement and Rust, wearing a slouch hat to hide his hair and a scarf up over his face to disguise his identity, stepped out from behind a tree. He coughed and spat into the dirt. Jack turned his steed and faced him.

Rust pointed at the bag, his eyes glinting greedily, "Is that the money?"

"It is."

"Throw it down and I'll tell you where the brat is," he rasped.

"No. You take me to my son and then, I'll give you the money."

"Are you alone?"

"Do you see anyone else? Of course, I'm alone."

They stared hard at each other. The silence was tortuous. Jack could see the feral gleam in the brute's eye. Rust finally spoke again, "Right. Follow me. Slowly."

Rust set off into the trees and Jack picked his way through the woodland behind the man. He strived to suppress the red mist of rage that was filling his eyes. The moon shone clearly highlighting a well-trodden route towards a ramshackle hut where a light burned. As Rust neared the hovel he shouted out, "It's me. Come on out!" Masters and McQueen appeared from the dwelling wearing scarves over their faces. "Step down from your horse. Bring the money. Your kid's in there."

Jack dismounted, took the bag and inched his way towards the men, who suddenly drew knives. Jack yelled with all his might, "Koorong!"

All hell broke loose as a crowd of aborigines who had been lying invisibly in wait came out of the forest, all armed with traditional weapons. They surrounded the men who tried to stave them off with their blades, but two dropped from the trees with nets and threw it over McQueen and Masters while Jack tackled Rust pulling off his hat and face covering. The thugs were swiftly restrained by the natives and tied up as Jack raced into the hut.

There was an unearthly bellow and a roar of anger from inside the shed. Jack emerged holding the limp form of Tom. Jack was numb, his face lacked expression as if Medusa herself had turned his heart to stone. He walked to the three killers, clutching his child to his chest. There was ice in his tone, which sent shivers up the spines of those listening. "He's dead. My little one is dead. You've killed my son."

***

That night, Koorong and his fellow natives were sitting around a blazing fire keeping the three murderers under close guard whose feet and hands were tied. They were bound tightly to a tree and gagged. They sat miserably in a huddle uncertain what was to happen to them while the Aborigines watched the flames leap, flicker and burn. The colours in the fire danced on the dead wood licking it ravenously, hues ranging from orange and red to yellow and blue. A goanna was being roasted on a stick but the natives were quiet and subdued and clearly waiting for someone.

There was a thunder of horse's hooves and Jack rode into the camp. His face devoid of emotion, his eyes were like those of a dead fish on a slab. He dismounted and removed a spade from his saddle and sat in front of the fire, chin in his hands, staring into the flames and listening to the snicks, snacks and crackles of the blaze. He appeared to make up his mind and called out decisively, "Koorong!"

Koorong looked across and Jack beckoned him. Koorong rose, left his friends and joined Jack who muttered something to him. Koorong stood up frowning. Jack was insistent, his tone brooked no argument, "Do it!" Jack passed him the spade.

Koorong called to two other villagers and the three of them disappeared along the path into the night leaving Jack to glare into the fire. He remained there sitting motionless like a stone sculpture until the moon had travelled across the dusky sky giving way to the first blush of the cerise tinges of dawn. The fire had almost burned out leaving only the smouldering embers to create more pictures in the heart of the dying cinders.

The three kidnappers remained under guard and bound to the tree as the natives awoke and walked around the camp stretching their limbs and yawning. One offered Jack a drink of water, which he refused. Jack stood and walked mechanically to the thugs. His voice struck fear into the criminals' hearts, "Are you prepared for today?" He ripped the gag from Rust's mouth making the villain wince.

"How d'you mean prepared?" said Rust suspiciously, his evil eyes closing to a mean slit.

Jack's bitter voice was without emotion, "Oh no! You wouldn't be, would you? No... You don't know what I have in store for you." Jack addressed the Aborigine guards and pointed at the men, "Bring them. Follow me."

The men were untied from the tree and the bonds on their feet removed. With their hands bound they were bundled after Jack. The natives prodded the reluctant trio forward. They continued to walk a few hundred yards, dragging their feet until they reached a large gum tree where Koorong and the two other villagers sat in the shade. The tree was filled with the happy buzz of chattering budgerigars that flew up as one colourful flock with the new arrivals. They set the sky ablaze with colour.

Jack halted the men and tore off the other two gags. Masters studied Jack's aloof expression and mumbled, "What you gonna do?"

Jack indicated three open graves already prepared and responded, "What's it look like?"

Rust gazed around showing the first flash of fear in his eyes and voice as he pleaded, "Please, Jack, Mr Dawkins. Please." His voice tailed off to a pitiful, cowardly yelp.

Jack continued almost machine-like in his instructions with a tone as dead as trees in winter. He gestured to the natives, "Make a circle. Surround these men."

The aboriginals waved their spears and made the men cluster in the centre of the ring. Jack ordered Koorong, "Untie their hands." Obediently, Koorong stepped forward and sliced the men's bonds with a large blade. Jack's next chilling words were said deliberately with venom, "You like to use knives, don't you? Here." Jack passed each of them a wicked looking blade and pronounced, "You will fight each other to the death. The man still alive at the end goes free."

The foul brutes who had never shown anyone else mercy either at the prison, or since being released, looked at each other in horror. Rust was the first to move. He took a lunge at Masters, who swiftly sidestepped, dodging clear. McQueen moved in to attack Masters and there followed a vicious brutal fight between the two, while Rust looked on gauging each exchange and waited for his own chance. Finally, Masters stabbed McQueen right through the heart and McQueen tumbled to his knees and fell forward with the knife still in him. Masters was now defenceless and Rust capitalised on this opportunity by leaping up behind him and slit Master's throat with a grunt. The blood sprayed out covering Rust's hands and his clothing. Rust breathed heavily with the effort. He scrambled up and Koorong removed the blade from him. Rust wiped his blood covered hand across his face looking like a medieval executioner and turned to go.

"Not so fast," said Jack slowly and deliberately, his face an iron mask. He indicated the bodies, bury them. The hard work's been done for you." He gave Rust a shove and stood over him as he dragged his fellow criminals towards the graves. Rust eyed the protruding knife from McQueen's heart and his eyes flicked around nervously at the natives and then back at the blade handle. "Don't even think about it," warned Jack throatily.

Rust kicked McQueen into one grave and waded back for the body of Masters. He repeated the action and brushed his hands off, picked up the shovel and began to pile the earth over his gang members. He mumbled wordlessly with each spade full of dirt that he threw and Jack stood like judge and jury watching distantly, his eyes and heart as numb and icy as the frozen mountains of Kiandra.

Koorong studied Jack's face anxiously and appeared disturbed by Jack's out of character hard chilling manner. Jack remained motionless as Rust completed his task and turned to go. Jack waited until he reached the edge of the circle and demanded, "Stop! Bring him back." Two natives caught hold of Rust and dragged him back before Jack who directed frostily, "Hold him!" It was then Jack drew his own cruel looking kukri.

"You said you'd let me go," protested Rust his eyes now wild with fear.

"You don't know who I am, do you?"

"You're Jack Dawkins."

"Let me nudge your memory." He paused, "You were going to 'ang me once; thought I was a threat, that I knew something 'bout you that others didn't. Have you guessed yet? No? I'm the Artful Dodger."

Realisation flooded Rust's eyes and he recognised the man who was once a boy. "... Dodger... you said you'd let me go."

"I lied."

Jack lunged forward stabbing Rust in the stomach and ripped upward almost eviscerating him. Disbelief spread in Rust's eyes as he struggled to hold his guts inside and he dropped to his knees.

Without looking at Koorong Jack commanded, "Bury him."

Koorong protested, "But, he's still alive."

"I know. Bury him." Two natives dragged Rust screaming and put him in the third grave. "Lie him on his back and cover the bastard."

Koorong threw down the spade and objected, "I cannot."

"Then I'll do it," growled Jack. He jumped into the pit, and turned Rust onto his back. Rust was still shrieking like a banshee. His face was contorted in pure terror as Jack leapt out of the tomb and grabbed the spade. He flung a shovel full of dry dusty earth over Rust's head. Rust spluttered and coughed as he fought to breathe and spit out the soil. A second spade of dirt showered over him and Jack continued to pile it on until the killer's screaming stopped. All that could be heard were the clods of earth as they landed on Rust's body. The Aboriginals looked on dumbstruck, their faces expressed their revulsion at the nightmarish actions of what they had just witnessed.

Jack then fetched the pitiful little bundle that had been his son and carried him to his horse and galloped back to the farm and the place where his 'family' were buried.

Jack gently lay his baby down and dug another small grave next to Edward and set his child inside. After the burial, Jack rose and stood at the graveside a while. He was almost unrecognisable. His lean saturnine face was devoid of humanity as if his heart had been ripped out and he had turned into some unearthly creature of the night.

23: Going Home But to What?

Jack galloped as if the Furies from Hades were pursuing him. Still in his old clothes, he raced onward. His ragged open jacket fluttered behind in tattered shreds like a winged creature from the Netherworld. He was a man demented and rode the track back to the road, unrelentingly and without care until he reached the town. People going about their business jumped out of his way as he spurred his horse onward. Bonnie was foaming at the bit and covered in a slick sheen of sweat but Jack didn't care.

He sped up the drive to the mansion, dismounted and tied up his steed. He rushed into the house through the now gleaming clean hallway. There was no sign of spilt blood, no sign that anything had happened at all. He marched along the passage to the drawing room and entered slamming the door behind him. He strode to the open window and closed the wooden shutters with a bang before locking the window and slumping in a chair. He was numb and devoid of emotion. He stared ahead pitilessly and a long juddering breath was slowly released from his lungs.

The door opened quietly. Jack didn't turn and didn't look to see who had entered, but remained rigidly in his chair. Amy crossed softly to him and tentatively asked, "Jack?"

Jack's voice was brusque, hardly recognisable and he didn't meet her eyes. The frost running through the blood in his veins came out in his tone and he said bluntly, "He's dead."

"What?"

His bald reply came back at her, "Tom's dead."

Amy moved closer but Jack did not stir. She knelt on the floor next to him and noticed the blood spatter that showered his clothes. She saw his hands still stained red. Unfazed, she attempted to put her arms around him but received no response. Jack stood up and removed her hands and walked away from her. Amy looked hurt and confused. She bit her lip and struggled with her own all-consuming grief and tried again, "Jack?"

Jack turned his back on her and remained stubbornly silent. His frozen eyes were filled with ice. He was unable to speak, didn't want to speak and the cloud of gloom that hung over him exacerbated his morose silence.

Amy waited but he still said nothing. She left the room feeling hopelessly lost.

***

Atwill, Dora and Amy sat in the kitchen together. Six weeks had passed. Dora's eyes were still red and puffy from crying. The atmosphere was melancholic and glum. Amy was the first to speak, "I've never seen him like this. It's as if he's just given up. I don't know who he is anymore. He's not the man I married. People are asking questions."

Atwill nodded, "He's broken, Mrs Dawkins. His life has been blown apart."

"So, has mine. I've not only lost my son but my husband, too. I've tried everything but he just won't talk. He just sits and stares into space as if I'm not there and never have been. At night **if** he finally does come to bed, instead of sitting alone in the drawing room with a bottle for company, he just lies there. I can feel his emptiness and abject despair penetrating through to my bones. We're like strangers as if our marriage and son never existed. I just can't take anymore." Amy struggled not to cry.

Dora and Atwill exchanged a glance. They could think of nothing to say that would comfort her. Atwill finally spoke, "I had to write to Miss Bonnet's brother. A letter had arrived from him asking where she was."

"What did you say? Did you tell him...?"

"I couldn't. How could I explain we'd covered up a murder and buried her?"

"What did you say?"

"I said she had died and it was sudden. That Jack had buried her privately at a prime spot where she would lie peacefully."

"That much is true. I feel as if I will never be at peace again... Do you think Mr Bonnet will pursue it?"

Atwill shrugged, "I don't know, Mrs Dawkins. Time will tell."

They continued to sit entrenched in sadness until Dora finally spoke, "You said you wanted to speak to us, ma'am?"

Amy nodded, "I did. I need you both to know that I am thinking of going away. I cannot stay as things are. It hurts me more than I can say. But I cannot live like this. I am grieving, too. I want you to come with me, Dora."

"Where? Where to?"

"I'm thinking of going back to England or maybe to the captain and his family. I haven't made a decision yet but I know the captain will welcome me back. There is nothing for me here now, not without Jack. At least, I can't live here in this frozen atmosphere. I have to get away, away from Jack. I need time to heal, as we all do. I can't do it here. I feel as if I am stepping on eggshells all the time, tiptoeing around him. This enforced silence, his mental isolation and shutting me out... it breaks my heart."

"What about me? What do you want me to do?" asked Atwill.

"Jack will need someone. He will need you. The house still needs to be run. You can do that."

Atwill nodded miserably, "I'll look after him. I promise."

"Then all that remains is for me to tell him." Amy rose and left the kitchen.

***

Jack was sitting alone in the drawing room an open bottle of whiskey in front of him. He glared at the liquid as if it was somehow responsible for all that had happened. His normally clean-shaven face was bristly with a straggly unkempt beard. He lounged around in his work clothes and seemed to have lost all pride in himself. He took another swig of his drink when he heard the door open. He didn't look up or turn around but just sat hunched in the chair. He didn't even move when he heard Amy's sweet voice.

"Jack?"

He said nothing.

"I am leaving today. I can't live like this anymore." She paused slightly and added quietly with a catch in her voice, "Tom was my baby, too."

At the mention of Tom, Jack stood abruptly. His eyes darkened. He marched past her to the door and stopped. He didn't turn or look around and answered roughly, "There's no need for you to go. You stay. I'm goin'. The place is yours. You won't want for nothing, I'll see to that." He strode out the door leaving Amy shocked and staring after him with her mouth agape.

***

Jack rode his horse hard all the way to the farm, as if the devil was chasing him. He dismounted and removed his small bag from the pommel and threw it on the porch before settling his horse with water and some food. Night was falling. Stars splattered the navy black heavens and the ghostly face of the moon swabbed Jack's face as he sat on the porch.

The hours ticked by; yet Jack still sat, unmoving and slumped as his haunted eyes drooped. It was as if he was deliberately punishing himself, scourging his body and mind. The demon in his head ranted and raved out of control. There was no angel to temper it, no voice of reason, no placating spirit; just his thoughts castigating him and thrashing him with its tongue.

Jack didn't move, didn't retire, had nothing to eat but just sat like a ghoulish spectre waiting for the day to break and reduce him to ashes. The sun's face peeped over the horizon and stretched its orange fingers of light across the land and on Jack's hardened face but it didn't warm him or melt his glacial heart.

It was late afternoon. Soft footfalls came almost silently down the track as Koorong approached the farm buildings on his horse. He dismounted and tethered his pinto to a wooden strut where the hen coop once stood in the yard.

Jack didn't move.

Koorong stood for a moment and stared at his friend, who had become a bizarre version of himself sitting silently.

Koorong stepped towards Jack who didn't acknowledge him but kept his eyes fastened stonily ahead. "Jack, the chief wishes to see you." Koorong's voice seemed surprisingly loud in the humid heat. "I will get your horse and we will go to the village." It was not a request and Jack turned his dead eyes on his friend of many years and rose but no greeting came from his lips. A lazy fly buzzed around him and settled in his beard but he never flinched. Koorong stepped forward and batted at the creature and Jack blinked.

Koorong strode to the stables and brought Jack's horse around to him and handed him the reins. He waited until Jack mounted before retrieving his own steed. He jumped on its back and turned the animal. He glanced over his shoulder and instructed, "Follow me." And like an automaton, Jack followed.

***

A large fire burned in the chief's hut. Its flames threw misshapen shadows in the corners and the mood was sombre. Jack and the chief sat on straw bales in front of the fire separated by Koorong who translated all that the chief said.

"My honoured chief wants you to know that he is aware that you have been our friend for many years."

"I have." They were the first words that Jack had spoken in a long time and Koorong was aware that his self-enforced silence had affected Jack's voice. It was more guttural as if he needed to clear his throat.

The chief continued and Koorong explained, "The chief knows what has happened to you and he feels great pain for you." Jack acknowledged the statement with a curt nod. "He asks when you last rested."

Jack replied in a low monotone, "I don't remember."

"He wants to know why you are not with your son's mother?" Jack didn't answer so Koorong pressed him again, "The chief asks why you are here?"

"Because he asked to see me."

"He says, he knows you seek his help." Jack remained silent. "Is that the truth, Jack?" There was still no response. Koorong spoke more firmly and insistently, "Is that the truth, Jack?"

Jack's dead eyes lifted. They were devoid of any emotion, which matched the emptiness inside him. He took a deep breath and finally responded quietly but monosyllabically, "Yes."

Koorong nodded believing he was getting somewhere, at last. "Good. Is there no one who could help you in your world?"

Jack said without hesitation, "I could have talked to Edward, but that's impossible, now."

Koorong repeated Jack's answer to the chief who nodded sagely and replied. Koorong listened nodding his head in agreement and translated, "You still can." Jack swivelled his head and stared at Koorong, his gaze was disturbing. "Our chief says, because *his* dreaming is over it doesn't mean you cannot talk to him."

Jack turned away once more and said heavily, "But he cannot answer."

This time Koorong spoke to Jack himself, "He does not have to answer. If you talk to him you can also listen to yourself and if you listen to yourself you may find the solutions he would have given you." Jack's expression remained implacable. Koorong suggested gently, "There is another way."

Jack showed a mild flicker of interest before dropping his head and murmuring, "What is that?"

"You can change your Dreamtime. My father and I talked of this many times before he died as has the one who is with us here now... This is what I have learned; if a man is troubled he can find an answer when he is out of reach of other men. When a soul has lost its way there is something he can do to put things right but it must be done alone. He will unearth the remedy from inside himself." Jack said nothing but it was clear from the sudden tension in his body that he was listening so, Koorong continued. "There is a cliff near a waterhole, which you have passed close to many times. Further on past the lagoon follow the path from the creek, until you come to the steepest part and face the cliff. Ask it to show you your life. Request this of Bunjil, the giver of life. Be sincere and he will answer. Take me at my word, Jack. You must stay there until you are shown your problems and it will reveal to you what has made you into a lost dreamer. You will then find a way to forgive yourself and when you do, your dreaming will change... You will have to take with you the means to make a fire. You must become naked as you were when you came into this world and plead for help. Do this, for yourself and Edward." Jack lifted his head from its dropped position and narrowed his eyes from which no light shone.

***

The solitary figure of Jack walked out of the village carrying a bundle of kindling on his back. He left his horse, Bonnie, at the camp and plodded onward mechanically, one step at a time as if he was counting his paces. Koorong watched him through shaded eyes until his figure disappeared from view.

Jack passed the lagoon with its cascading waterfall and continued doggedly around it up the precipitous path to the creek until he reached the designated spot. In his numbed state he was unable to admire the breath-taking view with its jutting moss covered rocks and its stony steep fall to a slow moving, snaking river that glittered and sparkled as the sunlight played on the cool crystal water, throwing prismatic light shows on the cliffs and lush greenery that was a few hundred feet below. It was an enchanting place but the hollow void in Jack's corporeal body was not heartened by the sight.

As the late sun hit the pluming splashes of water, which feathered the rocks, it cast magical rainbow arcs of radiance that gave it an ethereal feel of spirituality, tranquillity and peace. But, Jack in his traumatised state could not appreciate the stunning beauty of the vista before him. He selected a spot and built a fire, gathering brushwood to add to the kindling he'd brought. He took his tinder box and lit the sticks. Soon, he had a roaring crackling fire where fire imp flames leapt and danced.

Jack sat in front of it and stared into the heart of the blaze. His mouth was set in a grim petrified line and sweat beaded his brow. Koorong's instructions rang in his head. Unemotionally, he stripped off his shirt and then his work trousers and sat once more, naked as the day he was born. He took a deep breath and exhorted the giver of life. His voice had found some strength and he raised his arms in supplication and implored, "Bunjil, show me my life. Tell me what I need to know." There he remained until the daylight hours had faded and he was enveloped in the blanket of night and only stirred to feed the fire.

The full and contoured mottled moon lit the sacred place with a silver glow. A change in the air accentuated his lonely desolation with a sharp drop in temperature in spite of the heat of the sputtering crackling flames. Jack stared resolutely into the intense core of the blaze. His concentration deepened and the snicking sounds appeared to hide the whispers of a thousand voices.

So absorbed was he in the power of the living heart of the fire, he began to discern changes, quite subtly, at first, which then became clearer as scenes from his life unfolded. He watched himself as a small boy when he was forced to scrub the steps to the workhouse and the wrath that rained down on him with the buckle end of a leather belt that whipped and beat him and the face of the workhouse master who dealt the punishing blows and the pleasure he got from inflicting pain.

Time moved on swiftly to being courted by Fagin and dragged into the den of thieves where he was pulled up by his ears and thrashed for not being able to pick a pocket without detection. Fagin's leering face rammed into his own, which, at the time, had sparked fear into his core to 'get it right'. He saw himself being dragged from his filthy mattress and poorly covered bed by Bill Sikes wielding his stout cudgel and striking him. Bill's face alive with hate and brutish insanity when he was out of control and beating him just because he was angry at something else and not for anything he had done. The pictures continued, his treatment on the prison hulk, his transportation on the convict ship, the chains and fetters biting into his skin, scarring him forever. The dread on his face when he saw what the sadistic Captain Dowson did to Gipps and the preacher. The merciless scenes were unrelenting but Jack's expression didn't alter from its blank and vacant look, although he was seeing and watching all the horrors of his life, of everything that had been done to him unfold, until he came to the root of his current state. He saw himself carrying Tom's limp body from the hut. The grief and anger was plainly etched on his face and Jack felt a sudden rush of something, he didn't know what, which seemed to consume him as he continued to watch.

He observed as he baldly told Amy of their son's death. This time, he saw Amy's pain at the loss of their son and the anguish she suffered at Jack's cold, detached manner and unwillingness to talk. He saw her agonised tears fall and a catch caught in his throat. He watched as his demonised form ripped into Rust's stomach letting his entrails protrude and the villain's screaming face as he tried to hold his insides together before buckling to his knees.

He stood at the side of Koorong as would a spectre and watched himself ordering Rust's callous burial and heard Koorong's vehement protest ring again in his ears. "But he's still alive… He's alive… He's alive," echoed around the hallowed ground. And he heard his own cold, cruel response, "I know. Bury him." And Jack, the watcher, flinched.

He looked down as if floating from above at Rust's vile and screaming face in his earthen tomb and heard himself ordering he be turned on his back and saw the shock and horror on Koorong's face in his refusal to do this.

As if in some sort of delirium, he surveyed himself leaping into the grave and the Aboriginals' looks of revulsion and disbelief. He viewed the evil and rage emblazoned on his own countenance, and saw a man so fuelled with vengeance his features were distorted into that of a demonic entity.

As the nightmare vision continued Jack saw himself lying in that same grave with him throwing clods of earth over his own face and body. He felt the choking soil closing his windpipes and filling his lungs; he felt the searing agony of evisceration, he felt the dim spark of light being eclipsed from his eyes and he screamed a cry so terrible it echoed around and around the cliffs before he collapsed into a juddering sobbing heap. It was as if his soul had returned from torment and he fell into an exhausted stupor, not stirring even when the sounds of the night resonated around him. He was deathly still and conscious no more.

***

As the first fingers of the sun's rays explored and stroked Jack's face, Jack began to wake. He became aware of another presence. He was now covered with a blanket and he gazed about him blinking in the brilliant sunshine. Koorong was sitting close by, his face a picture of love and compassion. As Jack roused himself and sat up Koorong passed him a water bottle of kangaroo skin filled with crystal clear, cool water, which Jack gratefully accepted.

"You have rested for two days, my friend."

Jack wiped his hand over his tear streaked face and felt the grime on his skin from lack of care. He rose and walked to the waterhole and immersed himself fully into the cool water like a cleansing baptism and vigorously washed himself all over.

Koorong watched and waited.

As Jack emerged dripping wet, he asked Koorong, "You remember where we buried the kidnappers?"

"I do."

"Will you take me there?"

Koorong nodded, "I will."

Koorong studied the morning sky and position of the sun and set off in his chosen direction followed by Jack, no longer plodding unfeelingly like a merciless tyrant, instead there was something of a softening in his gait and manner.

They walked for what seemed like thirty minutes until they came to a large tree which cast a long shadow on the land. It was where Koorong and his native companions had sat waiting for Jack after digging three graves.

Koorong stretched out his hand and indicated the three burial mounds, "They are here."

"I remember," said Jack softly.

He studied the three mounds and Koorong stepped back. "I will leave you and wait for you yonder." He jerked his head at an acacia some fifty yards away.

Jack acknowledged him with a solemn nod of his head and paused until Koorong had given him space. Jack purposely ventured to where Rust had been entombed alive in the earth. He took off his hat and scrutinised the mound of earth and uttered definitively, "There is no doubt in my mind that you deserved to die for what you did. But... you didn't deserve the death I gave you and for that alone, I am sorry. Forgive me."

Jack stood there awhile and looked about him before studying the grave as if he expected something to happen. It didn't. He replaced his hat, turned and walked towards Koorong and began to follow him back when a single yellow budgerigar flew into the branches overlooking the graves. It hopped from branch to branch and looked inquisitively about it, but it did not sing. Jack didn't see it and kept right on walking.

They reached the village where he had left his horse and turned to Koorong. "Baiame bless you, Koorong, your chief, and people. I will return, but first there is something else I must do."

Koorong nodded assent, "May your God go with you."

***

Jack rode like lightning through the countryside and back into the town. He urged his horse onto the mansion. He entered the gates and pulled up short as he saw the carriage outside the front of the house. Amy stood there overseeing Atwill who was loading trunks and luggage into the carriage. Amy saw Jack ride up and dismount. She bit her lip and turned away. The hurt in her eyes was plain to see.

"When...?" Jack stopped.

Amy replied quietly, "The ship sails this evening."

Atwill pushed in the last case and climbed up into the driver's seat.

"I'll drive her."

"Yes, sir." Atwill climbed down without hesitation and stood back as Jack went to help Amy into the carriage.

Amy's hand trembled and she murmured, "I can't stay... I can't."

Jack took Atwill's place and shook the reins spurring the pair forward. They travelled in silence as the vehicle swept down the drive and out onto the road that led to the town and docks. All that could be heard were the clip clop of horse's hooves on the cobbled street. The sound echoed hollowly about them, piercing holes in the silence between them.

It wasn't long before they reached the poorest part of town and trotted down a stinking alley where street urchins ran after the smart coach and begged them for money. Vagabonds stared sullenly at the carriage. Men and women were raucous in their chatter as they swigged from bottles and stumbled around, some losing their footing in a giddy drunken reel. The rancid stench of unwashed flesh, urine and faeces together with stale alcohol, assailed Amy and Jack's nostrils. The obvious squalor and poverty was appalling. Jack stared about him at the depressing scenes that surrounded him and the carriage came to a gentle stop.

"What are you doing, Jack? I shall be late for the ship," asked Amy in a puzzled tone.

The numerous children with filthy faces in their ragged clothes swarmed to the carriage holding out their hands and begging for food and pleading for money in small pitiful voices and Jack stared as if bewitched. He watched a burly well-dressed landlord strut out of a slum property followed by a weeping mother holding an infant. Several scruffily attired children followed her crying. The mother rushed to the man and attempted to pull at his arm entreating him to have pity. He raised his stout wooden cane with a silver top to strike her. Another child, about ten years old, made a clumsy attempt to pick the man's pocket. The landlord swung around suddenly and caught hold of the child trying to remove his watch. He raised his cane and viciously struck the youngster and continued to beat him mercilessly.

Tears streamed down Jack's face as the urchins tried to clamber up still pleading and begging for help. Jack took out his wallet and thrust some money at the children who went wild. He emptied his wallet and pocket, throwing out all the coins and notes on the ground where the children scrambled for it in excitement and Jack wept.

Amy felt Jack's acute distress and managed to ask, "Jack, what is it?" Tears flowed down his cheeks and he looked back at Amy's sweet, concerned face and he struggled to answer. "Jack?"

"There's something we could do... together... if you've a mind?"

The children had jumped from the carriage and were fighting over the paper money that was blowing down the alley. Coins rattled and rolled down the narrow passageway that drunkards fought to retrieve. Amy stood up in the open carriage and put her arms around Jack's neck and Jack held her tightly and sobbed.

Amy closed her eyes, the warmth of human contact stirring emotions in her that she had thought lost for ever and she whispered, "Take me to Tom's grave, please."

"But the ship..."

"There will always be another. Let's go."

Jack stifled his choking sob and wiped his eyes and nose on his sleeve. He turned the carriage away from the dock area and pushed the horses through the crowded ginnel where the children still scrambled after coins and cash.

***

They drove through the evening and dewfall into the countryside and to the farm. They took the journey steadily, without haste and they did something they hadn't done in a long time.

They talked.

24: Ideas, Plans, Fruition

The silver claw of the moon had all but disappeared as birds were waking from their night-time slumber. The pink light of dawn dyed the sky that was low to the horizon where it stretched and grew to a deeper crimson, as the sun dependably began to rise in the heavens. It set the air over the land shimmering in the heat haze, which accentuated the sound of crickets chirruping. Dust motes floated like tiny orbs in front of Jack's eyes and drifted aimlessly as they travelled. He stopped and stepped down from driving the carriage and helped Amy out by the treeline overlooking the meadow with its wind and pheasant tail grass rippling in the gentle breeze.

Jack led her to the most perfect resting place for their child that was set apart from that of Edward, Miss Bonnet and Fred. Amy dropped to her knees. She fell forward and placed her hands on the dried earth as if she could touch the soul of her son. Jack knelt down beside her and lifted her hands bringing her back to face him. They clung together and in their mutual all absorbing grief, they wept. They remained in that overwhelming embrace for many minutes.

Amy finally released him and tried to say a few words but they just wouldn't come. So, Jack cleared his throat and removed his hat. He talked quietly and with affection, "There ain't nothing to hurt you now, Tom. You is here with the best family I got. Your mum's here, too... with me. We've come together. You can run free in the meadow now and ain't no one ever gonna hurt you again. I got 'em, Tom. I got 'em good. They ain't never gonna thieve or murder again. You're safe now with your Uncle Edward and Aunty B. He tried to save you, honest he did. They both did. So, did I. I've not been the best I could be since you were so cruelly taken. But your mum and me... We're here now and we've come to tell you that life won't never be the same again without your sunshine smile and gurgling laugh. But, from this terrible deed, we both want good things to come. Both of us. You will always be our son, our precious son."

Amy listened to Jack's words with a lump in her throat and more tears streamed down her cheeks. Jack replaced his hat and took Amy's face in his hands. He studied her sweet countenance and gently smudged away her tears. "We could make something good together. We could. You'll see. We'll make it work."

**

That night they remained at the farm. They sat on the porch together to watch the stars and fireflies as they darted in the almost perfect dark, even though the night was cool in winter. It was still much warmer than England. They talked and talked and discussed their plans. Amy snuggled up to Jack who placed a protective arm around her. He sighed, this time not in despair, but with a note of hope and anticipation in his voice as he said, "We start as soon as we get back, tomorrow."

"Tomorrow," agreed Amy and she entwined herself in Jack's warm embrace. They gazed up at the benevolent crescent moon, which hung in the sky, no longer looking like a sickle or a weapon of the grim reaper, but lighting their faces with the soft glow of optimism and expectation.

That night they cuddled together in the tender glow of love. Jack leaned up on his elbow and gazed at his wife's face. He explored every inch of her visage, every contour of her body, every available expanse of her fair skin and caressed her as he had on their wedding night. Their union was sublime, almost divine and as they lay together in each other's arms, Amy whispered, "And to think I nearly lost you..."

Jack's fierce passion returned and he held her even closer than he thought possible and his lips brushed her fragrant hair and he said, "Never again. Never again will I lose myself to such darkness that it would take me away from you."

***

Invigorated, Jack jumped down from the carriage as they reached the mansion steps. He helped Amy from inside and she followed him up the stone steps and smiled as he burst through the front door, calling out at the top of his voice, "Atwill, Dora... Where are you?"

Dora hurried along the passageway from the kitchen and entered the hall as Atwill came down the stairs. They both looked curiously as Amy entered behind Jack and she was smiling. "Mrs Dawkins is staying." Jack could not keep the delight from his voice.

Dora rushed to Amy and hugged her tightly, her face wreathed in smiles while Atwill entered the vestibule and pumped Jack's hand, "Well done, Jack." He was clearly as elated as Dora.

"Thank you, Atwill," said Jack beaming.

"Welcome back, Jack. I've missed you, sir."

"I've missed me, too." He eyed his staff, who were also his friends, with a fervent glint in his eye and he rubbed his hands together. "Everyone to the kitchen. We have much planning and a lot of work to do. Come, follow us and Mrs Dawkins will explain all."

Jack chattered excitedly as he led the way along the corridor and Dora slipped her hand into Amy's and squeezed it as they all withdrew to the scullery. There was an air of exhilaration and elation as Jack instructed them, "First thing to do after we've talked is to open all the shutters on every window in the house. Let the light into every room. But now, listen to what we have decided." Jack was animated, motivated and could scarcely contain his eagerness to impart all his ideas to them. Dora and Atwill leaned forward in their seats. They were just as keen to hear the scale of Jack's plans as Jack was to tell them.

The next few weeks galloped by and events whirled past with breath-taking speed. Jack and Atwill visited carpenters inviting them to tender for work for alterations at the mansion. They trudged around furniture stores in the port. Many beds were ordered as well as desks. Amy began a round of interviews assessing women for the posts of governesses, kitchen staff, nurses and specialist teachers. A queue of women waited that snaked from outside the drawing room through the hallway and partway down the drive.

Carts pulled up several times a day loaded with goods. Decorators stripped down walls and painted them. There were dust sheets everywhere. Books arrived together with beds, linens, desks, writing implements, toys and small baths.

Atwill examined the book titles as they arrived by Thackeray, the Brontë sisters, Goldsmiths, Dickens, Sheridan and collections from the Brothers Grimm, Aesop's Fables, and other anthologies of favourite children's stories.

The women hired as teachers and nurses were fitted for smart, cream uniforms that were clean and attractive without looking authoritarian. In record time the mansion was transformed by the army and variety of workers that busied themselves tirelessly and who were overseen by the eager team of four. The mansion became a comfortable, well equipped home for lost and disadvantaged children, orphans and street urchins.

The time arrived for them to open their doors. All they needed now were the children who needed love and care to inhabit this proper home environment.

***

Jack, Amy, Atwill and Dora gathered around the kitchen table again. Their manner was vibrant, their conversation dynamic, eyes sparkled as they had completed their final tasks of preparation. Amy sat upright, her words were accompanied by enthusiastic gestures, "Jack and I will collect the children and you will both wait in the carriage. They will be confused in the beginning. So, give them a toy and find out their names. Try and keep them entertained." She turned to Atwill, her face was alive as she spoke and Jack watched her, feeling a burst of pride as he listened. "Mr Atwill, when you have four children, bring them back here and the nurses will look after them. Then come back to whereever we last saw you."

"Yes, Mrs Dawkins."

Jack continued and he took his wife's hand, "We'll go down tomorrow morning. I've seen these kids and I know the sort that will need our help. There shouldn't be any trouble. Now, let's all have a drink and an early night. Tomorrow will be a big day but I promise you, it will be fun."

***

Atwill and Dora waited in the carriage in the desperately poor Fletcher's Alley situated close to the docks. The pungent smell of poverty and all that it meant was heavy in the unusual winter heat. Crates of rotting vegetables added to the putrid odour as decaying juices ran through the alley mixing with urine where chamber pots had been emptied outside. Dora wrinkled her nose in disgust. "I have never seen anything or smelt anything as bad as this. Look over there." Dora indicated two small children playing in the gutter. The little girl had long hair that was matted and tangled, her face was dirty, her clothes, far too big, frayed and tatty. "Hand me downs," she said to Atwill. "I came from a big family. I was the youngest. Never had me own clothes only others' cast-offs. But my mam always kept us clean. To see these kiddies like this playing in all this filth tears at my heart," she suppressed a sob.

Atwill turned his attention to the small boy who was crouching down throwing pebbles into a small pot. His nose was running and he had scabs on his face and body. He stood up to retrieve the pebbles revealing his bottom showing through his canvas breeches where they had been torn. Once he had the stones he began the game again. Atwill frowned, "We may have been poor but nothing like this. My mother taught me to read and write. She improved my learning until she was taken from us with consumption."

"I never knew. That's like Edward... his mother..."

"I know... That's what made me get into trouble, trying to survive. I got caught thieving to put food on the table and got lagged. I'm not proud of it. It was harsh. There's no proper justice."

"Or help for kids like these."

"Makes my heart bleed. It's a wonderful thing they're doing, Jack and Mrs Dawkins."

Atwill nodded and looked away, his eyes had misted up. The conversation stopped as they continued to watch the two small children who were completely oblivious to the attention they were receiving.

At that moment, Jack and Amy returned, each carrying a very small child. They passed them to Dora in the carriage. "Take them back, Atwill. Mrs Dawkins and I will find the last four. These two are brother and sister. Their mother sold them to us." Atwill's face registered his shock. Jack added, "I know. But I also know their lives are about to change for the better. Go now. Meet us back here as soon as you've dropped them off into the care of the nurses. Instruct them to get them clean, dressed and fed."

Atwill climbed into the driving seat from the carriage and set off happy to leave the squalor behind, along with the appalling rancid odours that abounded in the alley.

Jack turned to Amy who was shaking and looked extremely distressed, "Are you all right?" he asked concerned for her state of mind.

"Yes... thank you. It's just... it's so desperate here. I had no idea."

Jack said gently, "Come on, now, Amy. One more time." Amy nodded and followed Jack to another part of the docks, passing through the worst of the slums of Port Jackson. They avoided the drunks that brawled and watched where they stepped until they reached Oatley Road where a small alley branched off, into which Jack turned. They progressed through the narrow back street littered with bottles and old newspapers, which blew in the breeze and wrapped themselves around Jack's legs. The hems of Amy's skirt were drenched in some distasteful substance. One sniff in the air confirmed that the gutter was running not with water but something else. As they neared the end of the alley they spotted a small child, a little girl of about six. She was standing like a sentry at a scruffy door where the paint was peeling and the wood warped and cracked. She stared ahead with fear in her eyes. Amy was touched by the child's large eyes that had seen more than her fair share of sorrow. She approached the girl and tentatively asked, "Hello, where's your family? Do you have one?"

"Don't have no family. It's just me and me mum."

"Where is your mum?"

"In there," and the little girl pointed at the seedy looking door. Amy smiled at the child benevolently and was about to move on when the door opened. A man came out adjusting his clothes followed by a woman.

"Get inside, Molly," the woman ordered.

Molly pointed at Amy and said, "Mum, she was talking to me."

The woman looked Amy up and down and said roughly, "Yeah? What d'you want?"

"I was asking if she had a family."

"What's it to you?"

"If she'd been alone I was going to take her in."

"Take her in? Take her in where?"

Jack came to Amy's side. "My husband here and I have opened a home for children that need care."

"Well, she don't need no care. So, push off."

"Good day to you," said Amy and turned to Jack. "Where shall we go now?"

"We could go anywhere in this area. There are so many of these poor waifs." The two walked on leaving the woman looking after them curiously and the little girl stepped out of the doorway and hid behind her mother's skirts. They watched until Jack and Amy had disappeared from view.

The Dawkins progressed hurriedly through the run-down district and ventured closer to Yarnell Alley that was nearer the docks and famed for its street urchins and derelict shacks. A gang of kids were playing a game in the alley. They were unkempt and looked half starved. Jack stopped to question them. The bigger children scattered leaving two scruffy little mites who stood together. They were pitifully thin and dirty. Jack stepped closer to them, "Don't be afraid. I'm not going to hurt you. Do you have a mummy or daddy?"

The kiddies looked at each other. The girl looked down and wouldn't meet Jack's eyes while the boy sniffed, "Who wants to know? What you gonna do?"

"Nothing bad. We're trying to help children, give them a safe place to live and look after them."

"You expect us to work?" said the slightly older boy.

"No, we hope you'll be learning."

"Like at a school?" said the boy and the girl looked up with a semblance of interest.

"Something like that. You'd be fed and well looked after."

"I'm hungry," said the girl.

"So, do you have a family?"

The little girl shook her head, "It's just us. Has been for a long time."

"What happened?"

"Our dad left us when I was three,"

"And your mum?"

"Dead," said the girl.

Jack beckoned Amy across who was talking to a woman who had come out to see what was happening. "What do you want to do? Would you like to have a new home, grub in your belly and learn?"

"I would," said the girl.

Jack looked at the boy. "I'll give it a go."

"That's all we ask." He turned to Amy, "Two more here."

Amy replied, "The woman over there says they have no one. Not since their mum died. She does what she can but she can't afford to feed her own brood let alone an extra two mouths."

The two waifs went along with Jack and Amy, and the woman watched. Her face, initially creased into a frown, broke into a smile and she nodded in relief before going back inside her house.

"That's it then," said Jack with a satisfied grunt and they made their way back to the waiting carriage retracing their steps.

They handed the last two orphans to Dora inside the carriage and Jack helped Amy in before he climbed up beside Atwill. Atwill shook the reins and the carriage began to roll back along the disreputable streets.

They clip clopped past Oatley Road and the alley where they had seen the single mother and child. Suddenly, there was a raucous shout, "Stop! Please stop!" Amy looked back and saw the child, Molly, holding her mother's hand and they were chasing the carriage. "Stop!" the mother shouted.

"Stop, Mr Atwill, please," said Amy. The carriage ground to a halt.

The woman raced alongside and asked, "This home you've got, how much does it cost?"

"Nothing, but..."

"Take my daughter, please."

"I'm sorry, we have all that we can manage."

"But, I can't look after her. You saw what I was doin' with that man back there. That's the only way I can care for her. Please, missus, take her. She shouldn't grow up like this..."

Jack intervened, "We'll take her." He took some money and passed it to her. "This will help you for a little while."

The mother looked at the cash and threw it back at Jack. "I'm not selling her. She's mine and I love her. I just can't keep her."

"What's her name?" asked Amy gently.

"Molly."

"Molly? Molly come here, darling."

"No, I'm staying with me mum," Molly said stubbornly.

Her mother pressed her, "Please, Molly, please."

"Don't want to."

"Go with the nice lady. She'll look after you now. It's for the best. Please."

The child clung to her mother's legs and shook her head vehemently, "I ain't going."

Amy looked at Jack. Jack turned to the mother, "Would you like a job?"

Her face lit up, "Oh, yes. Yes, please." Then she frowned suspiciously, "Doing what?"

"Looking after children?" said Amy with a question in her voice as she looked at Jack again and he smiled and nodded.

Molly and her mother climbed into the carriage and Atwill set off for the mansion.

***

The late evening sun gave way to dusk and the fading of the light. Nevertheless as Jack and Amy guided the children towards the mansion entrance the mother gazed in amazement at the splendour and size of the place. Jack ran up the stone hewn steps to the front door and opened it. The newcomers trooped in staring about them wide eyed at the candlelit hallway. They moved to the drawing room, which was now a more child friendly area with toys and books, and scatter cushions on the floor. There was a log fire blazing in the grate shielded by a big fire guard. Some of the children were playing with a doll's house. The children that had already settled were clean and dressed in fresh clothes.

The latest arrivals came in slowly and uncertainly to be greeted by the nurses and whisked upstairs. Amy followed them to help but Molly clung to her mother who was still gazing in awe at her surroundings. She eventually murmured with a sigh, "It's so pretty."

Jack paused as he studied her closely and chewed the inside of his mouth, "You always liked pretty things, didn't you... Maudie?"

"How do you know me name? You been with me? You a mark?" Maudie was both irate and puzzled at the recognition.

"It's me, Maudie... It's Jack."

"I don't know no Jack."

"Dodger. I'm the Artful Dodger."

Maudie's face suffused with realisation showing not only shock but absolute delight. "Dodger? It can't be. Oh, Christ... you made it." She threw her arms around Jack and hugged him fiercely. "You bloody made it." She began to cry tears of joy. Her daughter Molly looked on in amazement not understanding the meaning of this odd reunion.

Amy came into the room and looked curiously at the emotional embrace. Jack smiled at her and beckoned as Maudie finally released her arms. "Amy, this is Maudie. Maudie, this is my wife, Amy." He went on to explain, "Maudie helped me to escape from the stockade. I wouldn't be here now if it hadn't been for her."

Amy smiled broadly and shook her hand, "Maudie, you're very welcome here. I am more than grateful to you."

"Thank you." Maudie was now bursting with questions, "Where's the little one... Edward, isn't it? Ain't that his name?"

Jack's eyes flashed with pain and Amy answered for Jack, "He died."

"What? How?" said Maudie aghast.

Jack swallowed and replied, "It's a long story. Let's go to the library and have a drink."

Amy suggested gently, "Perhaps Maudie would like to change first, Jack?" she indicated Maudie meaningfully with her eyes.

Jack nodded in understanding, "Of course, I'm not thinking."

Maudie looked down at her ragged, dirty clothes and at the pristine surroundings and Amy's fine attire. She touched her grimy cotton skirt and said wholeheartedly, "Oh, yes please."

"And Molly, too. Come with me." Amy led them out of the room.

Jack sighed and looked about him at the freshly washed, neat and tidy children playing on the floor and went and crouched down with them and began to engage in their game.

**

That evening Jack retired to the library and sat by the fire as he quietly reflected on the day's events,. The door opened breaking his reverie and Amy entered with Maudie. Amy was looking proud and pleased, and Maudie looked vastly different in one of Amy's dresses. She was fresh and tidy, her hair was styled and instead of the painted face she usually wore, her appearance was clean and wholesome.

Jack nodded appreciatively, "Maudie, you look lovely." He smiled at Amy in recognition and thanks.

"Yes, she does," said Amy pleased.

Maudie gave a little twirl like an excited child, "It's pretty isn't it?"

"It is indeed." Jack rose and went to the decanters and poured them each a glass of port. He passed them around, "Let's sit down."

Jack and Amy sat together on the loveseat and faced Maudie who shook her head in disbelief, "Who'd have thought it? We all thought you'd died. Your missus told me what happened... I had to ask."

There was a slight hesitation before Jack continued, "Well, now you know. We were lucky. Very lucky... Has Molly settled down, yet?"

"She's playing with the others," said Amy. "She really is a very pretty little girl."

"Like her mum," said Jack with his lopsided grin.

"Now, that smile I remember," said Maudie with a laugh. "If I look real hard I can still see the boy in the man..." and she scrutinised Jack's face making him laugh.

"So, where's Molly's father?"

"Gawd knows. I don't even know who he is."

"No?" Jack arched his eyebrow.

"Well, you know what I was doing in the camp, Jack. And when I got out that's all I knew. I suppose I'm a natural born bangtail. Her father could be anyone. I mean if you eat a load of beans you don't know which one made you fart, do you?" She looked from one to the other, first at Amy's serious face, and then Jack's slightly embarrassed demeanour. "What? What did I say?"

Amy's expression crumpled as she wrinkled her nose and began to giggle, which turned into a full blown laugh. Jack felt the corners of his lips tug up and he smiled and as Amy's laughter grew and mounted, Jack threw back his head and he, too, chuckled uproariously.

Maudie gazed in astonishment at the two of them, "What? Go on, tell me... What did I say?"

Amy clasped hold of her stomach with one hand and gripped Jack's hand with the other. She could hardly speak for laughing, "Oh... that is the funniest thing I've ever heard." She leaned forward and said with absolute glee, "Oh, Maudie. You are so welcome here!"

***

The next few days set the tone for the rest of the children's young lives. Jack and Amy ensured the children felt happy and secure. They played and learned, had food in their stomachs and were clean and well cared for. There were a few hiccups with one lad who couldn't believe that they were allowed to share in everything that was provided and he would steal items away and hide them including food. Jack tried to explain to him, "You don't need to take nothin', Freddie. It's all there for you. You and the other kids. There ain't no need to pinch things." The boy looked suspiciously at him as if it was some kind of trick.

"You mean, we really live here? With you? For 'ow long?"

"As long as you want. You're safe here. No one is going to hurt you. I promise."

The little boy sniffed and struggled not to cry, "Why you doing this? What d'you get out of it? Everyone is always out for summat."

"I just... I just want for you what I never had. And that's what makes me 'appy."

Freddie screwed up his face and shook his head. He was someone who had survived on his wits on the street and who found Jack's selfless acts of kindness hard to understand. The boy sniffed hard and Jack studied the little one's face. His eyes were sunk into his head and his skin was mottled and blotchy. His thin body was emaciated through lack of good food. He was hot in spite of the fact that there was no fire lit that morning and the mansion was cold inside, even in the winter sun. The boy looked feverish.

Jack was concerned, "Freddie, you feeling okay?"

The boy nodded, "Just a bit tired that's all."

Jack put his hand on the boy's forehead. It was clammy. "Wait here, Freddie. I'm just gonna get a nurse."

The boy nodded, too tired to care and he slipped over onto the floor. His eyes rolled back in his head and he began to twitch and tremble with jerky body movements. Jack leapt up and called Amy, "Amy get a nurse. Come and sit with Freddie. I'm going for Dr Long."

***

Jack dashed from the room. He shouted to Atwill to get the carriage and follow him to the doctor's house before he raced to the stable startling the newly hired stable boy and ostler. They hurriedly tacked and saddled Jack's horse, Bonnie. Jack leapt on her back and urged her from the backyard, passing Atwill doing up his coat as he hurried to follow Jack's orders. Jack galloped down the drive through the elite neighbourhood and onto the road leading to the town.

He passed busy people moving to and from work, mothers with children dressed to go shopping and went on up the road past the Victoria Hotel, where he slowed Bonnie to a trot on the cobbled street. They soon reached Dr Long's residence and surgery. Jack jumped off Bonnie and secured her to the gate before he ran up the path and hammered on the door. Mrs Long, a rosy cheeked comely woman opened the door. "Yes? Oh, Mr Dawkins, is all well?"

"No, one of the children. There's something wrong with him. I need the doctor to come, now."

"Come on in." She shouted up the stairwell, "Philip! Mr Dawkins is here. Something about a sick child."

Dr Long came running down the stairs, "Fetch my bag, Mabel." Mabel scurried off to get what the doctor needed. "Have you got the carriage?"

"No, I'm on Bonnie. Atwill is coming with it. He shouldn't be long after me. I wanted to alert you and tell you about his condition."

"What is it?"

"I don't know. I don't know the child's history. I've only known him a few days."

"Tell me his symptoms."

"His eyes are sunken and he's got a fever, clammy to the touch but he collapsed on the floor, started twitching and moving strange like."

"What about his diet?"

"He's thin, wasted. Don't think he's had no proper food till he came to us."

"Sounds like convulsions caused by malnutrition."

"Can you do anything?"

"The fever could be a sign of his body shutting down. If he's not gone too far he will recover with proper food and care. I'll have to see him." He called to his wife, "Mabel I'm going with Mr Dawkins. I'll wait outside for the carriage."

Mrs Long scuttled in with the doctor's bag and handed it to him, "I hope whoever it is will be all right."

Jack nodded and left with the doctor. They waited at the front gate until they saw Atwill arrive with the carriage. Jack untied and mounted Bonnie. "I'll see you both back there."

Dr Long acknowledged with a nod and climbed in the chaise. Atwill turned the coach and set off back the way he had travelled.

Jack took the journey home more slowly. His mind was racing and he prayed that they hadn't taken Freddie in too late. He prayed that proper love and care with good food would build the boy up and save him from digesting himself. His body shutting down didn't sound good at all.

Jack turned into the street that led to the Victoria and he almost pulled up short when he saw a face he recognised. Skulking around the corner was a disreputable looking man with greasy, lank hair and unmistakeable twist to his mouth. Jack breathed the loathed name under his breath, "Charlie Coombes."

His anger rose but this time it did not consume him. He was more measured in his reaction. He knew he had the important care of Freddie to deal with but then Dr Long was already on his way; he would be surplus to requirements and he didn't want to get in the way. However, this murdering criminal needed to be brought to justice and he had sworn an oath at Fred's grave that his death would not go unpunished. But, this time, he vowed he would not take the law in his own hands.

It was clear that Coombes hadn't spotted Jack as he didn't look back, kept his head down and continued on his way. Jack held back to observe and watched where the villain was going. Coombes had come from the direction of the port and was making his way to the rats' run of alleys and back streets that had sprung up, in the very area that Jack and Amy had scouted to find the orphaned children. He kept at a safe distance and noted the name of the alley and logged the number of the door he went inside. He waited awhile but Charlie didn't come out.

Jack turned his horse and went in the direction of the fort. The very fact he was nearing the stockade made him sick to his stomach. He had to steel himself to move onto the fort where two sentries stood on duty at the main gates.

Jack approached them, rode up and jumped down, "I need to see Sergeant Phillips, please."

One of them indicated an office inside the main drill yard. Jack led his horse through the gates to the building and knocked. An officer came out and looked at him quizzically, "Yes?"

"I need to get a message to Sergeant Phillips. It's urgent."

The officer looked Jack up and down and noticed he was dressed as a gentleman, "Who shall I say wants to see him?"

"Tell him it's Jack. Jack Dawkins. And I know where to find Charlie Coombes."

The officer called a young soldier across and sent him off with a message while Jack waited. He shifted his feet nervously. He didn't want to stay there any longer than necessary.

A few minutes later Sergeant Phillips returned with the private and acknowledged Jack with a wave. "Jack! What's this about Coombes?"

"I saw him, Sergeant. He went in a house, number 9 in Bardolph Alley."

"Are you sure? Last I heard, he'd gone up to the Northern Territories and lost himself in the bush."

"I saw him. I'll never forget his face or what he did."

"And you're sure?"

"Positive. What you gonna do?"

"I'll issue another warrant and take my men. He'll not escape the charge of murder. Denton was a good man and a fine soldier."

"So was Fred… a good man. He was done in by Coombes."

"Isn't that just rumour?"

"No. And I believe he was responsible for the mass poisoning of the Aboriginals in Bathurst."

"Sad to say that won't carry much weight."

"The man's a paid assassin. He tried to poison the captain of a small garrison at Windsor. Talk to him. You'll have more than enough."

Phillips nodded, "Tell me, is there a back route out of Bardolph Alley?"

The alley is part of a back to back housing system. So, yes. The ginnel at the back needs to be covered, as well as the front."

"Thanks, Jack."

"I shouldn't take too long. He's more than likely here to do a job. He needs to be stopped."

Phillips assented with a nod and they shook hands, "Don't worry. We'll get him. You have my word."

Jack mounted Bonnie, "I hope so. I don't want to have to take the law into me own hands."

"That's not advisable, Jack."

"I know. That's why I've come to you."

The men eyed each other. They had reached an understanding. Jack turned his horse and rode from the fort. Although he didn't show it, his guts were churning. He made his way back to the home to see what Dr Long recommended.

25: Mrs Buddings

Jack made it back in time to see the doctor and hear his recommendations. "It is as I thought, Mr Dawkins. A severe case of malnutrition, which can cause febrile convulsions. The lad is lucky to be here. A few more weeks on the street and he would more than likely be dead. Keep doing what you're doing. Good food and loving care will make all the difference. You'll see. I will come and see him again at the end of the week. Perhaps, it would be advisable for me to check over all the other children while I am here."

Amy and Maudie who had been attending Freddie looked at Jack and nodded in agreement. "That would be a good idea," said Amy.

Jack nodded, "As you wish, Doctor. And thank you. Maudie, perhaps you would take Dr Long to the drawing room and then bring the children to him one at a time. Stay for the examination and take notes of anything that's needed."

"Yes, Jack." Maudie's voice could be heard as she showed the doctor through the corridor. "They've all been deloused. No nits or fleas now but a couple of them have some other ailments it'd be good to remedy."

Jack waited until the door closed and he turned to Amy. "I had to visit the fort."

"Whatever for?"

"I saw an old enemy."

A flicker of alarm crossed Amy's eyes, "Who?"

"Charlie Coombes. The swine responsible for Fred's death."

"Oh, Jack... what have you done?"

"Done? I ain't done nothing. I followed him. Then, I went and reported it to Sergeant Phillips. I didn't go to the police. But Phillips is all right. He knows the mongrel and he's wanted for the murder of Private Denton amongst other things."

"Did this Coombes fellow see you?"

"No. I kept out of his sight."

"Then, you did the right thing. Let the law take its proper course."

"They should pick him up easy. Reckon there'll be an 'anging. Serves him right, the bastard."

Amy smiled and took Jack's hand. She looked him straight in the eyes. "Jack, I'm so proud of you." Jack leaned in and kissed her gently but they broke apart as Maudie returned. "Doctor's all set up. I'll bring one of the nurses down to help and he can see the kids one at a time."

Jack nodded and said gratefully, "Thank you, Maudie. If you need me, I'll be in the library. It's the only sanctuary in this house, now."

Maudie laughed and went off to assemble the children as Jack retreated. And Amy went off to teach her class waiting in the schoolroom.

***

Three weeks later, Freddie was up and about and looking stronger. He had a fresh bloom to his cheeks; the yellowing tinge had gone. Things were going well. Word had reached them that Charlie Coombes had indeed been arrested. He had been found with a quantity of noxious substances, toxic plant life and seeds. The house in Bardolph alley was kitted out like an apothecary akin to some sort of chemical workshop. Phillips had arrested and charged him along with another blackguard and a woman who had screamed abuse at them denying she was doing anything wrong. They were all taken into custody.

Jack was keen to hear when the villains would be tried. He and Amy were sitting in the library when the doorbell rang. "I expect that will be Sergeant Phillips now," said Jack eagerly.

"I'll go," said Amy. "I am eager to meet this sergeant, you speak so highly of him. Besides, Dora and Atwill are both busy now."

Amy opened the door with a smile of welcome when she saw the sergeant in his full uniform. "Sergeant Phillips. How lovely to meet you. Do come in."

"Thank you. What a lovely place you have here." Two clean, healthy looking children raced past them giggling and dashed down the corridor to the kitchen.

"Don't run!" called Amy.

The children skidded to a halt and murmured, "Sorry, Mrs Dawkins."

Amy smiled, "Apologies, Sergeant."

"No, it's delightful to see children so happy."

"We do our best. Step this way, Sergeant. Jack is in the library. I believe he has a drink waiting."

"That sounds good to me."

The sergeant followed Amy to the library where he was warmly greeted by Jack. They all took a seat, a drink and talked before Phillips concluded, "It seemed that once separated the three criminals turned on each other. Each one accusing the other and Coombes continued denying it was him, saying it was mistaken identity. Claimed his name is Bob Blackmore."

"Blackguard more like," said Jack.

They chatted on and Phillips praised what he and Amy had set up in the mansion. "You are the talk of the town, greatly admired everywhere for all that you are doing." He rose. "Good luck to you both. I'll send word of the trial date. He'll not wriggle out of it this time. The captain from Windsor is coming to identify him and he'll be for the drop. I'm sure of it."

"And that, Sergeant Phillips, has made my day."

***

Word spread through the port of the capture of wanted felon and murderer, Charlie Coombes along with two others engaged in making poisons from plants and seeds. Rumour had it that a local landowner had hired him to perform a mass poisoning of Aboriginals at a camp to the east of the town where land was fertile and very much in demand. Coombes and his cronies were being held securely and taken to the fort, imprisoned to await trial and a date had been set.

Jack was eager to see justice done. He took time off to visit the courthouse and watch from the public gallery. A sullen looking Coombes was led into court in manacles, flanked by two guards. His accomplices followed and stood in the dock to listen to the charges made against them.

The list against Coombes was long. He kept his head down as each charge was pronounced and peered up shiftily through his tangled hair to scrutinise the members of the jury and those seated in the gallery. He spat on the floor at one point and was reprimanded by Judge Carstairs.

Jack was fascinated by the speed of the proceedings, not that he had any sympathy for Coombes, but it did reinforce his view that the legal system was flawed, usually leading to rapid convictions with little proof although in this case there was a mountain of evidence against this killer and Jack knew he would deserve all he got.

He listened to the legal jargon and opposing arguments, although it had to be said the defence had very little good to say about the man. It was almost like a double prosecution. The number of witnesses that came forward, and there were many, were only too eager to damn Coombes and when the jury retired it took them just six minutes to come to a verdict. The court was amazed at the speed of the judgement. The public gallery had only begun to vacate their seats when the jurors filed back and the public scrambled back hastily to hear the verdict. The foreman of the jury rose when asked and pronounced that Coombes was guilty of all charges.

There was a hush in the court as the judge prepared his final summation and passed judgement. He reached into a box under the bench and pulled out the black cap, a square of black material and placed it on his head. "Charles Coombes you have been found guilty on four counts of murder, perverting the course of justice, and conspiracy to murder. I hereby decree by the power vested in me that you will be taken from here to a place of execution where you will be hanged by the neck until dead. May God have mercy on your soul."

Judge Carstairs ritualistically broke his pen with which he'd taken notes during the trial after he made the pronouncement. He rose and left the chamber leaving the other two felons to wait another day for the completion of their own trial.

Jack turned to the man sitting next to him and asked, "Why did he do that?"

"What?"

"The judge. Break his pen."

"Because he doesn't want it to be used again for another judgement. The very act of passing the death sentence on someone is considered so unholy that the pen automatically becomes sullied. So, it's destroyed. It also means no one can question his decision. Only a superior court would have the power to override it. I've even heard he breaks it out of guilt."

"Guilt?"

"The power of taking a life rests with God but being human he's only carrying out his official duty that is bound by rules."

"So, by breaking the pen he's declaring he's only carrying out his official obligations?"

"Exactly."

"I see."

"Will you be here tomorrow, for the rest of them?"

"I don't think so. I came to see and hear what I needed."

"Me, too. May see you at the hanging then?"

Jack shook his head, "I doubt it. I take no pleasure watching someone die at the 'ands of Jack Ketch. Even those that deserve it."

The man nodded, "I know what you mean... but, I'll be there. I need to see he doesn't escape the hangman."

Jack rose and left the court. He looked up at the bright sapphire sky and murmured, "It's done, Fred. You got your justice. You can now rest in peace." Jack collected his horse, Bonnie and trotted back through the town towards home. He felt lighter, easier in his heart, now he knew Fred's death had been avenged.

Curiously, when he handed Bonnie over to the stable boy as he walked back to the front of the house he glanced up at the sky again and saw some wisps of cloud like strands of hair that traced shapes in the sky. One had a long curling tail, which combined with another wispy tendril that resembled a heart. Knowing how Fred and Mrs D enjoyed looking up to the heavens Jack took it as a good sign.

**

Two years later and Jack and Amy's home had achieved high standing in the community. The children in their care were well nourished, educated, loved and happy. They flourished. Even young Freddie who had been severely malnourished had grown from strength to strength and was eager to study and learn. He had ambitions to be a doctor and spent time with Doctor Long when it was permitted and Jack was keen that the boy should be able to qualify in medicine when he reached the right age. He determined that all the correct research would be done and he would be helped as much as was humanly possible.

That afternoon, Jack and Amy sat in the library discussing Freddie's educational plans and had arranged for Dr Long to join them to discuss how best to proceed, when the doorbell rang. Jack looked at the clock, "Crikey, he's early. Show him in here. I'll get us all a drink." Jack rose and selected the glasses and placed them ready next to the port decanter as Amy left.

Amy answered the front door where a tiny blonde woman stood. She was not quite five foot in height even though she was wearing heeled black button boots. The woman was in Bombazine black and wore a black mourning bonnet with folded, black, slightly ribbed silk, trimmed with folds of black crêpe, and black ribbon ties and neat black lace gloves. She was the epitome of someone dressed in sorrowful funeral garb for the loss of a loved one.

Amy studied her curiously, "Hello? May I help you?"

"Oh, I do hope so," she gushed. "I am looking for an Edward Hargreaves."

"Edward?" Shock flooded Amy's face. "I think you'd better talk to my husband. Please come in."

The woman followed Amy down the corridor. All the while she looked about her taking in the grandeur of the place. Amy entered the library and Jack turned with a smile to welcome the doctor but his face registered surprise when he saw the woman.

"Jack, this lady here is enquiring after Edward."

Jack frowned and arched his eyebrow, "Please, sit down."

"Oh, pray do forgive me, I haven't introduced myself. I am Constance Buddings, Mrs Constance Buddings."

He indicated himself, "Jack Dawkins and this is my wife, Amy. You were asking about Edward?"

"Yes." She smiled broadly, "I am his aunt."

"Oh dear," said Amy with clear signs of distress.

"I am sorry to tell you, Mrs Buddings, but Edward died two years ago."

"We are talking about the same Edward? Edward Hargreaves?"

"That's right."

"But, I have come halfway around the world to see him."

"I'm very sorry."

"Oh dear, I wish I had come sooner. I lost track of him. After his father, my brother, Ben... Benjamin Hargreaves, died on the railway, Edward and his mother moved. And then when I found where they had been I heard that she had died of consumption and that Edward had been um... sent away."

"Lagged, yes," said Jack. His eagle eyes studied the woman as she spoke.

"Lagged?" she said questioningly.

"Transported."

"Ah, yes, of course. How could they do that? He was only eight."

"Do you know why he was transported?"

"I'm not sure, something to do with a shroud."

"That's right. He took the shroud from his dead mother's face."

"Poor soul."

"Why did you come here? To look for him? I mean, to this house?"

"I asked in the town where there is a land office. They told me that he was here and had bought a house here."

"Well, me and him bought this house," Jack corrected.

"With what? He never had any money. Oh dear, what am I to do? After Mr Buddings died he left me a little money. I spent that on my passage here. I have nothing left and nowhere to stay." She removed a lace hankie and dabbed at her nose.

"Amy, could we have a minute together?"

"Yes, of course. Please, excuse us, Mrs Buddings."

Jack and Amy left the room closing the door firmly behind them. Jack took Amy's hand and led her up the stairs to the landing where they were well out of earshot.

"Poor creature. We must do something for her," said Amy.

"Something's not right here. Edward never said nothin' about no aunt. Not in all the years we knew each other."

"But she seems genuine," Amy protested.

"She came to Australia probably wanting money or something. She knows Edward was poor. Why would she spend her last penny comin' here? Nah! It don't smell right."

"What are we going to do?"

"Go to Atwill, now. Tell him to get Bessant. Bring him here immediately. In the meantime, I'll entertain Mrs Buddings, give her a drink. And we must try and reschedule Dr Long."

"I'll get Dora to do that."

"Perfect, ask him to make it for the same time tomorrow, if possible?"

"Right."

***

Portly Mr Bessant with his cherubic rosy cheeked face sat in one of the wing back chairs adjacent to Mrs Buddings, who sat primly in another, while Jack and Amy remained on the loveseat. Jack continued to watch and observe the woman's manner.

Bessant appeared to be doing a good job of emphasising Jack and Edward's partnership. "Mrs Buddings, Edward did, indeed buy this house. He bought it with Mr Dawkins."

Like a little bird she twittered the same response, "But he had no money."

Bessant beamed, "He had a stroke of good fortune and he and Mr Dawkins shared in it."

"That's right. We did." Jack's tone was measured.

Bessant fiddled with his cravat and smiled benignly at Jack, "Show Mrs Buddings the document, Mr Dawkins. It's in that file you were holding for me," he said meaningfully.

Jack rose and crossed to the bureau. He opened a drawer and removed a file. He passed it to Bessant and returned Bessant's disarming smile appearing deferential.

"Mr Bessant, could you give Mrs Buddings the document we signed?"

"But, of course." Bessant opened the file and removed the relevant paper. He passed it to her. "Here you are."

And all the while Jack watched. He observed carefully as Mrs Buddings perused the agreement. No one spoke until Mrs Buddings' eyes lit on the figures involved. She gasped, "But this is a fortune! A holy fortune."

"It is indeed, Mrs Buddings," said Bessant with obvious pleasure.

Mrs Buddings' prim and gushing manner became more hawkish, "I see that Edward didn't sign it all to you, Mr Dawkins. Only half."

"That's right," agreed Jack reasonably.

"So, as Edward's only living relative that means I have the other half."

Mr Bessant chipped in smiling agreeably, "It seems that way."

"But surely you have to prove you're Edward's aunt? I mean, you could be anyone... How do we know for certain?"

Mrs Buddings looked affronted and she straightened up even more in her seat and tutted. "What a disgraceful thing to say."

"Mr Bessant a word." Jack's voice was authoritative as he stood up followed by Bessant, who left the room apparently meekly and who had turned slightly pink.

Once in the corridor Jack pressed Bessant who fiddled with his cravat again. "I thought you had checked on Edward's relatives?"

"I did. But on his mother's side, not the father's," he explained.

"Then you'd better check on that as well."

Bessant's eyes widened in dismay. "But, that will take the best part of a year."

"So?"

Bessant looked slightly uncomfortable, "Look, may I suggest something?"

"I'm listening."

"Get your man to put Mrs Buddings into a hotel. Give her a little money and then we can go through this properly."

Jack paused slightly, "Yes, that's what we'll do. You come back and see me in the morning."

"Agreed." Bessant straightened his cravat once more and they went back into the library where Mrs Buddings sat, still holding the document. Jack retrieved the agreement, replaced it in the file and returned it to the drawer as Bessant watched.

Jack turned back and smiled placatingly, "Very well. No one wants to behave outside the letter of the law so this is what I suggest we do." Jack recounted what he and Mr Bessant had decided.

Bessant smiled effusively, his cheeks no longer pink. "This is most apt and I am sure any dispute can be settled most amicably. Mrs Buddings, Mr and Mrs Dawkins, I will take my leave. Until tomorrow at eleven o'clock sharp." Bessant left the room with a jaunty stride and a bob of his head as Jack rang for Atwill.

***

That night, when the house was still, the staff had retired and all the children were safely in bed, the library door creaked open. In the shadow of the night a faint figure could be discerned creeping into the library, which was Jack and Amy's domain. A sliver of silver moonlight caught the cream uniform worn by the nurses and teachers at the home and lit the clean hands of a woman who went directly to the bureau drawer where Jack had placed the file with the documents and his and Edward's agreement. She secreted it under her apron and tiptoed stealthily from the room closing the door quietly behind her. She left the house silently and went out into the dark.

A carriage was parked outside the fence to the property where the insectile Spanner waited nervously. His jaws clicked as he grinded his teeth in apprehension. Ever on the alert, he kept his eyes focused on the fence boundary.

A bush rustled in the warm night and the crickets' song stopped momentarily. Spanner's spindly legs stepped out from the carriage and with his coat tails flapping like a cockchafer preparing to fly, Spanner clicked his way to the fence. A woman dressed in cream removed the file she had taken, from under her apron, and passed it through to Spanner who snatched at it avariciously, his twig-like fingers almost piercing the folder, his grip being so tight.

The woman hurried back the way she had come like an outlaw from the bush. Spanner's feet ticked on the road like a death watch beetle. He scuttled back to the carriage and with remarkable control urged the horses to move off. Their hooves were muffled with some sort of material and Spanner melted into the night as silently as he had arrived.

From a top bedroom window in the house that overlooked the road stood Atwill. He had witnessed the whole exchange. He remained there a moment longer before finally deserting the window and disappearing into the room.

***

The following morning, the benign sun spread its golden warmth across the land and rose in the sky. Prompt to the minute as the hall clock struck the hour, the doorbell to the mansion rang. Jack padded down the stairs and opened the door to see Bessant, clearly in an extremely good mood, standing on the steps. "Good morning, Mr Dawkins," he said cheerfully.

"Good morning. Come in." Jack opened the door wide for the lawyer to enter. He followed Jack along the corridor to the library and couldn't resist humming a little ditty to himself as he walked with a lively spring in his step.

They entered the library and Jack appearing infected by Bessant's good humour asked with a smile, "A drop of port wine?"

"Most certainly, yes, please." He sat with a flourish in the wing back chair and beamed as Jack poured the drinks and passed him one before Jack sat at his desk.

Bessant, unable to contain himself, was clearly overflowing with excitement. He studied Jack's quizzical expression and began to chuckle, the chuckle turned into full blown laughter and he held his sides because he laughed so much, it hurt. He finally managed to pant out in between a few hoots and whoops of merriment, "Oh, this is a sweet moment for me, Mr Dawkins. Very sweet."

"What do you mean?" asked Jack looking perplexed.

"What do I mean? Ha! You have nothing. I have made sure you have nothing. Mrs Buddings has the document that Edward signed, giving you half. And I will provide her with papers to prove that she is Edward's aunt. Once she destroys Edward's agreement she will inherit everything. And you will have nothing." He growled the last word, nothing with exaggerated ferocity. "Dawkins, I have beaten and destroyed you." And he took a swig of port before starting to laugh again.

Jack eyed him closely and once Bessant paused in his laughter, he spoke. "You have forgotten something."

"And what is that, pray?" Bessant's eyes twinkled in delight.

"The file I have that proves your embezzlement."

This comment only served to set Bessant off into another fit of giggles. He took another mouthful of port. "Oh, this is good. So, good. Indeed, it warms my heart," and he downed the rest of his drink, while Jack looked at him with a steely glint in his eye. "And what file would that be, Dawkins?"

Jack opened a drawer and then another looking extremely concerned. He glanced at Bessant who grinned inanely and shrugged before giggling again until Jack removed a thick file and set it on the desk top in front of him. "This one."

Bessant's expression changed and his jaw dropped. He looked questioningly, "It can't be... How...?"

"Oh, Bessant...Bessant." Jack shook his head feigning sorrow. "I've been onto you from the start. Come with me."

Bessant scrambled from his seat. He went to grab the file but Jack took it and put it under his arm. He wagged his finger at Bessant as if he was a naughty schoolboy, "Nah, nah, nah! Come."

Bessant's manner altered and a flash of uncertainty crossed his eyes as he entered the corridor and walked behind Jack to the drawing room and entered.

Assembled inside were Amy and Atwill looking severe. Mrs Buddings stood trembling in a nightdress with a robe on top. Spanner was in his trousers and a shirt. He looked cowed and shame-faced and Maudie was unsmiling, in her cream uniform. Bessant looked aghast at their silent faces and the first flash of fear entered his eyes.

Jack crossed to Maudie and asked, "How much did Bessant promise you, Maudie?"

She answered clearly without hesitation, "Three hundred guineas."

"You shall have it. And you, Mrs Buddings? How much?"

"The same, three hundred guineas," she said looking bewildered.

"Well, you did your job and you will be paid." He turned to Atwill, "Would you tell us what happened, Atwill?"

"It was just as you said, Jack. Maudie gave Spanner the file." Amy gasped in disbelief. "I watched from the window, like you said. Then I went to the hotel. Spanner and Mrs Buddings were drinking and laughing together. Then they went up to her room, together." Atwill emphasised the word 'together' and Mrs Buddings coloured up. "That's where I found them this morning. Oh, I put the file and that document I found on her back in your desk as you requested. That's it!"

"Good work," praised Jack.

Amy could scarcely contain herself as she reprimanded Maudie. "Oh, Maudie, how could you? After all that Jack's done for you..."

Jack leapt in and said reassuringly, "Maudie did nothin' wrong, my love. She came straight to me as soon as she was approached by Bessant. We played it out just as he wanted. I was onto him well before Mrs Budding arrived."

"What!" exclaimed Bessant.

"Maudie would never betray us."

"Never!" agreed Maudie. "I fed him stories about Edward and he coached her." She indicated Mrs Buddings who began to sob.

"What are you going to do with me?" wailed Mrs Buddings.

"Nothing. I thought you played your part very well. Very well indeed. With the money Bessant is going to give you, you can make a brand new start. Start anew, a second chance. And the money will come out of your pocket, Bessant, not mine."

Bessant stifled a cry and bit his fist. Jack took Mrs Buddings' hand and pushed up the sleeve of her nightdress, revealing her convict scars from having worn fetters. "It's no wonder you kept your gloves on. And in this heat, too! It would have given the game away instantly."

Bessant was now red in the face and almost apoplectic. He finally grunted, "But… What about me? And Mr Spanner?"

"I ain't doin' nothin'. Let it sit on your conscience. I will give you a bit of advice though. You're not very good at being a crook, are you? You've been caught three times now. I'd think about going straight, if I were you. That's if you call being a lawyer going straight – never trusted them meself. That's why I've always been on my guard even before this." Jack cleared his throat and grinned seemingly enjoying the moment. "Now… You will pay Maudie and Mrs Buddings their three hundred guineas each. You will pay them today. No shilly shallying. Oh, and Bessant, as you are feeling generous you may as well give Atwill three hundred guineas, too. I don't have to tell you what will happen if I hear of anything like this happening again to anyone else. Maudie, show 'em out. Atwill, accompany Mr Bessant to his place of work and secure the dues you are all owed."

Atwill grinned, "Yes, sir!"

Jack took Amy's arm and swept her from the room. They returned to the library where Amy was bursting to speak. "Why didn't you tell me? You knew all the time."

"I thought it would amuse you."

"It did. But I doubted Maudie."

"She's all right is Maudie," said Jack with his lopsided smile.

"Yes, she is."

"And now those shenanigans have been dealt with we must prepare for Dr Long. He should be here any time soon. Is Freddie ready?"

"I'll go and fetch him but not before I've done this," and she stepped onto tiptoe and gave Jack a gentle kiss.

"What was that for?"

"Nothing. Just for being you."

26: The Return of Captain Dowson

Life continued peacefully and uneventfully for a while. Jack and Amy continued to work hard to do their best for the children. The original children were growing up fast and Freddie who had struggled so much initially with ill health and the fear of having things stolen away, had completed his education at the home with merit. He was a very bright lad and accompanied Dr Long on many visits and helped out at his surgery. He was set to work alongside the doctor until he could go to medical school in London and gain his qualifications. Jack had promised to sponsor him when he came of age and Freddie had sworn to return and put his degree to good use to work locally in health care. He was hoping, not only, to become a capable doctor, but had a great interest in scientific research. There was much to be done. Infant mortality was high in the slums at the port and elsewhere. There were other illnesses that were devastating killers or cruelly disfiguring, like Yaws. Yes, Freddie had aspirations to cure the world. Jack and Amy did their best to encourage him in his ambitions.

Little Molly was getting prettier every day and very popular at the home amongst the other children. She had determined that she wanted to grow up to be a teacher like Amy and care for those less fortunate. Her ultimate goal was to open her own school, but that time was still some way off. And as Maudie said, 'children often change their mind.'

Maudie continued to live in the house and help look after the children, even though she was now a wealthy woman in her own right, such was her loyalty to Jack and Amy, but, on her days off she had taken to frequenting some of the hotels in the town, where she would meet up with some old friends from her days as a working girl. She often returned with the latest gossip and had exciting news of Daniel and Bobby who had finally married the two sisters, Minnie and Josie, and were leaving their parents' farm for a life in hospitality now Edgar was getting older. He wanted a more relaxed way of living but needed a male figure at the bar to help his daughters run the place. Although, Minnie and Josie had protested that they were more than proficient, it just wasn't done to have a woman solely in charge.

Jack would listen to Maudie's exuberant chatter with an amused expression and did wonder if she was returning to some of her old ways, after all she had called herself 'a natural born bangtail.'

Amy had chided him, "Don't be so suspicious, Jack."

"I can't help it. It's instinctive... easy to me. Good job, too, when I think of the con merchants and charlatans that try to inveigle and deceive anyone that'd listen."

"Have you ever thought that she might have met someone?"

"Have a beau, you mean?"

"Dora thinks so. She says she's quite taken with a gentleman who gives her flowers and all sorts."

"Well, good for her. I hope you's right."

***

Maudie was sitting with two old friends from the fort, who now frequented and worked the dockland area, Effie and Kate. "It's so lovely to see you both. I 'ad the surprise of me life when I saw you two walk in here. You still working?"

"Got to," said Effie. "Need to put food on the plate somehow."

"Well, don't you worry nothing about grub today. I'm gonna buy you both a slap up meal. That's what."

"Thanks, Maudie. You really landed on yer feet, didn't you? It was Emma told us you sometimes popped in 'ere, when you was in town. We thought we'd see if we could find you. Been coming 'ere a while now in the 'ope of catching yer," said Effie.

"Tell me, whatever happened to Emma and her kid? I ain't seen 'her in a long while."

"Oh, Lordy. You don't know? She's dead," said Kate.

"Dead? How?" asked Maudie her face registering shock.

"She was bludgeoned to death by some sadistic pig, who enjoyed hurting women."

"No? That's horrible."

"He got done though. Had the morning drop. Coombes, 'is name was. Devil's own spawn," added Effie, pulling a face.

"I heard about him, what about her kid?"

"Dead." Kate shook her head sorrowfully.

"Gawd. How?"

"Had some sort of infection, gave her the squits and terrible sickness," continued Effie.

"Why didn't she come to me? I could have helped her."

"Too proud, I think. Didn't want to put on yer."

"That's daft. Course I'd have 'elped."

"What about this grub then?" pressed Kate.

Maudie laughed and went up to the bar to order two specials.

Effie nudged Kate and murmured, "Lookee out! One of Maudie's old regulars has just come in. D'you remember 'im?"

"Oh, yeah," said Kate. "I wonder if she'll notice."

"Notice what?" said Maudie as she returned to her seat.

"A bloke you used to know."

Maudie turned to see a strikingly handsome man, who was finely dressed in elegant fashionable clothes. She frowned, "Can't say I do,"

The man caught sight of Effie and Kate and looked curiously at the well-dressed woman sitting with them and screwed up his eyes. He walked across to their table, "Ladies, aren't you going to introduce me to your friend?"

"It was the smooth toned voice that gave him away and Maudie realised who it was, "Crikey! Never thought I'd see you again. It's me, Maudie."

The gent looked more closely at her, "Maudie, well I never. I would never have recognised you. What did you do? Did somebody die?"

"No. I work for a living now and not on my back. I am now a woman of means," she said proudly.

"And yet you still like to mix with your... 'old' friends?"

"Friends is friends. That don't change."

"Maybe not. Perhaps I could persuade you to pleasure me again," he said hopefully.

"Nah! Not me, not now. I'm proper decent, now."

"In that case, maybe you'd like to accompany me on a walk in the park sometime?"

"Maybe. Yeah," said Maudie with a smile.

"Until then," said the gent and touched his hat before moving away to join his male friends in a game of cards. He looked back over his shoulder at her and winked and Maudie actually blushed!

***

The summer was almost over and the leaves were starting to turn. Amy pleaded with Jack, "Oh do, let's. It will be fun. I promise you. Just like the days when we first got together."

"A picnic? Why not? Where? If we have one in the grounds we will be overrun by children."

"What about Hyde Park? It has some wonderful spots for a picnic."

"Hyde Park it is. But away from the barracks. I'll get cook to prepare us a hamper."

***

Amy and Jack took the carriage and drove to the park, where people walked and enjoyed the gardens. Jack spread a woven blanket on the ground with a couple of cushions and helped Amy down, careful not to catch her dress, which sometimes had a mind of its own and would whip up, the petticoats almost covering her head.

The sun beamed down happily and the rays cast their golden light on the two of them, as they sat under a spreading tree beginning to wear the garb of autumn. Amy put up her parasol as the sun shone radiantly through the leaves that were a wonderful mix of reds, golds and russets; colours that would enjoy resting on an artist's palette.

Jack opened the hamper, "Now, what we got here? There's ham, cheese, even a bit of chicken and a tub of cook's kisses."

"I remember when you first had those," said Amy.

"So, do I. I think I made you blush."

Amy laughed, "I think I did that myself. I didn't realise what I was saying until I said it!"

"I didn't mind," said Jack grinning lopsidedly.

265

Amy twirled her parasol before putting it down. "I can't hold this and eat. Imagine the mess I'd get into." She shaded her eyes as she saw a couple approaching, "Well, I never!" Amy waved madly, "Maudie, Maudie, over here!" And she beckoned them across.

Maudie was holding the arm of an extremely handsome man in his late forties. He had dark hair and a chiselled, clean cut face. She beamed at them and waved back excitedly.

"Maudie! How are you? I'm sorry we haven't seen you in a while. Jack's been busy organising work placements for some of the older children." Amy looked curiously at the gentleman with her.

"Don't need to worry about that. I've been fine. We can catch up any time, after all we do live in the same house." She giggled and felt Jack eyeing up her companion. "Oh, do excuse me. Let me introduce you. This is my intended, Mr Valentine." She turned to him and added, "Mr Valentine, these are the friends that I told you about, Mr and Mrs Dawkins."

"Pleased to meet you, I am sure," he said doffing his hat. His voice was rich and smooth.

"Your intended?" said Jack arching his eyebrow.

"Mr Valentine has asked for my hand in marriage and I have said yes."

Jack leapt up delightedly, "Well done, Mr Valentine. Congratulations, Maudie! I am so pleased for you."

"Congratulations to you both," said Amy. She put out her hand for Jack to help her to her feet. Maudie stretched her left hand out and wriggled her fingers, showing off her large diamond and sapphire ring. "That's so beautiful, Maudie."

"It is pretty, ain't it? I like it."

"Only the best for you, my love," said Mr Valentine smiling down at her.

"When is the day?" asked Amy.

"Very soon," said Mr Valentine. "It's next week. Maudie wanted something really romantic."

"We're getting married on a boat," she said excitedly. "Jack, I wanted to ask you something. I know I'm older than you, but..." She looked at Valentine who nodded and encouraged her with his eyes. "Would you give me away? Be my dad for the day?"

Jack's eyes misted over and he took Maudie in his arms and hugged her. "I'd be honoured. Thank you for asking."

"Oh, I'm so pleased. It will make my day perfect. Molly will be a bridesmaid. Mr Valentine is kind enough to welcome both of us into his house although Molly has already said she wishes to stay with you until she's finished her education, if that's all right with you?"

"But, of course," said Amy. "And if there's anything I can do to help with the arrangements, just say." She tucked her arm in Maudie's and said brightly, "Don't mind if I steal her away for a moment, Mr Valentine? I want to hear all about these plans. It's such a surprise."

"Not at all," said Valentine. "But don't keep her too long, will you? I am missing her already."

Jack laughed, "I believe Maudie will have enough romance to talk about so as to make my wife jealous, Mr Valentine. Come, let us sit and talk awhile. I suspect my wife will be more than a minute or two. She loves weddings. Perhaps, you can tell me in what ways I can help?"

***

The week raced by. The mansion was bustling with activity as the carriage was prepared for the wedding. It was decorated with garlands and flowers. Jack and Amy waited in the hallway dressed in their formal attire. Jack shoved his finger between his neck and restrictive collar. Amy tutted, "Jack, don't do that. You'll untidy your cravat. Hang on, I'll just get something. Wait there."

Jack shifted his feet and struggled not to scratch his neck. Amy soon returned with a pot of something. "What's that?"

"It's new. It's healing jelly, stops chafing and rubbing."

"Won't it stain?"

"Not if I'm careful. Come here." Jack moved cautiously towards her. Amy put some on her finger and gently wiped around the red mark on Jack's neck where the stiff collar had rubbed. "There! How's that?"

Jack turned his head from left to right, "Bloomin' marvellous. Why haven't you done this before?"

"I told you, it's new," said Amy with a smile. She popped the small pot into her reticule. "In case we need it later."

It was then that Maudie appeared on the stairs with Molly.

Jack and Amy gasped, "Maudie, you look lovely!" said Jack. "And look at Molly, pretty as a picture in her bridesmaid outfit."

Molly beamed, "Thank you, Mr Jack. I love my dress."

Jack announced, "Ladies, your carriage awaits as does your betrothed."

Maudie squealed with pleasure, "I'm so excited. Ain't never been wed before. Never thought it would happen... and to such a lovely man. I'm really lucky, ain't we, Moll?"

"Yes, Mum."

"Come on, we have to pick up Mr Valentine. Let's go."

***

The day was perfect. There wasn't a cloud to be seen to mar the clear blue sky and the sun warmed the earth. Birds sang sweetly in the eucalyptus trees aligning the avenue as two carriages paraded towards the town and the docks.

Amy, Maudie, Molly and Mr Valentine sat in one beautifully adorned carriage that Jack drove. Following behind was another equally decorative carriage with Atwill, Dora and three of Mr Valentine's friends inside. There was much merriment and laughter from both carriages. It was a joyous day.

They drove along the cobbled street that led to the quayside where a tall ship was moored. It stood like the carapace of some unholy creature, a sentinel, from hell, its tall masts and sails blocking the sunlight that flashed through the gaps as the boat gently rocked in harbour. But, there was nothing gentle about this ship. A feeling of evil pervaded the air mixed with the stench of death, vomit and disinfectant.

Valentine called out excitedly, "Here it is. Pull up, Jack."

Jack stared at the Aurora trying to suppress his horror and the memories this devil ship brought with it. He halted the carriage sharply and the occupants all tumbled out happily. Jack stepped down and shuddered. He forced himself to try and look calm while inside he was churning in turmoil and disgust. Amy saw the revulsion in Jack's eyes and asked quietly, "What's the matter, Jack?"

Jack forced a smile and he attempted to reassure her and swallowed hard, as the bile in his stomach rose up to his throat, "Nothing, my dear."

The wedding party strolled towards the gangway. Maudie and Mr Valentine led the way followed by Amy and Jack. Amy glanced sideways at Jack whose dismay, although well-hidden to the others, was more than apparent to her. She took his hand and squeezed it; it was clammy.

Some sailors were on deck mopping the boards and two marines guarded the top of the gangway. A tall, sturdy man with a bushy, but now greying moustache, remained at the head of the guards at the front. It was the same marine sergeant from over twenty years earlier who had accompanied Jack and Edward on their abysmal journey from England to Australia. Something caught in Jack's gullet and Amy glanced at him again in concern but Jack had plastered a smile on his face so as not to betray his acute inner revulsion.

Mr Valentine addressed the marine sergeant; he was smiling effusively, "I am Mr Valentine. Please tell the captain we are here."

"Yes, sir. We have been expecting you. Step this way."

The marine sergeant ushered Mr Valentine and Maudie together with the rest of the party onto the ship towards the bridge where stood an imposing, daunting figure that appeared to loom over them. He had an abundance of wild white hair giving the appearance of a mad professor or erudite cleric, but when he spoke his booming voice struck terror in the heart of any person who had encountered him before. "Welcome to you, all," he pronounced.

"Christ!" Jack whispered, unable to contain that one small word that no one heard or noticed.

"Mr Valentine! You are most welcome," Dowson's voice bellowed, drowning out all other sounds, and he grinned revealing his sharp, white pointed teeth, which reminded Jack of a crocodile preparing to strike.

"May I introduce you to my guests?" asked Mr Valentine with a smile.

"Please do," the captain assented.

"Everybody, this is Captain Dowson, he will be marrying Maudie and me."

The captain nodded with an arrogant toss of his head as each person was introduced to him and he shook hands with them accordingly. His grip was vice-like and crushing, even to the ladies who winced slightly in his grasp, all except for Molly to whom he merely bowed. Once official introductions were over his plangent voice requested, "Shall we go straight to the bridge?"

He led the way followed by everyone else who shuffled into some sort of order while Dowson picked up the same heavy black leather bound Bible emblazoned with a gold cross, now looking worn at the edges. He turned to face them.

Loathing for the man filled Jack's body and he tried to look unruffled as he brought Maudie forward. They faced Dowson who stood centre opposite Mr Valentine.

Dowson's voice thundered with authority, "Give me the ring, Mr Valentine and we shall begin."

Maudie smiled up at Mr Valentine as Captain Dowson addressed the company, "We are gathered here in the sight of God to join these two people in Holy Matrimony."

Suddenly, Maudie shrieked, "My ring! Where's my bloody ring?"

Jack looked concerned, "Whatever's the..."

Maudie held out her left hand where she had worn the impressive engagement ring she had received from Mr Valentine, "I had it on just now! Jack, I was just wearing it. I swear. Oh, Gawd! My engagement ring's been nicked. My beautiful ring." Her eyes filled with tears and she looked in despair at everyone.

Jack attempted to placate her, "You must have dropped it, Maudie. It could have fallen off." He clapped his hands, "Look lively, everyone. Look on the deck. It could have rolled somewhere."

Everybody scrambled around the immediate area hunting for the errant ring. "Where the bloody hell is it?" wailed Maudie.

"It has to be somewhere," insisted Dowson.

"Nah! Someone's nicked it. Come on, it's not funny anymore," said Maudie. There was a flurry of questioning whispers as the group continued to look on the ground and then at each other.

Jack said soothingly, "No one's nicked it, Maudie. Why would they do that? We've all come to see you wed and happy." Maudie began to cry. "All right, all right... if it makes you feel better," said Jack. "Look!" and he turned out his pockets, held his arms aloft with his hands open. "You see! Nothing! It ain't with me, Maudie."

Amy opened her reticule, for everyone to see, "I have nothing. It wasn't me."

Dowson roared, "Sergeant!"

The marine sergeant hastened up the steps to the bridge and saluted the captain, "Sir!"

"It would appear we have a thief amongst us."

The marine sergeant seemed to know the drill, only too well, almost rolling his eyes. "Yes, sir. Right! Everyone turn out their pockets."

Mr Valentine looked affronted, "Must I?"

The sergeant murmured sympathetically, "I'm sorry, sir. It has to be everyone."

Mr Valentine sighed, "Very well. Although, this is somewhat ridiculous. However, if it must be done..." and he emptied his pockets. "You see, I have nothing, either." His other friends laughed finding the whole thing amusing but followed suit without any acrimony. They too had nothing. Neither did Atwill or Dora.

Molly shrugged, she didn't have any pockets but just carried a posy of wild flowers and she shook them to prove there was nothing secreted amongst them.

Dowson looked bemused, "Well, that's everyone." He eyed Maudie and spoke in an overly condescending manner, "Perhaps you forgot to wear it, my dear. You must have made a mistake. After all, everyone has been searched."

"Not everyone," said Jack firmly.

"How do you mean, sir?" asked the marine sergeant looking puzzled.

Jack looked at Dowson, pointedly, "The captain wasn't searched."

"What! Search me? I am the captain of this ship. I will not be searched," he said imperiously.

The marine sergeant spoke judiciously, "But, sir... They have all submitted to being searched, Captain... even the bridegroom."

Dowson was enraged, "Well, I will not submit. This is highly offensive. I am next to God aboard this ship and what I say goes. I will not permit this and be treated like a common criminal."

"Sounds as though you have something to hide," said Jack meaningfully.

"How dare you! I am above reproach," and he shook his head violently, his wild white hair accentuating a look of madness.

The marine sergeant remained calm and he said quietly but forcibly, "Captain, if you do not submit, I will be obliged to call over the marines and we will force you to be searched."

Captain Dowson's face suffused with rage and he growled threateningly, "You will pay for this, Sergeant! I will see to it."

"No doubt I will, sir."

Captain Dowson snorted in fury. He raised his arms above his head and the marine sergeant, patted him down and searched him.

"What's this, sir?" said the sergeant accusingly as he removed his hand from Dowson's pocket and held up Maudie's diamond and sapphire engagement ring.

"What do you think you're doing?" blustered the captain. He eyed the expensive engagement ring, which glittered in the sunlight, "Where did you get that?"

"It was in your pocket, sir. Andrews! Johnson!" called the sergeant and two marines popped their heads up from below. "Take the captain below." The men began to cover the deck to mount the steps to the bridge.

The captain was practically apoplectic, "You have absolutely no authority to do this. I am the captain of this ship and no one has power over me! I am the law here!" he roared.

The marine sergeant countered, "That would be so if we were at sea, but we are in port, in Australian waters and you must surrender to local authority here. Take him below." Jack was convinced he noted a flicker of pleasure in the marine sergeant's eyes. The marines had just reached the bridge and took him by each arm, although Dowson continued to protest vehemently and struggled against them. "This is outrageous!"

"But, what about the wedding?" objected Jack.

"Sir?"

"The wedding... we have paid for a wedding. What happens now?"

"There's nothing I can do, sir," said the sergeant apologetically.

"Then, perhaps the captain could be persuaded to perform the ceremony while we wait for the police to arrive?" suggested Jack.

"You can go to hell," screamed Dowson red in the face.

"Well, it was just a thought," said Jack in a matter of fact tone as the officers led Dowson away. It was hard to suppress the grin that yearned to manifest on his face.

The wedding party were led back off the ship and stopped to decide the best course of action.

Jack suggested, "You could get wed in church. You've had the banns read, it's not your fault the captain was a thief."

Mr Valentine frowned, "Do you think we could do that? Or maybe we could visit the town hall or courthouse and see if there is a magistrate prepared to perform the ceremony."

"I don't care where we go as long as we can get it done," said Maudie. "We've got the meal all booked for us in the town."

"Why don't you and Mr Valentine and friends visit the courthouse, in the carriages. Atwill and I will wait here for the police to arrive and appraise them of the situation. The scoundrel mustn't get away with it. We will come along as quickly as possible. Or someone can collect us. If not, we can always have the meal first and then see you married," said Jack.

The rest of the company seemed to agree that this was a good idea and they set off in both carriages, while Jack and Atwill sat silently and stared at the Aurora, which held such horrific memories for Jack until the wedding party had moved on.

Atwill was the first to speak, "I never thought I would set foot on that ship again."

"What? You, too?" said Jack in surprise.

"Same bastard ship and same bastard captain. In all my life I have never seen a colder, more vicious killer than him. When I came over he murdered four men. And all in the name of God." Atwill snorted derisively, "Well, his God."

"It was three that died on my voyage. I almost puked when I heard his voice. Fair turned me insides out, cold-hearted villain."

"Didn't think he was the type to steal, though. Just goes to show, you never know."

"Maybe he ain't. Maybe it was a moment of madness. He certainly looked insane with that hair." Atwill grunted in agreement and Jack went on, "Or maybe, just maybe someone helped him."

"What do you mean?" asked Atwill looking confused.

"Let's suppose that someone else put the ring in his pocket..."

"You never...!" Atwill began to grin.

"I never said it was me what done it. But, then again, suppose there was someone who had a deep hatred for the man. Suppose that bloke, whoever he was, wanted to stop other prisoners suffering at Dowson's hands... Suppose that man was known as the Dodger. What then?"

"I'd slap him on the back and congratulate him... Bloody hell, Jack. What d'you think will happen to him?"

"He'll do time. He's bound to. And it will be hard time. He'll spend his sentence with a lot of men he transported, men who hate him, like us. Those prisoners would love to see him again."

"That they will. The bastard will suffer."

"Count on it. I don't fancy his chances inside the stockade."

"Jack, you're a bloody genius."

"If it was me that done it, I would agree with you. Hey up! Here come the police."

"I will enjoy watching him being taken away. Hope they put the swine in chains."

"We might not get the chance for that, here comes one of Valentine's friends in the carriage with Amy."

She beckoned to them smiling. Jack and Atwill scrambled up. They stopped and exchanged a few words with the police and promised to deliver statements if called.

Amy opened the carriage door, "It's all fixed. Maudie won't be disappointed. Let's hurry."

Jack grinned at Atwill and winked.

27: Problems for Maudie

Maudie and Mr Valentine emerged from the courthouse followed by the wedding group and were showered with rice. Mr Valentine had hired a photographer to record their first moments of married life. Maudie was amazed believing that it was some kind of magic that would capture their images and couldn't wait for the pictures to be developed and presented to them. The photographer, a tall, lean man who dressed flamboyantly, was keen to explain to the guests or anyone who would listen, how it worked and the processes involved.

Molly stood with her mouth agape as she heard all about William Henry Fox Talbot and his incredible, revolutionary techniques for calotype negatives and salt print processes. Molly's enquiring mind continued to ask questions of the man and he was only too delighted to answer. She was especially interested to discover new words and their meanings. "I always thought salt was something you put on food, used to preserve it and add to taste."

"It is, it is! But, it can do so much more," said the photographer. "And I'll tell you something else, the word calotype comes from the Greek words kalos and tupos."

Molly listened wide-eyed, "But what does it mean?"

"It means, beautiful… impression," said the photographer with a smile.

Molly dashed across to her mother as they all stood chatting while they waited for the carriages to be brought around for them. "Mum, I learned some Greek. You know you are kalos."

Maudie said with a laugh, "Whatever does that mean?"

Molly replied, "Beautiful!"

Maudie kissed her daughter fondly on her head as Mr Valentine agreed, "Yes, you are. And you're all mine, forever."

Amy watched the interchange with a fond expression on her face. She was clearly touched. Just then the carriages arrived and halted as the sound of marching feet approached. Jack turned to look as the group climbed into the carriages. He stared hard as the marines neared the courthouse accompanying a manacled Captain Dowson who was now silent but red in the face from anger. Jack was almost tempted to say something but thought better of it. He turned the carriage and shrilly whistled Edward's favourite song, 'This Small Violet I Plucked From Mother's Grave.'

Dowson turned his head and glowered at Jack who gave him a cheeky salute and spurred the carriage forward as the marines led their prisoner into the courthouse whilst the wedding party made their way to The Mansfield Hotel. Jack was keen to see how the proprietor and other waiters would react when they saw Atwill enter as a guest. The thought of their possible reaction amused him and he laughed, very loudly much to the confusion of everyone else.

Jack turned to the occupants and explained, "I am in an excellent mood!" And he laughed again.

***

Captain Dowson's case was heard in the magistrates' court and although he vehemently denied any wrongdoing and protested his innocence, the evidence against him proved too strong. He had been caught with the ring on his person and the judge refused to listen to his complaints. His previous character and occupation counted for nothing. In his final summing up the judge decreed, "You are the foulest of men who has fallen into the habits of those very criminals you have transported here through the years. What else have you done for which you have escaped retribution? No one has ever questioned your authority before."

Captain Dowson shouted, "I am above the law and stand next to God in my authority."

The judge hammered his gavel to silence him, "Be quiet. You are not the law in my courtroom. I am. You have no one to attest to your character not even the marine sergeant who has accompanied you on many voyages. He tells us a very different story of other crimes you have committed against man. Be glad I haven't taken those into consideration. You have been tried and convicted for full thievery of a very expensive ring. The theft of that item of such high value would normally constitute a hanging offence, flogging and skin. But because of your long standing service to the penal colony I am being more lenient, sentencing you to thirty lashes and removal of your right ear after which you will be incarcerated for a period of no less than ten years. The flogging will take place in three days' time as will the removal of your ear."

Dowson reeled in the prisoner's dock. His dishevelled white hair looked wild and he called out pleadingly, "No, it was not me..."

"One more outburst from you and I will increase the sentence." The judge waited and this time, Dowson said nothing. He hung his head in despair and began to sob. The judge ordered, "Take him away."

Two policemen flanked him and led him from the court.

***

Dowson, in manacles, was marched to the stockade by soldiers. The noise from inside the stockade reached them. It was almost deafening as word had spread through the prisoners that they were receiving a new inmate who would be very familiar to many of them. The gate to the enclosure opened where a mob of prisoners had gathered. They fell silent at the sight of Dowson. The prisoners parted like the waves of the Red Sea and stood creating an avenue lining the sides of the prison camp.

One soldier removed Dowson's shackles and the captain rubbed his wrists, which were now red raw. He stopped dead and his eyes ranged across the mass of faces of men and women he had transported and he was gripped with fear, "You can't leave me here. Please. No."

The soldiers said nothing and retreated barring the gate securely behind them.

Dowson initially stood frozen. He shrank back fearfully as the deadly silence engulfed him and spread through his body. After the shocking voices he had heard on his march to the stockade, which had filled him with panic, this muzzled, alien quiet seemed to scream at him. He bowed his head in sheer dread. The lack of any sound or vocal clamour was more deadly and terrifying than the vile noise he had heard before.

He could not hear a whisper, could not hear a breath and with trepidation he stepped forward. Even his own footsteps made no sound on the earth floor. His faltering movements did not disturb the lethal hush that was filled with menace as he made his way through the seemingly interminable line of prisoners whose hatred for him penetrated his very bones filling him with doom.

**

Maudie was delighted to be starting, as she called it 'respectiflul' married life and her first few weeks were filled with hope for the future firmly believing that she was now a reputable married woman. She had aspirations to improve and better herself. Her face was permanently fixed with a smile at this new-found success and change in her social standing.

However, she felt she needed accomplishments as other ladies in Valentine's circle of friends possessed and she sought their advice, but they weren't the most amenable towards her. It was as if they all knew of her past life and were unaccepting of her. She felt somewhat demeaned by them and said so, "I don't know what I've done to them. They's really unfriendly. Stuck up, I say."

"Don't worry, my love. You have accomplishments that none of them could even hope to have. And thinking about that, why don't you get yourself upstairs and wait for me. Prepare yourself, rosy your cheeks, colour your lips, put on your best seduction wear." Maudie looked surprised and a little put out. "Just for me, please," he wheedled. "I am your husband. This is our honeymoon period." He patted her bottom and indicated the stairs with his head.

Maudie reluctantly picked up her skirt and went up the stairs.

**

In the library Jack poured Atwill a glass of port, as Atwill had come back from town flushed with excitement. Jack looked his friend up and down, "What is it? Has something happened?"

Atwill nodded, "Dowson's dead."

"Dead? How?"

"We're not the only ones who hated the bastard and loathed the way he treated us like he was some sort of vicious demi-god."

Jack's mouth pursed into a thin line, "The man was a sadistic swine. We knew he'd have it tough inside. What happened?"

Atwill licked his lips, he was clearly going to enjoy recounting events as he had been told. "I met your friend, Sergeant Phillips at the port. He told me Dowson survived just over three days."

"Did he do himself in or...?"

"Oh, it's better than that. Once inside the prison with their own convicts' law, they allowed him to walk through them towards the living quarters in silence. Dowson moved slowly with his head down staring at the ground. The place was deathly quiet. It was as if collectively the whole prison had sent the brute to Coventry. I gather there had been discussion amongst the men to punish Dowson and demean him as if he were nothing. Not talking to him, but letting him live with the threat of what was likely to happen, was more abominable than any beating he could have had. Like being thrown in the lions' den he could see them around him, their teeth, their eyes, see their faces, if he dared to look, and if he did look he'd see their rampant hatred of him. He ate alone. Men shunned him as they would a leper, he always ate alone. Folks would move away from him like he stunk worse than a dung heap. No one would go near him except to spit in his food. He was treated as if he didn't exist. Ignored to the end, just like our cries and pleas went unheard on that damned ship. Dowson experienced a different terror that punished him, to what he did on the Aurora. He terrorised every man and woman that sailed under him or was transported. Now, he was getting a taste of retribution. So, he got what was coming to him. It's only right."

"I'd like to have seen that. He murdered innocents on my trip that were good hearted men, even a preacher hung himself," said Jack bitterly as he remembered the atrocity they'd all been forced to watch.

"But the best bit is, they stretched it out. The menace of silence was more terrifying than anything else. Their revenge was complete."

"How?"

"Cos they wanted him to have his lashing and his ear lopped off. They enjoyed his public flogging and seeing his ear ripped off, but none of them made no sound. No jeering, no mocking, nothing. He went back to that solitary existence of odium, and the convicts continued their ever increasing disgust of him, which plagued Dowson. He daren't sleep, in case he was attacked. The man was gibbering and hallucinating from three days of being snubbed and ignored. Like those poor perishers that got boxed."

"So, revenge was served. What was his end?"

"They found him strung up in the yard. He'd hung himself. Imagine him living not knowing, which day would be his last," said Atwill taking a sip of his drink.

"But, he knew that one day it would happen. The threat of not knowing when is somehow worse."

"So, what happened, next?"

"They left him strung up and dangling for all to see. He won't be terrifying no one else ever again."

Jack raised his glass, "I'll drink to that!"

Months passed.

***

Maudie sat slumped unhappily on the floor. Her face was now a ghostly white as if all her blood had absconded to her extremities. She stared blankly into space. Maudie brushed away a tear and left the house. She made her way along the road with no idea where she was going. It was early and people were not yet out and about. She walked stiffly and was shivering, even though the early morning was seasonably warm.

Maudie breathed in hiccupping gasps as she tried to control her urge to sob. She rambled on, stumbling on the cobbles. A man setting off for work saw her blank stare and untidy appearance with a stained dress and messy hair that had come loose from its hairpins and ties. He approached her and asked, "Are you all right, ma'am?" Maudie didn't respond but just plodded onward silently.

She continued walking in a daze and found herself entering the grounds of the mansion. She stopped and looked up at the house, where the children were still asleep. Only a few of the staff were up and about, preparing for the day ahead. She gazed up at the landing window and saw Amy speaking with one of the nurses who seemed to be listening to some instructions. The nurse nodded and bobbed a curtsey and moved on. Amy stepped towards the window and peered out and was surprised to see Maudie standing there looking up at her. Amy tentatively raised her hand in a wave but there was no response from Maudie so she hurried down the stairs and opened the front door.

"Maudie? Whatever's the matter? Come on in." Maudie teetered up the steps and went inside. Puzzled, Amy asked again, "What's happened?"

Maudie spoke in a flat monotone, "I've left Mr Valentine."

"Oh, Maudie, no... Why?" All Maudie could do was stare blankly ahead. It was as if she had been struck dumb or suffered something unspeakable. Amy waited but there was no response so she continued, "Come on into the library. I'll fetch Jack."

Maudie followed Amy like an automaton. She sat down to wait looking numb, her eyes wide and despairing, her shoulders drooped and her whole demeanour was one of hopelessness. As she sat and waited, a rush of emotion flowed through her and she began to cry. She removed her dainty lace hankie from her sleeve and dabbed at her nose. "This ain't no good," she whispered to herself. "Can't catch proper spillage from me nose," and she wiped her nose across the sleeve of her fine dress and then berated herself for doing it. "What you thinking of, Maudie? You don't deserve nothin' nice," and she snivelled again.

***

Jack and Amy sat and listened to Maudie in utter shock. They had assumed Maudie was happy and settled and couldn't understand why she had left her husband, who they believed to be a fine man who, from what they had seen, obviously adored her and she, him.

It was hard for her to gather her thoughts and speak. Her throat was constricted and tight and the words just would not come. Jack probed gently, "Come on, Maudie. Something must have happened to make you feel like this. We're your friends. You know you can tell us anything. We will never judge you. Please, what is it? If we can help, we will."

Maudie took a deep breath and sighed trying to control the tremor in her voice, which cracked with emotion. However, it seemed that once she had started to talk she couldn't stop. Her words babbled out like a mountain spring and Jack and Amy listened.

"You see, I knew Mr Valentine from before. You know, when I worked on me back? He was always a bit lively. He was known for it with me and the other girls. Liked it all ways, if you get me meaning? Well, after we was married I thought he'd settle down, but he was worse. When I was a bangtail, I learnt all the tricks and things to do, to pleasure a man and keep him happy. I thought, well I hoped, that once we were wed we should be respectful and he would treat me as such. But no, he wanted to do it all the time. Some days I could hardly walk. It was like he had to do it or he couldn't function. It got worse when he wanted me to do all the things that I did when I was a doxie. I told him, 'no'. I didn't want to be treated like that. I wanted to be treated proper like a decent married woman. This is so hard..." She turned to Jack and asked, "Can I have a drink?"

"Yes, of course." Jack rose and poured her a glass of port, "Here."

"Thank you," she took a sip and some colour returned to her pale cheeks. "He wanted me all rouged up like I was before. If Molly wasn't there he'd pester me to walk around with me titties hanging out. It weren't decent. When his friends came for a game of cards he'd expect me to do the same, wanting me to do it with his mates. I said I wouldn't but he told me I was his property and if he wanted to share me, he would."

Amy gasped in horror, "Oh my God, Maudie!"

"Do you know what he said? He told me I was his private little whore and he could do with me as he wished. When I dug me heels in and stopped doin' what he wanted he went all quiet. Wouldn't talk to me at all."

Jack gazed at her in sorrow, "Maudie, I am so sorry. I had no idea and no inkling the man was like that."

"Why would you? He hid it well. But what went on in that house..." She started to cry again. They waited for her to continue. "I went to meet me old friends from the fort the other day and they told me, he'd been down to the docks and done it with Nell, more than once. I don't blame her, she needed the money but that really hurt. I mean, Nell was my friend. You remember her, Jack?" Jack nodded. "He's supposed to behave like an honourable married man. He was married to me!" She wiped her eyes on her hands and sleeve again. "Look at me, not even behaving decently meself, now. But, that's not the worst of it. Last night he brought women home. Him and his mates and when they'd gone he said, he couldn't wait for Molly to grow up and me to teach her my pleasuring ways. I don't know what came over me. I stuck him like the pig he was."

"What do you mean, stuck him?" asked Jack looking even more concerned.

"I grabbed the letter opener from the bureau and stabbed him good. He's dead."

"Christ! Are you sure he's dead?"

"He's dead all right. I sat by his body for the rest of the night. Oh, Jack! What'll I do? They'll hang me. What about Molly?"

"Oh, Lord... Amy please fetch Atwill. And hurry! We have to move fast." Jack began to pace in the library as he thought and Maudie sat there quietly sipping her drink.

Moments later, Amy returned with Atwill, who looked anxious. Jack had urgency in his voice as he explained to Atwill about the predicament Maudie was in.

He instructed him, "Atwill, take Maudie to the farm tonight. She'll be safe there. We can hide her here today. Molly can stay here as normal... Tomorrow, I'll go to the docks. Maudie, you're not a lifer. I remember you telling me in the stockade. You said you could go back to England if you'd a mind. Well, I'll find the first ship sailing home, get tickets and you and Molly will be on it. I promise you. Amy will get some food and drink to take to the farm for you."

Maudie was now looking calmer, "Oh, thank you, Jack. Thank you, all. I don't know what to say."

"Just be ready after dark. I'll be waiting for you," said Atwill.

"I will come and see you tomorrow at the farm and bring clothes and things for your journey."

"How you gonna do that? They're all at the house," said Maudie. She downed the rest of her drink and placed the glass down.

"You can have some of my clothes," said Amy. "And Molly has plenty here so that won't be a problem. We can pack a case for her for the ship." Amy took Maudie's hands and raised her to her feet. "Come with me." Suddenly, she wrapped Maudie into a close embrace and said sadly, "Oh, Maudie I shall miss you."

"And I'll miss you, too and so will Molly. We have been so happy here. Now, let me go or I'll start crying again."

***

That night as planned, Atwill took Maudie in the carriage to the farm. They unpacked her things in the farmhouse and Atwill laid out a hamper of food in the kitchen. "You'll be safe here," said Atwill as he turned to leave. "Remember, if anyone comes knocking don't answer the door. Stay inside. Even if Koorong comes calling."

"Who's Koorong?"

"Aboriginal friend of Jack's. He's a good man. So are his people. They use the farm from time to time, but I'd advise you to stay out of their way."

"But if they're Jack's friends..."

"It's safer that way. Although, I can vouch for Koorong and a few others, I wouldn't trust all of them. There's good and bad in all races, as you well know and if the police have found Valentine's corpse there's bound to be a price on your head. You need to be careful."

Maudie nodded, "I will. And thank you."

"Don't thank me yet. You can send me a postcard from England and then I'll be happy. I'll be back for you, once we know when there is a place for you on a ship. If

I were you, I'd lock all the doors and keep the curtains shut. We don't want anyone seeing you. No one."

Maudie nodded and gave Atwill a quick hug, "You've been a good friend to me. I'll not forget you. You'll have your card from England, I promise."

Atwill smiled and bade her goodbye. He slipped out of the door and waited until he heard the key turn in the lock before getting back to the carriage to journey back.

Maudie sat in a kitchen chair and looked about her. The only light came from the bright moon outside that filtered in through the window. If she closed the curtains she wouldn't be able to see. She studied the place. It needed a good clean. She thought that after she had explored the house she would see what she could do to tidy it up. She hoped there would be something around that she could use to wash the floor and the corners of the room. But now the place was really dark as the moon's face had been hidden by a wandering cloud. She needed to find a candle or a lamp. She couldn't stay in the darkness. It frightened her.

Maudie got up from the chair, which squeaked in complaint and she crossed to the kitchen sink with its water pump and tested it. As she worked it, water gushed out. She stopped pushing the handle and it stopped to a slow drip. Maudie rummaged under the sink and found candles and a tinderbox. She sighed in relief and set about lighting the candle and went to explore the rest of the house. She found the main bedroom and a lamp on the bedside table, which she lit. It filled the room with a soft ,warm glow and Maudie closed the curtains tightly hoping nothing would spill through the gaps before retreating back down the stairs. She was hungry and was surprised that she could eat. But, it was going to be a long night and she didn't know how many days she would be there.

***

Port Jackson was alive with the news of Valentine's murder. His body was discovered by his friends who had turned up at the house for their usual game of cards. Everyone was on the lookout for Maudie Valentine. Valentine's friends had stumped up a reward of twenty-five guineas for information that would lead to her arrest and capture. Word soon spread around the town and the police came to the mansion to interview staff as to whether or not they had seen her.

Atwill was adamant that he didn't know where she was as did the other mansion house staff, and when Jack was questioned he just shook his head, saying that she no longer worked there. He suggested they check amongst her friends at the docks. He breathed a sigh of relief when the militia accepted his answer and went off to do just that.

Jack took the carriage and made his way to the passenger ship's company offices and made enquiries about the next sailing for England. The clerk was helpful and Jack managed to purchase two first class tickets with a luxury cabin to travel to Liverpool on the Champion of the Seas. He bought them in her maiden name of Summers and prayed no one would realise the truth of her identity. The ship was to sail in two days' time at eleven o'clock in the morning. Jack returned and prepared an envelope of cash to sustain them both on the journey and to help them on arrival in Liverpool.

When Jack returned home, he asked Amy, "How can we disguise Maudie so she's not so easily recognisable?"

"I don't know. Have you heard anymore?"

"No... perhaps we could pad her out and make her look fat?" suggested Jack.

"But then none of her clothes would fit her," countered Amy.

"Hmm!" Jack frowned. "Maybe cut her hair?"

"What and disguise her as a boy? She'd attract more attention with short hair... But, maybe that's the answer," said Amy. "Make her dress outrageously. No one would expect her to look so obvious..."

"You could be right. Keep thinking," agreed Jack.

"I had heard the authorities are going to post pictures of her from her wedding day. She looked so happy then," said Amy sadly. "What a terrible state of affairs."

***

Koa, was a young aboriginal that Koorong was trying to teach about selling wool bales and the lad had accompanied him to the quayside in Port Jackson. They were travelling back through the farmland skirting the house when Koa's eagle eyes spotted a flickering light coming from the dwelling. Koa drew Koorong's attention to it, "Look. A light!"

Koorong warned, "Ignore it. It's more than likely a friend of Jack. None of our business."

"But..."

"Koa, no!" Koorong was vehement. "Jack is our friend. If someone is here with his knowledge it is nothing to do with us."

"But, what if it's not?"

"Then we will check in the morning but for now, leave it," said Koorong sternly.

Koa fell silent but his mind worked feverishly as they returned to the village to be met with great celebration for their successful trading. The chief had prepared a feast in their honour.

Minjarra begged his uncle, "Next time, take me. Please, Uncle."

Koorong laughed, "We will see, Minjarra. We will see." He did not see Koa slip away after he had eaten. He had told his mother he was going for a walk and would be back soon. No one was aware of his absence and no one missed him.

The boy slunk away through the gorge, past the lagoon and waterfall and walked back to the farmhouse. His keen eyes had adjusted to the dark and he observed the house. There was a flickering light shining through a chink in the kitchen curtain.

Koa crept through the brush and sneaked up to the window, disturbing the crickets' thrum. A small snake slithered on its nightly hunt for lizards and other small mammals, and Koa flinched. He stealthily lifted his head up to the window and strained to see inside the kitchen where the light flickered.

There was something familiar about the woman he watched moving around the room making herself something to eat. He scrutinised her face and realisation dawned. It was the woman from the wedding picture he had seen posted around the docks when he sold wool with Koorong. Whosoever knew of her whereabouts was promised a reward of twenty-five guineas if she could be found.

Koa sat back on his haunches. He knew that he had to watch and wait before informing the authorities and claiming the bounty; and that he determined he would do.

28: The Best Laid Plans...

Jack had managed to purchase tickets for Maudie and Molly. Amy had helped Molly pack some bags for herself and her mother. They just had to wait until Atwill could collect Maudie from the farm and hide her out at the mansion overnight until they could safely get her to the quayside.

It was a tense time at the house as the authorities were all on the lookout for Maudie. Her photograph had been posted all over town, in the hotels, along the docks and the rough bars in the slums of Port Jackson. Maudie's friends tore down any posters they saw in the hope that it would help.

Atwill readied himself for his clandestine trip to the farm. He had placed rugs in the carriage that Maudie could hide under if anyone glanced inside the carriage as they passed through the town but first he had to fetch her.

Jack shook Atwill's hand firmly, "Thank you, my friend. Come back safely."

"I'll do my best, Jack. Maudie's a great woman. She don't deserve to die."

Jack nodded and watched him retreat around the building to get the carriage.

***

Koa had waited until the light had been extinguished before he returned to the village. He spent a restless night as he worked out what he could do. He knew he had to be up at first light and be gone but not attract any unwanted attention from Koorong or anyone else.

The galahs had begun to chitter as the first blaze of sunshine splashed over the horizon washing the emerging day in scarlet and burnt orange creating a shimmering haze in the warming air above the ground.

"Koa! Where you go?" said his mother as he tried to sneak out of the hut.

"I'm going walkabout, Ma. I need to think, clear my head after yesterday."

His mother nodded in understanding and settled back down to sleep as her son left.

Koa hurried back to the farm. He didn't want to be followed and was careful not to leave any tracks in spite of the fact he was dressed in clothes and boots as worn by the white men, which made his passage clumsier. Koa settled down under cover to watch and confirm that the woman was still there.

She was.

Now, he puzzled what to do next. Should he stay? Or should he make his way back into Port Jackson and report what he'd seen? He hung around for a while before he decided that he should start back for the port. It would be a long walk.

Koa set off, he kept off the road and travelled through the outlying farmland, but although close to the road he stayed well out of sight. He stopped for a drink at a creek. That was when he heard the rumble of carriage wheels coming towards him. Koa laid down low and saw the carriage turn down the track to the farm. He immediately assumed that the carriage was going to collect the woman so he doubled back to watch.

***

Atwill arrived in the yard and looked about him. Maudie came out and Koa strained hard to listen. "It's done. You and Molly have a berth on 'Champion of the Seas'. It sails tomorrow at eleven in the morning."

Maudie said something else, which Koa didn't catch but Atwill's firm voice reached his ears easily. "In the name of Summers. As soon as it's dark we'll head back. There's a rug to hide under if someone gets too close and peers in. Now, I could do with a drink of something." Atwill followed Maudie inside the house. They bolted and barred the door.

Koa slipped back into the bush. As he saw it, he had two choices. He could hide himself under the carriage and travel back to the port and then he would know exactly where the woman would be hiding. Or he could start walking knowing he'd reach the port before morning. He would find the authorities and report what he knew. The twenty-five guineas would surely be his? Koa grinned from ear to ear. He'd start moving now.

***

Maudie stayed in hiding in Amy and Jack's bedroom until it was time to go. She was dressed beautifully and wore a magnificent hat with a wide feathered brim that hid her face. Every time she turned her head, if someone stood too close, the feathers would tickle their nose. Atwill had already sneezed several times much to everyone's amusement.

Atwill brought the carriage around. The trunks had already been delivered to the docks. Molly came out from her geography class and climbed into the carriage. No one wondered where she was going and Maudie was looking finely dressed like a first class passenger. She had received the tickets from Jack and climbed inside the carriage. She sat with Amy and Molly as Jack drove. He was determined that if they did get caught, Atwill would not be held accountable.

Maudie clutched hold of Molly's hand and whispered to Amy, "Never felt so scared in all me life. Me heart's thumping like a blessed Kangaroo jumpin' about in me chest."

Amy tried to soothe her, "You must stay calm, look as if you belong with the gentry. You look wonderful and that hat hides your face. Just be confident."

***

At the quayside, Amy, Maudie and Molly alighted. Jack hopped down and took the remaining bag onto the dockside. They didn't linger but said their goodbyes quickly. As Amy hugged Maudie, she whispered, "Look assured, as if you own the shipping line and you'll be fine."

Maudie's smile was tight, "I do 'ope you're right. I'll do me best. Performance of a lifetime." She turned to Jack, "You have been the best to me. Promise me that you'll look after Moll if anything goes wrong."

"You know I will, but, nothing's gonna go wrong. Believe it and you'll carry it off. Good luck." And he hugged her tightly before saying a swift goodbye to Molly. "Now, go on. Got your tickets?" Maudie nodded, holding them tightly in her hand as she stepped towards the ship's officer welcoming passengers aboard.

Maudie held Molly's hand and they stepped towards the gangway, showed their tickets and walked through before entering the bowel of the ship as Jack and Amy watched anxiously.

Amy held tightly onto Jack's arm. Jack muttered under his breath, "Go on, girl. Go on."

They waited nervously for what seemed an eternity but was, in fact, just a few minutes until they saw Maudie and Molly step out onto the deck from where they waved at Jack and Amy.

Amy sighed in relief and said quietly but happily, with a tear in her eye, "She made it. Oh, she's made it. Thank God." Amy began to wave back joyfully but the wave faltered, stopped and she bit her lip as a ship's officer and a policeman come out onto the deck behind Maudie. The policeman took Maudie's arm and she was led away followed by Molly. Amy cried in despair, "Oh, Jack! They have her."

Jack's face showed his shock and disbelief, "But how did they know? How? It's like they were waiting for her. We never saw no policeman boarding."

***

Maudie's indictment was swift. She was taken to a holding cell almost immediately after she was secured and interviewed before being taken to the courthouse. Jack and Amy followed the evidence of the prosecution closely. They portrayed Maudie as a common prostitute whose character was completely immoral. It was suggested that she had planned the murder of Valentine in order to gain his fortune, which made no sense at all to Jack. Valentine's friends rallied around describing her as a common whore whose behaviour within the marriage had been more than questionable.

Jack bristled with anger at the blackening of her character. He approached the defence counsel to speak up on her behalf but Amy was worried it might do more harm than good, if his identity and past came out in court and so, she decided to speak up for Maudie.

Amy stood in the witness dock and described how Maudie had become a valued member of staff at the children's home and was a reformed character. Amy depicted a woman pressed by a need to survive that had led her into that line of work after she left prison. She was not that woman anymore. Frustratingly, she was prevented from explaining the ways that Valentine had humiliated her. As the man was dead there was no one else to deny or verify the truth. Valentine's friends painted the man as a paragon of virtue. It was clear that the judge and the male jury had already made up their minds of her guilt and refused to accept any mitigating circumstances. The fact she was a mother was never even taken into consideration.

After giving her testimony Amy joined Jack in the public gallery to hear the outcome and judgement. They both went cold when the judge took out the black cap and placed it on his head. His words slurred in Amy's head and she struggled not to sob aloud as she heard the pronouncement.

"Maud Valentine you have been found guilty of the wilful and vicious murder of Patrick Valentine. You will be taken from here to a place of execution where you will be hanged by the neck until dead. May God have mercy on your soul."

The judge turned to the guards and instructed, "Take her down." He then broke his pen before the clerk called for all to rise and he swept from court.

Amy clung onto Jack's arm, "Oh, Jack! This is so unfair and so wrong. Isn't there anything we can do?"

Jack pursed his lips and said slowly, "There may be a way."

***

When Jack and Amy returned to the house, Atwill was waiting to meet them together with Dora. Atwill took one look at Amy's face and murmured, "Oh, no."

Jack sadly confirmed their worst fears, and Dora burst into tears and rushed to her room. Maudie had been popular with both staff and children and an air of despondency fell across everyone at the mansion.

Atwill followed Jack into the library, together with Amy and Jack poured them all a drink, "Think we need it after that," he said. He marched to the window and looked out. "The judge refused to grant the right to appeal the sentence. We have to try something else."

"What? What can we do?" asked Atwill. "She's to be hanged tomorrow morning early."

"I have a plan but we need a friendly priest to help us."

Atwill looked puzzled, "Help us? How?"

"We have to borrow a cassock and biretta," said Jack mysteriously, "and get Percy Golding in here. I need to speak with him."

"Before we do that, there is something you need to know," said Atwill mysteriously.

Jack arched an eyebrow, "What?"

"Rumours are flying around the town. I mean, how did they know it was Maudie on that ship? She was barely recognisable in that garb."

"Funnily enough, I thought that."

"I heard they were looking out for her and knew her name to be Summers."

"But, that's impossible!" exclaimed Jack.

"That's what I thought and so I did a little digging."

"And?"

"You're not going to like this, Jack."

Jack frowned and waited expectantly for Atwill to speak. "While you were in court I went down to the docks and chatted with a few of the merchants, pretending to be interested in the scandal. It seems the police officer was already aboard the ship and waiting for Maudie's arrival. They knew she was travelling under the name of Summers and the information had been given to them by a young Aboriginal man who tried to claim the twenty-five guinea reward."

"I don't understand. No one knew of our plan except us. And we didn't say nothing to no one."

"Nor did I," assured Atwill. "It could only have happened at the farm."

"But how?"

"Someone from the village must have known, or seen us or heard something."

"So, did this young man get his reward?"

"Apparently, after Maudie's capture, he did."

"Then a visit to the village will test that out. An Abo with that amount of cash will be obvious. No one could keep it secret. But, first things first. Get Percy Golding."

Percy was the ostler and groom who tended the horses in the stables. He was a lively character and a friend of Jack's. Atwill hurried to fetch the man, and then brought the carriage around for Amy. She and Atwill set off for St. Mary's church, where Amy was friendly with the clergy.

That night, Jack obtained permission to visit Maudie in her cell. As soon as she saw him and he was admitted, she fell into his arms. "Oh, Jack. Whatever's to be done? I don't regret sticking the man. It'll save another woman going through the torment I suffered but I am worried for Molly."

Jack released her and said earnestly, "Now listen, Maudie and listen good. Dry your eyes." Jack looked about him to see if any of the guards were listening and lowered his voice, "When I escaped from the stockade you dressed me as a woman."

"I remember," said Maudie listening carefully and scrubbing away her tears with her sleeve.

"I've a friend. He's the same size as you, height and build. In the morning, an hour before you're to hang," Maudie gulped, "he will come to your cell dressed as a priest. He'll be there to give you the last rites."

"But I'm not a Catholic and I ain't religious."

"That don't matter. When the two of you are alone he'll give you his clothes. You tie him up with this," and Jack removed a length of rope that was tied round his middle. "Hide this under the mattress for now and when that's done, cover him over with that blanket. Then, you knock on your cell door. They'll let you out. Keep your head bowed. Don't say nothin' or you'll give the game away. I'll be waiting outside. Walk slowly to me and get in the carriage. Do you understand?"

Maudie nodded vigorously, "Do you think it will work?"

"I hope so, Maudie. I'm countin' on it."

Maudie's eyes searched Jack's, "And if it don't, will you be there when my time comes?"

"Don't talk like that. It'll work. It's got to."

The two old friends embraced again and Jack knocked on the cell door to be released. He turned to her, "Be strong, Maudie."

Maudie's eyes filled with tears and she murmured, "Thanks, Jack."

Jack nodded as he heard the iron keys jangling outside threateningly. There was a resounding clang as the guard unlocked the door, which slammed shut behind him and Jack left quickly. A nervous sheen of sweat had manifested on his face and he felt unbearably cold.

***

Mantled in the darkness of night, Atwill drove the carriage to the wicket gate at the side of the prison. The horses pawed the ground fretfully as if they were aware of the importance of the event. Jack and his friend the 'priest' stepped out of the vehicle. Percy had on a biretta, a square cap with three flat projections on top and a pom-pom usually worn by Roman Catholic priests. The cassock covered his clothes and he clutched a black leather Bible. Percy shivered and looked uncertainly about him.

"Keep calm. Breathe. Keep your head down. Good luck."

Jack knocked at the wicket gate and slipped back into the shadows. It opened and the 'priest' went inside. Jack returned to the carriage and sat next to Atwill where they both waited tensely. Atwill kept studying his pocket watch. Time seemed to move very slowly. Not a word was spoken between them.

***

Percy Golding followed the stocky turnkey along a shadowy passage. Their feet clattered on the stone floor echoing ominously in the gloomy darkness. The guard stopped at a cell and his heavy iron key went into the lock. The door opened revealing Maudie sitting quietly on the bed.

When she saw the 'priest' enter she stood up, expectantly, a glimmer of hope in her eyes.

***

The first flood of crimson colour rose in the heavens as dawn broke and the sun peeped over the skyline bringing with it a welcoming warmth. The horses stamped their feet anxious to be off and Atwill tried to soothe the animals and calm them.

Jack had his eyes fixed on the side door of the prison. He was relieved to see the door open and the 'priest' emerge. The 'priest' walked slowly towards the waiting carriage and got in. Atwill flicked the reins and the carriage moved off. They rounded a corner where Atwill stopped the coach. Jack turned and the priest looked up at Jack. It was his friend, Percy Golding and not Maudie.

"What the hell happened?"

"The turnkeys stayed with us the whole time. We weren't left alone for a single minute. Sorry, Dodger," said Percy sorrowfully.

***

Crowds had begun to gather in the prison yard, looking forward to the spectacle and sport of a hanging. Jack and Atwill pushed their way through the jeering throng until they reached the front. They waited with heavy hearts and trepidation as Maudie was brought out to the gallows and forced to climb the steps to the platform and hatch.

Two turnkeys held onto her as her eyes searched the crowd. She cried out plaintively in a tight small voice, "Jack? Jack!"

"Maudie, I'm 'ere." His voice choked with emotion and he struggled to keep the tears spilling from his eyes.

Maudie caught sight of him and even in her terror of what was about to happen she managed a half smile and pleaded, "Look after Molly, Jack."

"I will," Jack said, nodding fiercely, in between gulping hard.

A black hood was placed over Maudie's head and then the noose was tightened. She was propelled forward to the hatch and a hush fell over the crowd as the executioner reached for the lever to open the trap and Maudie dropped. There was a roar from the crowd and Jack unashamedly wept. Atwill put his arms around Jack and held him close as would a brother. He, too, felt his cheek wet with tears and a howl from the crowd rose up as they clamoured in glee at 'justice' being done.

There, the two stood as the crowd dispersed to return to their safe lives chortling at the 'entertainment' they had just experienced. Jack remained there trembling in Atwill's embrace in their shared misery.

Finally, Jack broke free and murmured, "We have to claim the body, Atwill. We can't leave her to be buried anonymously in prison grounds. She deserves that much."

Atwill nodded, "I'll come with you, after all... She was my step-daughter, wasn't she?" he said meaningfully.

Jack nodded, "Let's do it." They walked to the prison entrance and gained admittance to make their plea.

***

The following day, Atwill and Jack returned to the prison and were taken inside. They were accompanied down a corridor to wait outside the mortuary. A prison guard, whom they had seen before, opened the door and beckoned them inside, his face was solemn, "You can come in now."

Jack and Atwill entered almost reverently removing their hats. A coffin was open on a table. Maudie's body lay inside covered in a shroud. He lifted the veil from Maudie's face and she appeared almost angelic. Her eyes were closed as if asleep, she had a blush to her cheeks and looked peaceful. The cloth was replaced and at that moment a man dressed in a filthy white apron entered the room carrying a tiny, bloody linen bundle and laid it in the coffin with Maudie.

Jack looked curiously, "What's that?"

The turnkey said regretfully, "I'm sorry. When she dropped, her insides fell out."

"What do you mean?"

"She was pregnant."

"Christ! No!"

"Thing is that if we'd known she was pregnant, she wouldn't have been hanged."

Atwill and Jack exchanged shocked glances. "Do you think she knew?" asked Jack.

"Surely, she'd have said," murmured Atwill.

"Must have been Valentine's."

Atwill nodded. "This is a most shocking revelation. Should never have happened."

"No. Maudie had a good heart. If it wasn't for her..." Jack trailed off.

"I know," said Atwill comfortingly.

"We will make this right. Come." Jack closed the coffin lid and together they lifted the small casket and carried it from the room. Jack noted that there was hardly any weight to it, which wasn't much of a surprise, as Maudie had been very petite. But he couldn't control the myriad of thoughts of her that flashed in his mind: her cheeky smile, her laugh, and her engaging sense of humour and he swallowed hard to prevent himself from crying out loud.

Once they had loaded her coffin, they travelled back to the mansion to collect Amy, Dora and Molly. It would be another few hours before they would reach the farm.

***

The late afternoon sun was bright but not scorching at that time of year and the humidity levels lower than the summer. All in all, it was a pleasant day to be at the farm and at one with nature. The small, solemn funeral party trooped from the farmyard towards the skyline of trees that sheltered the past family graves and overlooked the sweeping meadow with its flowing pheasant tail grass.

Silently, Jack and Atwill rolled up their sleeves, took their pickaxes and shovels and began to dig. The ground was dusty and hard and their tools clanged as they hit the dirt. They had seen little rain this winter, which was unusual. Both men worked up a sweat as they broke up the ground. Molly clung to Amy's skirt and she tried her best to comfort the child. Dora had tears streaming down her face as her eyes fell on Edward's grave. She whispered to Amy, "Oh my love, my Edward," Amy took her hand and held it tightly. "You have great company now, Edward. Look after Maudie... I know you will."

Jack and Atwill lowered Maudie's coffin into the ground and shovelled earth over it. No one spoke. They stood there with their heads bowed. Jack took the basic, rough cross they had made and placed it at the head of the earth mound and Jack spoke, "We go back a long way, you and me, Maudie. You 'elped me when I needed it most otherwise I'd not be here now nor living the life I got. That's down to you. I'm sorry, Maudie, so sorry. Sorry, I couldn't 'elp you. Sorry our plan never worked and sorry you had to suffer what you did, with Valentine. You're at peace now, and I promise you, I've made a vow that me and Amy will look after Molly like she's our own. She won't want for nought. You can look down on us and see we'll do right by you."

The motley group stood silently and reverently saying a prayer to themselves for Maudie before plodding back to the carriage. Jack turned to them all, "You all get back to the farm and wait there. I have one more thing left to do." Amy looked questioningly at Jack. "I need to see Koorong at the village."

"I'll come with you," said Atwill.

Jack shook his head, "No. You stay with the others. Give me three hours and I'll be back." Jack pulled down his slouch hat and trooped off down the dusty track towards the gorge and the Aboriginal camp.

29: Tribal Law

Jack made his way to the canyon and walked through to the village where the children came running out and danced around him, calling, "Mr Jack, Mr Jack!" He bent down and spoke to them charming them with a few of his pick-pocketing tricks that they loved so much. He stood up as they giggled in delight and went onto play their own games and to try their hand at 'Jack's magic' but with little success. Jack laughed as he watched them, while he waited.

Minjarra emerged from a hut with Koorong and they smiled in welcome as they crossed to Jack. Minjarra had become a strongly built, powerful, young man and Koorong, many years Jack's senior, was now grey, his face weathered and wrinkled with the sun and age. Jack gave the friendship gesture and Minjarra spoke with enthusiasm, "Uncle Jack! We haven't seen you in many moons. You have stayed away too long."

"My work at the home with the children keeps me busy. I am doing my best but cannot visit as often as I would like." He looked Minjarra up and down, "I cannot believe how much you have grown. He will soon be overtaking you in height, Koorong."

"He still has a few more inches to grow yet," said Koorong with a smile. "I have promised him that he can come with me next time I sell the wool bales. It is time he learnt and took over from me. I am getting too old for the haggling and bartering. Besides, he will soon be starting his own family."

As Koorong spoke a young woman came out rubbing her belly; she was clearly pregnant. Minjarra beckoned her across, "Jack this is my wife, Bindi."

"Yes?" said Jack with a grin. "That is wonderful. Minjarra, a father... I had always hoped you might have come to school and learned with our children."

"That is not the way of our people. I would always be afraid that he would learn things he shouldn't from the white man."

"Ever suspicious, eh?"

"Not of you, Jack. You have always played fair with us and been our friend. Baiame blesses you for it."

"So, how have you been? Who has become your prime pupil in sheep husbandry?"

"I have taken a few to town with me to learn the trade. We will get by. Last time it was the turn of Koa. He is already an expert shearer, like Minjarra. Now, he needs to learn the business side of things and then he and Minjarra will make a good team."

Jack nodded and his eyes narrowed, "Did Koa accompany you on your last trip?"

"He did."

"I should like to meet him."

"Would you could, but he has gone across to Bobby and Daniel's old place. The farmer there is selling a horse."

"And Koa has the means to pay for it?"

"He's been saving, a little here and there." Koorong studied Jack's face, "Where's this leading, Jack? Why the interest in my companion at the sale?"

"You know me too well. Tell me, did you notice anything happening at the farm that night on your return?"

"We did."

"What?"

Koorong was hesitant, "Why do you need to know?"

"I just want to be sure I have the right person. I am not accusing anyone of anything... Yet. What did you see?"

"Nothing much. Just a flickering light. I told Koa to ignore it thinking it might have been a friend of yours."

"And did you?"

"What?"

"Ignore it?"

"I did."

"And Koa?"

"Why all these questions, Jack?"

Jack took Koorong by the arm and steered him away out of earshot from Minjarra and the playing children. He turned to Minjarra. "I won't be long. I am just borrowing my old friend here for a moment." The children continued their games and Minjarra looked after them puzzled.

Jack spoke in a low tone, "I don't believe that you, Koorong, would do anything to hurt me or my friends. What I have to tell you, is for your ears alone," and he explained all that had transpired at Port Jackson.

Koorong was aghast, "That is truly terrible, Jack. But surely you don't think one of us would betray you?"

"I have it on good authority that it was a young Aboriginal man. Tell me, when you got back from the sale, can Koa's movements be accounted for?"

"We will find out. I will ask his mother." He turned to a woman with a baby and asked, "Jedda?" She pointed towards the communal hut and Koorong went inside.

He came out a few moments later shaking his head in disbelief. "It seems he said he went for a walk after we got back and then when he returned, he left again before daylight to go walkabout." Koorong paused. "Jack, if it was Koa and he did betray you, our trusted friend, he will receive payback in tribal law or he will be sung."

It was Jack's turn to look confused. "What is payback? And sung?"

"Payback is our way of dealing with incidents. Parties involved meet and negotiate a way to restore balance so friendships can continue. If the victim wants retaliation the offender must agree to accept physical punishment; or pay a lot of money or give gifts to the victim, until satisfied. It prevents ongoing feuds and retribution."

"It sounds quite mild," said Jack pointedly.

"Believe me. It's not. It can sometimes be very deadly. After our first invasion, payback was given to settlers who abducted and abused Aboriginal women. Their payback was death."

"What physical punishment are you talking?"

"Spearing. Into the thigh or calf. The punishment fits the crime. If you so wish, after mediation, you can claim the boy's life."

Jack thought awhile, "I don't want that. It could be argued, he didn't know a crime against Maudie would be a crime against me... What is the other?"

"Being sung or pointing the bone. We would ask our most potent elder, who has the power to call on the spirits, to do ill to someone who has committed a crime or abused our culture in some way. In this instance, betrayal of trust, of a loyal friend who has done so much for us would qualify."

"What happens?"

"If he's sung by a Featherfoot, anything could happen. I know of a man, Dural, who dared to steal another's wife. His forty-year-old scars from his tribal initiation ceremony suddenly burst open and erupted into festering wounds filled with pus."

"So, a Featherfoot is a kind of sorcerer or wizard?"

Koorong nodded, "What do you want to do?"

"I don't want more death on me 'ands. I've seen enough of that. And I don't need no money. You've taught me much through the years. What would you do?"

"I cannot speak for you, Jack. It is your decision. Wait until he returns, talk to him and then decide. But, I will say this, if it was Koa then he disobeyed me by going against my wishes to visit the farm."

Jack nodded, "I'll need wise counsel. Can you help?"

Koorong considered Jack's words, "Come with me." Koorong led Jack into another hut empty of all but a fire, a pot of some bubbling liquid with clay mugs, a pan of salt and rugs, on which to sit. "We will call on Baiame. He will show us Koa's heart and then you will know."

Koorong fed the fire and built it up. He ladled some of the milky liquid into two vessels and passed one to Jack. It smelt aromatic but the taste was bitter. Koorong drank his own in one draught and urged Jack to do the same. Jack stared at the opaque liquid mustering up the courage to swallow it down.

Koorong stripped off his shirt and sat cross-legged on a rug in front of the blazing fire. The light played on their faces casting shadows in the lodge. Koorong muttered something in Awabakal and began a low chant.

Jack removed his slouch hat and shirt. He, too, sat with his legs crossed and drank down the liquor and made a complaining face at its sour taste and tried his best not to retch.

They both stared into the flames, which leapt and danced, gorging on the new wood the fire had been fed. Koorong raised his arms and prayed. "Oh, great and powerful father, our creator, Baiame, bless us and allow us to see into the hearts of men that we may know their truth. I bring to you our people's good friend for your wise guidance and help. Show us what we need to know."

The milky drink and the heat of the fire was starting to take effect on Jack who began to sweat. His pupils were now heavily dilated making his eyes look black and his body began to tremble uncontrollably. Koorong, too, started to drip with perspiration. For an old man his body looked polished and well defined in the firelight. Misshapen shadows congealed and clumped together in the corners of the hut as the flames crackled and hissed.

The sound of the chant penetrated Jack's mind. He began to swoon and sway as if in a trance. It was clear that Jack had embarked on his vision. He could see pictures form in the fire and this led him to dream. His vison was of a young boy about to reach adulthood. Jack could see inside him, the workings of his body, his major organs and his heart pumping forcefully. Blood that resembled a tarry substance appeared to travel through his veins. He had a winning smile and very white teeth. A bird flew around him and settled on his shoulder. It was a crow.

Suddenly, the boy appeared to stop breathing and fell into a dead faint. Koorong and other elders went to the young man and opened his fist, which contained a bone and a fistful of money. A woman rushed to his side and began to wail and the boy jumped up. He leapt onto a fine ebony stallion and rode like the wind, through the brush. The horse reared up as a king brown slithered before the horse's hooves and the youth fell off, tumbling down and down and his body split and black worms writhed from his heart.

Jack shuddered at the powerful images and became more aware of Koorong's low chant, which echoed in his head. He continued to stare ahead into the flames, which gambolled and frolicked in swathes of intense colour. The colours appeared to wrap around the body of the youth and a white light shone down engulfing him and healing his wounds. The youth turned and he had Jack's face. Jack flinched and blinked and the images faded away.

Koorong leaned forward and threw a handful of salt into the fire, which snicked and snacked and burnt in a muddy orange glow. He rose and turned to Jack. "You have seen. What happened?"

Jack shook his head, "How can I translate what I saw into truth? It all seems so back to front."

Koorong smiled, "I don't pretend to have all the answers but I know someone who will. Come. We will exchange our visions and you will come to a decision."

***

Jack and Koorong redressed and exited the hut into the caressing warmth of the sun. Jack followed Koorong to a ceremonial hut further into the village. The outside was adorned with feathers and other implements. Magic signs and symbols were painted on the walls. The aura of serenity emanating from inside surrounded the hut. Koorong entered first and bade Jack to wait. Jack stood there trying to remember all the details of his vision so that the wise man would be able to interpret what he had experienced.

Koorong introduced him to the Featherhead, Kuparr, who could commune with the spirits and they sat together on the floor. It was hot in the hut and the sage studied Jack's face. He spoke in Awabakal to Koorong who translated to Jack. "You are unusual for a white man. You have senses that connect you to the land and the netherworld. I see you are much loved and have spirits that surround and guide you in life. Trust your instincts, they will serve you well."

Jack shifted uneasily on the floor. He was uncomfortable with this kind of talk but he had to admit that he had always had inklings, feelings that could almost be called premonitions that had served him well through his life. The old man was right and he trusted his gut more than anything else.

"Tell me what you saw."

Jack recounted the vision as he remembered it. The Featherhead listened carefully to Koorong's translation and nodded knowingly as each part of the dream was revealed to him.

"The youth you talk of is Koa. You saw a bird; a crow and crows can be good or bad. They can be harbingers of death and very clever tricksters. This is Koa. He is split. His white teeth and winning smile show the promise of good but the pitch in his veins also reveals the probability for evil."

Koorong relayed all to Jack and then asked for the next part of the vision. The sage thought and explained, "The dead faint signified his fear of getting caught and in his hand is his crime and punishment. The money he received for an ill deed and the bone to be pointed."

Jack took all this in and asked Koorong, "What about the rest? Of the dream?"

Koorong repeated the next stage of Jack's symbolic trance experience and the old man stroked his chin thoughtfully. "His mother was the woman crying for her son's soul. I see the black horse was some kind of reward for his bad deed. If left unpunished, he will go on to do more and worse. The serpent came to try him and the cleaving of his body reveals the wickedness in his heart."

"What about the white light?" asked Jack. Koorong translated.

The Featherhead thought for a moment, "The final resolution. It could mean, death and the forgiveness of Baiame as he walks into the light or..."

"Or...?"

"Your own demise, where you are blessed for the good you have done. You embrace the light to learn. To be a guide for future generations."

Jack paused and murmured to Koorong, "What do I do? And what did you see?"

Koorong turned to the sage and detailed his own enlightening revelation. The old man nodded sadly and tears fell from his eyes. Koorong explained, "Our wise man weeps for the soul of the boy. He asserts punishment from pointing the bone as in your vision. He emphasises the need for punishment as there is a chance his soul can be saved but he fears the dark shadows will win. You should know, Koa... his name means crow."

Jack shuddered. "But what did you see, my friend?"

"Much the same as you but mine went further. I saw future betrayals of our people if something is not done. The snatching of our land and death of our people at the hand of the white man aided and abetted by Koa. This was all for coin to bring Koa the accoutrements of the white man. He yearns to live in the farmhouse, not just use the sheds for shearing and bale wrapping. He desires to control the wool trade that you gave to us. Your gift has meant we can flourish, your acceptance of us has counted for much in the Port."

Jack nodded in understanding but his heart was heavy.

A huge hullaballoo outside broke the tension in the hut. The Featherhead turned and indicated they should leave. He informed them that Jack had a decision to make and he would comply with whatever was determined. The noise outside continued to rise and there was a gunshot.

Jack and Koorong hurriedly left the wise man and went outside to see Koa riding a fine black stallion as in Jack's dream. He was waving a rifle and had a belt of ammunition draped across the horse's neck.

Koorong addressed the youth and a sharp exchange passed between them. The horse reared up in the air and Koa galloped off firing his rifle into the trees sending the birds perched there screaming into the sky. Koorong turned to his friend. "It is as you say. He admits it was he that claimed the reward. He saw no wrong in his act. He bought the horse and the gun from the farmer. There is bound to be more trouble. What do you want to do?"

Jack said decisively, "Point the bone."

Koorong nodded and they embraced before Jack made his way out of the village and walked back towards the farm.

***

Weeks rolled into months and life at the mansion was hectic. Children who had been nurtured and educated moved onto independent lives. Freddie had worked alongside Dr Long and since travelled to England and gained his medical degree. He had returned and vowed to put back into society what he had gained and went into practice with the good doctor and agreed to be the medic on call for the home. Jack was proud of the lad and how he had turned out. He knew the decision he'd made all those years ago had been the right one.

A new twelve-year-old arrival scooted past Jack on the stairs almost knocking him over. Jack caught hold of the banister and called out, "Slow down, lad. You almost had me over." The boy whooped and skidded to a halt. Jack shook his head and entered the foyer and put his hand on the boy's shoulder. "No one wants to spoil your fun but just take care, especially on the stairs."

"Yes, mister," he said looking down before he trotted briskly towards the kitchen as Jack made his way to the library.

Jack went inside and closed the door with a sigh. He poured himself a glass of port as was his habit in the afternoon and settled in the wing back chair, which he had turned to face the French Windows overlooking the garden where Amy had a class of children sitting looking adoringly at her. Jack smiled as he watched his wife walking around and helping each child and he took a sip of his drink.

The door to the library opened quietly, Jack's eyes lifted and looked at the reflection of the cheeky new arrival in the window. He sat quietly and watched as the boy moved to the table. His eyes lit up as he saw a silver spoon lying there. His fingers reached out and he nimbly picked it up and studied it, examining the hallmark and design of the implement before he slipped it into his pocket.

"Hello, son." The boy jumped in alarm, spun around and stared about the room. Jack turned and peered around the chair, "You don't have to nick that, you know?"

The boy stared at Jack, "Nick what?" he said innocently.

"That spoon."

"What spoon?" The boy had an impish look about him and a cheeky expression. It reminded Jack of himself when he was a child.

"The one in your right pocket," said Jack in a measured tone. There was no accusation in his voice.

The lad patted his pocket and took out the spoon feigning surprise, "Gawd! How did that get in there?"

"You don't have to pinch it. It's yours."

The boy looked confused, "How d'you mean?"

"Well, everything here is yours."

"All mine?" he said looking puzzled.

"It's all yours and everybody else that lives here. You all share everything."

The youth examined the spoon again and reasoned, "If it's mine I can take it."

"Not much fun nicking what's yours though, is it?"

The lad screwed his face up as he considered what Jack said. He looked at the spoon again, "Nah, I s'pose not."

"You're very new here."

"Yeah. Came today."

"What's your name?"

"Ain't saying."

"What were you transported out here for?"

The boy grinned. "Thievin' spoons."

"How long you get?"

"Don't matter. I got caught."

"That's still the only crime, isn't it? Getting caught?"

The boy looked curiously at Jack and walked around to the window and Jack sitting in the chair. "You're all right, you are. What's that you're drinking?"

"Port wine."

"Never tried that. Only had gin."

"Wanna sip?"

"Nah. You the one they call Papa Jack?"

"My name's Jack," Jack said in a matter of fact manner.

"You're all right, you are." The lad studied the spoon again wistfully before he put it back on the table and then he scooted back to Jack. "I'll see you around, Papa Jack." The lad turned to go but stopped, he looked back and said, "Me name's David." Then he scurried from the room. Jack turned back to the window with a broad smile on his face. He finished his port and rose, before going in search of Atwill.

***

Jack sighed as he looked at the farmhouse. He got down from the carriage. The sound of sheep bleating was all around them. There were two makeshift pens in the yard and aboriginals were taking sheep into the shearing shed and penning up the newly shorn animals in the other pen.

"I was happy here, Atwill. This place gave me my start."

"You were lucky, Jack."

"I was."

Jack studied the aboriginals to see if Koorong or Minjarra was among them. He waited, enjoying the gentle caress of the sun on his face as he drank in the familiar atmosphere, the smell of lanolin, the sound of the animals mixed with bird chatter and the buzz of flies.

His patience was rewarded when he saw Minjarra open the shearing shed door and look out. He waved at Jack delightedly and came out to see his visitor, "Uncle Jack! They told me you were here." He ran down to meet them. "How can I help?"

"Always a pleasure to see you, Minjarra. Is Koorong here?"

Minjarra shook his head, "He's back at the village. Can I help?"

Jack paused, "I wondered if there was any news?"

"News?"

"Koa."

Minjarra rolled his eyes, "It's bad, Uncle Jack. You need to see my uncle he will explain."

Jack didn't question Minjarra further. He just nodded and murmured, "Good luck with the shearing."

Minjarra gave Jack a one fingered salute and watched Jack as he climbed back into the carriage. Atwill got into the driver's seat and flicked the reins. He headed the carriage towards the canyon entrance to the village and was instructed to wait while Jack went in search of Koorong.

***

Jack found his old friend in his hut and the two sat down together. Koorong eyed Jack knowingly, "You wish to know the outcome for Koa?" Jack nodded. "Oh, Jack, who would have thought it?"

"Tell me."

"Koa denied what he did was wrong. As you thought, he complained he did not know it was a crime against you. But, he had no excuse for disobedience. As you wished the bone was pointed. Three days later he fell into a raging fever. His body was covered with sores. His mother Jedda begged for forgiveness as did Koa and I truly believed this would be his turning point. He would come to the right spiritual native path… but…"

"But?"

"It was as the Featherhead told us. Koa had a choice to follow a good path after he healed or…"

"Follow the dark path?"

Koorong nodded, "And bring himself harm."

"What happened?"

"He tried to move into the farmhouse on a part-time basis so not to arouse too much suspicion for his intentions. Some nights he would be at home, others he was at the farm. From there he made trips to the port dressed like a white man and visited a big land agency. Jack, he volunteered his services to scout out prime territory to be stolen from our brothers."

"He didn't bring them here?"

"No. But he would have. He has betrayed our brothers in Bundaberg and further up the coast. Word came back to us of a massacre by poisoning; he used the pretext of supplying a fiery rum to them for relaxation. It was fiery all right. It burnt their insides out. They died in agony. He laced supplies of flour with arsenic and strychnine. Then he joined the Native Police with other black hearted men to work with the white men whose goal is still to eradicate our race."

"How did he die?"

Koorong's voice choked with emotion and his eyes misted up as he remembered the atrocities Koa had been involved with. "He got more than payback. He caught the illness that has ravaged our people brought over by the white man and he died alone, a terrible death. You call it the smallpox."

Jack nodded, he knew the disease and he shivered. "Then, justice has been served for Maudie's death. He had his chance to reform. I have no sympathy."

"Nor I. Except for his mother. She has been ostracised by many. The sins aren't hers but she is paying a price."

"Will your people forget? It was not her fault."

"Give it time, Jack. She has to pay a penance in the eyes of some as she brought him into the world."

"Your law is your law and I respect that."

Koorong smiled. "We understand each other."

The men embraced as Jack murmured, "Not sure when I will be back, but you know where I am if you need me."

Jack left the village and Koorong watched the familiar figure in his slouch hat until he disappeared from view. "Goodbye, old friend." He smiled reflectively. "You don't know but I know what is to come for you."

30: We All Grow Old

Jack woke and winced as he stretched his arms above his head. His elbows twinged and his shoulders ached. It was no fun growing old. He looked towards Amy still sleeping peacefully. She sighed and turned over with a slight murmur and her eyes fluttered open to see Jack gazing at her. "What?" she said sleepily.

"Nothing. I was just thinking."

"About what?" she said moistening her lips.

"How we got here."

"We climbed the stairs last night," said Amy with a giggle.

Jack grinned, "No, I mean where has the time gone? I can't believe it. I feel exactly the same inside as I did when I met you. It's when I catch sight of myself in a mirror and think who's that old man? Then I realise it's me. Makes me wonder if I resemble my mother or father, but that's something I'll never know."

Amy raised her hand gently and caressed his face where his whiskers were sprouting through, "What's brought all this on?" She pushed herself up on her elbow and looked deeply into his eyes.

"I'm not sure. Perhaps, it's our shared birthday coming up and me not knowing exactly how old I am. There is so much I don't know."

"What we don't know won't hurt us. I've been looking at some books about star signs and I think we got it about right. Everything I've read makes you a Capricorn."

"Capricorn?"

"An old goat..." and she laughed.

"If I'm an old goat, what are you?"

"A nanny goat and probably considered an old goat, too."

"You're not so old... Yet."

"I'll be seventy in a few days' time."

"And I'll be seventy six or seven or eight."

"Or five or four. It doesn't matter."

Jack flopped back on the pillow and Amy snuggled up to him. Jack sighed contentedly, "Tell me more about being an old goat."

"Well, remember not all of this will apply to you but much of it does."

"Then what applies to me, also applies to you?"

"Yes."

"Tell me more," said Jack enjoying watching her explain it to him.

"They are ambitious to the point of being workaholics and persistent in getting what they want. That's definitely you. Although, it's said they can be something of a pessimist."

"A pessimist?"

"Someone who fears the worst but you're not really like that. You have always shown positivity. I would describe you as a visionary, an idealist. I mean look at what you have done here. They are very practical, which you are. A man of the land with a fiery temper, and that's you, too. Not necessarily me. They never forget anything and will often remind you of things that happened a long time ago. They lack tolerance and won't forget if you have wronged them in some way."

"So, that's me, is it?"

"Some of it. Why?"

"Just keen to know, that's all. I have an enquiring mind. Is that on your list?"

Amy thought for a moment and shook her head, "Don't think so."

"Pity. I was going to ask what you wanted for your birthday."

Amy patted Jack's cheek playfully, "I have all I want in you."

"Nevertheless, I think this year should be different. You will be seventy. It's a milestone. We should do something special for you. My celebration can wait."

"We've always had a double birthday before," said Amy with a pout.

"Well, this year we won't," said Jack. "I've made up my mind. Does it also say that goats are stubborn? You better add that to the list."

Amy smiled resignedly. "You're forgetting that I'm a Capricorn, too and I can be stubborn. I do know that once you make up your mind it's hard to change it. But I also know, you would do anything for me."

"And?"

"My present will be a joint party."

Jack smiled amiably, "Very well, but make sure everyone we want to see is on the list of invites, Freddie and Dr Long with his wife."

"And Molly. Don't forget Molly."

"She's grown up to look so much like Maudie. Pretty little thing."

"Married with two children and expecting another baby. Maudie would have been so proud."

Jack's eyes filled with tears. "Yes, she would. I'll leave you to organise that. Get Dora to help you. I wish Atwill was still here."

"He was a good friend to you."

"To both of us," corrected Jack. "Why did he have to die?"

"It was his time. Heavens, he would have been a hundred, now."

"I know. But, I do miss him." Jack leaned up on his elbow and leaned across to kiss her. "We've had a good life together, haven't we?"

Amy nodded, "We have and it's not over yet. As my mother always said, the best is yet to come."

***

Jack sat in the library a concentrated expression on his face. He looked across at Amy. "We have to pay Bessant a visit."

"Bessant? Why?"

"We need to be prepared and I need you to be there and read the documents he has set down ready for me."

"I didn't know you had seen him, lately."

"I keep tabs on him. Make sure he's not walking a crooked path again. He did have a good little practice for a while, from what I understand. Should be all above board now. But, I also heard rumours."

"What kind of rumours?"

"He's not doing as well as he was. There's no loyalty these days. Folks are taking their business elsewhere. I think he's having a tough time."

"Serves him right... So, when do you want to go?"

"Now. Tell Percy to bring the carriage around."

Percy Golding, the ostler and groom had now been upgraded to drive the carriage as well. Amy went out to the foyer and rang the bell for the maid, a chubby cheeked lass who had gone through the home herself and stayed on to work for Jack and Amy.

"Ah, Clara. Could you ask Mr Golding to bring the carriage around please?"

Clara bobbed in obeisance and went off to find Percy. Jack and Amy put their outdoor clothes on and left the mansion to wait for the carriage, which didn't take long. Jack instructed Percy and the carriage set off for town.

Jack was paying particular attention to the roads as they passed along them and acknowledged those who waved or recognised them. They soon reached the town and Golding drove the carriage to a stop outside Bowkett and Bessant, where they alighted and Golding settled down to wait.

Jack noted, a 'For Sale' sign outside the building and a germ of an idea glimmered in his eyes as they walked up the path to the entrance.

Once in the inner sanctum the insectile and now ancient Mr Spanner fawned over them using wheedling tones and waving his arms like an ant's antenna as he begged them to sit while he alerted Mr Bessant.

The door opened and Bessant puffed out clearly unnerved by this surprise visit. He was perspiring heavily and welcomed them inside. "Mr and Mrs Dawkins. What a pleasure." Although, there appeared to be no sincerity in his voice. Jack and Amy were ushered into his office and the door was closed firmly. "What can I do for you?"

"The papers I asked you to prepare, are they done?"

"But of course, all they await is your signature."

"Good, take them out and give them to my wife Amy, she will read them for me to see if you have written my wishes to the letter."

"But of course, Mr Dawkins," he huffed, mopping his plump and surprisingly unwrinkled brow with a hankie. "It is hotter this summer than a blast furnace and I'm afraid I don't have the means to purchase one of these new-fangled ceiling fans. We have to make do with anything we can lay our hands on." He passed Jack and Amy some stiff pieces of card to waft and create a draught. "It wouldn't be so bad if there was something of a breeze, but I digress. You wish to see your will?"

Amy looked up in surprise as Jack nodded, "Just need to make sure it's all fair and square."

"Of course, of course." Bessant crossed to his filing cabinet and rummaged through it and removed a sheaf of papers in a folder and handed them to Amy, who began to look through them. "It's everything as you wanted. All assets and gold payments to be transferred into Mrs Dawkins' name with a proportion set aside to fund the home and continue to look after and educate abandoned children at the mansion. And in the event of her passing the same title with the same agreement to pass to Molly Summers."

"What about the farmland?"

"Mr Dawkins, as I explained, Aboriginals are not allowed to hold title of land or property."

"But, I have an agreement with them now and I intend to not only honour it but allow it to continue."

"It cannot be made legally binding as a bequest." Bessant shrugged his ample shoulders.

Amy spoke up, "Surely, you can insert a codicil that the property will have a covenant for the people of the village to continue to use the land for their own purpose and lifetime? And that promise to roll on forever."

Bessant thought, for a moment, "It may be possible, if we can word it that the land cannot be sold, bought or used by any white person or foreigner... Until the law changes that would be the best I could do."

Jack nodded agreeably, "That sounds very good... In a backward way it would only be aboriginals that could use it."

"Yes, yes. It would. Excellent idea. You could also enclose a letter of intent should the law ever change."

"Then prepare those papers now. We will wait and have a glass of your excellent port wine, while my wife examines the rest of the documents."

Bessant trotted from the office and went to see Spanner. They listened as Bessant explained to Spanner, who took notes, exactly what was needed. They heard a sheet of paper being inserted into a machine and the click, click, clack, of a typewriter in use.

Jack rose and poured himself and Amy a glass of port and watched his wife's face as she read through the paperwork. Amy nodded and looked up. "It all seems to be in order. We will need two copies; one for us as and one held here."

Jack nodded, "That makes sense. In fact, it's high time these two retired. I will suggest it and maybe even surprise them, too. A good surprise," he added with a wink.

"Oh, Jack! Whatever next? After all their double dealing and attempts to steal from you?"

"Don't worry, it's nothing massive, I assure you."

The typewriter continued to clack away in the outer office and Bessant finally returned with the papers. "Here we are, Mr Dawkins. Your will and your letter of intent."

"We will need two copies," said Jack passing both documents to Amy to look through. "And I believe we need an independent witness?"

"Surely, Mr Spanner and I will suffice?" said Bessant colouring up.

"If you don't mind, I'll just ask my man to come in and witness this." He left the office to return a few minutes later with Percy Golding.

Amy set out the papers and indicated where Jack should sign and Percy happily witnessed all signatures. Bessant whisked one set away for his files and gave the other to Amy. Jack finished his drink and turned to Bessant, "I would have thought that you should be retiring soon."

Bessant shook his head, "Alas, Mr Spanner and I can ill afford to do that. We have to keep working to live."

"In that case, I have a proposition." Bessant looked up with interest. "I will source and install your ceiling fan for you, to improve your living conditions."

Bessant smiled agreeably, "Thank you, Mr Dawkins. That would be gratefully appreciated."

"Tell me, who owns this building? How many rental offices are there?"

Bessant looked surprised, "It is owned by the port authority, and there are four offices in total. Why?"

"I wish to purchase it. See what you can find out. If successful, you can remain here rent free for as long as you wish and you will be responsible for collecting the rent for the other offices, which you can have as income. When you eventually pass on, this building comes back into the mansion's assets. No jiggery pokery, no malarkey. How does that sound?"

Bessant's jaw dropped in amazement. He was completely stuck for words and was visibly moved by Jack's offer. "I don't know what to say."

"Say, yes. And then you will be able to retire, you and Spanner."

"...Er yes... yes... YES!" Bessant stepped forward and pumped Jack's hand vigorously. "Thank you, Mr Dawkins, Mrs Dawkins. Thank you. I will draw up the papers on your behalf and contact the port authority. Why thank you. May I ask why?"

"Why what?"

"Why you would do this for me... us... when..."

"When you tried to cheat me?"

"Er... yes." Bessant had the good grace to look shamefaced.

"I heard you're not doing so well. Word gets around. People taking their business to other law firms and such... I believe strongly that everyone needs another chance. I know I gave you two but you've behaved properly since then and as I was blessed with good fortune by Mr Fred, consider this to be a helping hand."

"Why, thank you. Thank you both." Bessant was beaming and Jack was sure he could see the glimmer of a tear in his eye.

"Get it done as quickly as possible."

"I will. I will."

Bessant followed them out of the office and watched them get into the carriage before racing back inside to tell Spanner the good news.

Amy turned to Jack, "Why, you really are an old goat! You never cease to surprise me. You have a heart as big as..."

"A bucket?" said Jack with a laugh.

"A bucket," said Amy decisively.

***

January 1st 1901 arrived. The mansion was decorated with bunting, banners and coloured balloons. There was a great feast laid out on tables on the lawn. Silver bowls containing a fruit punch complete with ladle and cups was available as was ale and port wine.

Port dignitaries arrived to pay their respects to the couple, well known for their kind generosity and philanthropy. Old friends, Bobby and Daniel turned up with their wives Minnie and Josie, leaving the Victoria in the capable hands of their children, who were now grown up.

Jack was delighted to see Molly arrive with her husband and two little children. She moved, as quickly as her pregnancy would allow, to Jack and Amy, and embraced them, "Papa Jack, Miss Amy. Happy birthday!" She turned to her husband who was smiling idiotically at her and he passed her a posy of flowers and a wrapped box. "These are for you. I picked them myself, from the garden, and added some finer specimens from the florist to make this little bouquet."

Amy took them and beamed in delight. "Molly, they're beautiful. Thank you. But just you coming today would be enough."

"What! And let a milestone like this important birthday go unnoticed." She turned to Jack, "And this is for you."

Jack unwrapped a box of chocolate sweets, "Thank you, Molly."

"I know you have a sweet tooth, but there's more... look underneath." Molly watched eagerly as Jack lifted the box away from the wrapping. There was a handmade book called 'Memories'. It was filled with photographs and dates with little captions. There was even one of Maudie in her wedding dress together with Molly as bridesmaid, Jack, Amy, Atwill and Dora.

Jack's eyes filled with emotion and he could hardly speak. "Oh, thank you, Molly. You couldn't have done anything better for us."

Amy's eyes glistened and she embraced Molly again. "What a wonderful gift. Thank you. It will be treasured by both of us."

***

Jack watched as the staff ensured everything ran smoothly and the children ran around the grounds playing their games and laughing. He and Amy sat together on the terrace watching everyone enjoying the celebrations.

The smiling face of the sun beamed down on them and refused to share the glory of the azure sky with any clouds. Jack rubbed his rheumy eyes that sometimes played tricks on him. He no longer saw as well as he did and he rubbed them before reaching for his old slouch hat to shade him from the sun's rays.

He squinted as a tall young man in his late twenties climbed the steps to the terrace to speak with him. He was in the company of several other young men who scrutinised their grand surroundings in wonder.

"Hello, Papa Jack. Do you remember me?" asked the gentleman.

"Step closer," said Jack and peered at him from behind the brim of his hat. The young man smiled and came nearer. Jack contemplated the man's face and recognition flickered in his eyes as he said, quietly, "Still nicking spoons, David?"

"You do remember?" said David with obvious pleasure.

"Might not want me to broadcast that though," he said with a wink. "But, I'm very glad you're here, David."

Amy beamed at him. "Oh, David... It's so good to see you. Tell me, what is your employment, now?"

David said proudly, "I work in banking."

"And I thought you'd be doing something honest," said Jack with a wry smile.

David laughed and one of his friends, a plump, short man, coughed. He was clearly keen to become acquainted. He had a certain air about him that demanded attention. Amy studied the man but there was just something about him that she couldn't quite identify. Something she didn't like.

David was eager to introduce him and immediately apologised, "I am so sorry, Sir Henry. Sir Henry, may I introduce Mr and Mrs Jack Dawkins our host and hostess. This is Sir Henry Rhymer. Our chairman."

"Mrs Dawkins, a pleasure," said Sir Henry with a short bow.

"Sir Henry," acknowledged Amy courteously.

"Dawkins," said Henry with a supercilious twist of his mouth.

"Sir Henry. Please call me Jack."

"I'd like to talk to you, Dawkins." It was more of an order than a request and Amy bristled. She studied the man and decided she didn't like his flat blue slate eyes that appeared cold and unfeeling. He had an arrogance that obviously came with his title.

Jack arched an eyebrow and said simply, "Why?"

"Men like you interest me. You've done very well for yourself." It was more like an accusation than a statement.

"Thank you," said Jack and offered nothing more.

"I'm interested in anyone who has made a lot of money."

"Looking for the secret?" said Jack with a return of his impish expression.

"No. Wondering if they made it honestly."

There was an awkward silence. Amy bridled and David looked uncomfortable.

Jack, however, seemed unfazed. "...And?"

"Would you say you were an honest man?"

"As an honest man yourself, what would you say?"

"I would say, yes."

"So would a dishonest man," said Jack in a matter of fact tone.

"You haven't answered my question," pressed Sir Henry rudely.

"Haven't I?" said Jack noncommittally.

Sir Henry paused, clearly not used to anyone avoiding his type of questioning and changed tack, "Do you follow the cricket?"

"Yes."

"Which team will you be supporting in the Ashes?" he asked with a hint of mockery in his voice.

"The best one," said Jack simply and David hid a smile.

"Which is?" demanded Sir Henry.

"The one that wins."

Sir Henry could no longer attempt to disguise the tetchiness in his voice, "Tell me, Dawkins. Have you lived in Australia all your life?"

Jack smiled as he answered, "Not yet." Sir Henry's cronies couldn't help themselves, they all laughed. A flash of annoyance crossed Sir Henry's face. Jack turned to David and said politely, "Excuse me, David. Please make yourself and your friends comfortable."

Jack rose to leave with Amy and Sir Henry barked sharply, "I haven't finished talking to you yet, Dawkins."

Jack continued to turn away, "You weren't talking. You was questioning."

Amy faced Sir Henry, "May I say something?" Her cheeks had grown quite pink.

"Of course, Mrs Dawkins."

"Sir Henry, I wonder that you dare interrogate my husband in his own house. By what right do you do this?" Amy looked and sounded angry.

"My dear lady, I..."

"Do not 'dear lady' me, Sir Henry. You come here with your fancy title and an entourage that flutter around you like a bunch of..." she searched for the words, "constipated starlings. They hang on your every word as if you had something important to say, which by the way, you don't!" Jack's eyes opened wide in surprise at his wife's sudden outburst and they glimmered with something else... his eyes shone with pride.

Amy spun around and lambasted David, "And you, David! I am ashamed of you. Jack always taught you to be your own man not someone's puppet. I believed you would turn out better than this; bringing someone here prepared to demean Jack without whom you wouldn't have had your good start in life." Abashed, David hung his head and couldn't bring himself to look at her.

Amy was now even more fired up and began another blistering verbal attack on Sir Henry with such great force and fervent energy that everyone stopped in astonishment, "Your sort, come over here and take all that this great country has to offer, raping the land, taking what you want, removing, dividing it and selling it, when it wasn't yours to begin with. That is full blown thievery. The profits go back to London where it swells the pockets of your shareholders in the banks. You put nothing back into this country whereas my husband gives his wealth back to the people. He has helped so many less lucky than he has been. I look at him and I look at you. He is worth ten million of you."

Those guests and staff who were within earshot stood listening with mouths agape and nodded in total agreement. Sir Henry, now red in the face turned to Jack and said sneeringly, "So, Dawkins, do you let your wife speak for you?"

Jack stood next to Amy and spoke quietly but firmly, "I don't *let* my wife do anything. She is her own woman. But, I will tell you one thing, Sir Henry, she has always been the better part of me." Jack put his arm around her.

Amy looked up at him, her eyes shining, "Why, thank you, Jack, that means everything to me."

Jack and Amy started to leave but Amy had not quite finished. She stopped and turned to Sir Henry again. "And there's one more thing, *Sir* Henry," and she leaned heavily on the word Sir. "Your title 'Sir Henry Rhymer,'" her voice was heavily laced with sarcasm and she added... "It means less than shit out here!"

Jack couldn't stop the laugh that erupted from him and continued even longer as she said sweetly, "Please enjoy our hospitality. If you will excuse us," and the two moved away leaving Sir Henry speechless and dumbfounded.

Jack bowed his head to Amy and whispered, "What kind of language is that for a lady to use?"

Amy smiled and Jack winked at her. He moved back to Sir Henry, "Pardon me, Sir Henry. Does this belong to you?" He held up a gold watch and chain.

Sir Henry immediately patted his waistcoat pocket. His face registered surprise and he blustered, "Yes, it does. How did..."

"You wants to be a bit more careful, Henry. You must have dropped it!" Jack passed the watch and chain back to Sir Henry and strolled back to Amy's side. He whispered to Amy, "First time the Artful Dodger ever gave something back... Must be losing me touch! What was all that you told me about being a goat? A fiery temper? Think you displayed that extremely well."

Amy smiled up at him and smacked his arm as if he was a naughty boy and caught a flash of something in his eyes, "Are you all right?"

Jack laughed derisively. "Bloody colonists! They all think you're something unpleasant under their shoe. He's somethin' else, ain't he?"

Jack put his hand up to his head and swayed unsteadily for a few seconds.

Amy looked concerned, "What's the matter? What's wrong?"

"Aw, it's nothin'. I'm a little tired, Amy. That's all. It's been a big day." Jack patted her hand and smiled his lopsided grin that she had told him she loved so much. "Think I'll go and sit in the library and look at the book Molly made for us. Have a glass of port."

They strolled together inside the mansion, arm in arm as the celebrations continued outside. "It's been a wonderful birthday." Jack gazed tenderly into his wife's eyes, "Thank you, Amy."

"For what?" said Amy bemused.

"For sharing your life with me... and your birthday." Amy flushed with pleasure and smiled up at him as he repeated, "Thank you for everything, my love."

31: Making Plans

Jack and Amy had returned from signing all the sale papers and his will, which had all been done in record time. Jack suggested that the speed may have had something to do with his offer of assistance to Bessant. Amy inclined her head in agreement, "I think you're right. Amazing how quickly someone can work when it is to their advantage. But, still, it was all done correctly."

"It was indeed," said Jack. "Thanks to you and your eagle eye. You went through all the documentation with a fine toothcomb. You don't miss a thing. No nits in our house," said Jack with a laugh.

Amy looked serious for a moment, "Jack? Changing the subject..."

"Yes?"

"I have asked Molly to visit. As she is to be my successor it may be an idea to show her how I do things and to see if she would be willing to take over at the right time."

"Do you think she might not want to?"

"I'm sure she will but she has got two little children, soon to be three."

"I expect it would work the same way it did for Maudie."

"But better to discuss it with her," said Amy. "Especially as it will be such a big responsibility."

"Remind me what her husband does again," said Jack thoughtfully.

"I know that look," observed Amy. "You have a plan burning in your brain."

"Isn't he something to do with accounting?"

"Yes, I believe he is."

"Good. Then he could do all our books for the charity and the home. It would save you a lot of headaches and keep everything in the family, so to speak."

"That's an excellent idea," said Amy with a big smile. The front doorbell rang and Amy looked up. "I expect that's her now."

Soon there was a knock on the door and Clara entered, "If you please, Mrs Dawkins, Molly is here to see you."

"Tell her to come in, Clara." Clara genuflected and opened the door wider to let Molly pass. Her baby bump was considerably more noticeable as she was nearing the end of her term. She eased herself gratefully into the chair that Jack pulled out.

"Thanks, Papa Jack. Think I'm bigger with this one than the other two. Hope it's not twins!"

"Surely, they would know by now?" said Amy.

Molly grinned, "Of course. I'm joking. I'm only expecting one. That's enough. I can't wait to have him or her and get back to work."

"That's what we wanted to talk to you about."

Molly's face fell, "I'm not losing my job am I?"

"No, nothing like that," said Jack reassuringly. He turned to Amy, "Perhaps, my love you'd better explain."

So, Amy outlined the plans that Jack had for her. Molly clapped her hands delightedly. "Oh, oh this is more than I could ever have dreamed and to involve Stephen as well. He will be thrilled. Thank you. Thank you so much for your trust in me."

Jack smiled and raised his glass to her, "To you, Moll and the family. I know I've said it before but you are so much like your mum. She was one of the best."

Molly's eyes filled with tears, "I know. But then so are you. Mum loved you both very much." Molly winced as she rose, "God damn, I am feeling so uncomfortable in this heat. What a time of the year to pick. Been getting these twinges all day. Arrgh!"

"What is it?" asked Amy concerned.

"The baby. I think it's coming. Oh, I'm so overwhelmed, I think that's what's done it. Oooh, no!" She bent over and there was a whoosh.

"Whoa!" exclaimed Jack. "I think her waters have broke."

"Well, I haven't peed myself!" said Molly. "Aw, Gawd. What now? The last one came really quickly, they say the next one will be faster."

Amy rang the bell, "I'll get Clara to help her upstairs and call for Dora. She can go in our bedroom. Better get Percy to fetch Freddie or Dr Long." It was apparent that Molly had started with more severe contractions as she doubled over. "Quick, Molly breathe. Breathe through it. It will help with the pain."

Clara came into the library and took one look at Molly, "Oh, Lord. What's happened?"

"Help me to get her upstairs and then get Dora and send Percy for Freddie. Hurry."

For once Jack stood looking on helplessly not knowing quite what to do and then he appeared to become more alert, "I'll get Percy. You get her up to bed. What about your husband? He should be told." Jack answered his own question, "I'll fetch Stephen; where does he work?"

"Argh, thirty-three Main Street. Quick, please hurry. Argh!"

Jack slammed down his glass and made a bolt through the French Windows as Amy and Clara helped Molly from the room.

***

Jack sat with a worried looking Stephen in the library who sat stiffly clutching his glass of ruby port and looked at Jack, "Do you think she'll be much longer?"

"They say each baby comes quicker than the last. I say the baby will come when it's ready." Jack swallowed hard. It was so reminiscent of his own wait for the birth of Tom when he sat with Atwill and Edward that he became quite overcome with emotion.

Jack rose unsteadily and gripped the back of his wing back chair. "Are you all right?" asked Stephen looking concerned.

Jack forced a smile, "I'm okay. Just took me back that's all. To the birth of me own son."

Stephen stared curiously. "Didn't know you had a son," he said softly.

"I don't. Not no more."

"I'm sorry," said Stephen sincerely, but looked uncertain as what to say next.

Jack was saved from further explanation when the cry of a new born baby came from upstairs. Stephen rose doubtfully, not knowing whether to be excited and rush upstairs or wait to be called. Jack could see his dilemma, "Sounds like a healthy one with a lusty pair of lungs. Go on up. Go on."

"Do you think I should?"

"If you don't, they'll come looking for you."

Stephen set down his glass and started for the door as Clara rushed in beaming with joy, "Oh, sir," she said, her face flushed with excitement. "You have a son, a beautiful baby boy. Come on up." She looked across at Jack, "You, too, Mr Jack. You're wanted, too."

Clara scurried out and raced back up the stairs followed by Stephen. Jack swayed and took a deep breath. He followed them to the foot of the stairs and climbed them slowly gripping the banisters firmly.

***

Freddie was washing his hands and turned as he saw them enter. He grinned broadly, "A remarkably strong baby with robust lungs. And a good size too." He packed away his scales, "A most excellent eight pounds three ounces."

Stephen sat at his wife's side and touched the little one's hand and the baby grasped his finger firmly. Jack leaned against the door and a tear trickled down his cheek, which he hurriedly brushed away. Amy glanced across at him and knew instantly what her husband was thinking.

Freddie completed packing his medical instruments away and rolled down his sleeves, "So, what are you going to call him?"

Stephen looked at Molly, "I've a name in mind, if you agree?"

"I have, too," said Molly.

"I'd like to call him Jack," said Stephen.

Molly's mouth dropped open, "So, would I." She engaged Jack with her eyes, "Would you mind?"

"Mind?" said Jack. "I'd be so proud. Prouder than you know."

Freddie picked up his bag and coat and turned at the door, "Sounds like we have another Jack in the family." Freddie smiled again and began to leave the room where a few curious children and staff members had gathered. "Baby Jack," he announced to them. "Jack! A good strong name for all that it stands for." Freddie made his way to the stairs still grinning inanely.

***

311

Jack sat contentedly in his chair sipping his port wine and looking out onto the lawn where a few of the older children still played. Amy stood behind his chair and watched with him. "Amy?"

"Yes?"

"Would you do something for me?"

"Of course."

"Play me some Beethoven. I haven't heard you play in a while. The Moonlight Sonata like when we met."

"I'm a bit rusty."

"That don't matter. I'd love to hear it again. Go on. Leave the door open so I can hear it all."

Amy opened the library door and went into the foyer and sat at the grand piano. She lifted the lid and began to play. The soft, gentle music was like a lullaby and Jack listened, a smile playing on his lips. He set down his glass and closed his eyes to be transported back in time to the church and Amy with her sausage curls playing this poignant piece so beautifully. He rested his hands on his chest to enjoy the languid strains that filtered into the room. And sighed.

***

Amy closed the lid on the grand piano and flexed her fingers. It felt good to play again. She had forgotten how much she had missed it. She glanced at the big grandfather clock in the corner, twenty minutes had passed. She walked back down the corridor to the library and asked, "I really enjoyed that, Jack. Did you like it, too? I'm not as nimble with my fingers as I used to be but I can soon get practising again... Jack?"

There was no answer and Amy crossed to his chair and smiled, "I must have sent you to sleep. That's a good sign... Jack?"

Amy stroked his shoulder and his head fell forward. Amy touched his neck for a pulse and righted his head. She stooped down and sat at his feet holding his hand. Her eyes filled with tears that yearned to be released and there she sat until the sun went down in a blaze of glory.

***

Four ebony horses sporting black plumes pawed the ground as they waited for the instruction to pull the black and gold carriage. The driveway to the mansion was lined with crowds of mourners. Many children both old and young lined up behind Amy who stood proudly serene.

The doors and windows to the mansion were all open and fires burned upwind outside. Minjarra and other villagers were gathered and fanned the aromatic smoke inside the house as was their custom. Amy had a faint smile on her lips knowing how Jack would have appreciated this ritual from his friends.

The carriage began its journey down the driveway and into the town. Amy's eyes were fixed in front. If they hadn't been, she would have recognised many people: Bessant and Spanner, Effie, Emma and Kate who were now wizened and looking like old crones in their rags. Military men, too, from the fort, alongside Captain Phillips, who now held the rank of major. Daniel and Bobby together with Minnie and Josie and many, many more.

News had reached them that halfway around the globe in Osbourne House on the Isle of Wight in England, her majesty Queen Victoria had suffered the self-same fate on the self-same day 22nd of January 1901 just three weeks after Jack's last birthday party. He, of course, didn't have the titles of Victoria who was by the Grace of God, Queen of the United Kingdom and Ireland, Defender of the Faith, Empress of India and she held the record for ruling longer than any other monarch in history at sixty-three years, seven months and two days. She was eighty-one, when she passed away. No one knew the age of Jack Dawkins, the Artful Dodger and never would, not exactly. But the crowds that visibly mourned in Britain were not more than here, proportionally. Jack was well loved.

The funeral procession moved out of the port and along the road and then, the dusty track to the farm where it stopped before the line of trees overlooking the meadow full of fragrant summer blooms.

Freddie, Percy, Stephen and David lifted the casket from the carriage and lowered it into a grave next to Tom. Amy watched and a soft gentle breeze blew her wispy grey hair as lightly as a butterfly wing that would flutter in the summer sunshine. To the other side of Jack were the graves of Fred, Edward, Maudie and Atwill.

Amy was reassured, he was laid to rest amongst his greatest friends and of course, their beloved son. The rest of the Aboriginal villagers led, by the aged Koorong who was now eighty-five and chief of his tribe. He had been given the title, after the untimely passing of the old chief's son, Yindi. The villagers were all there in force and stood silently but proudly in Jack's honour, for in truth there had been no one quite like Jack.

Amy tossed a simple posy of wild meadow flowers on top of the casket and whispered, "Goodbye, my one true love and dearest friend. I will miss you." She dared not say more for fear her tears would flow again. She stepped back and Molly slipped her hand into hers and squeezed it. This modest act triggered Amy's pent-up emotion and tears streamed silently down her face as she turned away from the graveside and climbed aboard the carriage to wait for the other mourners to pay their last respects.

Jack Dawkins, the Artful Dodger, was dead. His dreamtime was over.

Epilogue

"It's strange, I'd had a burning pain in my head and closed my eyes just for a moment, listening and enjoying the wonderful music of Beethoven and I woke up here. My Dreamtime was over. I never thought I would live long enough to see my own funeral, but I did. Four black plumed, ebony horses that pulled the coach with my coffin in it was far grander than I expected. The casket looked so small, but then, I was always short for me height.

"A crowd of my loyal aboriginal friends waved smoke from large fires through the open windows and doors of the house as was their custom, to see me safely on my journey, cleanse the house of death and ward off bad spirits. Just like they did for Fred. There was a big procession that followed the funeral carriage with lots of youngsters that we had helped. Some of them was proper grown up now.

"Molly was there with her children and baby Jack in her arms. I am humbled by that and feel privileged. I just couldn't believe how many important people attended, for me, the Dodger! Not bad for a thief transported from London.

"And leading them all was my Amy, my love. My Amy, who taught me so much. She was the one who taught me the meaning of the word love. She made it so simple. She didn't cry in the procession but looked proud, serene and beautiful.

"I liked that they took me to the farm and put my coffin in the ground next to my Tom, my only treasured son. As I said, my Dreamtime was over. I am now in the real world. I won't tell you what it's like. It'll be a surprise, a wonderful surprise. You'll find out everything when you wake up."

*

You may also enjoy...

Cycles of
Norse Mythology

GLENN SEARFOSS